GONE TO GROUND

Morgan Hatch

Black Rose Writing | Texas

This is a work of fiction. Names, characters, businesses, places, events, and incidents are either the products of the author's imagination or used in a fictitious manner. Any resemblance to actual persons, living or dead, or actual events is purely coincidental.

ISBN: 978-1-68513-634-5
PUBLISHED BY BLACK ROSE WRITING
www.blackrosewriting.com

Printed in the United States of America
Suggested Retail Price (SRP) $22.95

Gone to Ground is printed in Cambria

*As a planet-friendly publisher, Black Rose Writing does its best to eliminate unnecessary waste to reduce paper usage and energy costs, while never compromising the reading experience. As a result, the final word count vs. page count may not meet common expectations.

PRAISE FOR
GONE TO GROUND

"Readers that choose *Gone to Ground* for its promise of heady action, discussions of personal transformation and impact, and discovery will relish how Hatch brings all these influences home to explore Los Angeles culture from a very different perspective."
–Midwest Book Review

"Morgan Hatch's *GONE TO GROUND* is a compelling critique of modern politics, violent gentrification, and the super-rich—all wrapped in a bittersweet coming-of-age story. A fast-paced, deeply engrossing book that's equal parts emotional, tense, and unafraid to include some jaw-dropping twists."
–IndieReader

"With a heavy dose of wit and an intelligently conceived plot, Hatch masterfully lures the reader into his unpredictable and absorbing world."
–Booklife Prize

"Fast paced and poignant."
–Kirkus Reviews

"George Jones is one of the most evil characters you'll ever find in a book."
–RG Belsky, award-winning author of *It's News to Me*

"A gripping, suspense novel set in the streets of LA."
–Reader's Choice Book Awards

To Anita

GONE TO GROUND

CHAPTER 1

Five minutes into class, Javier knew it was a wash. The post-lunch narcosis had set in, leaving everyone's eyes at half-mast. A flat-faced boy sitting along the side was completely out, his head back against the wall, mouth open as if ready to catch raindrops. At the front of the class, Mr. Patel stood stroking his mustache, a massive thing set off with dimples on both sides like parentheses. On the wall hung a picture of him from his salad days in private equity ringing a stock exchange bell, a moment that had launched dozens of indulgent stories, and Javier could see Enrique doing his best to bait another one out of him.

"So, hold up. It's called a *hostile* takeover?" Enrique asked, bug-eyed in wonderment. There wasn't a curious bone in his body, but he appeared suddenly seized with the spirit of inquiry.

Javier knew Patel was in on the act and would often parry these obvious bids to hijack his lessons, though today he seemed to welcome the diversion. By the time he finished with his mustache and went to recap the markers, the class had already started closing their notebooks and pulling out their phones. Javier never tired of the act, but as this was their second year with Patel, the anecdotes were getting recycled. He glanced over at Gio, absorbed in today's sketch, a human jaw so lifelike Javier found himself working his own back and forth like he was trying to pop his ears. Javier had already taken the class, AP Economics, last year. He was there for the view, nothing else. Patel's room on the second floor of

East Valley High was the only one with an unobstructed view of the lunch scene at Gaither Middle School across the street where his younger brother Alex now sat perched between two friends on the back row of some low-rise bleachers. Javier knew the two friends, Beto and Augusto, no problem there. Whenever Javier checked Alex's phone in the evening, it showed only these three in the chat. Dumb memes and gamer videos. But the signs were there, first with the sagging jeans, his denim crotch more like a hemline, then with the Raiders gear, a sartorial middle finger to the school dress code. And now this week's yo-homie flourish— one pant leg up knee-height, a throwback look that had been making the rounds on social media.

Halfway through lunch, the pair from Denker would arrive, Itchy and Scratchy, the former notable for his insistent, vacuous smile and the latter for his slightly forlorn appearance. They'd take the bleachers two at a time, stepping over lunch trays on their way to the back row. Itchy always had on a pristine ball cap turned at a jaunty angle, a shiny decal still affixed to the bill, and Scratchy, hands shoved deep in his pockets, wore a hoodie that bisected his skull and swung off the crown of his head as if glued in place. Itchy would plop down next to Alex, stick one hand in the bag of chips, then drape an arm over Alex's shoulder, a telling combination of coercion and brotherhood that had grown over the first semester. Three months ago, Alex would have given the boy all shoulder, kept his eyes on his phone. Here it was October, now with the dap and the head nods, a steady drip of street-love like water for the thirsty. Itchy, the salesman, brought the hype, and sad-sack Scratchy brought the promise of violence. Javier held the most contempt for guys like Scratchy, follow-ons who kept the whole charade going. Javier had known a handful of Scratchies—his friend, Chuey, exhibit A—and knew they had more choice in their lives than the Itchies of the world who couldn't help but inspire the worst in others. Scratchies lacked imagination, and without them, Itchies were just gas.

The Gaither lunch bell rang. Scratchy scanned the quad like a farmer looking for a good place to plant corn. He clutched the side of his jeans and climbed down the steps, a pop-and-lock that gave him the appearance of old age. Then Itchy stood, having sold Alex a vision of *vida loca* now for ten minutes, and offered the cherry-on-top out of view of the school cameras. His hands, belt-high and with the fluid grace of an interpreter for the deaf, flashed the Denker trademark S-R-V: the first letters of the three street names, Sepulveda, Roscoe, and Van Nuys, which bounded their neighborhood, Barrio Horseshoe, or as everyone called it, the Shoe.

There was no fourth street because the southern boundary of the Shoe was a lunar landscape called Dogtown, a 500-acre vacant lot in the middle of East San Fernando Valley big enough to site a football stadium. Fifty years ago, when this part of Los Angeles had been mostly farmland, the area had been a man-made lake. Seen from above even today, it resembled an enormous footprint minus the toes. On Google Maps, it was cryptically referred to as a hazard abatement area, a lake long since dried up and now a tent city for the Valley's destitute. Both code and law enforcement took a hands-off approach, certain that a close look would trigger enough paperwork to keep everyone behind their desks for months.

Javier watched Alex slow-walk to class like he was underwater. Another bad sign.

"Dumb and Dumber come by?" Raffa broke in.

Class was ending, Patel now returning to the mundane world of homework and Friday's quiz. Javier looked at the whiteboard and made a mental note of the page numbers to read and the problem set to finish. Raffa knew Javier had been watching Alex and the daily ritual. "He's in eighth grade, big brother. They're all stupid." Raffa zipped up his backpack. "Trust me. Jocelyn belongs in a cage." Jocelyn was his sister. "I say put 'em all on an island, come back in a year. Whoever survives gets to go on to high school."

Javier thought of smiling but couldn't. "Kid's a follower, and he's angry about something." He stuck his notebook in his backpack and watched Alex disappear around a building. "Those two mooks been working him since August." He couldn't shake the fact that it was Alex, not Beto or Augusto, who'd been the target these past three months.

The bell rang, and the class stood to leave. Javier nudged Gio who was now staring at McRibbs, the skeleton parked in the corner, its head tilted toward the floor as if he'd dropped a set of keys. Enrique was already macking on the girl next to him who had the hunched posture of someone expecting a bomb to go off. Javier, Raffa, and Gio left him there and walked into the hallway traffic, a human salmon run after fourth period.

Raffa turned to Javier over his shoulder. "Relax. He's gonna join a tagging crew, throw up his *placa* three times, get busted on the fourth when he shows up on camera." They wound down the stairwell and outside to the quad. "Then Mendez's gonna turn the jets on his ass." Raffa took out his water bottle, offered a sip first to Gio then to Javier; both declined. "Then you'll take him to Walmart to buy a new set of *chones*."

Officer Mendez was the school police officer who'd made it his life's mission to put wayward boys like Alex back on the path their mothers wanted them on. Twice a year he'd round up the Gaither frequent fliers and put them into a room with a group of *veteranos* who'd lived the life, done the time, and now put the fear of God into boys like Alex. Their facial scars webbed with stitch lines belied a history of violence, their jailhouse tats now blurred and illegible. Eight of them would put their chairs in a row, a firing squad for each of the Gaither bad apples.

See this paperclip? That's what Papi will use to ink his initials on your neck, entiendes? Then another would push in closer, an ugly, staring face with dead eyes. Each fatherless boy, an unexpected spark of need suddenly welling up, as if summoned by this stranger, so close now, he could hear the man's breath whistling through his nose. One by one, their chairs scraping the floor, until they formed an OG semicircle. One of them—whichever one still had his prison swole—would whip off his shirt to reveal a torso slabbed with muscle.

Gonna put salt on yo ass. Hahahahahaha. Yo ass taste better with salt. More riotous laughter then Mendez would get up and leave the room to take a call, and that's when some of the boys would pee themselves.

The three of them got to the main office where Raffa fist-bumped Javier and Gio and then pushed a shoulder into one of the double doors and disappeared inside. He worked two hours a day answering phones, sorting mail, translating for parents, and helping with the reams of paperwork that were forever breeding newer, smaller piles. Like Javier, Raffa was on a glide path to college. They had each, in fact, already accrued enough credits to have graduated by now.

"Only double-hinged joint in the body, Javi." Gio tried wiggling his jaw. "But mines mostly up and down, you know. I can still hear it click, though..." He smiled and trailed off. He and Javier had been mistaken as brothers in fifth grade when they first met. Most teachers had to look at their necks to tell the two apart. Javier wore a gold Our Lady, though their hairstyles soon diverged. By third grade, Gio's hair quickly became a mop he trimmed himself with school scissors. Javier, by contrast, had always been twos on the side and fives on top. The one other distinguishing difference was the scar over Javier's left eye where his father had taken batting practice, the dead white tissue of a slow healing wound stitched up country style back in Jalisco. In the pigmentocracy of the barrio, Javier and Gio were both slightly more on the almond end of things, though not coffee bean dark, with bee-stung lips framing their fish angled mouths.

"You ever notice how skeletons all seem like they're smiling?" Gio mused apropos of nothing. He made a Cheshire smile, revealing two rows of fun-house teeth. An orthodontist could look in Gio's mouth and see his daughter's college tuition. It was, in fact, Javier who had taught him how to brush.

"Spring'll be here faster than you might think, Gio," Javier said. "The Needles sisters are gonna change the locks, put your shit on the curb." Javier had been trying to chip away at Gio's blithe indifference to aging out, convince him to put in some job applications, start lining up food stamps. His eighteenth birthday would be his last as a ward of the county.

"Emancipated." Gio gave Javier a coy look and chuckled as if considering the full weight of the term, then wandered off toward the unlit section of the hallway past the main office, a no-man's-land that led to a stairwell with a pair of locked doors at the bottom. Kids went to vape there, some using it to take a leak when the bathrooms were locked. Halfway down the hall Gio stopped in front of a wall display, eternally lit by a pair of fluorescent tubes, trophies from generations ago, art projects from students now old enough to have kids of their own. He leaned in, trying to read something.

"Dinner, Thursday," Javier half shouted. "Ma's playing catch-up on *Rebelde*." It was Mama's *novela*, and over the course of two weeks while he slept on their couch one summer, it had become Gio's too. The saccharine storylines, a fifty-minute mental oasis for Mama and half the women of the Shoe, served as a stand-in for Gio's family narrative, his own like a phantom limb that he could feel but that no longer existed.

Gio kept staring at the display and nodded his response, his detachment sudden and complete.

Javier's phone buzzed, a text from Mama. She'd be working another double tonight which meant there'd be a frozen brick of noodle soup in the sink when he got home. The freezer was full of them, gallon Ziplock bags stacked like sandbags. She never said no to more work—and there was always more work—and she had the joint and back pain to prove it. Javier would often greet her when she returned from overnights with a tube of high-octane Mexican balm that he'd rub into her knees and shoulders but mostly her back where a couple of discs had turned to sponge. The doctors might as well have put a zipper between her L3 and L5 vertebrae she'd had so many surgeries.

The college off-ramp wasn't more than ten months away for Javier, and as much as Mama had insisted early on that education *es lo mas importante*, she'd been steadily dialing back the rhetoric as the medical bills had started arriving with big red letters stamped all over them. But more than that, she'd come to rely on him to keep Alex, a born rule-follower, from slipping further into the streets. Javier's carefully built Jenga tower had a couple pieces sticking out.

CHAPTER 2

Carlos rode the boom lift thirty feet up, stepped onto the deck of the viaduct, and worked his way through the final course of rebar, checking the snap ties as he went. By noon, it would all be covered with two hundred yards of cement, an act of finality that had left him sleepless and bleary-eyed. He got to the unfinished edge and gazed out at the yuccas standing in the morning sun, their knobby arms raised as if surrendering. The only movement, the only noise, came from the survey team a quarter mile ahead, hammering stakes and taking measurements through transits. His phone buzzed with a text from Raymond, the lead surveyor. It was an image of a tortoise craning its neck.

Carlos pulled out his walkie. "How many?"

A pause. "I count about twenty, twenty-five."

Carlos hissed. Nothing meant more trouble for projects like this than habitat issues, and the desert tortoise was at the top of the protected species list in this part of California. He kicked a water bottle off the deck, his head now flooding with a list of change orders, cost overruns, impact reports. The Sierra Club would have an injunction by the end of the week, his crew would scatter, and the job would be bad-mouthed in the trades, *falton* as they would call it. It was the bane of every publicly funded project. Things were always stop-and-go, and for subcontractors, consistency was king.

"We'll need some video. Get a geotag on it and send it over." He paused then added, "Tell your guys to go home. We gotta pull them off the job."

A moment later Raymond came back on the radio. "One more you need to see."

Carlos opened the next text. It showed the flat underside of one of the tortoises, four legs helplessly splayed out. Along one edge of the shell, a small strip of aluminum had been riveted to it. The last picture was a closeup of the tag, showing a bar code and a set of Chinese characters.

■　　■　　■

Tasha passed through the metal detector and retrieved her phone on the other side. She saw Carlos had sent her a video then tapped the screen to see a clip showing a pod of tortoises ambling across the desert. The image needed no explanation.

Muthafucka.

In her two years as Communications Director for Senator Rittenhouse, she'd had to learn ways to corral her temper—deep breaths, long drinks of water, long drinks of Grey Goose—but today all she wanted to do was throw her phone across the capitol rotunda. The rail project was her ticket to Washington, with or without the Senator. If things went pear-shaped here in Sacramento, she'd be back running school board elections in Los Angeles.

She arrived in the back of the Senate chambers in time to catch the last legs of the reauthorization debate. Support was split for the bullet train, which was now so far over budget it would require a fourth round of bonds. An eleventh-hour deal with a large off-shore hedge fund had given the project new life. The Speaker could bring the reauthorization up for a vote either now or tomorrow. Three hours ago, it would have been a lay-up for Tasha. She'd already put in an offer for a two-bedroom condo in Georgetown.

The vote count on the screen and the adjournment clock ticking down lent the usually staid chambers a charged air. The Speaker stood at the rostrum, gavel in hand, talking with a staffer over his shoulder. From the steps below, a senate page reached up and slid the Speaker a note. He read it and pulled out his phone, scrolled through some texts, then brought down his gavel twice. The vote would be delayed until tomorrow at 8 a.m., an eternity in the deal-making days of late August in Sacramento. Careers often turned on these votes, and Tasha felt hers slipping away. The Sierra Club was probably already setting up the presser with their righteous refrains. She'd done her best to curry favor with the green slice of the electorate, keeping the Senator at or above eighty percent favorability. Coastal set asides, old-growth logging regulations, that stupid little fish in the delta. And this had come at considerable expense to the donor list, a hit she knew was worth the points he'd scored with the base.

All those years triangulating, positioning, counter messaging, all the miles on the road, in the air, prepping, dodging, deflecting, polling, vetting, all that code-switching, hi-watt smiling, all the hours briefing and debriefing, and for what? So that a thirty-second video could expose him as an environmental hypocrite? Tasha knew this was no accident, and she knew who was behind it.

*   *   *

The video feed to the twin-engine Gulfstream had been in and out, the result of a typhoon over Micronesia, delaying the meeting for another ten minutes. George Jones couldn't stand long flights and hated meetings even more, so here he was thirty thousand feet over the Pacific about to combine the two. He poured himself two fingers of Glenmorangie and contemplated the fate of several hundred displaced tortoises. He could wrangle and return them to their country of origin, collect his six-million-dollar deposit, or he could let them wander the Mojave and mystify subsequent generations of herpetologists at a loss to explain how this particular species made it from the Gobi Desert to the I-15 corridor of Southern California.

The video link refreshed, prompting Jones to throw back his Scotch in one go and come off mute. His screen filled with thumbnails of the ten committee members. All but two, both of whom were clearly on the upper deck of their respective yachts, had their cameras off, their names anonymized.

Jones got right to the point. "We've been looking at LA for about ten years now waiting for the right time, and an opportunity has arisen that pencils out," Jones said. The fund's specialty was transit node development, and Jones was its fixer. "I'll give you the haiku version. Stir shit up, drive values down, then back the cash truck up and remodel the place." Very wealthy people came to the fund to park their money, earn massive returns, and reduce their tax liabilities. "With a little pressure, we'll be looking at a 12 to 1 return over the first five years." He knew it would probably be twice that amount.

Stir shit up. A little pressure. The committee took a position of willful ignorance to these aphorisms. Rate of return was all that mattered. The methods and means were none of their concern which is why they skipped past any due diligence motions and went straight to the vote. Fifteen minutes later, the screen was once again empty, and Jones had the fund's blessing.

The plane made its descent into Sacramento International where Jones had one more appointment before a six-hour drive to Los Angeles. The Gulfstream taxied into the hangar where the pilot cut the engines and dropped the gangway. Jones appeared at the doorway where an attendant handed him a hot towel to wipe the sixteen-hour flight off his face. He descended the stairs, and at the bottom, a man in jeans and leather jacket handed him a burner phone.

"For our friends in the white van. Image uploads, crypto transfers, confirmation texts only." Jones toggled through the settings. "This group likes to keep tabs on their clients. Whenever the burner is on, they'll know where you are, and no way to disable the geolocation."

The man then reached inside his jacket and pulled out a Walther P38 and handed it to Jones, grip first. Jones wracked the slide, chambered a round, and flipped the safety on. Then he climbed into a matte black Land Rover and put the burner in the cup holder.

An hour later, he self-parked at Torento, one of the few spots in Sacramento that could still be relied upon for discretion. He walked past the hostess, straight to a corner booth where Senator Rittenhouse sat alone, hunched over a bowl of pasta. He saw Jones approach and dipped his head slightly to indicate an empty seat. Jones ignored the Senator, instead pulling up a rattan chair from a neighboring table, took a seat as he shot his cuffs, and waved off the waiter who appeared instantly with a menu.

The restaurant was dimly lit, the high-backed booths upholstered in oxblood leather, the room awash in hushed tones of last-minute horse trades. "Your train is coming in," said the Senator without looking up. "But I suspect you already knew this." The Senator went at his pasta like it owed him money, his torso rocking with each spin of the fork. "Something about turtles." He finally looked up and let out a breath. "I hear they're on loan from the Zhang Zhao Preserve. They must have cost you a small fortune." Then he shoved a forkful of pasta in his mouth.

"They're tortoises, not turtles, and I have no idea what you're talking about," said Jones.

The Senator pulled out his napkin and dried the sweat from his upper lip, then stabbed at something in the sauce. "Turtles, tortoises. No one cares. All I know is they're slow, and there's too many." He took a swallow of wine. "You have my ass in the air, and the vote is tomorrow. Seems like your reputation is well earned, Mr. Jones." He broke off a piece of bread and dragged it through the white sauce. "Prague, Athens, Hyderabad," his mouth finally empty. "Some biblical shit."

Jones had actually flirted with the ministry at one point. "Pox and pestilence, death of the firstborn, rivers into blood. Moses didn't fuck around, and neither do I." A college girlfriend had once examined the headline of his palm, straight and uncrossed, and proclaimed it a sign of either intense religious conviction or a tendency toward psychopathy. "If there's a transit node involved, I'll salt the earth myself." He made a show of checking his watch.

The Senator leaned back, let his hands rest flat on the table, as if ready to make it levitate.

"We're prepared to reroute the line to Panorama City. Just know you're the ghetto option." He folded the napkin and looked at Jones. "And as we both know, bullet trains don't stop in the ghetto."

"Of course it's coming to the ghetto, Senator. There's nowhere else to stick it." Jones ran a hand down his pants to flatten a wrinkle. "Ghetto for now, Senator." He nodded at the Senator's bowl of pasta. "But I'll bet you another bowl of that alfredo you seem to love so much that in a year, you'll be making offers on our condos before they're even out of plan-check."

The Senator gave Jones an appraising look. "Have you seen Panorama City lately, Jones? Great town if you're a pole dancer. They have a tent city the size of Rhode Island."

"For a curious man," Jones said standing, "you ask the wrong questions." He passed his gaze around the room. "Your work is done, Senator. Time for the ground game."

When he got to his car, Jones pulled out his phone and placed a call before getting inside. "We're up." Across the lot he spotted the tail he'd picked up just outside the airport. The car had back-in parked, the only one in the lot to do so. "I'm on my way."

Once inside the Land Rover, he grabbed the burner from the cup holder, and typed in a text.

VDL go

.   .   .

The man in the boat hadn't had a bite and didn't much care. He came for the solitude, the stars, and the sounds of the reservoir at 4 a.m. Most people fished during the day from the dam wall where it was wide enough to park their coolers and fold-out chairs. Van der Lipp Dam itself was the third largest in the western United States and the oldest by a decade. A sluice had been built at the base of the dam's southern end, a failsafe option for a uranium enrichment plant from the 1950s. The plant had long since been dismantled, though the sluice, which emptied into a dry lakebed in East San Fernando Valley, remained.

A vehicle approached, the light wash of high beams coming through the pine trees. The man in the boat had never seen anyone use the access road. It was a white transit van, and it very quickly turned, reversed, and backed up ten feet from the water's edge. The rear door opened, and five men climbed out, two of them in wetsuits hoisting scuba tanks from the back of the van. They worked without talking, testing the respirators, buckling their weight belts, and in less than a minute, they were walking backward into the water, each clutching something the size of a shoebox. Soon, the only evidence of either of them was a trail of bubbles rising to the surface.

The man took out a pair of binoculars he kept for birding and watched two other men walk out onto the dam's catwalk. The first man carried a coil of rope slung over his shoulder; the second wore a backpack and a climber's harness. When they were about one hundred feet out, the first man sat down and tied himself onto a railing stanchion and belayed the second man over the edge of the dam. The team worked noiselessly, their movements practiced and efficient. In twenty minutes, the divers surfaced and took off their flippers and tanks. Soon after, the man in the harness reappeared on top of the dam.

As they loaded up to leave, a fish took the man's lure and pulled the rod off his lap, hitting the aluminum gunwale. A second bang followed when the reel hit the bottom of the boat. The noise echoed across the reservoir. All five men stopped what they were doing and looked in the man's direction. The man, still hidden in darkness, froze. Five seconds passed. Then ten. Finally, one of the men reached for something in the front seat and disappeared into the woods. The other four climbed back in and drove back down the access road to somewhere called Panorama City.

Ten minutes later the man in the boat lay face down, hidden among the tule in the shallow water of the lake, two in the chest and one in the head. His boat lay at the bottom of the lake, also with three holes shot through it. The shooter had collected the six empty shells then walked the eight miles back down the access road to the city street. He'd boarded the 154 bus which would take him to meet up with the others. Someplace called Dogtown was about to become the newest body of water in Los Angeles.

CHAPTER 3

The six blocks from school to work took Javier past a collection of defeated storefronts, inside each a tableaux of some hasty retreat, papers littering the floors, cabinet drawers pitching off their guides, as if Godzilla had shown up at one end of Van Nuys Boulevard and spotted Rodan at the other. Only two shops did any noticeable business. The first, Mantrap Nails, was the neighborhood haven for local women looking to get out from under, catch up on *chisme*, and be on the receiving end for once. The second was a block further north and across Van Nuys, a bar doing its best to stay hidden, no sign, no windows. On Wednesday afternoons, the owner doused the place in bleach and left the front door propped open, revealing a handful of men bent over their beers as if in prayer. It wasn't until Javier got to the sixth block, a strip mall featuring a Salvadoran restaurant, a Korean donut store, a barbershop called Deez Cutz, and a small grocer who sold nopales, that Javier noticed any effort to actually attract customers.

Behind these stores stood Valley Savings, monument to steel-rush Panorama City of the fifties, now ten looming floors of abandoned office space. Its most striking feature, a bizarre set of flying buttresses arcing off its roof, looked like an enormous pair of luggage handles which now served no purpose other than to give junkies a landmark to get their bearings. *Just look for the, you know, suitcase.* Valley Savings had turned into the Shoe's shooting gallery for needle users, but to Javier it was a bit of a shrine. It had been the first place he and his brother Alex could call their own when they first arrived ten years ago. They'd grabbed two office chairs from the fifth floor, lugged them up five flights to the roof, and spent every day after school for the next three months watching the traffic on the 405 go by. It was a strange view of a strange land, the two of them more accustomed to the upper branches of their mango tree back in Jalisco. Atop Valley Savings, Javier wondered sometimes to himself and sometimes aloud to Alex why they'd come here in the first place. Though violence had been a more intimate fact of life in Mexico, they were never strangers there which, to Javier, was more corrosive, their family starting to rust in this place. They'd gone from a family of five to three in the first two years, though neither loss ever drew any mention. Yanira's memory was still an active minefield, roped off by Mama who was yet to come to terms with her oceanic guilt. The annual *offrenda* always featured the same picture of her, a gap-toothed smile and hair like a raven's wing. In contrast, their father's absence hardly warranted mention. A man who never said no to a shortcut, he had always given Javier the impression of someone waiting to get off a bus.

His phone buzzed, his girlfriend Leslie Facetiming him, no doubt with another round of go-here-do-this.

"Check your calendar, Javi. Next month. Meet and greet with Lupe's board." She often called during his walk from school to work, speaking in bursts like her phone was about to die. She was playing Sherpa guide on Javier's ascent up Mt. Scholarship, and, by Leslie's account, this Lupe person's program was the summit.

He had no idea what a board was. "I dunno, Les."

"You'll get to meet Lupe." A choir of angels every time she said that name. Leslie had gone all in on this Lupe lady, apparently a barrio-beater who'd made it out of the Gardens and was now living *maximo* in the hills. "She totally gets it, Javi."

The front end of Delilah was just pulling out of Mission Tow, its diesel burble growing louder as the flatbed approached. Betzaida was driving and leaning across the front seat to open the passenger side door as she pulled even with Javier.

"10-54, *ponerse las pilas*, Javi." A 10-54 was police code for a hit-and-run requiring an ambulance, double dips in the towing world—one invoice for the tow and another for the storage until the investigators could get there. "Later for lovergirl," Betzaida said. She was his half-sister and owner of Mission Tow which made her technically his boss. Javier waved at the phone and clicked off.

Betzaida and Javier shared the same father, though Betzaida had been born in the States, the black sheep, the one with short hair and the name from Aztlan in a houseful of pocha names like Madison. It was hardly a surprise to anyone when Betzaida came out in high school, though her mother, having construed her daughter's sexuality as a knock on her parenting, made a clean break of it with a dramatic closet toss out the alley-facing—not even pool-facing—window.

"*Te ves como un hombre!*"

Broad-chested, no hips, and small ankles, Betzaida had the physique of an upside-down traffic cone. Customers mistook her for a guy all the time.

"They're not man-boobs," she'd eventually announce.

Valley tow companies competed fiercely, and Betzaida had carved out a reliable piece of business with CHP near the 101 and 405 interchange. Officers liked Betzaida because she never bent their ears with theories of skid marks or how the Lakers were doing. She arrived almost as soon as fire and rescue, cleared the lanes quickly, and was "wracked and rolling" faster than any other company in the Valley.

"Every swinging chippie dick has to stand in front of the LTs once a month and talk lane clearance rates." It was the only piece of guidance she got from Janson, the previous owner, and it was all she needed.

"Fat Man is gonna try to move on this one," Betzaida said, checking her rearview. Fat Man was Kristops Bergosian, corpulent rival who'd started running trucks into Mission's stretch of the 405. "Cocksucker aint stepping in front."

The interior of Delilah was pristine. The dash and seats, usually the first items to relent to the Valley heat, were still looking almost new, even at eighty thousand miles. Betzaida's only full-timer, a wiry guy named Lester, made certain Mission rigs "rolled correct," chrome polished, panels waxed and buffed, tires dressed.

Javier buckled up. "I thought Lester was driving today."

"He's doing repos." Betzaida stole a glance at Javier flipping through the stack of bills lying between them and finally pulling one out. "I know what you're gonna say, and no, we're not switching agents. Letty's my girl." She checked her traffic app and began signaling her lane changes. Javier opened the envelope with their insurance premium inside then blanched at an umbrella policy with exotic coverages.

"No, you're right, Betz. Makes sense, you know, if Russia and China both invade at the same time, we'll be in good shape." He'd been making the same point for six months, annoyed because Betzaida never suffered fools but was letting loyalty get the better of her. It was her blind spot, and her margins were too thin to be sentimental. He then tore open a bank statement and scanned it. More bad news. The business was running off Betzaida's personal credit. "You need to finance your receivables, Betz. This ninety-day-late shit is killing you."

She side-eyed him and shot him some boss-talk. "Front wheel drive on this hook, so make sure you clip inside the bushings." Fire and EMT were already on scene. A matte black Land Rover was pinned against the k-rail separating the north and southbound traffic. The passenger side of the car looked like it had been through a can opener, the front and back doors nowhere to be seen. The front-end suspension was gone, leaving the car in a kneeling position looking like a wounded animal. A bike cop directing traffic saw Betzaida approaching, nodded and waved her past the phalanx of rescue vehicles walling off the scene.

The driver of the Land Rover was already on a gurney being loaded into a waiting ambulance. It was a bloodless scene, airbags still bundled away. The guy would be treated and released in a day. Wrinkle patterns on the hood ran lengthwise, suggesting the car had been pinned against the median by a larger vehicle. If Javier had to guess, this was no accident. Most people swerve quickly on contact, but not the other driver in this collision. They'd have kept their hands firmly on the wheel for some time, a hundred-yard hip check into the median.

Javier got out and went to put the Land Rover in neutral. The interior was immaculate, a high-end sports package with paddle shifts and terrain dials—a waste of money in Javier's mind. This car never went anywhere that wasn't paved and was probably hand-rubbed once a week. Glass shards were splayed out on the black leather seats like uncut diamonds. A pair of wipers wagged back and forth, oddly typical for high-impact collisions. As he went to turn them off, he noticed a burner sitting in the cup holder blinking a text.

VDL package delivered

An Amazon update or something.

He opened the glovebox to put the burner inside and saw a gun sitting there, the barrel pointing straight at his chest as though expecting him. He had to suppress an urge to pick it up, feel its heft. Instead, he stuck the burner inside and quickly shut the door like it was Pandora's Box.

CHAPTER 4

Los Angeles City Councilman Jesse Delatorre arrived at the gym as he always did at 5 a.m. He wore headphones not so much for the music as to let others know he wasn't there to chitchat. In the months prior to an election, he took off the headphones and nailed on a smile, but his next primary wasn't for another two years. He benched four sets, hit the squat rack, and then the treadmill before ducking into the locker room, as was his custom, at 5:45.

He always chose the same locker in the same bay, the same set of faces with the occasional old baggy-balled man parading around. A plumber in a blue jumpsuit was bent over one of the touchless faucets that never worked. Delatorre worked the combination on his lock, got out of his gym clothes, wrapped a towel around his waist, and hit the shower for his three-minute routine. When he returned still dripping, he noticed the lock dial was now facing the other way. And the plumber was gone. He quickly flipped the lock, spun the dial left right left, and pulled open the locker door. His wallet and watch were both still there. He let out a breath and grabbed his dress shirt off a hook, and as he did, a legal-size manila envelope flopped over. He pulled it out and looked at the contents, a collection of pictures of his drug-addict son and what he recognized as a set of charging documents issued by LAPD to the district attorney. He reviewed them one at a time then stared at the ceiling wondering how long this was going to take and what the final price would be. Developers looking for variances were conniving little shits.

He indulged in a moment of fantasy, a drive up the coast against traffic to Zuma Beach, watching the waves on a fold-out chair and plucking beers from a cooler full of ice. Instead, he summoned what scraps of resolve he could muster and went outside into the gray dawn. His driver was there, on time as usual, holding the door open to his city-issue.

A middle-aged man with gray hair in a dark suit and white shirt, no tie, was sitting inside. "Thought we'd share a ride downtown, Councilman."

Delatorre paused, managed to conceal any surprise and got in.

"I see you got some mail," said the man, nodding at the envelope. The Councilman started to say something to the driver, but the glass divider was already halfway up, the car already turning left out of the gym parking lot.

"Who are you?" asked Delatorre. The man in the suit handed him a card. "False imprisonment is a felony...Mr. Jones," he said, looking at the card.

"So is possession with intent." He took the envelope from the Councilman, reached inside, pulled out a set of eight-by-ten glossies one at a time and placed them on the car seat. "Seems Junior has a bit of a habit...Dad. But that's not news to you." Jones stuffed the pictures back and left the envelope sitting on the seat. "Probably not the extracurricular activity USC is looking for these days. Second offense, so no program. He's looking at three years in Corcoran." He stared out the windshield, letting it hang there. "Minimum."

Delatorre looked at Jones. "What do you want?" Salty but tempered.

"Same thing as you. To make the bad people who feed your son's habit go away." The car slipped down the onramp diamond lane past a long line of commuters. Delatorre turned his attention to a woman driving an enormous SUV in the lane next to theirs. She was applying mascara in her rearview mirror while driving.

"Well, that's a noble goal. Let's put a committee together and study the problem." Shakedowns were part of the job, but this one cut close to the bone. His son had sustained a football injury in high school, been prescribed painkillers, then quickly moved up the opiate ladder, which these days took less and less time.

"Denker Park across from Roscoe Gardens is an open-air drug market. Junior is on a first-name basis with all five crews. Get rid of the Gardens and you get rid of his supply." It went unsaid that the Councilman's son would soon find another source, but that didn't seem to be the issue.

"It's public housing. You can't take it down." He added just enough tone to push back on this guy.

Jones took a moment. "Consider this your red pill moment, Councilman." Delatorre was a mid-tier politician going nowhere. In a few years, he'd term out, then either be forced to pursue higher office or sign up to take the realtor's exam. "The Gardens will be gone in six months. Get your head around that, then picture in their place the LA terminus of a bullet train to Vegas."

Delatorre looked at Jones like he had two heads. "You're a fuckin' nut."

Jones looked out the car window and peered up at the sky as if trying to assess the chance of rain. "We don't have much time, Councilman. I'm getting out at Alvarado."

There was a long pause before Delatorre ran a hand over his face. "I'm not gonna even pretend what you just described is even remotely possible." He knew Corcoran Correctional Facility would ruin his son, a sensitive kid who'd get punked before his first lunch arrived. He chinned at the envelope containing the charging documents. "How do I know you can make this little problem go away?"

"You don't."

Outside a freeway sign on an overpass announced Alvarado was two miles away. Traffic was unreasonably light today. "And what do you want from me?"

Jones angled his body toward the Councilman, put his arm along the top of the seat. "The HUD mortgages at the Gardens could have been prepaid five years ago, but you've just never had the motivation." It was the truth. "Or the stones." Also true. The original developer, G and K Holdings, could get out from under the regulations any day by simply paying off the mortgage. "Your committee needs to get the ball rolling."

"You make it sound so simple." He didn't like being lectured to. "It's not just a committee vote. The tenant association has to agree on move-out terms." He kept his tone flat. "They get five years sometimes to pack up their shit. And you seem like someone with a more aggressive timeline." Delatorre watched the lady in the SUV now apply lipstick using her rearview mirror to inspect her work, turning her head left then right, her vehicle drifting across the lane. Delatorre actually hoped there would be contact. "There is one vote in the association, the local *abuela*, been there since the place was built, and she will fight you tooth and nail."

"Won't be an issue." It was a loaded response. Delatorre studied Jones who returned the look with a pair of waterless eyes that never seemed to blink.

"Stop pretending you don't want the Gardens down too, Councilman. Tear them down, and you will have done more to get rid of drugs in the Valley than any other public official." The Gardens had been home to Denker Street, the local wholesale narcotics distributor for the past three generations. "It's going to raise your profile, put you in line for state office, maybe Congress. Don't doubt I can help you." Again, not a throwaway line. Jones was painting a bigger picture.

Delatorre resented how well this man—his kidnapper—saw inside his head, saw his own ambitions, once outsized and now beginning to wither on the vine. The Gardens were a millstone to the Twelfth District. He'd blocked the vote for prepayment twice already, had knuckled under to his westside contributors who'd financed much of his campaign to keep public housing on the east side of the Valley.

Jones tapped the glass partition behind the driver's seat. The driver hit his turn signal and started changing lanes.

"What else, Mr. Jones?"

"Later today, your office will be receiving a master development plan which includes the terms of a partnership between the city and my firm, Solano. You'll notice it's going to require enactment of state and federal enterprise zones, disaster relief, and eminent domain." Jones gave Delatorre a moment to consider all this, then proceeded. "The governor is on board, Councilman, and he'll have his eye on you for the next six months, so it may be time to cap those teeth and think about some plugs." Jones shot a glance at the Councilman's thinning hair. "Be ready. Kickoff is in two nights." They were on the exit ramp now, a panhandler approaching the passenger side, holding a cardboard sign. "Some people flip homes. I flip zip codes, Councilman."

Delatorre let his eyes fall to study Jones' shoes, often his quickest measure of the competition, and noticed, with chagrin, the hand stitching, the deep luster, his own already on their fourth set of soles. He was outgunned and outplayed, his entire career suddenly cooked down to an action item for this prick Jones. He was staring down the barrel of a dozen ethics violations if he didn't walk away right now.

He tried switching fields, suggesting Jones was wearing a wire. "Don't ever pull a stunt like this again, Mr. Jones. I'll start a RICO investigation if I ever see you again and your lobbying career in this great city will be over." The car took a right turn, then quickly came to a stop.

Jones got out and pulled up his shirt revealing only his stomach and no recording device. Then he tucked his shirt back in. "Councilman, in three months you're going to be cutting a lot of ribbons in the Shoe, smiling for a lot of cameras, and I'll be sure to come by to shake your hand. And when I do, I have a sneaking suspicion you'll be the one opening the car door for me." He waved at a car across the street that immediately pulled out, did a U-turn and pulled up alongside Delatorre's. "I'll be at your committee meeting next week to see which side of things you're gonna be on." With that, he got into the waiting car, and sped off.

CHAPTER 5

When Javier got to work the next day, Betzaida was off and Lester was out doing repos. Lenders paid well to recover their cars when loans went unpaid, the only hiccup being when the delinquent borrower suddenly appeared in their slippers and bathrobe waving a pistol. Most repos were uneventful but in this corner of the Valley, some of the owners were drug-addled and half crazed on a normal day. Two weeks ago, Lester'd been chased and shot at, and a week before that followed all the way back to Mission Tow where Betzaida greeted his pursuer at the gate clutching the twelve-gauge looking like Geronimo.

In the middle of the Mission Tow yard was the trailer office, the Box. It had one three-inch solid core door with a variety of sliding and deadbolt locks and one window with two-inch Plexiglass where people came to pay their fees and claim their cars. The interior consisted of a microwave, a mini-fridge, a flatscreen that ran news with no sound continuously, and two workstations that sat on desks pocked with cigarette burn marks from Betzaida's smoking days.

Javier pulled out the drawer where Betzaida's stuffed anything that might bear witness to the financial health of Mission Tow: work orders, invoices, credit card statements, receipts, handwritten notes. A few months ago, he'd started putting some systems in place to manage payables and payroll, but the money that was due, the revenue, was mostly in the wind. He reckoned

Mission was sitting on fifty thousand in receivables, an asset he could borrow against, but without a balance sheet and tax returns, no lender would look at a loan application.

A black Mercedes pulled into the yard, quickly enveloped in a dust cloud as it skidded to a stop. Javier got up and went to the door of the Box to see who it was. A young man stepped out like an arriving general. He had short hair and a short beard, wearing a pair of glasses that were, in Javier's estimation, trying way too hard. Javier came out of the Box but only crossed halfway across the dirt lot.

The man, squeezing a blue ball in his right hand, met him in the middle. "Are you Javier?" It was more statement than question.

"How 'bout we start with your name since you're the visiting team."

The man smiled and nodded. "You're right. Sorry about that. Name's Dana Booth. The 405 always puts me in a mood. Westside is bad enough, but I hate coming to the Valley. No offense."

"What can I do for you?"

"You towed in a Land Rover a couple of days ago. Belongs to my boss, and I came to pick up the phone that was left inside." He looked around, spotted it. "Right there. That one."

He pointed at the Land Rover, still missing two of its doors and its front-end suspension.

"Right." He kept looking at the guy's frames feeling fated to hate this guy. "How's your boss?"

"Fine. Couple of stitches from the airbags and a bad headache, but nothing major."

Nope. Wrong answer.

Javier chinned in the direction of the Land Rover. "Car is part of a hit-and-run investigation. Can't release it."

The guy waved a hand. "Right, understood. I'm just here for a phone that was in the car. My boss needs it."

"Just need to call him then to get authorization." Javier started walking to the Box waiting to hear the guy's plan B.

"Of course, but yeah, he, ah, is getting on a plane right now for New York." There was a pause. "That's why he sent me." He put the blue ball in his other hand and continued squeezing.

Javier stopped and turned. "Your boss, who pays you to run errands, like driving to the Valley to get his phone...flying red-eye." Anything leaving out of LA at this hour would be overnight to New York.

The guy studied the ground, hands on hips. "Look, I understand I'm asking you maybe to bend the rules a little, but he expects me to have that phone back tonight, and he's not a guy who likes to wait, if you know what I mean, so here's a little something for your trouble." He pulled out his wallet and produced two hundred-dollar bills.

"I'd lose my job," Javier lied.

The man stuffed the bills back in his front pocket. "Well, how 'bout I just wait until Betzaida returns." He tried to make it sound like they were good friends.

"She's on a plane to New York."

The guy looked around the yard now realizing he'd driven into a boxed canyon. "Didn't realize you guys had such a wide service area. Guess I'll have to cancel Triple A." He stood there impassively, looking unsure, then abruptly got back in his car, backed out, and made a hard left on Roscoe as quickly as he had arrived.

When Betzaida returned thirty minutes later, Javier was working his way through a folder of invoices using a twelve-key machine. "That guy come by for the phone?" she asked, going straight to the mini-fridge and pulling out a cardboard carton of something.

"He's not the guy."

"How'd you know?"

"He said something about stitches and airbags."

"And..."

"The interior's clean. No blood and no airbags. Numbnuts was lying."

Guys like that usually came back, perhaps hoping to find someone else on duty, and maybe next time it's Lester working, not Javier, and maybe the offer is five hundred and who knows, maybe the poseur gets what he came for.

Javier wasn't going to let that happen. He went to the Land Rover, opened the glove box to see the burner once again blinking a text.

VDL package set to open 2130

A firearm. Coded texts on a burner, and now people coming out of the woodwork asking for it. The gun didn't bother him, but the burner promised only trouble, like some portal into another world he wanted nothing to do with. Javier got them both out of the Land Rover, brought them to the Box, and placed them inside the safe. He checked the vehicle registration for the Land Rover. Some guy named Jones. The sooner he got here to claim them, the better.

■   ■   ■

"Donde hermano?" Mama said as Javier walked through the door, the phone wedged between her ear and her shoulder as she stirred a pot on the stove. Javier wasn't sure if she was talking to him or the person on the other end of the call until she twisted her body slightly in his direction and mouthed something he couldn't make out, all the while stirring whatever was in the pot. Three things at once, Mama's life story.

"No se. I told you. He turned off his GPS two months ago." Javier flipped through the bills stacked on the end table, pulled out the ones with big red letters and stuffed them in his back pocket. There was a laundry cart from the *lavenderia* full of folded towels and linens by the door, reminding Javier that the machines in the complex were broken again, and he would have to do the other two loads tonight across the street. He pushed the cart back and forth to make sure all four wheels worked. Mama had a habit of taking the first cart she saw. If only three wheels actually turned, she'd

still drag the cart home leaving a long plastic skid mark the whole way.

The couch showed signs of her nap, the pillow still cupped from where her head had been, the brown and white blanket in a heap where her feet rested. A box of tissues was on the floor, leaving Javier to wonder if it was from *Rebelde*—still on, though thankfully muted—or if it was something else. He folded the blanket, put Mama's pillow on the sofa, clicked off the television, then went into the kitchen and stuck his nose over the pot. Oxtail stock for the minute noodles. Mama assuaged her maternal guilt for relying on frozen dinners by periodically making *cola de buey*. The kitchen was a riot of smells, aromatic chilis going toe-to-toe with the stink of death coming off Mama. No matter how many latex aprons and double-knit jumpers you wore to a slaughterhouse, *hedor a muerte* found a way through to settle on your skin, perhaps the residue of transmigrating souls departing the luckless cattle and hogs.

Mama was in high-gear Spanish, one hand stabbing the air. It was work-related, as usual. The supervisor—*¡flojo!*—was making an example of one of their colleagues—*¡povracita!*—by docking her wages—*¡cabron!* Mama worked at an abattoir in Pacoima, staffed almost entirely by not just undocumented Mexicans but those specifically from Jalisco, and even more specifically, from the same village. Management often underwrote coyote fees specifically from this village, which were then worked off once the recruits arrived, creating a modern-day mix of indentured servitude and a baseball farm system. It was a rite of passage for village girls to receive a set of boning knives before their first communion. Not surprisingly, violence against women was uncommonly low in this village.

The microwave beeped, and as if on cue, Alex came through the door trailing a microclimate of angst. Mama wrapped up her phone conversation and turned the stove off. "No text, no nothing. *Nada, mijo.*" Mama pulled off her apron. For a moment, it looked as though she would throw it at him. Instead, she took a breath and walked over to Alex, taking his chin in her hand. He wriggled out of her touch as if it stung.

"*Todo dias llegando tarde a casa.* I worry too much."

He finally brought his eyes up to meet hers. "What?" The tone, a sonic boom of disrespect.

Javier could tolerate many things but couldn't take even a hint of shade for their mother, a walking testimonial to sacrifice. "*Grosero.*" Javier moved within an arm's length of Alex and eye-fucked him, hoping Alex would raise up so Javier could drop him. "Apologize." Had it been Javier using that tone, Mama would have taken off her *chancla* and given him five swats on his *culo* plus Wednesday evening mass for a month. Not Alex, though. He was her baby now.

Instead, Mama shook her head and smiled, unmoved by Alex's slight and unwilling to chastise Javier. "*Noodles esta noche. Posole manana.* A real sit-down dinner with real food." She gazed at Alex standing wordless and looking lost. She didn't like having to always rely on food, to make the dinner table the centerpiece of the family, though she took some comfort knowing it had been that way for generations. She put on her coat, gave Javier a cautionary look, and left, the screen door bouncing twice before clicking shut.

Javier nodded at Alex's leg. "Not showing off your ankle now, huh?"

"Fuck you," Alex said without looking up and disappeared into the bedroom they shared, leaving his backpack, not much more than a prop these days, hanging on the back of a chair. Two years ago, it was full of textbooks, weighing more than Alex himself. Now, it was covered with tags written in white-out marker, inside only a broken Chromebook, its keys mostly pulled off, and school fliers from last year. Javier divided the noodles into two bowls and put them on the coffee table in the living room. Alex returned from the bedroom wearing a Primitive T-shirt and a new pair of Vans. He sat down on the sofa and wiped a fleck of dust off the pristine nap of his shoes. He looked at the bowl of noodles in front of him. "I ain't hungry."

Javier knew Alex didn't have the money to buy his own shoes, but he also knew that anything that he said just then would be combustible. He added four shakes of Tapatio to his own bowl, took big bites, and was quickly done. Alex was on his phone playing Candy Crush.

"I can still beat you any day of the week," Javier said.

Even four months ago, he would have just snatched the phone and cleared the game for two players. Now, no way. "Look, Alex, those guys you meet up with at lunch..." Javier paused, watched Alex's eyes. "Not Augusto and Beto, the other two." Still nothing. He pressed on, doing his best to soft-pedal his tone. "Those guys are just looking to recruit—they score points when they bring you in."

Alex kept staring at his phone. "Sounds like someone's been watching too much *Blood In Blood Out*."

Javier let it pass. "All that down for the barrio bullshit is just meant to make you feel like you're one of them, like you count. And I get it, Alex, that stuff goes a long way in middle school." Javier could hear the lecture creeping into his voice but plowed on. "It's like this experiment these guys in Finland or someplace did. Put a frog in a pot of boiling water, and of course the frog hops right out." Alex's thumbs stopped for a moment. "Put a frog in a pot of water at room temperature, then heat the water slowly, bring it to a boil over an hour, and the frog never notices, ends up boiling." This last part came out didactic, freighted with meaning.

Alex stood. "Sucks to be a frog." Then, finally, some eye contact. "You done?"

It had been the same thing, more or less, every night now for the past two months, Alex all attitude leaving Javier having to find new ways to zero out his anger. Today he just gazed at the picture on the opposite wall next to the door. It was a framed ten by fourteen of himself, Alex, and Yanira back in Jalisco under the mango tree, their innocent expressions belying an afternoon of mischief. Yanira, one hand behind her back, most likely had one of Alex's shoes.

"You're wearing Ma out." He said it mostly for his own benefit, certain the mention of their mother and her self-emptying love would get a rise.

Alex didn't bite. "Only one golden boy per family, *hermano*," he said, suddenly grabbing his backpack and walking out. Their dog Flaco appeared, his tail wagging, as though sensing he might now have a shot at some food.

Javier stared blankly back. "Every fool for themselves tonight, Flaco."

CHAPTER 6

Javier and Enrique leaned against the side of the school auditorium waiting for the others to arrive. The morning street scene was notable for its lack of conviction, traffic barely outpacing the receding shadows, kids schlepping to school like hooded penitents on their way to see the bishop. Pigeons sat frozen, plump and heedless on the overhead wires. Small clutches of girls, sleep-dazed from the twenty-four-hour firing squad on social media, stood mute and droop-shouldered. Only the skaters, one legging it on the sidewalks, seemed in a rush to go anywhere, the sound of their skate wheels puh-tunking across the concrete seams like rail cars along sections of track.

Enrique's resting face was one of sly expectation, as if catching him in the middle of an amusing story. He ogled a girl walking past them. "Thank you, Jesus, for giving me a last name that puts me directly behind that ass in math." He'd cupped his hands over his mouth as he said this last part and aimed it at the girl looking to get a reaction. He had a lanky grace and led a frictionless life. He should have graduated by now, had been held back once in kindergarten and once again in third grade, but of all the guys, he enjoyed school the most. He clowned and flirted during class but generally earned a long leash with the teachers. His comments were often on point and sometimes insightful, but as for actual work, he never did any. Wouldn't pick up a pencil if you paid him, and at one point, his mother had tried. Most teachers had a hard time failing him, though, most privately conceding that his weightless charm would take him farther in life than public education ever would.

"Nah, man, if Jesus was doing his job, her last name would be Anchovy, sit up front, because the girl can't see shit," Javier replied. "I sit next to her in math. Girl copies everything off me."

Across the street, Dogtown, the expansive tent city, lay mostly inert, its residents on a staggered schedule to rise and shine. The drug-whacked among them, who generally cloistered together in a section called Methistan, would emerge at all hours and scratch themselves comprehensively. They were a minority, however. Most folks in Dogtown were simply sitting this life out and preferred to do so on their own terms. There was a third group— the temporarily dispossessed looking to get back in the game. They held down jobs, sent their kids to East Valley, and were the only ones in Dogtown up at this hour. Then there was Oral-B, his own category, so named for the toothbrush always tucked inside his mouth. Rail-thin and hyperkinetic, he was the Shoe's metal man, forever pushing a shopping cart with whatever he could lay his hands on. He usually wore a winter coat and nothing else underneath, revealing a torso cut like suspension bridge cable.

Raffa arrived, hiking a thumb in Oral-B's direction. "Dude makes an ant look lazy." He was holding a tamale from Dolores's cart. Enrique snatched it out of Raffa's hand, took a bite, and handed it back.

A squat woman, made to look even more so by her rhomboid apron, Dolores was the Shoe's *abuela*. Her ample cheeks were at odds with a shelf-like brow that gave her a sour countenance. Most people assumed she was angry, convinced she was holding a rolling pin under that apron. She had listened to three generations of *gente* from the Shoe, knew more than anyone what was happening and, more importantly, what was going to happen in the six-block barrio. She sold *pelote* when it was cold and shaved ice during the Santa Anas. Boys who stank came to her for deodorant, and girls with hard-work hair came for five-dollar umbrellas if there was even a hint of rain. She knew what your sweetheart liked before you did and parceled out advice only when it served the greater good. She sold on credit and knew who owed how much, and she collected. Today's special confection was an outrageous combination of what looked like Gummi Bears in blood. Diabetes in a bag.

Javier wandered over to her cart, wanting to find out what Dolores could tell him about what Alex was up to at the park.

He asked first about her cats. *"Como esta los gatos?"* Dolores lived in the Roscoe Gardens and was one of the few residents who insisted on taking the steel mesh off her first-story windows so her cats could come in and out on their own.

"Todo bien." She pulled out her phone and thumbed through a few pictures, Javier nodding and wondering what the big draw was with cats.

"Mi hermano." He didn't have to elaborate. She knew all the families, all the dynamics. "I think he's in the park." He knew she'd understand the reference.

Dolores snatched a bag of chips off her rack and handed it to a mother pushing a stroller with a baby in it, its bulging eyes threatening to explode. She made change for the mother, shaking her head. *"Malas semillas, mijo."* Bad seeds. "He doesn't fit, that one. His group," she looked at Javier, *"Pistolas.* And the drugs." She pulled a face, not so much for Alex as for the Gardens where she'd lived since the 1970s, back when people left their front doors unlocked. "Southeast corner." Dolores couldn't hide her contempt for what went on there. "He's a *burro.*" A mule. Entry level work that confirmed Javier's suspicions.

"Gracias Dolores." He stuck a twenty-dollar bill in her tip jar, then looked across the street to see Leslie and a friend coming out of Starbucks. They caught each other's eyes and smiled though Leslie, thankfully, refrained from the added pinkie and thumb "call-me" gesture. There was a small tribe of her Quincy classmates now moving en masse in their hallmark uniforms—pleated skirts,

blazers, and ties. She went to Quincy, a charter school that routinely creamed some of the high-fliers off the neighborhood schools like East Valley. Parents in the Shoe loved the uniforms, but they rarely got past the sea-wall admission process that required a series of "informational" meetings before they got anywhere near the application. Most parents could get to one, maybe two, before they gave up. Leslie had talked her way through most of the application process herself, and when the school asked to meet with her mother, who never took time off from work, she produced a letter from a pro bono lawyer who'd cited several sections of the state education code. Leslie was offered a spot the next day.

Javier wandered back to the guys, arriving at the same time as Sergio.

"Make Mexico great again." Sergio bumped fists with Raffa.

"*Chale*, how 'bout 'Make Guatemala tall again'?" Raffa made a show of peering down on Sergio, a good six inches lower. Sergio was Guatemalan, generally known for their short stature. What he lacked in verticality, he made up for with hacking skills. Freshman year he'd learned how to override the digital chime that announced the end of every period and replaced it with a five-second clip of "Baby Shark," all from his phone. He could beat any firewall, favored Metallica T-shirts, leather wristbands, and kept his shoulder-length hair ear-tucked on the right side only.

"New day, and you're still ugly, Raffa." It was Chuey. Raffa was movie-star good-looking. "And you smell like ass." Also wide of the mark. Raffa worked high-end retail on the weekends and smelled as good as he looked.

Raffa looked at Chuey and gestured toward Javier. "Why don't you try to be useful for once in your miserable life. Denker's puttin' their hooks into young Alex."

Chuey despised gangs, called them all homos—that is, until Raffa came out. On the first day of sixth grade, a skinny pelon three years older than Chuey called his mother a *puta*, tipped his head back *¿Y que?* style. Chuey snorted, then shot his right hand into the boy's crotch and clamped down on his balls like he was trying to crack a pair of walnuts. The boy bent forward in pain, his throat running into Chuey's other hand coming up. Chuey then walked him backwards across the quad and pushed him into the girls' bathroom. A loud bang followed by a distressed girl running out screaming.

"Fuckin' pussies." Chuey sent a stream of spit through his front teeth and pulled out his phone. "Lemme see who's around." It was a reference to his army of cousins who were on perpetual standby.

Javier knew it would end badly. "It's cool, Chuey," he said. The first period bell rang which mostly got the snooze-alarm treatment—six minutes until the gates locked. The inner clocks of most students were as accurate as Swiss-made movements when it came to knowing the absolute last second they had to start moving.

During fourth period, Javier hadn't even taken out his notebook when he noticed Alex shoulder to shoulder with Itchy and Scratchy, roaming the quad, having left Augusto and Beto still sitting in the bleachers. Javier watched Itchy wander off to a row of lockers and scrawl his tag, then waved Alex over to contribute his *placa*. It was the first rung of the knucklehead ladder. In a month or so, Alex would get jumped in and be full-on Denker. Javier couldn't stand to watch and let his attention float back to the front of the class. Gio was angling today's artwork toward Javier, a horse's head cranked at an impossible angle, a man, open-mouthed and anguished, simultaneously savage and comical, a glimpse into Gio's world. When the bell rang, Javier looked down at his desk and saw a Post-It Patel had stuck on his Chromebook. *See me.*

At the front of the class, Patel was recapping his dry erase markers, usually bone-dry and useless within days of coming out of the box, giving him fits at the whiteboard. His lectures, carefully scaffolded toward the teachable moment, then dashed by a rock-hard chisel tip.

"My God, what was so wrong with chalkboards," he would tell himself before turning to the class. "None of you grew up clapping erasers?" The class would just stare back, each wondering if there might be a story they could tease out, chew some clock.

Patel held out a plastic container. "My wife's samosas. Try one."

Javier peered inside. Odd-shaped, deep-fried, reminding him of Mama's fritas. He took one, held it up, and studied it before taking a bite. He made his yum-face out of reflex but found himself quickly going in for another bite.

"Compliments to your wife." There was a familiar salty crunch, but the background flavors were unlike anything he'd ever tasted. And then the heat. He opened his mouth and quickly pulled a water bottle out of his backpack.

Patel laughed. "I'm so sorry, Javier. I should have warned you. Indian heat is more delayed than Mexican heat, sort of sneaks up on you." He undid his thermos and held it out. "Would you like some *chai*?" Javier shook his head, tilting his head back to let the water pool in the back of his throat. "Maybe next time," Patel said, taking a paper towel and wiping his hands.

He took a beat, then threw his eyes at the window. "I had a brother too, Javier."

Javier shifted his weight from one foot to another, sensing an ambush.

Patel explained. "A colleague of mine works at Gaither and has your brother in his homeroom. We got talking over the weekend."

"Ah. Got it." This was going to be about Alex.

"Back in India, when I was your age, I had a younger brother too, Javier. Went through phases, got in trouble, seemed to drag the whole family down." His eyes settled on a stack of books. "So hard-headed at that age," he said, looking up. "And like you, I'm guessing, I had to work to help my family pay the bills. Made bricks for two dollars a day each afternoon, seven days a week." He held his hands up, turned them back and forth. "Oven mitts at one point." He laughed. "We were very poor." He reached again for the container and offered another samosa to Javier who demurred this time. "One-room tin shack with dirt floors, and five of us all crammed in there, neighbors on three sides. Slums for miles, Javier." Patel ran his hand out in front of himself, miming the expanse of impoverishment.

Javier tried to picture the dirt floor, somehow everyone in the mental image also barefoot. "Do you have gangs in India?"

"Where I come from, it's not like here. Yes, we have gangs, but it's really just organized crime, you know, protection rackets, all those internet scammers, I'm afraid to say." He trailed off. "But here, here it's like a status thing, an identity thing, very different. My brother, so deluded, wanted to be a big movie producer and had to find a pot of cash to make his films and throw big parties, and he just fell in with the *gundas* who saw him as an easy mark. Lend him ten dollars today and expect twenty tomorrow. So, he got in over his head very quickly, and I had to go collect him from the police station...which was a disgrace for our family." Patel stuck the Tupperware back in his bag. "In my country, shame is a very powerful motivator."

Javier looked out the window contemplating Alex, a portrait of remorselessness.

"I'm telling you this, Javier, because I recognize your struggle. Family first, right?" Patel waved a hand. "Total hogwash. And I am telling you right now, if you abandon your plans for college to stay at home, to keep Alex from disappearing into the streets, to help your mother pay the bills, you will never forgive yourself, and you will never forgive your mother." Patel paused. "And you will break her heart."

Javier wasn't sure if he liked where this was going. He'd been expecting a little chat about the recent test. Instead, this little show-and-tell session had Patel trying to draw him out. "What happened with your brother?"

"Judge gave him one chance to change his ways." Patel pulled out his phone, scrolled through some pictures. "Here he is, last year. Junior account manager for a pharmaceutical company."

Javier nodded, impressed. "Suit and tie." He passed the phone back to Patel. "Guess we need to move to India."

Patel absently scrolled a few more and came to one with the brother in a hospital bed with family beside him. "He's recovering right now from some burns he suffered several months ago." Patel went briefly off into himself, his voice dropping into a sullen mutter before pulling himself back out of it. "Your brother, what's his name?"

"Alex."

"Alex has to learn his lessons on his own too. You have been the older brother and—I'll go out on a limb here—father too." He put his phone on the table and crossed his arms. "No one is looking out for you, Javier. And your mother, a saint I'm sure, will go to sleep and wake up thinking about Alex before all else, just as my mother did for Surjit."

This was pushing it. Only the guys were allowed inside this fence, and even so, their role was mostly as Greek chorus, chipping in with their own tales of dysfunction, a few pats on the back, some *got-you-bros*. Only Gio really understood the contours of his family, could parse the signal through all the noise.

"You handle your sister's books, am I right?" Another curveball.

Javier just nodded wondering where this was all going. He rarely spoke with teachers about anything, much less what went on at home. Patel unfolded his arms, put his hands in his pockets. "While you're staring at Alex, you leave your QuickBooks open on your laptop, Javier, and I can see all the accounts you have to balance." A little ball of guilt landed in Javier's stomach.

"I'm trying to line up some AR financing for my half-sister's tow company. I'm sorry—"

Patel waved another hand. "You're in AP Economics, man. I should give you extra credit, but I'm afraid my gradebook doesn't go that high." He looked at Javier. "Would you like some advice?"

Javier wanted to tell him he'd been giving it away for the past ten minutes. "Sure."

"Look out for Javier first." Patel studied him. "I know, I know, it sounds bad, sounds selfish, and it is. On some things, Javier, you have to be selfish. Trust me, though you may not think it now, your family will survive without you."

He'd never heard anyone speak so plainly about the colossal undertow of family. It was like he'd been breathing smoke for so many years, and here was Patel offering oxygen, too rich for his lungs.

Javier nodded at the chai. "Maybe I will try some of that." Patel found a cup and poured him some. "It looks like chocolate milk, but don't expect anything sweet." He handed it to Javier who sniffed it, took a sip, but couldn't find much enthusiasm for it. He took the rest in one gulp.

"Second piece of advice—lucky for you, two for one and no coupon needed." Patel took a sip of his chai. "Exceed your grasp. You have what it takes to go far, Javier, but college is just a gateway. Opportunity is floating all over this place." He swung his head in a loop meant to represent *this place*. "You're a natural with numbers, Javier. You can read a set of financials better than most MBAs."

Javier shifted his backpack to the other shoulder. "Just hate to see money go to waste."

Patel pulled out a pen and a piece of paper. "You should call this person." He wrote down a name and a phone number. "She does a bit of everything, very successful, and will underwrite some unconventional loans like your sister's." He handed Javier the paper.

"Half-sister, but—" He read the name and paused. Lupe Rodriguez. "Is this the same lady—" He couldn't figure out how to finish the sentence.

"Probably. She's everywhere in the community. Very successful, and, it should be noted, was the last student I ever taught who had as much natural ability with numbers as you, Javier."

CHAPTER 7

When Javier arrived at Mission Tow, the Land Rover was gone. Lester, a man of few words but an abundance of presence, was the only other person there. Javier had only spoken with him a few times since he'd started three months ago but found the short exchanges revealed a lurking perceptiveness, like he was cataloging his terrestrial experiences for a return trip to Mars.

"Po-lice impound." Lester was doing a brake job in the garage. An air wrench hung from his arm like a pendulum. "Dude in a suit came by, and I gave him the lot number at LAPD."

"Young guy with a beard? Glasses?"

Lester shook his head. "Nah, older guy, gray hair. Gucci loafers." Lester knew footwear like Betzaida knew makes and models. "The shoes maketh the man."

Javier nodded sagely, as if considering this maxim. "There was a burner and a gun in the safe that belonged to the guy. D'you give him those?"

Lester sucked his teeth and took a moment to rummage around his memory. "Nah." He went back to pulling a brake shoe off, and Javier went inside the Box then called the number Patel had given him for the increasingly all-purpose Lupe. Someone answered on the first ring. "Rodriguez Group, with whom do I have the pleasure of speaking?" The hyper-correct grammar and aggressive chirpiness took Javier off guard.

"Hi. I'm trying to reach Ms. Rodriguez. My name is Javier Jimenez."

"I'm sorry Mr. Jimenez, she's in a meeting. Can I give her a message?"

"What is this regarding?"

"I'm looking for a business loan."

"Wonderful, Mr. Jimenez. I would be happy to assist you with that." Apparently, you had to deal with this one to earn the chance to speak with the boss. She sent Javier a link on the Rodriguez Group homepage, asked him to send the financials and Schedule Cs which was going to be a dealbreaker since Betzaida had never done a tax return in her life. Javier thanked the woman and said goodbye then uploaded what he had and hit submit. No way he was getting this loan.

He didn't even bother telling Betzaida about the loan request later that night as they sat parked outside Winchells listening to news radio and watching a man standing at the service window pour an endless stream of sugar into his cup. Javier kept expecting the coffee to eventually crest the rim and spill out, but it was like a magic trick where the coffee never gets displaced no matter how much sugar the guy poured. In this part of the Valley, people were coming and going all hours of the day and night, graveyard shifts the bread and butter for the most recent arrivals, and donut shops pushed the two things most of them needed—sugar and caffeine. With its enormous windows on three sides, Winchells was a human terrarium, the ladies in their aproned outfits hustling their trays out of ovens and into the display cases. It was a nocturnal oasis, the only lit spot with any signs of life for several blocks, a stand-in for kitchens everywhere, the promise of something warm and sweet coming out of an oven.

"What's up with Alex?" Betzaida brought her hands off the wheel and rested them in her lap.

Javier stared out the passenger window at a skater trying to do kickflips under a sodium light, the board always skittering away from him. "Boy is out of pocket." His voice was thin and distant. "Denker's recruiting him, and he ain't playing hard to get."

Betzaida caved at the waist like she'd been gut-punched. "Alex, a gangster?" She banged the heel of her hand on the steering wheel. "Been tellin' y'all. Time to move."

She'd helped raise both Alex and Javier for a year soon after getting booted from her own place. She'd instituted a morning routine that came as a bit of a stunner to the two boys: school supplies inventoried like they were going to live on the moon for a year, a homework check with a point system. Before leaving the house, they both needed to have five pencils each sharp enough to draw blood.

Javier wasn't up for told-you-so comments. "We can't put the move-in money together. Medical bills are killing us. Christ, Betz, why I gotta remind you?" Javier wiped his fingers, put the napkin in the takeout bag and rolled it up. "Ma's killing herself and that fool..." He shook his head and looked back at the skater now joined by someone else.

"You try talking to him?"

"Can't get there. He shuts me down, throws it in my face. Just wants to play victim."

The scanner came to life. "All units, 4-92 Sepulveda and Roscoe," a rare undertone of urgency in the dispatcher's voice.

"4-92?" Betzaida reached for the ignition but stopped.

It was a radio call just south of "officer down" in terms of response, and anyone within a mile was coming lights and sirens. "Sepulveda and Roscoe? That's Dogtown." A dozen units responded before dispatch pushed them off to other channels. The second scanner, this one for fire and rescue, announced six alarms, meaning at least a dozen rigs and wagons rolling to the same scene.

Javier turned on the news radio station.

...of the Van der Lipp Dam has given way and water is currently coming down through the old Raytheon spillway. Flooding is being reported in the northeast Valley near the intersection of Sepulveda

and Roscoe. Our KABC air patrol Sky Lord Dan is in the area. Dan, what can you tell us?

Betzaida cranked the ignition, sending a tremor under the seat then glanced over her left shoulder before bolting across four solid yellows. Javier leaned forward to look out the windshield and saw the blinking red and green lights of several news-copters hovering in place. A police airship was already flying a tight circle, its searchlight a silver finger pointing toward the scene. Betzaida pulled over to let several police cars pass, their engines double-throated cop-turbo. Close behind came her competition, two Bergosian flatbeds. "Aw, hell no," she said calmly then floored the accelerator.

Only one section of the dam has caved, and the water is emptying into what—well, I'm being told it's a dried-up lake bed that is now a homeless encampment many in the local community refer to as Dogtown. Our Jane Coleman is live on scene. Jane, what can you tell us?

They arrived at the staging area on the northeast corner of Sepulveda and Roscoe, a sea of red and blue flashers offering strobed images of a slow-motion disaster. Ladder trucks hit their thousand-watt night-suns, the rising surface of the floodwater looking like it might suddenly stand up and breathe fire. The "town" part of Dogtown was starting to come loose and disintegrate though there was oddly little panic on what was now shoreline. An officer was on the bullhorn giving directions, urging everyone to remain calm and leave the water, as though there were any doubt about that. Tarps sagged and tents sprung free then folded. People, hundreds of them waded around collecting whatever flotsam they could get hold of whether it was theirs or not.

The flood was gently having its way. Dogtown was going underwater.

Javier got out of the rig and ran down to the water's edge. Personal items bobbed everywhere in the murky darkness: food containers, old clothes, children's toys, plastic bags. He made out a piece of plywood floating with a stack of textbooks and recognized one of them from his history class. To his right, he saw Oral-B hoisting a large cooler on his shoulder. He was holding the hand of a little girl who was wearing a long braid and glancing around as they walked toward shore leaving a small wake behind them. Javier wanted to shout something but couldn't think what to say. The little girl could not have made a better choice of savior. Instead, Javier scanned the water's surface, all inky images splashing about, and spotted an elderly lady talking to herself, stuffing whatever she could into a trash bag. He walked over, the surface now to his waist.

"Ma'am, can I help you?" The woman was jabbering to herself, her house dress beginning to billow out like she was sitting on a pool toy. Javier could feel the current's press and knew her frail body would soon likely relent.

"Ma'am, I think it's time you got out of here. There are people on shore who will be able to help you." Still no response. "Listen, lady, there's nothing here worth saving. In five minutes, this is all going to be under water." He stuck his face a few inches from hers and noticed her eyes had that crazed, dissociative glint of someone with the lights on but no one home. "You have to leave!"

She fanned at him and continued grabbing items from the water and sticking them in her bag. "Okay, ma'am, I apologize in advance for this, but it's time to go."

He got behind her and picked her up, a collection of bones under loose skin. He could feel his fingers settle in between her ribs now certain he would break one. She screamed and started kicking, her feet splashing in the water like she was learning to swim. The fire department had launched inflatable rafts, each with several rescue workers in waders walking alongside them. When Javier saw one approach, he walked over and hoisted the lady up as far as he could. Someone in the raft reached over and pulled her on board at which point she was suddenly lucid, the water's spell now broken. She looked at the men in the raft and thanked them.

People with nothing now had even less. In thirty minutes, the water, now up to Javier's armpits, had risen at such a rate that the surface area seemed to have doubled, the shore's edge now creeping up to the tires of some of the vehicles that had parked earlier. Javier decided he had done all he could and climbed out of the water then looked at the scene along the shore. Victims were being unloaded from rafts and were then wheeled to a triage area. No one seemed to be gravely injured though some were soon shuttled into the back of ambulances. A few tents bobbed on the surface, oddly serene as prayer candles. A doll rested on the shore, its arms spread wide. Commotion was noticeably absent, as though there was a competition to make this catastrophe as quiet as possible.

Betzaida came toward Javier through the water carrying a kitten in the crook of her elbow like a football.

"Where is everybody?" Javier asked, looking around.

"Over there." Betzaida used the cat to point across the water. On the far side of the lot, Javier could see the front end of a bus poking out from behind a retaining wall, lights on, the driver standing outside. An odd sight made even more odd as a line of victims from the flood stood in a queue to get on, the now double- homeless residents of Dogtown wandering onto a modern-day Ark. Behind them sat a parking lot with at least a dozen buses.

It was as bizarre and as unexpected as the dam break. Not only had Dogtown disappeared like Atlantis in a matter of hours, but buses were cued up to cart the refugees off. Javier studied the scene, an epic catastrophe now with a hint of premeditation, like a disaster movie where you can see a boom mike hanging over the set, the whole thing now a fraud.

Betzaida whistled from the truck. "We're outta here. Pile-up on Sepulveda, and Fat Man's already rolling on it."

Javier took one last look at the scene, the expanse of water still growing, and walked backwards to the rig, still scanning the other side of the water for some explanation. Inside, Betzaida was laughing. "*Menso* went down Woodman—one lane with construction." Javier couldn't understand what passed for humor with his half-sister sometimes, but for her, any miscues by Bergosian were comedy gold.

He climbed in. "Where'd the cat go?"

She chucked a thumb toward the backseat. The cat sat staring out the windshield, unperturbed, as if this had been the plan all along.

Reports are coming in now—one body has been recovered from the Van Der Lipp Reservoir, apparently an unrelated gunshot victim. We are monitoring the situation closely...

CHAPTER 8

Enrique was the first one there the next morning, one foot in front of the other, slalom style, one hand clutching an imaginary tow rope, the other waving in the air. He was riding the make-believe wake of a make-believe boat on a surprisingly real lake. A crowd stood along the sidewalk straight as lamp posts, transfixed by the sight. An entire body of water had sprung up overnight, displacing the reliably depressing eyesore that had been Dogtown.

"Time we learned to waterski!" Enrique'd sent out a short video panning the area, telling the guys to hurry over before school. Having witnessed the whole thing last night, Javier just stood next to him, unable to feign any surprise.

"Saw it all go down."

Enrique gave Javier a *you-crazy* look but didn't break his pose. "No shit? How'd it happen?"

Javier wasn't sure how far down this road he wanted to go. He shrugged. "Heard the same thing you did. Van der Lipp finally cracked." The school grapevine would be buzzing today, and he could imagine his name floating out there attached to some half-baked conspiracies about buses appearing to cart the homeless off to the desert and into a waiting spacecraft. He steered the conversation in a more benign direction. "Oral-B was there, and I think some old lady cussed me out."

Enrique quickly lost interest and went back to wave-hopping in his mind. "Go get your damn boat, Javi! Hashtag *lakemistake*," Enrique shouted, then elbowed the person next to him. "Get it trending!" A few chuckles but the large majority just simply stood still, witnessing what certainly would be one of the most extraordinary moments of their lives.

The lake was now half again the size of what it had been when Javier'd left last night, roughly the length of a football field and twice as wide. Truth was, waterskiing wasn't out of the question. Javier studied the far side where he'd seen the buses loading the homeless, but in the morning light, the place looked different, felt different, as though, overnight, stagehands had struck the set to make ready for some new production.

"What the fuck?" Raffa came up behind the two of them. "You do this?" He looked at Enrique as if he were a dog standing in the middle of a kitchen floor covered in trash.

"Yeah, and next I'm gonna part the waters to free my people, except your ugly ass." Enrique made a show of giving Raffa the once-over. "Hair lookin' sharp today, Raf." He sniffed and nodded. "Nice...citrus."

The crowd was now three-deep on the sidewalk and getting larger. On both sides of the street, news trucks were doing live stand-ups, the reporters with brightly lit faces and humorless expressions. Local tradesmen stood watching from the strip mall parking lot across the street clutching their coffee and donuts, sussing out future work. On the far side of the lake, skip loaders were already making piles out of the leftovers from last night, their sudden appearance only adding to Javier's suspicions. Less than twelve hours out and the heavy equipment was already on scene.

The evening's detritus bobbed eerily. Puzzled seagulls hovered, confused, their morning meal no longer available. Dogtown, among its many code violations, had an open-air trash pit that serviced a large chunk of the landlocked gull population. The Shoe was now remade, everyone on hand looking slightly disoriented. In a neighborhood where every inch of ground was paved or developed, the dam break seemed like a welcomed disaster. The news people were generously calling the body of water a "reservoir," though the term robbed the scene of its sense of wonder. No doubt local priests and pastors had dug out their King

James to brush up on Noah's little adventure and would, as was their stock-in-trade, try to weave current events into their version of the gospel.

"Big improvement if you ask me." Chuey arrived taking large bites out of a Pop Tart. "Fuckin' pervs and flipperheads," he added, spitting crumbs, waving his breakfast in the direction of Dogtown. "Hasta la pasta." The crowd had started to spill onto Van Nuys and nearly had one lane shut down. School police had arrived and were telling students to start heading to class though it was clear the cops weren't going to be writing any tickets. They were just as mystified as the kids.

Gio snuck up on Javier's right. "Where'd they all go?" Javier knew who Gio was referring to. Largely indifferent to his own circumstances, Gio had savant-like abilities when it came to the world around him.

"Some buses were here last night." Javier half-regretted saying it. "On the other side. Past Pan City."

Gio shook his head and burped at the same time. "Accident my ass. Shit was planned." Gio reached into his backpack, produced a school burrito, shot through with enough preservatives to embalm a corpse. He had an endless supply he collected at the sharing-is-caring table during lunch. "Watch." He used his teeth to open the burrito without looking at it. "Place is gonna look like Miami Beach in a few months." He bumped his head to the far side of the vacant lot on the opposite the lake. "Construction fence is already going in. Someone's got plans for the place. The flood just saved them a shit-ton of legal fees clearing the place out."

·   ·   ·

For two weeks, the East Valley principal ended each day with a cautionary announcement to stay out of Lake Mistake, thereby ensuring twice as many kids would be coming home in wet clothes. It was one of those rare occurrences where the novelty never wore off. The lake, in fact, had spawned new heights of applied learning. A flotilla of improvisational rafts was quickly launched, some for socializing and others for combat. Lovebirds floated on the water in one area, while the dreadnaughts went at each other on the other side, propelled by poles, oars, and, in a matter of days, two-stroke gas engines—converted weed whackers with metal-shop propellers. If there had been an elective during the school day simply titled "Lake," it would have had a waiting list.

No one expected the lake to become a permanent feature, assuming that it would either drain out or evaporate like a big puddle, come and go like Circus Vargas in the WalMart parking lot. But it didn't. Instead, it actually grew. Lake water now even crested a section of sidewalk, dam water still sluicing down from Van der Lipp, some days more than others, as if someone was turning a faucet left and right. On off, trickle gush.

It reminded Javier of a drainpipe he'd noticed when he'd first arrived in the Shoe. It had been tall enough to walk into and equally fickle in its output, one day bone dry, the next, a torrent so strong you'd have a hard time standing up in it. It mystified him, and he sold Leslie on a plan to spelunk it to its source on a bone dry day, though they only made it fifty feet before a constellation of bats' eyes, twinkling in the flashlight, sent them screaming back the way they came. It was the last of what had been a year of adventures for the two of them, both ten at the time. That afternoon, Javier returned home, came through the door, the story fresh in his mind to share with his father who had hours earlier left his house key on the kitchen table and done a runner, bringing the freewheeling part of Javier's LA childhood to a hasty conclusion.

Gio had been right. By the end of the month, the construction site next to Lake Mistake was crawling with excavators, skip loaders, graders, a collection of blades and buckets to flatten and prepare the site, now large enough to land a spaceship. The first real sign of what was to come appeared two months later: four foundation cutouts deep enough for at least six levels of underground parking. Out of nowhere, the Shoe suddenly had aspirations, as if it had gone to sleep as a collection of strip malls and woken up wanting to be Dubai.

CHAPTER 9

The office on the third floor of a nondescript municipal building on the corner of Third and Broadway had a forgettable view of a parking lot. Councilman Delatorre could see his own car, buried now in the stack despite his insistence that he be parked up front, even pointing as he always did, to the City Council placard on his dash. No one who worked at the lot even looked at the placard, never bothered to listen to his insistence that he would be out in two hours and had an important meeting on the Westside. He'd tried his best to charm a smile out of them, but they never went along. Worse, they seemed to always step up their banter— some Eastern European language with a lot of "zh" sounds—once he got out of his car. He made a mental note to check with Building and Safety to see if the lot had any code violations, and if not, to start issuing some, shut it down while men in the hard hats leaned on their shovels and watched a backhoe tear up the pavement.

The conference room was a morose space that seemed to reflect the pointless nature of much of the work that went on inside. The coffee service—an aluminum silo, spigot, handles, and a cherry red light—was the only hopeful sight in the whole room. The drop ceiling showed dark plumes around the registers where cigarette smoke had once been sucked in. The Councilman himself had been an intern just as the smoking ban had gone into place and could recall how people still smoked here months after Governor Wilson had signed the law. It made a favorable impression on his young mind: the lawmakers of the local jurisdiction flouting the laws of the state in a show of cross-party, nicotine-crazed unity.

Every other Thursday at 10 a.m. it was the site for the standing meeting of the Housing and Community Development subcommittee, a third-tier assignment for mid-career politicians going nowhere. Here in Los Angeles, your star was either rising or you were irrelevant, and this committee was a political backwater. Delatorre took his seat in the middle of the dais and surveyed the twenty or so people in attendance, mostly staffers, some visitors and invited guests, and three members including himself. He dragged a finger over the chipped edge of the faux mahogany veneer and recognized the pen mark he'd etched during a particularly dull meeting, back and forth like a tuned-out high schooler.

He tapped the microphone to signal it was time to get started. The reaction of the group was a little too casual so he brought the gavel down, didn't pretend he was unannoyed, and quickly proceeded. "The meeting will be called to order. I see Ms. Garcia and Mr. Beltran here," he said without smiling, "so as we have a quorum, I'm going to pull the chocks and get things going." It was an Air Force reference which no one got, and he didn't care.

"First item: The Van der Lipp Dam break was without question one of the worst disasters in the city. Ever." He then went on to reel off the perfunctory pledges to rebuild and to thank the first responders. "I am happy to announce that federal relief money has been requested, the area declared a disaster zone, and I am happy to announce preliminary plans the city now has to redevelop the area." He clicked through a set of slides featuring renderings of three ten-story residential towers, each with decks sprouting off the sides, and a fourth deckless tower, presumably office space. The last three slides showed mock-ups of a retail esplanade composed mostly of repurposed shipping containers, referred to in the trade, as Delatorre informed the audience, as cans. A few heads started popping up, and some journalists in the back smelled a scoop and started taking notes furiously. Page one news often got leaked through a committee.

"In conjunction with nearly a dozen of the leading tech and entertainment companies that will be opening offices on the site within the year, we have begun construction on a project which will be the envy of not just the city but the country. You are looking at the next LA hotspot: *Can City*." It was a play on the colloquial shorthand version of Panorama City, Pan City, though no one seemed to get it making him oh-for-two on the references.

The journalists in the back row were now holding their hands up like schoolkids with the correct answer. Delatorre motioned for them to put their hands down, nodding as he did so to let them know they'd have a chance later to buttonhole him for specifics, and they'd have their story.

"Item number two. As the council member representing the Twelfth District, I am constantly reminded that opioid drug use is the number one cause of death in the age group of eighteen to forty-five. No one is immune to the scourge, least of all me and my family." At the mention of family, the room descended into silence. Rumors had been circulating about Delatorre's son and his drug habit.

He'd known he was planting a flag, that the political and the personal had now merged into one. There'd been a lurking need for several years to speak out on the issue, to do something, if not for his constituents, then for his own child, and the fact that it had required Jones to finally force his hand only stoked his eternal flame of self-loathing. "It is common knowledge that most of the opioids in my district and, in fact, all five Valley districts, originate in the Roscoe Gardens. You—," he motioned to those assembled, "—might go to a farmer's market for arugula like people—," a catch in his voice, "—people like my son...go to Denker Park for their drugs. And it is no secret that all of the drugs sold at Denker first pass through the Roscoe Gardens." He fanned his attention out over the audience as if looking for challengers. "Therefore, today, I am making a motion that the Local Housing Affordability Plan be amended to include the following language." The Councilman looked down to read the verbiage. "That G and K Holdings be empowered to prepay their HUD 232 mortgage and remove all federal and local restrictions and encumbrances such that the land and all improvements thereon no longer be subject to any obligations, duties, or regulations by any public agency or elected body.

"I've invited two of the vice presidents from G and K." He paused and looked out at the audience. "Can you hold your hands up?" Two men in suits, accustomed to being attacked in public hearings, hesitantly raised their hands. "Gentlemen, with a second on my motion and a roll-call vote, you will be able to propose to the tenant association your plan for relocation and move-out assistance to help the residents of Roscoe Gardens find new housing, forthwith." Delatorre punched the last word with the gravity of a hanging judge.

Then smiling, "Once vacant, you, sirs, may do with the Gardens as you see fit." The city would issue housing vouchers to families to continue their rent subsidies elsewhere, though Delatorre went on to say that he would be visiting the Gardens later that week to deliver the news in person and to encourage residents who may be in the business of selling drugs "to please find housing outside District Twelve."

He hardly recognized the conviction in his own voice, and for once regretted winding up his speech and almost missed the arrival of George Jones who was leaning against a doorframe in the back. The Councilman heard the motion, took the vote, and banged the adjournment gavel then ignored his two colleagues sitting on either side of him, and took his time wending through the crowd, a few strange faces angling toward him, thrusting their hands forward to shake. The two journalists descended on him with their phones out, but Delatorre just snapped his finger and drew a line in the air between them and his aide, miming his wish for them to get on his schedule. For one small moment in his meaningless career, he had owned the room and felt reluctantly proud that Jones had been on hand to witness it. When he found him in the back, there was no hint of celebration or mutuality, only a cool regard for each other.

"And so it begins, Mr. Jones." He waved at someone without smiling. "You do realize the one snag in your plans will be the move-out, the tenant association."

"We've made a very generous offer and are confident the Gardens will be empty in ninety days."

The Councilman couldn't help but laugh. "Now you're starting to sound like me. In my world, *confident* is just another way of saying all hat, no cattle." He inched in toward Jones. "We both know you need all five votes on the tenant association, and you only have four." He studied Jones' face for a moment, looking to see if this little showstopper might have somehow skipped past him. "Our friend with the pushcart, so you know, is the most beloved person in the Shoe, and she's got nowhere else to go. She once told me she'll be going out in a pine box before anyone tells her it's time to go. And old-school *abuelas* are the most stubborn...I mean, I got two of 'em."

Jones didn't seem interested in Delatorre's family dynamics. "I suppose you're wondering when we break ground on Can City."

Delatorre's face fell. "You make it sound like I'm only along for the ride, Jones." The Councilman canted his head. "Don't forget whatever comes down or goes up in the Twelfth needs my blessing."

Jones looked over Delatorre's shoulder, then pinned him with a hard glare. "And you make it sound like your son isn't facing prison." No edge to his voice, only a flat delivery. "We're still on a thirty-day trial basis, Councilman, you and me. Full membership is still a few weeks away."

Delatorre's aide came up and stood expectantly, wagging an iPhone, apparently the signal they were running behind. The

Councilman flicked his head telling the aide to get lost. The two men in suits from G and K stood smiling, expectantly off to the side, wanting to thank Delatorre. He took some pleasure in making them wait.

"I watched a drone sit over Valley Mercado yesterday for half an hour, just hovering with that dumb ass sound. If I'd had a gun, I'd have plunked it. Four weeks of this shit, Jones."

Another meeting was scheduled for the room, and some new faces were beginning to dribble in and set up. An easel with an aerial picture of an intersection was plopped next to a lectern, suggesting a crosswalk hearing about to get underway. He could smell booze coming off someone nearby.

"*Tiempo al tiempo*, Councilman." Jones spoke as if Delatorre had been too quick to believe and too slow to comprehend. "In a couple of weeks, you're going to get a chance to break out that Brown-Lives-Matter speech you've been practicing all these years. And you'll have every network sticking microphones in your face while you do." Jones offered his hand for the first time. "*Vive la raza.*"

Delatorre paused, unsure what he was buying into, his lame duck life now buoyed by Jones and his cataclysmic vision of urban renewal. He imagined the two Eastern European car attendants chuckling over how far back in the stacks they'd stuck his car.

He grabbed Jones' hand and shook it firmly.

"*Si se fuckin' puede.*"

CHAPTER 10

The Roscoe Gardens Tenant Association meeting was now more than an hour long, the mothers with young children having called it quits long ago. By HUD regs, management had to provide free childcare during these meetings, though the practice had been quietly abandoned years ago. In reality, even a hint that someone else might watch your kids for three hours guaranteed a truckload of kids in the multipurpose room, though in the meeting itself, the number of actual parents could fit in a two-door car.

The three vending machines in the back, currently the only source of sugar and salt within walking distance, had long since been emptied. Kids back from school had paraded in and out for the first thirty minutes of the meeting, dropping f-bombs when they realized management hadn't restocked anything, until someone stuck a broomstick through the door handles. The Korean grocer across from the Gardens had already pulled up stakes. Once the notices to evict had gone out, he'd backed his truck up and emptied his store overnight leaving the Gardens devoid of any ready source of booze and junk food, leaving everyone a little bit twitchy. A growing sense of inevitability prevailed, U-Hauls starting to show up like lifeboats circling the Titanic.

About fifty or so tenants had shown up for the meeting, alert weariness on their faces. A couple of guys from management were in the back, discreetly angling their phones toward the front where Roscoe Gardens Tenant Association sat ready to answer the fourth round of questions about the eviction notices. Lenora Matias, the chair of the meeting and third-generation Gardina, made no secret of her impatience with head-in-the-sand tenants. Her trademark ruby lips, somehow the focal point of every meeting, were peeled back in a smile that came across as more of a grimace. The eviction notice, she proclaimed, was her sign from God to "get your ass moving," a comment that drew blank looks despite her allusion to a personal relationship with the Almighty. She went on to list out all the wonderful things that had happened to her since she had heeded *la llamada*, the Call, and started boxing her things.

It was the type of lead-balloon leadership that Dolores expected from Lenora. The next thirty minutes was a constant volley of questions bordering on accusations that Lenora treated like a wave of locusts. The other three board members, apart from Dolores, did what they could to deflect some of the incoming, but it was evident their hearts weren't in it. Lenora had lit the fuse with her trademark blend of ignorance and ego. As always, the initial hullabaloo burned itself out, at which point Dolores, sitting at the end of the table, asked for the microphone.

She quietly thanked everyone for coming out before saying *feliz cumpleanos* to the only other septuagenarian in the room, Sr. Rodriguez, who sat against one wall, hands perched rakishly atop his cane. Dolores spent the next fifteen minutes summarizing her history in the Gardens, how her father, a Vietnam veteran, had never intended to have his family live there for more than a year, but then one thing led to another, the common refrain to family histories in the Gardens. They all had their version of this story, and Dolores's recitation gave the group a shared footing, a spark of conscience.

She stood, her scowl now double deep. "And I will vacate the Gardens, and I will miss all of you. But I will leave when I am ready." A ripple of interest went through the audience, heads popping up from their phones. Dolores stared at the two observers from management diligently recording the meeting on their phones.

"And make sure you get my good side for your video, young man doing the filming." A few whoops from the ladies in the front who immediately got it, their knee-slapping bringing a few more heads around.

Dolores fanned a hand over the empty chairs at the table. "Six of the eleven board members have already moved out, voted to accept what management offered, then fled. *Huyó.* I know firsthand that three of them," she held up three fingers, "are now living in nice four-bedroom homes in Santa Clarita." She paused, no doubt each person there picturing a turquoise pool in the back. "And they own these homes, despite living only on disability. With bad credit." Again, she was describing half the people in the audience. "So, I ask you, why were they the first to leave?" Silence. "Are any of us going to find ourselves in new homes in our names?" Heads starting to shake. "Must we accept what management tells us?"

Someone in the back shouted something in Spanish.

"*Sí*, Alfredo. We negotiate." A burst of applause from the audience and some nervous glances from the other board members.

Lenora stood. "We love you, Dolores," she put a hand over her heart, "but we have already voted, and what's done is done. Ninety days." Then once again addressing the audience. "Clock is ticking." She spoke in the sing-song voice used on a ten-year-old.

"We need more time," someone shouted. Some murmured assent, the group consciousness now in search of a galvanizing voice to steamroll Lenora. It was the moment Dolores knew would come. She pulled up her canvas carryall and reached in. She held up a sheet of paper, some in the audience leaning forward to make out the letterhead.

"This is a letter from an attorney who oversees Section 8. We all know these are Section 8 units, and this means that they must follow federal regulations." The two from management, angling for the door, had put away their phones. "The attorney has sent us, the tenants, this letter," she waved it like courtroom evidence, "to tell us that the board vote regarding terms of the move-out must be unanimous, and as you know, I voted no which means it is time to negotiate."

The audience erupted. Dolores handed the letter to Lenora who took it without looking at it. Some in the audience stood and applauded, others whistled and stomped. Dolores, still standing, reached into her bag one more time and pulled out a folder. "And if our friends from the management company would like to come forward, we have here our first proposal. A two-year extension."

The two men, halfway out the door, froze and sheepishly turned around. Dolores finally smiled and waved the folder at them like they'd forgotten what they came for.

■   ■   ■

October meant special foods and decorations for the *ofrendas*, and Dolores's supplier had the best selections and the best prices on Tuesday mornings. His loading dock was on a back alley off Roscoe near Blythe Street. She bought two hundred dollars of sugar skulls, plastic marigolds, and *papel picado* which the owner loaded into her trunk and back seat. He gave Dolores a hug and returned inside.

She cranked the engine, slid the seat belt across, and then saw in her rearview someone bringing another box toward her car. She rolled down her window which is when the man dropped the box and produced a needle that he deftly sank into her neck. The alley was empty, though a white panel van quickly pulled up, producing another man from the back who teamed up with the first man to pull Dolores's limp body out of her car and into the back of the van. A third man got into Dolores's car and drove off in it. The van followed down the alley and headed west on Roscoe.

A motorcyclist found Dolores's body later that day on Woodman Avenue, her feet sticking out of the bushes. A pair of skid marks led off the road and across the sidewalk. Dolores's pushcart, now empty, lay twenty feet further in the bushes, a mangled heap.

The wounds were consistent with a hit-and-run, though the three sets of security cameras from neighboring businesses had all had their CCTV cut that very same night.

News of her death spread quickly. A roadside memorial with candles and flowers sprung up by the next day. At all three local schools a collection was taken for her funeral. At East Valley, the graphic arts kids had printed out an enormous farewell poster featuring a picture of her with the closest thing to a smile she could manage. Hundreds of students signed it, most leaving short messages, simple gratitudes, vignettes from their lives, and pledges to take care of her cats. When Javier took his turn, he noticed a one-liner, more message than remembrance.

woodman wuz slim charles

Javier understood it immediately, knew it was Gio's handwriting. There were two street vendors in the Shoe and Woodman bifurcated the neighborhood like North and South Korea, only it was east and west. The east side was Dolores's and the west belonged to a beanpole of a man, Slim Charles. Neither one of them would ever do business in the other's route. Farmers never harvested their neighbor's crops, and *callejeros* never poached business outside their routes.

CHAPTER 11

The flat screen in the back of the Box was, as always, showing the news, a segment about the Van der Lipp clean-up underway. Javier, seated at a desk, had just finished printing a set of financials that Lupe had requested upon reviewing his loan application. To his astonishment, she had suggested he ask for a larger loan and wanted a set of projections based on that amount. He stapled the papers then sensed rather than saw someone behind him in the doorway. He turned to see a figure looming there backlit by the Valley sun.

"It was open," the figure announced. "Hope I didn't startle you."

Javier stood. "What can I do for you?"

"You towed my Land Rover last month." The man took a step inside, throwing off the balance of the room. "My name is George Jones. LAPD sent me back here because there were a couple of items that were missing from my car." Jones surveyed the Box's modest interior and then let his eyes return to Javier. "A phone and a gun."

Javier could feel the man measuring his response. "I'll need some ID."

"Of course." Jones reached into his suit coat, pulled out his wallet, and produced a license. Javier took it and checked the name like it mattered which, at this point, it didn't. He wanted this guy and his personal property gone. The man stood there casually, hands in pockets, an aura of profound withholding coming off of him. Javier knew nothing about suits but could tell that the one this man had on was expensive. "Anyone else come by for them?"

"Yeah, one guy. Said he worked for you." Javier left it there.

"No kidding." Jones didn't sound surprised or even interested. His phone rang. "Excuse me." He stepped back outside to take the call.

This guy Jones was clearly from some other world Javier wanted no part of. He went to the safe and knelt in front of it, his pulse juddering in his ears, his heart starting to move toward his throat. He overshot one of the numbers of the combination, tried to reset his mind and looked up at the flatscreen. Something in the news crawl caught his attention. *VDL Clean Up Underway.* In the background, the now familiar scene of Lake Mistake.

VDL

A zap of recognition. The texts on the burner.

VDL

Jesus, why hadn't he seen it before. *Van der Lipp.* Of course, those texts, the cryptic messages, the pieces now miserably coming together. Outside, Jones continued to talk, his back to Javier but now starting a gradual rotation, casting his attention around the yard like the beam of a lighthouse. Javier tried the safe again, a sense of dread beginning to weed into him. The safe door opened, the gun and the phone still sitting there like two aliens from the same doom-filled universe. He pulled the gun out, placing it on top of the safe.

Then he reached for the phone.

It was blinking a picture icon

Javier tried to beat back a morbid curiosity, to turn the phone over and glimpse whatever ill-fated image was on the other side. He glanced toward Jones, his head now in profile looking like some kind of reptile, a lizard sensing a fly nearby. For a few swollen seconds, Javier, nerves humming like struck piano wire, sat there in teetering confusion. He dropped the burner, clattering to the floor and landing screen-side up.

A picture of Dolores appeared.

Oh, Jesus.

A surveillance shot of her and her cart.

Javier ran a hand over his face and tried to wall off his shock. Jones would be finishing his call any moment leaving Javier with a decision to make very quickly. His first reaction was denial, to ignore it. It was all mere coincidence, the texts and now the picture of Dolores. He checked the date on the text, noted it had been sent three days ago, two days before Dolores's body had been found. For a moment, he thought of slamming the door shut and grabbing the shotgun, and perhaps, as if sensing this too, Jones came up the steps, placed a shiny Gucci loafer on the threshold of the door, and reached inside his coat. Javier's stomach lurched. He raised a defensive hand as though getting ready to catch a bullet.

"Ever been to a Lakers game?" Jones pulled out a business card and held it out for Javier, too lost in his panic to figure out if he was supposed to answer the question or take the card. "That's my card with our client website. Choose your game, call that number. That was my office just now, and I told my assistant to add your name to the list. Skybox. All you can eat."

Javier's mind was a blender. "I really can't accept them, Mr. Jones."

Jones made a small take-it motion with the card. "Not many people with your quick thinking, Javier. Most people would have just given the first guy that came here what he asked for." It didn't slip past Javier that he'd never given his name to this guy. "You saved me considerable time."

Javier wanted him gone as quickly as possible, and Jones seemed unaccustomed to taking "no" for an answer.

Javier took the card and slid it into his pocket. "Thank you," he mumbled, handing Jones the phone and holding the gun out grip first. Jones grabbed it, popped the magazine, quickly slammed it back in, then stuck the gun somewhere inside his coat like someone who lived each day with a concealed carry.

Jones thumbed the phone screen awake, no doubt getting a look at the last picture ever taken of Dolores. Javier had to guess this was some kind of head game where Jones waited to see if Javier flinched or said something or did anything that might betray his knowledge of what was on the phone.

"Enjoy the game, Javier." Jones let his eyes linger on Javier a second more than necessary before turning to go. As soon as Jones rounded the gate, Javier punched up one of the street cameras Betzaida had installed on a telephone pole and followed Jones down the street to his new SUV, a Porsche Cayenne. Javier zoomed in on the tag, took a screen grab and emailed it to himself. Javier sat down as some new anxiety found his throat and made him cough. He couldn't pretend like he had a choice about what to do next, though his mind kept forking off trying to avoid it.

■   ■   ■

Years ago, the guys had discovered an abandoned set of orange, wide wale corduroy sofas that sat on a small rise in a vacant lot overlooking Dogtown. It had been the go-to spot for meet-ups during the sixty daily minutes of interregnum between school and home. The guys called it "study hall," a cover they'd invented in fifth grade after they'd made the rookie mistake of telling their mothers, when asked why they were late coming home from school, that they had been "chilling."

Porque "chilling?" *I no like this chilling. You no* chill.

Thus, the anodyne "study hall" was invented. When the mothers saw it in the group texts, they bumped their brows in pleasant surprise. By high school, time no longer their own, study hall became more a site for birthday cattle calls and occasional Friday wind-downs. More than one of them had spent nights there when things at home started coming apart. *Need some Switzerland.* It was their code to get out of their house before the pots and pans started flying. Enrique's mother in particular had a fascination with men who liked to fill the top shelf of the refrigerator with Modelos, monopolize the remote, and eventually big-dog it. Even Enrique had his limits, so when things broke out into the open, his mother would start in with the excuses, and Enrique would grab a few things to spend a night on one of the couches.

Javier's head was swimming, that last knowing look of Jones ricocheting around his mind. He texted Betzaida to tell her he wasn't coming in. It was dark out when he got to study hall, and he grabbed some construction-site cast-offs, plywood and two by fours. He took the lighter and starter fluid the guys kept beneath one of the sofas, and then watched sparks rocket into the blue-black night sky before vanishing. Across the lot, he could make out two construction cranes, blinking red lights affixed to the end of each jib. They'd sprung up only weeks after the dam break, harbingers of something very tall. Javier shot his feet out and crossed his ankles. He imagined getting on a Greyhound and not getting off.

Out of nowhere, Gio appeared on the other side of the fire, eating a burrito, dressed in ill-fitting clothes as if pulled off of laundry lines on the way over.

"Jesus, Gio. What the fuck?"

Gio took a seat on the couch opposite Javier. "Some Illuminati shit goin' on." He pointed with his burrito at the cranes.

Javier stared off at the cranes. "That?" He pulled the stick out, the end burning until he waved it around. "Tip of the iceberg, Gio."

"What are you talking about?"

"Dolores. The dam break." Javier tossed the stick on the fire. "*That* was some Illuminati shit. And wanna hear something crazy?"

Gio cocked his head and burped.

A sudden burst of sirens from Van Nuys drew their attention for a moment. Javier waded into his big reveal, well aware Gio would quickly see the big picture. "I found a burner. Proves neither was an accident. Dolores wasn't a hit and run, and the dam break was intentional."

Gio slowly took a seat.

Javier took a beat, wondering to himself what purpose it served to drag Gio into this apart from unburdening himself. "Came across it a couple weeks ago on a tow. Some texts about the flood. And a picture of Dolores two days before they found her body." Whatever regret he had about telling Gio this soon gave way to relief. "And not like selfies either. Like surveillance pictures, you know." Javier could see the wheels spinning in Gio's head. He would be like a dog with a bone once he heard all this. "What does VDL mean to you?"

"Van der Lipp." Gio didn't have to even think. "So lemme guess, you picked up a phone with a bunch of texts like *VDL this* and *VDL that...*" Gio titled his chin in the direction of Lake Mistake. "No way that was an accident, all those buses."

Javier couldn't deny his sense of relief, someone else to share his private hell. "I saw what you wrote on Dolores's tribute poster. About where they found her."

Gio put his feet up on a giant cable spool, its edges worn down from years of shoes resting there. "Woodman was Slim Charles. Everyone knows that." Gio slapped both thighs with his hands. "Do you still have the burner?"

Javier shook his head. "Owner came by to pick it up today. I was gonna just give it to him, you know, be done with it, but when I saw Dolores's picture..." He studied his shoes now wondering if a problem shared was a problem halved or doubled. "I still gave it back to the guy, and now I'm wondering if I should try getting it back, you know? I mean, that burner does nothing but announce major crimes."

Gio pulled his legs in, sat forward as if getting ready to get launched off the sofa. "My mother, God rest her miserable soul, used to be hung up on shaming me, Javier, like she was trying to win the shame Olympics. I mean degrading, crazy, whack-a-doodle shit, would have made Hitler blush, you know. But the thing that really makes me angry, Javi, isn't what she did, you know, it was what my father *didn't* do, what he could have done instead of just sitting there, Javi, 'cause dude didn't do shit. Watched. In a chair. Like it was a gameshow."

Gio picked up a stick and started poking the fire, sending a jerky burst of sparks up into the sky. "Just sat there like a fucking zombie, and like my mother can't help it, you know, like major frame damage on that one, always gonna be pulling to the right, know what I mean?" Gio paused to consider the end of his stick, now a glowing ember. He swung it in the air a few times. "But the people like my father?" Gio eyes followed the neon light trail of his stick. "He could have done something."

Javier could only speculate about Gio's life, an all-star collection of traumas and deprivations from what bits and pieces he'd shared. Javier'd first met Gio in third grade, his feet, hands, and a mop of hair sticking out of a trash can. The bigger boys, who sensed weakness on the schoolyard like a drop of ink in a bathtub, had stuffed him ass-first into the barrel half full with lunch trays. Javier helped him out and saw the problem: a pair of bootleg Vans where the sporty line went down toward the sole instead of upwards. Even though he had been in the States for less than a year, Javier understood the shoe-show that went on in school. He asked Gio his size (he didn't know which meant Javier then had to take off his own shoe and hold it up sole to sole with Gio's, an exact match). The next day Javier showed up with a pair of Old Skools for Gio, paid for with money he'd borrowed from Betzaida who then told Javier he had to work it off at the place she'd just started working, Mission Tow.

Javier sat there staring at the fire for what had to have been half an hour, and when he looked up, Gio was gone. Javier pulled out his phone and sent Sergio a text.

need to clone a burner

A burner he first had to steal.

CHAPTER 12

The construction site that had sprung up next to Lake Mistake had the frenetic intensity of an ant colony. On his way to work most days, Javier would glance through the entrance as he passed to watch the cranes and the heavy equipment go at the site like grazing dinosaurs. Four massive parking cutouts sat in the middle of it all, like giant-sized gravesites, auguring something the Shoe hadn't seen in five decades: tall buildings. To the side stood a gray office trailer that looked like the Box.

It was a week after Jones had come by Mission, and there was his Cayenne parked next to the trailer. Javier took out his phone and pulled up the screenshot he'd taken from Mission cameras. The license plates were the same. It somehow made sense that Jones would be involved in whatever development was coming to this part of the Shoe. Moments later, Jones emerged from the trailer, climbed into his car, did a U-turn and exited the site passing Javier who had to duck behind the gate to avoid being seen.

"Can I help you?" A woman's voice came out of nowhere startling Javier. He stood up and noticed a speaker-camera combo hidden behind some grillwork built into the construction fencing.

"Hi!" Javier responding a little too brightly, already sounding guilty. "My name is Javier Jimenez, and I'm from East Valley High and—" He'd hoped by playing the schoolboy card he might get a pass. "I write for the school newspaper, the Daily Python, only it isn't daily 'cause—" East Valley had no school newspaper so he was grateful when the voice interrupted his riff.

"What can I do for you Mr. Jimenez?" *Mister.* Not good. He was reaching as far into the charm bag as he could and getting nothing. Javier pulled up a smile and walked closer to the camera. "I was asked to write...um...an article on...what the plans were for this...place?" He had no idea what he was doing, his words tumbling out on their own as if trying to escape his mouth. "Is there someone I can interview? Perhaps you?" He produced a notebook from his book bag and waved it in front of the camera like it was a press credential. He was in way over his head.

"Trailer, to your left."

Javier hoped perhaps the woman behind the voice would appear at the door and wave to him, beckon him over, make this charade easy. A diminutive woman dressed in a brown pantsuit with a tower of bleach-blonde hair met him at the door, looking like a human soft-serve ice cream cone.

"What can I do for you, Mr. Jimenez?" She gave him a smile that came off like a moat.

"Um, yeah, my editor asked me to come find out what's getting built here, you know, so we could do a story about it...in the..." He trailed off, sounding like someone going under sedation counting back from one hundred.

He wasn't sure if it was pity, but the woman stepped aside and let him in. The interior was a dimly lit place with no office furniture to speak of apart from the counter standing in the middle of the floor looking like Stonehenge.

The woman took her seat behind the counter. "In the Daily Python?" It took Javier a moment to realize she was finishing his last sentence. "You'd have to speak with someone from community relations." She handed him a business card. "They'll answer all your questions."

"Thank you." He took the card, yet stood there, his smile flattening. "Just one question, if I may." The lady's face was a fist. "A couple of months ago, you know, when the dam broke and Dogtown got flooded, there was a bunch of buses here picking up all the people who had been living, you know, where the lake is now." She looked at him as an orderly would regard an inpatient. "Any idea how those buses were just, you know, waiting? I mean, it was an accident, right, Van der Lipp and all that." She let Javier fumble for some kind of point. "It just struck me as a really huge coincidence that all those buses would be on scene just waiting to—"

She gave him a sad face. "I'm sorry, Mr. Jimenez. I wasn't here when the dam broke, and I can't say." Then she pointed at the card still in his hand. "They can help you, Mr. Jimenez," suddenly bright-eyed and smiling, as if cheered by the prospect of a happy ending.

A phone rang from her desk. "Excuse me for a moment, won't you?" Javier was surprised she hadn't just shooed him out the door. "This is Lonnie." She clicked her mouse twice and began typing. "Three-quarter copper." Pause. Another click. "Offload at the basement." Another pause. "Below the chimney." Pause. "Talk to Wilson when you get over there." Another call came in and she clicked over without looking up. Another short conversation, something going somewhere.

Javier looked around the office, tried to spot some hint of what was coming—floor plans, a scale model—but other than Lonnie-the-battle-axe and her hair, there wasn't much. The second call was wrapping up, a coda of "yeah, rights."

It was Hail Mary time. Javier pulled out his phone, hit record, and stuck it at the base of a faux birch tree at the end of the counter and then set his notebook on the other end. Lonnie hung up, and again turned to Javier.

"Anything else?" she said, clearly ready for him to get going.

He made a circle with his head, wondering if anything else might come loose and pop out. "Nope, not right now, very grateful for your time...and this number." He held the card up. "Appreciate your time Ms...." he added, hoping he could at least walk away knowing her name.

"Ms. Witherspoon."

"Thank you, Ms. Witherspoon." He made an awkward bow like they'd both just performed a one act play. Once outside, he crossed the street to Winchells and bought six bear claws and a coffee. He sat down at one of the press-board booths, carved up with initials, and drank his coffee. In the uppermost corner, a tube television sat bolted in at an angle, the fasteners rusting and cobwebbed, the whole thing looking like it could fall down any second. The weatherman on the screen, sleeves rolled up, was growing excited over what looked like more sunny weather. Fifteen minutes later he crossed the street again and walked into the trailer without knocking.

"Forgot something?" Lonnie was in her seat holding his "reporter's notebook" he'd left behind.

Javier dramatically hit his forehead. "Thank you. I got halfway home and..." He produced a bag full of bear claws. "Hey, you know what, I have an extra." He peered into the bag. "But forgot the napkins."

Lonnie's face brightened. It had to be a nun's existence, sitting in this trailer, alone. Even a breadcrumb-sized act of kindness had to make an impression. "I think we have some in the back." She stood and disappeared, enough time for Javier to retrieve his phone from the base of the tree, hit the stop button, and stuff it in his pocket. Lonnie reappeared and stuck a hand inside the bag and pulled out a bear claw. She took a bite, eyes closed, then held it up, a large half-moon-sized bite taken from it.

"Shit coffee, but Winchells knows how to deep-fry and glaze like no one else." She seemed momentarily transported.

Javier held up the notebook, thanked her, and made his second exit, this time without the bow. Two minutes later, he was back on the sidewalk out of range of the entrance cameras and opening the recording app. He scanned the readout and about three minutes in, he saw the telltale bump. He dragged the bar and hit play.

Just some kid from the high school doing an article about the towers...No, he just wanted to know what's going in, you know...Wanted to write an article...Jeez, relax...I gave him Abby's number...Last name Jimenez, I forget his first name.

Javier couldn't help but feel slightly insulted.

No shit? Pause. *Yeah, Javier, that's right.*

It had to have been Jones on the phone.

He did mention the buses, though.

Bingo.

Right, same time next week. She hung up.

Perhaps feeling slightly giddy on the success of his little ruse, a plan came to him, unbidden and outrageous, long odds at best. He called Bergosian's Tow and left a message for Mark Bergosian, son of Betzaida's nemesis Kristops. Mark was Javier's age, went to East Valley, and was actually one of those kids you couldn't help but like, even though Javier had tried his hardest not to.

CHAPTER 13

Dolores's funeral was standing room only at Immaculate Conception, its vaulted ceilings with hewn wood rafters and lead-stained glass the closest thing the Shoe had to the baroque cathedrals from her home state of Zacatecas. Attire was as diverse as the people who came, professionals dressed down in dark suits, *raza* in their pressed Dickies and chains, tradesmen in their jumpsuits having canceled a few jobs to come pay their respects.

Javier and Betzaida had a hard time finding parking and had to stand in the back beneath the second station of the cross rendered in fresco. To Javier's left, a man built like a barrel in a Raiders jersey with a large 818 covering most of his throat from chest to chin, audibly breathed through his mouth which itself was surrounded by a goatee marbled with scar tissue.

It was a hot Santa Ana day, prompting more than one of the remembrances to make note of Dolores's shaved ice, the chuckles completely gone after the third version. A young boy, a neighbor of Dolores's barely tall enough to reach the microphone, was the only eulogizer who didn't read off a speech, instead launching into a set of calculations he'd done to determine the mileage Dolores had logged in her thirty-odd-year career pushing her cart around the Shoe six days a week. "I hated math until she gave me this." He finished by holding up a solar-powered, blue calculator.

Javier checked the program and saw the next and last speaker was Lupe Rodriguez. She strode to the pulpit, the air bending around her as she walked, her eyes stashed behind a pair of dark glasses. Most in the audience were folks from the Gardens, knew Lupe and had known her family, its own cosmos of dysfunction. Lupe could have pulled out a gun and shot the huevos off three of the men in the front row, and no one would have held it against her.

"We used to say that life was cheap in the Gardens, *verdad*?" A private smile, a few heads bobbing in the pews. "The world can go terribly wrong." Sensing a pall, she veered back toward the firm ground of reminiscence, a first encounter. Lupe had been standing in line with a group of friends to buy something from Dolores. One of the friends challenged Lupe to hold her breath for as long as she could, and after a minute, Lupe's lips turned blue. She collapsed on the ground next to Dolores who then broke out her ammonia wipes to bring Lupe around.

"I woke up and saw Dolores hovering over me, scowling—I mean, let's be real, the woman could look scary—and I had no idea what had happened. I got up and screamed '*Llorona*!' and just ran as fast as I could." The congregation laughed, each with their own family version of *La Llorana*, the cursed, child-eating woman of lore. After ten minutes, Lupe climbed down from the pulpit, lay her forehead on the coffin, and then, walked down the aisle, her words still hanging in the air. She saw Javier and detoured in his direction while the priest led the audience in a final prayer.

"*Hola*, Javier." She took off her sunglasses and put a hand on his arm, her skin like polished wood. He felt suddenly illuminated standing in front of her, her attention so comprehensive as if her entire life had been a series of moments leading up to this encounter. She handed him a card. "Call me so we can talk." And then she looked at Betzaida and smiled. "You will have your loan in a week." Betzaida couldn't hide her confusion, unaware Javier had even applied for the loan. Then back to Javier. "You are coming to the barbecue?" Javier studied the blinged-out tennis bracelet on her wrist, then noticed behind her left ear an RIP tattoo. Leslie was right. From the projects to the hills.

"Yes," Javier managed.

"And bring Alex."

Javier's mouth flopped open like a landed carp.

Lupe gave his arm a squeeze. "I still have cousins in Denker."

She smiled, a shared moment passing between them before she moved off, leaving a void in her place. Lupe greeted a few others in narthex before exiting the church. A minute later, the mouth-breather followed leaving a vapor trail of cologne in his wake.

The priest gave a hasty benediction, followed by a church soloist with a resonant soprano that filled the sanctuary with three verses of *"Un Dia A Las Vez."* Finally, the pallbearers came to the front, grabbed a handle, and carried the coffin outside to the waiting hearse. Senior Rodriguez stood at the front of the hall whistling through his fingers and waving his hand.

"Venga! Comer." Senior Rodriguez stood and announced that it was time to eat. Then in English, "And no crying while you are eating!" A small ripple of laughter escaped as the doors to the adjoining parish hall swung open like a game show revealing one long row of hot serving trays, steam rising off of each. More food than anyone can eat and NO mariachi. Part of Dolores's Big Adios pact with Senior Rodriguez. I will haunt you until your last breath, Fernando, if I see one *guitarra*.

It was always a coin flip who would ambush you at these types of events, and chances were good it would spell fifteen minutes of planning your getaway while you stood nodding and making affirmative sounds. Betzaida and Javier stood off to the side, the crowd large enough to have people turning sideways to squeeze by. Betzaida suddenly dropped a heavy hand on the shoulder of a guy wearing a sport coat and tie. "Get your ugly ass over here." The guy turned taking a millisecond to put a name with the face, then lit up.

"Betz! I thought that was you." They hugged which, for Betzaida, was a rarity.

She held him at arm's length then tugged his tie like there was a bell attached. "Carlos, this is literally my brother from another mother—Javier." She put an arm on Javier's shoulder. "East Valley to UCLA, so don't start fillin' his head with anything that has him swinging a hammer."

Carlos had the easy presence of someone who, as an adolescent, would have looked for just enough but not too much trouble. "Your *hermana* and me, we spent more time in detention freshman year than in class." Then, through a fist, "Always her fault." Betzaida chucked him one on the shoulder.

Javier had heard bits and pieces about Carlos, mostly backstory he knew Betzaida preferred to keep tucked away. "Betz told me about you two back in the day." They'd been part of a car crew that dragged streets on Sunday night, sideshows and takeovers on Mondays, long before social media.

"This one," Carlos said, pointing a thumb at Betzaida. "Her Camaro, V8, 440, used to smoke fools."

"Roll up, hit 60 on the tach, and just pop the clutch straight into second."

"Double-hemi glory days, Javier." Carlos shook his head. "Dumb shit, really." The three of them watched a plate of taquitos pass in front of them too quickly to intercept.

"Speakin' of which, I'm gonna eat that dumb-shit little tie of yours, Carlos, if I don't get me a plate." Betzaida stood on her toes and scanned the hall, looking for the best path to the food tables. "You guys want anything?"

"Two of whatever you're gettin'," Carlos said. Betzaida headed off, leaving Carlos and Javier to play East Valley trivia for a few minutes. Carlos didn't know Patel but remembered Ms. Belcher the math teacher. "She always thought I was high." He chuckled. "Just allergies. For real."

Someone came up on Carlos' left, dapped him. They exchanged quick words through heavy expressions before the guy disappeared into the crowd. Carlos took a deep breath. "Homie and

I were here a month ago for another service." Carlos spotted someone in the crowd, shot a smile and waved. Apparently, the connection didn't quite merit a trip through the crowd. "You might have heard of him. The guy they found at the bottom of the reservoir when the dam broke."

Javier vaguely recalled hearing something about that on the radio from the night of the flood. The organist, who had relocated into the sanctuary, was suddenly playing the baby grand piano that was about two feet from the two of them.

"What do you do?"

"General contractor." Carlos pulled out his phone "Here. Check this out. Bullet train out of Vegas. My team does the piers for the viaducts, you know, uh, the platforms the trains run on." He brought his forearm up flat and eye-level to demonstrate what a viaduct was. The pictures showed the enormous Y-shaped piers standing like soldiers in a row with their arms over their heads.

"Vegas to LA, huh? Where they putting the LA station?"

"Was gonna be Rancho Cucamonga, you know through the 1-15 corridor, but now it's like a big secret." Someone off to their right started sobbing, heads turning, a flurry of tissue. "Here, check out the renderings for the Vegas station. It's sick." The pictures showed an enormous box-like shape in mirrored glass set in the middle of a sandy expanse. It seemed nearly invisible, the reflection and the actual landscape merging into one. Carlos flipped through a few more pictures.

Javier saw something. "Wait. Can you go back?" Carlos swiped the other way, one, two, three pictures. "There." It was an image of what looked like a groundbreaking, a dozen people leaning on shovels—all but one, men in suits looking awkward, in the middle, the lone female in jeans and a yellow bandana. "That's the lady who spoke today. Lupe?"

Carlos gave Javier a funny look. "Yeah, Lupita. You know her?"
"Not really." He recalled her hand on his arm. "Sort of."

Carlos craned his head apparently looking for her like she might be in the crowd. "Grew up in the Gardens, same building as me. *Ay guey*, whacko family. Most of 'em dead or in jail now, *gracias a Dios*." He poked at the screen. "'Cept Lupita. But trust me, she weren't no angel neither."

Javier gave Carlos a puzzled look.

"Schoolgirl and all 'til one of her older brothers, Victor, got shot." The RIP tattoo. "After that, pssshh, she went hard."

"Lupe?"

"Yeah, right? Like now, she needs to run for president, you know, but back in the day, watch out." He opened his home screen, dug into some folders, and whizzed through some old photos, then thumbed a few more until he came to one, showing an adolescent Lupe with frizzed-out hair sitting on a couch, eating cereal with a handgun in her lap. "Girl was in deep." He flipped through some more school-age pictures of Lupe. "Had a major crush on her. Loved the big hair."

Javier wasn't sure what to make of this, *chola*-Lupe a bit of a curveball. He kind of assumed she'd been a head-down, brick-by-brick grinder like himself. He looked closely at the image of her on the couch, her eyes heavy-lidded and staring at air, the countenance of a youth who'd already seen too much. "Can you go back to that other picture? The one with all the people and the shovels?"

Carlos flipped back and widened the image. "Ground breaking on the Vegas station, like, five years ago. All those fools," he said, pointing at the semicircle of middle-aged white men wearing the same smile. "Don't know 'em. Politicians going for the photo op, but Lupita, she wasn't just a contractor. She had skin in the game."

Javier gave him another look. "What's that mean?"

"She was an equity partner which meant she was gonna share in the upside." He stuck the phone back in his pocket. "Only it's been mostly downside lately." Betzaida was knifing her way through the crowd holding four plates. Carlos put his phone away. "Stories I could tell from the Gardens, but hey, why drag up people's past. She's like a bazillionaire now."

Betzaida started to hand Carlos his plate then pulled it back.

"Oh, hell no, Carlos. Javi is not signing up to saw cement or whatever you got in mind." Then she handed the first plate to Javier. "Young'un got a jobsite already, called UCLA."

.   .   .

Tasha was hearing it from the constituents, none more vehement than her own father who had lived in the Senator Rittenhouse's district for the last thirty-nine years.

"Like giant mo-squi-toes, girl, just wanna swat those little bastards." He was on the phone with her every other day, and today was a bad time to talk. She was standing in the back of the East Valley gym, a last-minute press conference the Senator had gone ahead and set up. A recent hire, a willowy blonde who had swanned into the office six months with no experience but a compensating set of teeth and hair was managing the event. Captain of her college tennis team, she'd had won the Senator over with her brio and apparently a world-class backhand, a fact made abundantly clear on her resume which featured not one but two pictures of her hitting winners. Tasha had been the first to see the resume and was ready to ball it up, when the Senator glanced over, noticed the full extension of the forehand and went in for a closer look.

"I know, Daddy. We've been trying to get them down but none of the agencies are taking responsibility, so—"

"I ain't a-lying, girl. I took out my service and dropped one of 'em like a bad habit. Felt damn good, and Freddy from the Elks, he's taken out five." Tasha knew he would be holding up all five fingers as he said this. "But remember, he was a sniper in the army so he's got one of 'em long guns with the scope, and I've just got my little pea shooter, but ol' Elroy—" Tasha didn't have time for roll call at the VFW.

"Daddy, just stay inside for now. Lotta Looney Tunes stuff goin' on. Maybe try doin' your dominoes online or something, you know?"

"Online? You got to be—"

"Gotta run, Daddy." She hung up. The Senator was working without a prepared speech and was coming off vague and evasive. Immigrant communities were slow to rile, deferential at first, but once indignant, quickly coalesced, and if anyone could inspire that kind of one eighty, it was the Senator. The tennis captain was in the hallway drinking a soda and talking on her phone.

As he wrapped up his speech, insisting that he didn't have time to take questions, a man stood, hat in hand. Tasha could see the Senator two-step behind the podium, perhaps unconsciously warming up to get the hell out of there. "I got a friend, ya know, a little behind with things, ya know ..." The man spoke with a heavy accent and fidgeted with his hat. "He's been told these drones do that—what you call it—facial something?"

"Facial recognition," the Senator said with a smile. Tasha'd coached him on his tendency to finish sentences. It made him come off as a know-it-all.

"Right, that, and like I seen guys on video getting cuffed, you know, for like back taxes and child support, and you know a lot of us get paid cash, right, and warrants and that don't seem right, ya know? I mean what's goin' on here, Senator?" He stayed standing, Tasha thinking *Oh, shit.*

At community events like this one, she watched heads and shoulders to read the crowd, measure the amperage. The Senator, old enough to have grown up with a father who spoke of the "Negro problem," was out of his depth here. The tennis captain should have drilled it into the Senator's head on the way over that this was a press briefing, not a press conference, and that he was not supposed to take questions. Warrants and child support and back taxes were simply not subjects the Senator had any business talking about, especially in the Shoe. He'd come off like the arrogant nob he generally was. Instead of giving the Senator the hook, the tennis captain was still on her phone, now waving over some food delivery. Tasha walked to the edge of the stage getting ready to steal the mic.

The guy went on. "My kids don't wanna go to school cuz they seen some black trucks parked out front, and they think it's ICE or somethin'. We seen the videos, ya know, school kids gettin' picked up. And you know, that facial thing, that facial thing is like—" His tone had grown slightly righteous, audience whispers growing audible. "I don't know how you say it in English, but we call it *jodido.*" Fucked.

Boom. Half the crowd shot to their feet like someone had just scored a goal. The Senator, his eyes suddenly wide, was now a stand-in for all the asshole *gabacho* homeowners who spoke to all the plumbers in the crowd (and there were a lot) like they were diminished in the head, to all the nannies (and there were even more) in the crowd who had to swallow their self-respect and withstand the *guera* mother (who couldn't even take care of her own *pinche* kids) flap her lips about dusting the stair railings with all that ornamental iron shit. It was a bad look heading downhill fast. Tasha was on the stage in two long strides, quickly grabbing the microphone.

"*Escucha, escucha,*" she boomed. "*Sé cómo te sientes. Estaba hablando con mi padre y me dice que acaba de dispararle a un dron.*" She'd always been able to improvise, respond under duress to whatever fix the Senator found himself in, but on this occasion, with a small revolution about to ensue, she didn't have time to think and told the crowd her father had just shot down a drone.

It worked. The crowd came to a quick standstill, unsure how a Black woman could speak virtually accent-less Spanish (maybe from Belize?) and why she was talking about her drone-shooting daddy. Tasha filled the silence quickly, explained who she was, shared her bonafides to let them know she was one of them and that her boss, the Senator, had a meeting with ICE for which he was already thirty minutes late.

"El senador promete que los drones desaparecerán pronto."

Had the Senator known any Spanish, he would have told her immediately to retract the promise to get rid of the drones. He gave a smile, mouthed a thank you to no one in particular, stepped off the riser, and then out the back gym door where his Town Car was idling, a getaway ride like he should be holding a bag full of cash wearing a mask. Tasha stayed behind to mingle with her new fans and reassure them that things would soon get back to normal. She scanned the crowd to find the man who had stood and asked the question but couldn't see him anywhere.

i need to get off my back foot on this shit

It was the Senator already texting from his car.

i look like an asshole

Tasha took a breath, reminding herself to add some cushion time between reading and responding that texts like this one.

"He got one thing right." Tasha turned to see a man peering over her shoulder, staring at her screen. It was George Jones.

"And who the fuck asked you anyway?" Next to Jones was the man who had been asking all the questions. Tasha could tell they weren't strangers.

Question-man looked at her. "Tell your boss to saddle up 'cause this is just the beginning, Ms. Granderson," his halting English and heavy accent long gone. He turned and walked away leaving Tasha and Jones standing at center court.

Jones' eyes fell back on her phone. "Your boy is one and done. Numbers are weak."

"Your breath is weak."

He smirked. "Nearer my God to thee."

Tasha dipped her head and glared as if trying to will him into flames.

"Your theme song, Tasha. The music the band played while the Titanic sank. Too loyal for your own good."

"Too loyal for your own good." She did her best mock white-guy voice. "You wouldn't know loyalty if it fell outta a tree and hit you in the head." She hated that he was right, her girlfriends making the same happy hour comments. *Girl, you need to RUN for office, not answer the phone for that ol' fool. Sheeeet.* However much she detailed the litany of functions she performed every day, her friends had it in their heads that she was a secretary for the Senator, taking messages and bringing the coffee.

"When the music stops, Tasha, you need a seat." He passed his gaze over the crowd, as if offering evidence. "Your boy never could read a room, and his district is skewing more beans than rice, if you follow me, so what you just saw, today, only gettin' worse for Father Knows Best." He turned towards her, his shoulders now squared up. "Just so happens the next chairman of Ways and Means in D.C. is looking for a chief of staff. He's asked me for a short list, and you'd actually be on the shortest."

"You got me confused with someone who falls for your shit, Jones."

A few constituents had started to draw close, wanting some time with the Black lady who spoke better Spanish than their kids. Tasha mouthed *Uno minuto.*

"Your boss has been sitting on some enabling legislation relating to some tax credits I feel would benefit *este barrio*, Tasha. Just sitting on his desk, constipating my plans and doing considerable disservice to the voters. I'm gonna primary the good Senator next year unless he signs it."

Tasha looked up toward the rafters where a collection of banners hung. "Three of those titles, I ran the backcourt, used to hang thirty a game." She juked her head like she was about to drive past Jones to the hoop, though he didn't flinch. "My daddy still plays the ponies at the OTB across the street with his 31st Airborne jump-buddies. Walks his constitutional at five a.m. every morning. Been that way since you were in shorts, Jones, and if you think you just gonna come up in here, treat this place, *este barrio,*" using air quotes, "like it's a board game," she leaned in toward him, "then I will find that enabling legislation and send it up your narrow, white ass."

Jones looked at her, his eyes two wet stones. "Offer stands, Tasha, for another twenty-four hours. Don't let loyalty be more curse than blessing."

She stuck a palm in his face and chicken-necked her reply. Really, she just wanted him to stop talking because the offer he was dangling, no doubt legit, would be keeping her up tonight.

CHAPTER 14

It was the fifteenth of the month, always a busy date in the towing business. Workers got paid in cash, went straight for the bars on Sepulveda that served heavy pours. Betzaida did a brisk DUI business on these nights. Her reputation with CHP had worked its way into LAPD dispatch who now called Mission to tow the "deuces," shorthand for drunk drivers.

They'd pulled up on a stop, two cruisers and the driver in cuffs on the curb bobbing his head to some private tune. They both got out, and as Betzaida went to go give the officer in charge a work order to sign while Javier pulled the ramp lever. A thin, high-pitched wail came from under the bed. Javier took off a glove, stuck a hand underneath the hydraulic controls and produced a finger covered in a red fluid. The master cylinder had a blown gasket.

"We're done, Betz." He held up his finger, and Betzaida's head fell back.

The offending driver had blown a .35 which is fall-down drunk. From the curb, he'd dropped the music and had started threatening litigation. Then came the ad hominem insults towards the officers by name and eventually threats of violence towards Betzaida specifically which veered off into very specific homophobic acts. The two cops conferenced with each other, and Betzaida overheard one of the officers tell the other that the driver had five priors in the span of two years and had been 10-91 (police code for off-leash animal which was cop-talk for being an asshole) on all of them. This mope was not only going to lose his license and do county time, his car, a BMW M8, would be seized as a "nuisance," stashed in Mission Tow at $120 a day for the next few weeks. She got on her phone and called Lester to get over there and ramp the car before dispatch made a call to another tow company.

Betzaida pulled a rag from her pocket and threw it at Javier who snatched it out of the air and wiped his fingers. "Time we go do a wellness check on that brother of yours," she said. A pair of working girls had emerged from the shadows and stood under a nearby light pole, smoking and watching the man in cuffs whose protestations had started veering toward self-pity. One of the girls, stick-legged and wearing a feathery top giving her the appearance of a flamingo, took a few steps toward him and shouted something. The man tried to turn and look at her but lost his balance, fell over on his side, and went suddenly quiet, perhaps concussed. A nearby cop chuckled and doffed an imaginary cap at the girl who just dropped her cigarette and ducked back into the shadows.

It was less than a three-minute drive to the park, its light wash visible from a block away. Denker Park, all two blocks of it, was essentially a shared backyard for the three hundred families that lived in the Roscoe Gardens. By day, young mothers watched their children climb monkey bars, chase each other and ask for change when Dolores came by. *Viejos* fed the pigeons and *vatos* pulled the belts on their engines, but when the sun went down, the retail end of the narcotics trade–the jugglers–bloomed along the periphery of the park.

Betzaida pulled up along one of the streets that ran perpendicular to the park and cut the engine then leaned back to let Javier get a view out her window.

She banked her head towards the street. "The walking dead."

A handful of hopheads stutter-stepped down the street on their way to score. To Javier, the scene was the two-legged version of Mama's jobsite, an abattoir, where he'd spent a sick day in third grade discovering how hamburger got made. She'd had no other option but to bring her fevered child and stash him in the lunchroom which served as the de facto child care/sick bay for all the mothers who worked there. Supervision was spotty, and Javier managed to slip out a door and take a self-guided tour where he watched cattle conclude their miserable lives with a short walk down a one-way chute to a room where an air compressed bolt scrambled their frontal lobes. Once unconscious, they were strung up by their hind legs and exsanguinated. He couldn't not look away, at one point watching Mama draw her knife across the carotid of a bull. He threw up then wandered back to the lunchroom, snuck back in, and spent the rest of the day curled up in a ball.

There were no signs of Alex, only a handful of crotch-grabbing jugglers. In the half-shadows of the handball courts were the *capitanes*, supervising the action like distracted dads at their kids' tee-ball game. It was a live action felony with little concern for law enforcement. The street sales themselves were drawn up like football plays designed to mitigate legal exposure. The first juggler would walk over to the passenger side window, collect the money, then finger-flash the order to another juggler a hundred feet away who would dash across the street, go around a corner, reappear with a small brown bag which he would drop in a trash can. The customer would pull forward, get out, and go collect the prize. No one holding cash or product. No actual hand to hand. Stood up better in court.

Police rarely had much success in street busts because the stash house changed every night. Occasionally a team of "knockos" (as in "Open up!" knocks of Housing Police) would play whack-a-mole if they had a tip on a re-supply, but the perps were usually Denker scrubs too young to shave which meant they would be kicked and back on the benches before the next shift. The game was changing though. Social media was taking a bigger and bigger bite out of street sales, and as a result, law enforcement had started moving their attention off the park, looking for new choke points.

Javier squinted at the far side of the park, a flurry of scooters pulling up and speeding off. "The real business is over there. With the plugs."

The plugs. Snapchatters and Instagrammers who took emoji orders. They gigged out delivery to anyone on a scooter which meant the barriers to entry in drug sales were coming down, leaving the biggest margins at the bottom of the ladder where the producers whacked up the product with baby formula and fed it into a pill press. And that end of the business was strictly south of the border.

"Word on the street is Denker's getting into production." Betzaida still had an ear to the ground courtesy of Janson, the previous owner of Mission Tow currently doing eight to ten on a manslaughter charge. "And cartels do not truck with that shit."

A black SUV with tinted windows drove the wrong way down the street, lights off, vape smoke pluming out the driver window, with a Canadian maple leaf on the chrome bumper and bullet-hole decals on the passenger side doors. A juggler came up to the driver side which was now curbside given the moving violation. The driver handed him a backpack, and then the boy gestured toward a second-story unit in the Gardens where a young girl sat propped in a window frame holding a cat in her lap, a storybook cover. She put the cat down and reappeared outside moments later with another backpack which she dumped in the trash can. The SUV pulled forward and a passenger jumped out to fetch it. The little girl was back in the window with her cat before the SUV turned its lights back on and pulled away.

"No Alex." Betzaida made one more scan of the park, fluttering her lips, head over the steering wheel. "Don't know if that's good news or bad."

"Ma doesn't know, so keep it to yourself."

Betzaida let out a clipped laugh. "Oh, she knows, Javi. Give your mother more credit. She might be in a little denial, but this shit," she bent her head toward the park, "she got friends at work who know more than you, Javi, 'cause their little hoodrat kids are up here too."

It was a revelation, and it took Javier a moment to absorb this little nugget, that perhaps Mama, the parent who wanted him, who had already lost a daughter, who came home wracked in pain, simply wasn't doing enough where it mattered most.

CHAPTER 15

It wasn't until his fourth beer that Terry Price finally felt his mood swing free. He was less than a year away from forced retirement, two words together that each on their own made him cringe. He was trying out different images of himself without a badge and gun, a mental slideshow of himself doing new things, and none of them fit. Plenty of agents could only sit out of the game for a year before they came back on a part-time basis. It was no secret that for agents, retirement came not with freedom but loss. You had to have another chapter underway, and Terry simply had never bothered with much beyond the job. He had no hobbies to speak of, didn't really find much use for RVs, golf, Kiwanis, or any of the other standard out-to-pasture pursuits. He stuck a hand up to signal for another beer.

"Your money's no good tonight, Ter." It was Richie, his partner on X-ray, reaching across the bar with a twenty. They ran over one hundred rigs through their machine an hour, looking for typical density footprints of weapons, bodies, and class IV substances like meth, cocaine, and heroin. They were star performers, Richie and Terry, year after year, thanks to the regular heads-up they got from Emme, Sinaloa, and Cali. No one in X-ray, either here in TJ, Calexico, or even Juarez, took down more *yayo* than Terry and Richie. They were legends, though less heralded was the far greater number of packages they let through. If the cartels gave out plaques for bent border agents, Richie and Terry could have built a house out of them. And that was the thing that Terry always circled around but could never admit. He wanted to keep his badge and gun, not for the enforcement end of his life, but the un-enforcement part.

There was no way around it—the game of cat and mouse at the border had given his life purpose. The high-wire thrill of playing both sides had transformed his Walter Mitty life with its brain-pounding routines into a meditation on death, and reciprocally, life. A few times a week he would dance with fate; his phone would buzz with the plate numbers five minutes before the cartel's driver pulled into his bay. Terry would take off his hat which was Richie's cue to override the X-ray footprint with one from a clean scan, a trick that was remarkably simple and also most definitely punishable with thirty-to-life. Then Terry'd wave the truck through, a simple act that vanquished his demons, turned off the loop in his head.

The bar was filling up, now shoulder to shoulder with college kids ready to cross over the bridge into Tijuana and let someone in a bandolero pour two fisted shots down their throat. He drained his beer, gave Richie a pat on the back

"Gotta go feed Furillo." Terry's one true love these days was his cat. He went out to the parking lot, got in his truck, drove the six miles to his house, hit the remote to open the swing gate, and pulled into his driveway. He spotted Furillo, perched on the first step of the porch stairs, his tail draped over his toes.

As he switched off the ignition, he noticed in his rearview a truck suddenly drive in through the gate which had not yet started to close. Terry got out and stood there.

He'd always known this day would come. Two men in cowboy hats got out of the truck, each carrying a sawed-off shotgun. Two more men remained in the backseat. One was drinking a Big Gulp through a straw, and the other was watching his phone.

Terry held his ground as they drew closer. "I can make it worth it for you."

They kept coming forward.

He put his hands up. "Double your product, same price."

The two men in their cowboy hats came to a stop, racked their guns and raised them to their shoulders. Terry put his hands down and stared past the gunmen at a rope of sunlight that sat just below a deck of coal black clouds. If only Furillo had not chosen this moment to come off that step and head for the front door, Terry's last thoughts might have been on the perfection of nature and its humbling effect, but the plaintive cries of his cat only filled Terry with a parting regret that Furillo would have no one to feed him.

CHAPTER 16

In a low-rent neighborhood of Phoenix called the Fairgrounds, a film crew rigged and lit an apartment complex. In the scene, ICE agents would descend on a second-floor unit and detain a man, once in English and then in Spanish. The director had agreed to spend a few days with everyone who lived there, most of whom didn't speak English, explaining that ICE was not really coming and that what they were filming was not an actual raid. The production company had catered a large lunch next to the empty pool to quash any fears. Through a translator, the director offered anyone who wanted one a walk-on role; the translator explained their daily wage as an extra, and heads bobbed up. *Comida gratis*, a few smiles.

"For this scene, a reporter from a local television station is filming a raid as it is happening." The director waited for the translation and then pointed to the parking lot in front of the building. "She will be out there and will follow the ICE agents—remember, they are not real—right in here." The director pointed to the staircase leading to the second floor. The residents of the building started chattering. Most of them had seen actual raids, many had been detained, some more than once. They spent a few hours blocking the scene, going through whose apartment was going to be raided, choreographing the breach, the distraught girlfriend, the lookie-loos. A few young children started firing their imaginary weapons first at the front door of the suspect's apartment then at each other.

"I hear Rudy Becerra is in this movie," a lady blurted out. "*Mi corazon!*" The women laughed and whooped.

The director nodded and grinned. "Rudy is currently filming in Columbia, but I spoke with him a few hours ago, and he says he feels this scene we are about to shoot is the turning point of the movie." Some of the women bounced on their toes, hands on their cheeks.

When it got dark, a cast of ICE officers in tactical gear descended on the complex. The mock news crew followed them in, the intrepid reporter wearing a Kevlar vest and a helmet, narrating the events in a whisper as the camera cut back and forth between her and the officers now climbing a set of stairs. The "extraction team" crept up on unit 212. The first officer tapped his helmet signaling the breach team to come forward and knock the door down. The door splintered and a handful of officers squeezed inside with weapons drawn; shouts and screams followed. Young children from the surrounding units spilled out onto the catwalk, dressed mostly in their underwear and T-shirts. They gawked and pointed at the lasers dancing in the apartment then drew back their fingers and stuck them in their mouths as a man was led out of 212, his hands zip-tied behind him. He was wearing red sweatpants and a blue Dodgers T-shirt, his hair mussed. Parents grabbed their children and pulled them inside then stopped and stared at the man being taken down the stairs.

The man shouted over his shoulder to his girlfriend, "*Llama a Manny y dile que se pase,*" telling her to call Manny who would presumably know what to do. He tried to project calm as the woman, in shorts and black tank top with Vegas! written in white cursive, followed behind, frantically trying to dial her phone.

She shouted, "*Pinche cabron*! You have the wrong man! What are you doing? I'm gonna sue you!" From behind a monitor in the center of the complex, the director nodded his head. Then she screamed, "Black lives matter!" The whole ICE team slowed down—not one Black life anywhere to be seen—certain the director would yell "Cut" and reshoot the scene. Instead, the cameras kept rolling. The man in the red sweatpants and blue Dodgers shirt got pushed into a waiting van which then sped off.

"Cut! That was brilliant!" The director made a point of coming over to hug the girlfriend who looked first relieved then overwhelmed, fanning herself with one hand while reaching out with the other to touch whoever was within arm's length. "One more time in Spanish." Everyone reset. The van returned, along with the man in the Dodgers shirt who got uncuffed and then returned to the complex, although they'd have to use another unit on the other side of the building to recreate the splintered doorway.

In the parking lot, the mock television crew took its position to film the second take of the detention. The reporter, still wearing her Kevlar vest, stared into the camera describing a "rash of ICE raids here in Panorama City as officers continue to pursue their suspects in the border shooting of agent Terry Price." She signed off then dropped her microphone as the camera light faded. "Okay, let's get some B-reel…go tight on one drone then go wide." The cameraman nodded and pulled his lens-eye off the camera to spot the one drone blinking over the apartment. Then he panned out revealing at a small cloud of drones, hovering over the apartment complex.

Then the cameraman reset the lens and finger-cued the reporter. "And we're back in 3…2…1…"

"Local officials won't confirm the use of facial recognition cameras on drones, but several of them have been spotted hovering at high altitudes over Panorama City. Additionally, we've heard from several concerned residents of the area that some supermarkets are now cooperating with ICE and sharing their video feeds. More on that at 11. For Channel 4, this is Evelyn Torres." She stared at the camera, her expression frozen for five seconds. The red light went off, she put down the microphone and blew out some air.

"Okay, *otre vez en español.*" Hair and makeup appeared out of nowhere and went to work on her like a Formula 1 pit crew. She looked at her watch, took a long drink of bottled water, and picked up the microphone, this time sporting the Univision logo.

Within twenty-four hours, the English and Spanish packages were ready for upload.

■　　■　　■

Back in Los Angeles the next morning, day laborers began to assemble by 4:00 a.m. at the Home Depot on Roscoe, thirty or so men of all ages standing in the parking lot, along the curb, backpacks slung over their shoulders, cell phones in one hand, coffee in the other. They waved at the contractors they recognized and followed some of the new trucks until they parked and started barking out their trades. The younger men with the stronger backs were gone by 5 a.m., the *viejos* left to wait for the painting trucks that arrived around 5:30. Most were undocumented and slept on floors next to strangers, earning less than one hundred dollars for a ten-hour day, seven days a week.

None of them paid much notice to the white van that drove into the lot and parked in the corner. No one looking to hire would have chosen to stop so far from the men. The engine didn't shut off. In the back was the latest in Israeli phone hacking technology—a stingray. It was little more than a cell tower that grabbed every signal within a quarter mile then scrubbed the metadata off each user before finally pushing out specious text messages using a familiar number. In this case, it allowed the men in the van to upload a message to every cell phone in the lot which included a link to a Spanish language television reporter detailing an ICE detention of a suspect wanted in connection with the shooting of a border patrol officer a week earlier. The video included footage of a man in a blue Dodgers shirt and red sweatpants being led out of his apartment by a team of commando-looking officers. The clip concluded with the reporter indicating that there were drones using facial recognition software.

The driver of the van could see the expressions of several men in the light of their cell phones, eyes wide, these men then elbowing the guy next to them, holding the phone between them to watch together. Then the friend would take out his phone and open a similar text from one of his friends. Of course, had any of them taken the time, they'd have noticed one of the hallmarks of a spoof: the time stamps were exactly the same.

The man sitting in the back of the van watched his display track the number of phones in the parking lot, the number of uploads, number of forwards, number of social media posts. Bad news like this traveled very fast *en la vin* since the only news these men ever trusted came from others like themselves. Panic would percolate up, would start gathering momentum later that day around the lunch trucks, would pass with bated expressions between mothers waiting for the children outside the schools, among the men and women waiting for the bus to take them home. The waxers at the car wash would embellish, each time adding more and more, word of mouth the least reliable messenger of truth but the one with the greatest currency in the Shoe.

Satisfied, the van pulled back onto Roscoe to repeat the same process at meat packing plants, construction sites. By the end of the day, seven hundred people, all of whom lived or worked in Panorama City, were convinced ICE was putting a dragnet on the area to find whoever had shot the border agent, their conversations with friends and family ending *"Cuidate."* Be careful.

CHAPTER 17

It was the 8th of the month, Javier once again on the wrong side of the rent date. He chastised himself for having to cough up two late fees, but what he hated even more was how it lumped him with the give-a-shits in the building, seemingly incapable of using a calendar, but here he was, no different than White Mike in 211 who was always whispering about great deals on flat screens and always seemed to have a rent notice taped to his front door. Javier rattle knocked the aluminum door at unit 2, the screen curling out of its frame along the bottom revealing four tiny fingers. Ana the manager, bouncing an infant on her hip, opened the door just enough to slip outside, stiff arming the toddler right behind her trying to make a run for it. Her human zoo was the only day care in the building. Javier could see four through the screen, each in diapers, gazing awe-struck at him, a sudden lull in the commotion as they studied him before the dog arrived, knocking one of them over like a bowling pin, restarting the ruckus machine.

"Javi, *como estas*?" Ana, one of those people whose smile reached their eyes.

"*Mas y meno.*" He looked at the *mucoso* wedged in her arm, a delta of snot collecting just below one of the nostrils. Javier handed her two months of rent in an envelope. "Sorry we're late. Business is a little, you know, slow right now." Ana took the envelope and wedged it inside her bra. She'd gone to school with Betzaida, knew the guy Janson who'd sold her the shop.

"This one right here," she bounced the infant, giving Javier I-get-you eyes, "Mom owes me for five months." She held up five fingers. The infant, thinking it was a game, pulled his hand from his mouth and made for a patty-cake. Ana grabbed his hand without looking and stuck it back in his mouth. "Reynosos had to move, *sin suerte* you know, in 105, had a boy your age, *que no?*" Javier gave a one-shoulder shrug. He never liked the kid, bit of a douche to Gio. "Anyways, tell your ma, okay?" Javier waved goodbye, grateful this germ colony was on the other side of the complex from his place.

He ascended the stairs, gave a wave to the *vieja* in 112, always bent at the waist, hovering over her herbs. She half-stood, a pair of rheumy eyes spinning in their sockets. She clutched her trowel like a weapon as if he was the cause for her dormant cilantro. Half the building was like this, assuming the worst of people, the other half, always in your business, wanting something, the fishbowl life of high-density housing.

Javier came through the door and didn't wait for Mama to start in with twenty questions. Alex had been ditching school, and he wanted her to know what was coming next.

"He hopped the fence. Gorjian texted me. He wasn't in class three times this week." Ms. Gorjian had been Javier's English teacher when he'd attended Gaither and now was Alex's. At Back To School Night, Javier'd stopped in and given her his number, asking that she'd keep tabs on Alex. "Might wanna bake some cookies for all the visitors we're about to get." School counselors made home visits when kids started spending more time off campus than on. "And remember to look interested when they give you the brochures." He leaned against the counter and gave her a knowing look.

Mama was bent over her mortar pulverizing green chilis, putting her full weight into it.

"*Aye guey*, not more brochures." The counters were full of cut potatoes, cilantro, and some frozen *asada* thawing on a plate. The kitchen window was open to let the air through, but the screens had long since rusted out leaving mosquitoes a clear path in. Mama had put a few saucers on the window shelf with water and three drops of dish soap. Mosquitoes were naturally drawn to the water but when they landed, there was no surface tension, courtesy of the soap, leaving the mosquitoes to drown. Javier looked at the latest batch of non-fliers, some dead, others still struggling. He usually saw the bugs with a mixture of pity and glee, but today it was all glee.

"You're only as happy as your least happy child," she said, spooning some ground habaneros out of her mortar into the *posole*. "Set the table for three. What is that gringo saying—build it and they will come?" She pulled Javier's head down to give him a kiss on his forehead then returned to her pot. She was exacting in her preparation of *posole*, a recipe that had been handed down at least three generations. It was the culinary go-to for the *malos tiempos*, the little family meltdowns and to welcome relatives who had not been seen in *demasiado largo*—too long.

She ladled out the servings and finished each with crème fraiche. Her hands were raw and peeling, the result of gloves which always chafed. "I've taken his phone, spoken to his teachers." She shook a brown spice out of her hand into the pot and continued stirring. Alex was past all that, and Javier had started to reckon his mother knew this. In their unspoken division of responsibility, Javier knew it was his job to play sheepdog to Alex, but ever since Betzaida had made those comments, he'd started wondering how clueless Mama really was.

"He's in the park," Javier said. He didn't need to elaborate, and if Mama was already aware of this, he wanted to call it out. "Or perhaps that's not news to you."

Mama turned to Javier and wiped her hands on her apron. She looked at him with a faint smile, her hair a nest. Javier couldn't recall the last time she'd had her nails done, had gone out to dinner with friends, or God forbid, gone on a date. She was a monument to sacrifice, and in the back of his mind, Javier wondered if perhaps she subconsciously thought everyone, including himself, should endlessly sacrifice themselves for family. "I am so sorry. Really I am." She stood there stock-still, her eyes suddenly wet.

The door swung open, and Alex sauntered in with a new haircut that did for his head what the equator does for a globe, leaving his forehead fringed with Romanesque bangs. It was a popular look among kids from Denker and had the added touch of "818" shaved in the back just above his neck.

Mama brought a hand to her mouth and crossed herself. *"Aye Dios."*

Javier chuckled. "Rockin' the Cesar." He went to rub his brother's head, but Alex ducked the move, dropped his bookbag, walked into the kitchen, and leaned against the wall arms folded in front. "Fun fact: that little area code in the back? Stand on your head, same number."

No one said anything for a moment, just staring at Alex's head like it was the backside of the moon. Flaco appeared, his tail knocking a cactus off an end table next to the sofa. Alex, grateful to shift the attention off himself, pulled something from his pocket, held it out for Flaco to eat.

"You're just in time for *posole*, Alex," Mama said. Normally she would have already hugged Alex, but today she hung back, unsure about this latest version of her youngest.

"Not hungry." Alex finally looked up and pulled out something else from his pocket and popped it in his mouth.

"You know the last thing Flaco licked before your hand was his balls." Javier stared hard at Alex, hoping he could draw his brother's gaze then smother it. Mama held out her arms and looked at the table, her nonverbal cue for the two of them to sit down, though neither moved.

"Comer," she said with just enough behind it to get her two sons to sit. She placed the pot in the middle of the table, pulled out her chair, sat down, and took a long look at Alex's head. She placed her hands on the table palms down, matriarch if only for the moment.

"*Ambos son lo mas importante para mi*—and I have missed these meals with all three of us." She took a spoonful of *posole*, and the boys followed. Soon there was only the sound of spoons on porcelain. "This serving bowl was a gift from your Tio Marco who neither of you remember." Mama crossed herself again and went on to describe how at her wedding Tio Marco, quite drunk, had toasted the wrong couple and been found later in the evening dragging first a finger and then his whole hand through their wedding cake. "He was a kind man, but I can never forgive him for what he did to that wedding cake," Mama said, smiling.

Javier chuckled at this and glanced at Alex for some reaction—nothing. Just the slurping sound as he ate.

"You know, Alex, you never liked *posole* as a boy." Javier noticed Mama's subtle implication about the passage of time. "You used to try to feed it to the dog, the one we had before Flaco." Alex slowed his spoon down. "You thought you were so clever. You would look out the window and point. '*Mira, Mama, un armadillo!*' and then you would hold your bowl under the table and let the dog eat it." She smiled. "That poor dog always got indigestion, and the gas we had to smell!" She waved her hand in front of her face. Alex bent further toward his bowl, trying to conceal a hint of a grin.

They took seconds and thirds and talked and ate until they had to tip their bowls to get the last, spiciest remnants. Finally, Mama put her hands back on the table, this time palms up, her cue to join hands.

"There are more important things than your haircut right now, Alex. *Las migra estan aqui* and they are—*como se dice*—" She scowled, unable to recall the word in English.

"Detaining, Mama," said Javier.

"*Si*, that." She pulled out her phone and showed a video of an ICE raid on an apartment complex in which a man with a blue Dodgers T-shirt and red sweatpants was led into a waiting van.

"They're even using—" She made a humming sound and spun a finger over her head.

"Drones?" Javier said, his soup spoon hovering over the bowl for a moment.

"ICE won't do anything," said Alex.

Javier let out a laugh. "Well, thank God we have the Director of Homeland Security here at the table."

Mama gave Javier a look but kept on. "They are chasing some man who shot a border agent. They say he is hiding out somewhere in *este barrio*." She'd lowered her voice as if the fugitive might actually be nearby. "We came here for one reason," Mama said, looking first at Alex and then Javier. "So that you could both have a better future." Her voice tightened. "There are only three of us now—"

Alex cut her off. "Yeah, well, why don't you bang out another kid, and then we can be four again."

Javier would have punched Alex if he'd been any closer, but the reach was too far. All he could manage was a slap, though it had enough behind it to turn his brother's head. Alex didn't react, almost seemed to welcome it.

"Javier!" Mama shouted and stood up.

Alex gave Javier a long look and then Mama a much shorter one, stood slowly, and pushed his chair in. "Thanks for dinner, Mama," he said, shooting Javier one more look before grabbing his backpack and leaving.

Javier and Mama sat there silently, the air pulsing. "Javier, you shouldn't—"

"Ma, he had it coming." He cut her off, though his anger had quickly come and gone like a rogue wave. Mama put her hand on Javier's, her skin calloused near the knuckles and soft on the pads.

"Don't ever hit your brother again, Javi." It wasn't a scold or plea, just a simple command like telling him to clean his room. "Be patient with him, but do not ever give up, Javi. Family is always first, *mijo*, and you are his only brother," Patel's reciprocal version of this same speech now eerily prophetic.

She took a breath and leaned in. "We live in the shadows, *mijo*, but remember, if they come to the plant, I will only be held two days at most. It doesn't mean we will be deported." She looked to their altar of Our Lady and made another sign of the cross. Javier couldn't remember the last time he'd seen her do this three times inside an hour. "The only way that happens is if one of us is in trouble with the law." She paused and sat back slightly; Javier could feel her eyes probing him. "If there is anything I need to know, tell me now."

He shook his head. "Not yet, at least." He glanced at her now glancing at him, certain she sensed evasion, but she had a bus to catch.

"He needs you now more than ever," she said, pulling a string only she could. He bit back the obvious rejoinder, that Alex needed her right now even more. She stood and took the plates to the sink, left them there, and grabbed her purse. "I'll be home in time to fix you *huevos rancheros*," she said then stopped at the door and put her hand on the frame, a sudden realization. "We actually felt like *familia* for a moment there."

CHAPTER 18

The noise. It was Javier's biggest adjustment to life in Los Angeles, the constant aural exhaust of human activity, nowhere more apparent than in the back alley that his bedroom window faced. It was an echo chamber of raised voices, wailing babies, hacking seniors, smoke alarms with low battery beeps, hair dryers, and more babies. The alley acoustics, much to his chagrin, could rival a concert hall, each sound distinct, creating a kaleidoscope of noise that kept him up, staring at the ceiling inventing new devices to turn off all electronics within a half-mile radius and put babies into a cryogenic sleep.

Back then though, one sound, a girl's laugh, floated above the din like a red balloon. At school, it was nowhere to be heard, not in the halls, the cafeteria, or even outside on the swings where girls pumped their legs and stuck their tongues out at the boys. On warm evenings with the windows open he could make out snippets of her conversations, meaningless jabber Javier threshed for clues. She was enigmatic and out of reach until one day he summoned all nine years of courage that had been gathering dust. He had to knock on four doors before coming to the right one, blowing right past introductions, and going in for the hard sell.

"He knows three tricks." Flaco stood there, tongue lolling, tail wagging, unaware of his role as a prop in courtship. The girl appeared behind a screen door as a veiled shape with folded arms. It was Javier's first taste of showmanship, a new kind of thrill, one that danced on his skin, made his back teeth float. He got through roll-over-and-beg before she laughed, and opened the door.

"C'mon in, Javier. I'm Leslie."

They'd gone to Chato's that first day to split an order of chili cheese fries, and ten years later, the same Chato's lifer who'd served them that first order came by, this time with a plate of nachos, and slid it across the table with enough force that Javier had to intercept it before it sailed onto the floor. The air was still suffused with grease smoke; line cooks still barked at waitresses before spinning the order wheel. A father-son team in their Day-Glo nylon vests, hot-moppers judging by the tar on their boots, perched themselves at a wraparound counter. At the other end a little girl in patent leather shoes and hair ties tried making herself dizzy on the spinning stool. Javier and Leslie were seated in their usual booth, a table between them and a picture window view of the parking lot full of pickups. Leslie was already going saucer-eyed with Lupe stories.

"Oh my god, you know she grew up in the Gardens, right? Whole nine horror-show, Javi, mom totally out of it, pervy uncles, and look at her." Leslie bent forward across the table as though divulging a secret. "Amazing house in the hills," now angling her head, presumably in the direction of the hills. "I've started interning with her a couple days a week, you know, little projects."

Javier tried to look impressed, recalling vaguely from some class that internships meant working for free. "Homegirl was in deep with Denker, Les. Full-on *chola*. Hair spray in one hand, gun in the other." He watched the waitress outside in the parking lot smoking a cigarette, taking deep draws and exhaling smoke through her nose while she studied her nails.

Leslie leaned back, a defiant flash in her eyes. "She's not proud of it, but she doesn't run from it either, Javi, and I kind of respect that about her." Leslie looked around for another waitress, made eye contact with one, mouthed *guacamole* and pointed at the plate. "I mean, you know what happened to her older brother, right?"

"I heard about it, yeah." He watched the father-son team attack their pancakes, Javier suddenly wishing they hadn't gone with the nachos. "Patel put me onto her for a loan, and I sort of met her at Dolores's funeral." The waitress outside took a few more long drags, stubbed out her butt, and came back inside passing the hot-moppers who were done eating, their whole breakfast taking less than ten minutes.

"She does it all, Javi." Leslie was leaning forward again. "And I gave you some shine." She smiled then laughed. "Even showed her your East Valley picture." That explained how Lupe had recognized him at the funeral. "So, you're coming then?"

"To what?"

"The barbecue, ding-dong. She's not the only vote for the scholarship. You gotta make an impression on the whole board." The waitress returned with the guacamole. Leslie's eyes followed her. "And there will be lots of me." Pause. "And Alex."

"Wait, what?"

Leslie had always taken an interest in Alex and kept tabs on him via his social media. "Figured neutral ground might be good for the two of you for, like, detente or something." She looked at Javier as she stuck a straw in his shake and went at it.

"Alex? Who's that? Probably calls himself Lil' Weenie by now." He grabbed some chips, dragged them through the guac and ate them in one go. "Blew past wanna-be straight into *gonna*-be." He was already sick of the topic and knew Leslie was soft on Alex. "He's already puttin' in work with Denker." He checked his phone like he was on a schedule. "Meetin' up with Chuey in five, Les."

He had more than an hour, and he knew that *she* knew that he was making excuses. It was true that Javier and Chuey met up most Saturdays and walked down Van Nuys to their respective jobs, but that didn't happen until 10 am and it wasn't even 9 yet. She reached across the table and took his hand, insisting that he look at her. "You have six more months until you're up and out of here. Six months, Javier. Use that time to get right with him." Javier met her gaze which flattened his urge for rebuttal.

He picked up the check, gave it a glance, and threw down a twenty and a pile of ones, saw the waitress thumbing her phone and then picked up the ones. They went outside into the late morning heat. Across the street, a man dressed in a suit was speaking urgently into a bullhorn, exhorting no one in particular that the end times were approaching, that the military drones buzzing overhead were a sign of the beast, and that the Four Horsemen had mounted their steeds and were headed this way. He spoke with the conviction of the converted or the insane, all in Spanish, and drew looks from passersby like he was a zoo animal. He had one helper with him, presumably his wife, handing out literature though there were few takers. "*Inundaciones e incendios,*" was his refrain. Floods and fires. No mention of Jesus the savior, only a paranoid warning.

"Probably trying to sell insurance," Javier said. He took a flier out of curiosity and scanned it, handwritten in hysterical all caps and double-sided. The author had underlined some key terms in case someone didn't feel like spending twenty minutes reading the screed: intrusive surveillance, the ubiquity of cameras, the convergence of AI and state-run databases to hold people hostage and become godless vassals of the state. Javier tossed the flier in the trash, but not before giving a quick scan of the skies.

■　　　■　　　■

Chuey was the least reflective person Javier knew, the whole world a binary system of good and bad, this or that. He was one of five brothers and a Mongol horde of cousins and uncles, men forever on high-alert for disrespect. Chuey was already earning a living wage at Home Depot, promoted every six months, and on pace to be a manager before he was twenty. Some days at school he came straight from an overnight shift doing inventory which occasionally turned into 4 a.m. forklift races in the parking lot. Most Saturdays, Javier and Chuey walked four blocks down Van Nuys on their ways to work, and usually never got past Tommy's Burgers and its salty-sweet grease smoke without stopping.

"I'm buying. What you want, a number six?" Chuey stuck a hand under his shirt as if checking to make sure his stomach was still there.

"Nah, I'm good. Just had nachos with Les."

Contractors came to Tommy's to wolf down meals in between jobs, but it was empty at this hour. Chuey ordered, then sat across from Javier and watched the traffic crawl south amidst the staccato of jackhammers. This stretch of Van Nuys was perpetually under construction. Two boys came in, placed their orders, and stood at a table on the opposite side of the stand. It was Itchy and Scratchy, though today unhooded and capless. Javier caught Chuey's eyes and nodded in their direction. Chuey took a glimpse, immediately getting the message. Scratchy was on his phone, but the other, Itchy, noticed Chuey look his way.

"*De donde*?" the boy asked, the usual throw-down, asking Chuey where he's from.

Chuey looked around, gave the boy a dramatic *who-me*? look. "Where am I from?" Chuey said with mock inquisitiveness. He took a long swallow of his soda. "I'm from a little part of LA called Up-Your-Ass."

This didn't draw much of a reaction, and Chuey started opening mustard packets, stacking them on top of each other behind his drink. "It's about two miles west of Suck-My-Dick." He bit into one of the mustard packets to open it and eye-locked the boy as he did this.

"You look like a faggot. I don't like faggots eating here," Itchy said.

Chuey made a sour face as though disappointed. "Well, unless your name is Tommy, that's not really up to you, pal. You see, faggots get to eat wherever they want these days, so you need to update your political views, hombre," he said, returning to his mustard packets.

Itchy ran a hand down his face. "By the time my burger gets to this window, you and your *maricon* best be outta here." He hiked up his T-shirt to reveal the grip of a gun tucked inside the front of his pants.

Chuey snorted, amused. "You got no belt there, hotshot, so when you pull that nifty gun out, we'll get a nice view of your bird legs cause your pants are gonna be around your ankles."

Itchy smacked his lips, happy to see things escalating. "Now I gotta fuck you up," he said, standing.

Chuey snapped his fingers. "You know what. I knew you looked familiar." He smiled. "I seen your picture, yeah, no kiddin', swear to God, seen it on your own fuckin' refrigerator every night when I come down for a snack after bangin' your bow-legged mama."

In an instant, Itchy came for Chuey who had already moved his drink to the side and was bringing his fist down on the pile of mustard packets. A stringy jet of bright yellow exploded from the table, forcing Itchy to cover his eyes and giving Chuey enough time to throw a roundhouse which turned Itchy's head and sent him reeling backward into one of the stools bolted into the floor. Itchy lost his balance and went down hard, his wrist popping as he landed. Chuey closed quickly and put Itchy in a sleeper hold, watched his head loll to the side, then rolled him over on his back and grabbed the gun out of his waistband, unclipped the magazine, slid the chamber open and checked each, both empty.

Scratchy, still standing at his table caught off guard, looked at his unconscious partner. Javier, a latent rage quickly flooding his blood, took three steps and grabbed him two-fisted, stuck a leg behind him, and put him on the ground face first. He pulled the boy's arm up behind his back and drove his knee into his neck. Javier was, for the first time in his life, overcome with a desire to hurt someone. He let his weight torque the boy's shoulder, producing a cry of pain.

He leaned within an inch of the boy's ear. "Stay the fuck away from my brother." And with that, he stuck the heel of his hand against the boy's cheek, pressed his face into the tiled floor, then grabbed his hair and lifted his head up, wondering if he could twist it off. Javier had expected some inner voice to signal "enough," but it never came. He hammer-fisted the bridge of the boy's nose, producing a crack then a stream of blood, bright red on the brown Mexican tile.

A siren chirped several times as a cruiser did a U-turn and pulled up next to Tommy's. Javier and Chuey looked at each other then took off at a full sprint in opposite directions, leaving the two boys lying there like two sacks of potatoes that had fallen off a truck.

CHAPTER 19

Jones was due back at Lonnie's trailer the next day, and Sergio had been out all week sick with some kind of stomach flu. Javier hadn't slept a full night in almost a week, trying to visualize his plan for the burner waking each morning to the same dream. In it, he'd launched a torpedo then watched its path on a screen, a green blip arcing out gracefully until eventually reaching its apogee then returning to where it came from. A week ago, he'd felt convinced, emboldened even, of his plan to retrieve the burner, but he'd had a week to ruminate on his plan. Had Sergio been absent that day, Javier would have taken it as a sign, scrubbed the mission and given up on the burner.

Instead, Sergio had returned, was seated, his hair hanging like a curtain, and hammering away at his keyboard. He didn't look up when Javier sat next to him

"Surveillance ain't for amateurs, Javi. And if the other guy is even halfway on the ball, he's gonna know his phone is hacked." He stopped typing and looked at Javier, his face pale and his eyes bloodshot. "But I knew after today you'd probably lose your nerve."

"Yeah, well, I don't have much choice." Javier was usually grateful Sergio never asked questions but half-wished he would today.

Sergio closed his laptop, pulled out a phone, and held up one end of a cable. "Lightning to USB. Then–" he held up a serial bus, "–plug and play." Sergio looked behind them to make sure no one was within earshot. "Scrapes everything off the burner you'll need to make a clone." He pulled out another device the size of a cell phone. "Duplicates the target sim card." He pulled out two sim cards, held them up like he was doing a magic trick, and then showed Javier what went where. "Last and most important step. Install a masking file." He showed Javier the sequence to go into the settings and perform the upload. "You sure you don't want me going with you?"

A student came and handed a note to the teacher who read it then looked at Javier.

"Main office," the teacher said before handing him the summons.

"I'm good." Javier told Sergio then collected the hardware and stuck it in his book bag, all of it suddenly looking unfamiliar, the instructions not even a vapor trail in his memory.

On most days, the main office had the look and feel of a walk-in ER. Two parents sat slump-shouldered on a bench looking morose, their own crappy adolescence now twice lived courtesy of their weed-selling child. Across the room, a rail-thin girl wearing long sleeves (it was over ninety-five today) and double-duty mascara schlepped down a hallway to a waiting social worker who banked her head to the side as if trying to get water out of her ear. In the back, Javier could make out a pair of legs rolling on the floor along the far wall, the rest of the body hidden behind a desk; a nurse was on the phone telling someone in Spanish to bring the medication. Then in English to one of the office techs, "Can't forget the brake fluid for that one." As the dramas eddied all around her, the principal, Ms. Smith, stood like an obelisk, talking to two men in suits, silver badges winking from beneath their coats. She spotted Javier and waved him over.

"Hello, Javier," she said with a blend of warmth and authority that made you feel both welcomed and worried. She knew him well, had signed her name to his honor roll certificates every semester for four years now. She motioned for the three of them to follow her down a series of hallways, sort of the backstage area, at the end of which was a conference room.

The four of them stood outside for a moment. "Javier, this is Detective Freemon and Detective Morales from LAPD," Ms. Smith sounding like a referee introducing fighters in the center of the ring. "You are not in trouble, and I have already spoken with your mother. She has given me her permission to let them talk to you." Javier trusted Ms. Smith, one of the few school muckety-mucks he'd known to always wield authority with the grace that kids responded to. "You're under no obligation to answer any questions you don't feel comfortable answering, and if you like, I can sit in on this interview with you."

Javier had received one piece of advice from his father back in Mexico: never look law enforcement in the eye. *Irrespetuoso*, though sadly, this one paternal nugget was culturally upside down with LAPD who mostly wanted to lock eyes and start drilling into your head.

"Thanks, I'm good."

"Anytime you want to, you can stop the meeting." This was more for the benefit of the detectives than Javier, letting them know it was her house. Javier nodded, already too busy trying to list out all the potential reasons for the meeting.

The conference room was three-quarters occupied by a table that looked like the rest of the school had been built around it. The detectives took their seats on one side, the one named Freemon, apparently the buttoned-up gravitas, the other, Morales, looking like he was on his way to a nightclub. Freemon motioned for Javier to sit across from them. He sat in the chair, unaware it was on casters, and felt it roll to the side, causing him to grab the arms in a small panic.

"Javier, as Ms. Smith said, my name is Detective Freemon, and this is Detective Morales, and we're with the Gang Unit of LAPD." Freemon's bearing, stock straight and humorless, suggested a life taking and giving orders. "I'll spare you the guessing game as to why we're here, Javier." He took out a pile of black-and-white photographs and laid the first one out like he was dealing a poker hand. It showed Alex taking a backpack from another young person, the Gardens with their prison-lite architecture serving as the backdrop. "These were taken last week." Freemon paused, letting Javier get his head around the enormity of what was to follow.

Then the next print, Alex walking into Gaither carrying the same backpack, the image taken from a security camera. Finally, two more prints in succession showing a cellophane-wrapped package and two handguns. "And this is what we found in the bag which we took off Alex this morning." Freemon leaned back, letting Javier study the full disaster storyboard.

Morales stuck a finger on the image of the wrapped package. "Something called 4ANNCP. Fentanyl precursor." He pushed the print toward Javier. "Street value, about four, five hundred dollars as is, but once it gets processed," he shrugged, "a thousand times that."

"And these too." Freemon pulled another eight by ten out of the folder, two Glocks and two clips, loaded. "Serial numbers filed off." The agent pointed to one of the gun's slide where someone had taken an etching tool to the serial numbers. "He's in custody right now," Freemon said. "Your mother is on her way to County to go sign for his release. Given his age, first offense and all, he'll be processed and out within a few hours. Which is why we're here right now, talking with you." Javier pinched the bridge of his nose, fighting off the image of Mama in her work clothes, having to wade through the collection of reprobates going in and coming out of lockup, signing the release papers.

Over to Freemon. "He'll have a chance to get out from under it. Probation, hopefully." Javier doubted this guy had much personal hope invested in this outcome, Alex just another face from the street.

Morales continued, his tone sounding like he'd done this routine several times already today. "Not sure if you keep tabs on the narcotics business, Javier, but the retail side is drying up. Any asshole on social media can set up shop. Buy a package—God knows what's inside but who cares—gig out delivery to any chump on a scooter, door-to-door service twenty-four seven." Morales glanced at his partner, the next part apparently a familiar punchline. "Drug addicts these days. Can't even be bothered to hoof it to the park." Morales sat forward, put his hands on the table like a big announcement was coming. "So Denker is moving into production." Pause. "Only it's like trying to bootleg iPhones, Javier. Apple ain't gonna just let you pimp their shit. Got lawyers with full-time jobs to look for IP encroachment." Javier got the feeling Morales was making a point of using a big word. "And Sinaloa? Emme? Same thing, got eyes and ears everywhere, and they do not truck with anyone, especially *en el norte*, trying to take a slice outta their pie. *Entiende lo que le digo*?" Javier was wondering when Morales was going to play the *espanol* card. He half wanted to *No hablar* the guy.

Freemon produced another eight-by-ten glossy, this one of a man sprawled on his driveway in front of an expansive ranch home with a splatter pattern like someone had dropped a balloon filled with blood from twenty feet. "The cartels are coming to shut it all down. This guy," Freemon tapped the photograph, "bent customs agent, normally not a target for the cartels. But he was letting the wrong things through, probably didn't even know it, but so what. They're clearing the board."

"And now the cartels got a pin in their map right where the Shoe is. Sending the gold-plated AKs in cowboy hats. And the first one to catch a bullet will probably be some unlucky putz like Alex." Morales was picking up steam, having probably delivered this same speech to countless older brothers in the past, had maybe even been the older brother himself judging by the way he was beginning to spit his words out.

Javier reached for the bottle of water and took a long sip. "Why am I here?"

Freemon crossed his arms, looking bored. "You and your family have a lot at stake right now," he said. "We could flag your file with this arrest, and you might all get picked up and put on a bus for the border this evening. That's how fast this stuff works."

"But let's say you don't get that knock for another—" Morales made an I'm-spit-balling-here face, "say, five, six years. Alex is going to juvie and will most likely come out worse than when he went in. We both know that, and none of us want that. But here's the thing, Javier. He's trafficking firearms and controlled substances, both of which are federal offenses. We can't just take away his Xbox."

Ping-pong to Freemon. "We need to know what Alex knows about Denker. That's it. Just hear what he has to say. Ask him a few questions to confirm a few hunches of ours. Doesn't need to wear a wire. Just needs to cooperate. Fully." Javier trawled his mind for the right response, the walls starting to close in on him. "We need to know some of the logistics. Locations, times, that sort of stuff. Like Detective Morales said, Denker is getting into production which means they have a lab. And that's pissed off the wrong people."

"You want me to convince him to talk," Javier said, stalling. The two agents nodded. "Why don't you just ask him yourselves while he's in custody?" He hoped it hadn't come off as impertinent. Alex, once just annoying, had become a potent liability.

Freemon again. "This little trip to County is like a promotion for him. His homies are gonna love him, but your mother is gonna have a broken heart, so he's not gonna be thinking straight which is why we usually have the most success goin' the indirect route. Older brothers or sisters."

It actually made sense to Javier. "Look, you should know, Alex and I barely talk right now. Me and him got into it little while ago, and he's just...not been around much." He could feel himself getting too chatty with these guys, giving them too much. "When do you need an answer?"

Morales glanced at the wall clock behind Javier, apparently ready to get going. "Talk to his lawyer first. She'll know the terms of the deal, but things are breaking pretty quickly so we'll need to know by Thursday." He scratched the side of his throat. "And don't forget your mother in all this." And there it was. Barrio-bro sent to work a little *madre* guilt on him.

Javier cast his eyes about, looking for a magical doorway he might crawl into and disappear but instead only finding shelves crammed with dusty books and enormous binders. A whiteboard on the far wall had some names and some arrows and in all caps the word LUNCH.

"Okay, I'll talk with him."

Morales slid his card over. "My cell phone is on the back." Both agents stood at the same time and waited, meeting over. Javier stood, walked back into the hallway outside the conference room, and the two agents followed.

"We'll wait for your call, Javier." No one shook hands. Ms. Smith, down the hall talking with someone, gave Javier a look to get a read on things. Ninety percent of her job was making split-second assessments based on facial expressions and body language. He gave her a nod. She broke off her conversation and rejoined the three of them.

"Thank you, Javier," another my-house reminder to the officers, giving him the first acknowledgement. Then she walked Freemon and Morales out leaving Javier to take the long way back to class, first sending his mother a text letting her know what had just happened then one to Betzaida, hoping she would drive over to County and lend Mama some support. The lockup waiting area was a special kind of purgatory, wives and mothers steeling themselves for the fools and monsters that would emerge from the holding cells.

Javier got back to class and dropped into the seat next to Gio who gave him an expectant look. The class had that low hum of student work, the clickety-clack of keyboards. Javier looked at Gio, his mind trying to work out the best way to convince Alex to turn snitch. Right now, he couldn't convince Alex to walk across the room for a bowl of ice cream.

"If it's about Alex—"

"I'm good, Gio," he said, cutting him off.

Gio put away his sketch pad. "Couple of Crown Vics in front of the school this morning," he side-mouthed to Javier, police cruisers without the misery lights. Javier ignored Gio and busied himself with a trig question, half wanting Gio to shut up and half wanting him to keep going. "You only get called out at the end of semester to have your picture taken for honor roll, and now...you look like your cereal box is missing the toy."

"They stopped doing that, Gio."

"Doin' what—takin' pictures or putting toys in cereal?"

"Toys."

"Not true." Gio sounded convinced and closed to rebuttal. "They got Alex on something, didn't they?" Gio and Alex had shared a brief but intense few weeks a couple years ago between foster family placements. The two of them had uncanny chemistry playing Battle Royale, had won five hundred dollars in a competition, and lived on DoorDash for three days followed by a trip to Magic Mountain. It spawned a friendship that always seemed to pick up right where it left off. To Javier, they were two puzzle pieces that just seemed to fit.

Javier leaned over. "Shit-for-brains committed not one but two felonies this morning." Gio nodded slightly like he'd already heard the news. "A gun and some of the precursors used to make fentanyl. Brought them to school." Javier took a quick glance at the rows behind him checking for snoops.

"Boy's acting out, cry for help and all that."

Javier gave Gio an annoyed look, underwhelmed with the observation. "No shit, Dr. Freud."

"What did Gorjian say last month?"

Javier looked at him, puzzled. "Gorjian?"

"At parent conferences last month. What's she saying about Alex?"

Javier looked away, trying to recall the conversation. Gorjian was a straight-shooter, knew her way around the jungle of adolescence, one of those teachers kids tended to orbit around. "She said he started falling off early, like, first week."

Gio made the duh face. "Origin story, Javi. He found something, you know, doing his research." Origin stories were an eighth-grade get-to-know-you essay, a deep dive into the elements of your childhood that made you who you were, always a minefield for a few kids. In Gio's case, it was like asking a Vietnam vet to go back and reconstruct Mai Lai. "There's your answer Javi. Alex found something."

.   .   .

Patel ran a chess club once a week after school in the library. Javier found him standing between two rows of players, none of the clock stuff going on. Projected on a screen standing off to the side was an image of a board, several pieces arranged mid-match, and a series of notations running down the left side in Patel's handwriting.

Javier came in quietly. He'd never understood the game. One year in middle school, they'd made checkerboards in art class out of construction paper and used pennies and nickels as pieces. The teacher, having watched Javier beat all his classmates at checkers, had broken out a set of plastic chess pieces, cajoled Javier into learning the game, then proceeded to ruin it with endless comments about various moves and strategies, at one point moving Javier's pieces for him. It was the first and last time he'd ever played.

Patel smiled. "Have you come to learn the royal game?" Javier never tired of Patel's stilted language.

"Royal pain, maybe."

Patel pointed a finger at him and grinned. "You, you, such excellent word play, this one. But perhaps in a few years, you will need something to decorate your fancy corner office, a nice marble chess set, hmmm?" He motioned to a long oak table next to the periodicals. One whole wall was covered with archaic encyclopedias and reference books, most likely last used when dial-up was just coming on the scene.

"You need a hobby, Javier." They sat opposite each other. "Only work and school, the candle burns at both ends."

"Photography." He was surprised at his answer, having never really given the subject any thought before.

Patel beamed. "How long has this been an interest of yours?"

"Since elementary." A memory flashed in his mind. "We made these things, pinhole cameras out of shoeboxes, and used a special photographic paper." Javier's eyes wandered the carpet, his mind floating back in time, his father sitting on the couch. He recalled telling him that he was taking his picture, that he had to be rock-still for twenty seconds while he uncovered the pinhole to allow the exposure. His father sat looking anxious, like he was late on a street loan, which was probably the case. "The images all came out grainy, mostly browns and whites. But it looked...like who he really was." It was the last picture anyone had taken of his dad, a liminal figure in Javier's life captured as mostly a blur.

One of the chess matches had ended, the players now shaking hands. Sportsmanship never got old to Javier, a small concession to the better selves of humanity. Patel folded his arms. "I like black and whites, so dramatic, so poignant, moments in time just snatched out of the air." He snapped his fingers for effect, then pulled his phone out and started scrolling. Pages of family pictures until the images went black and white. Patel slowed the scroll down, started skipping through some images. "These are some pictures I took a few years ago when I went back to my town, Hyderabad." They showed smoldering wreckage of some kind, twisted and charred metal beams, a thin man in shorts and a T-shirt rooting through the ashes.

"Is this where your brother got burned?"

Patel nodded. "Factory fire. He was one of the lucky ones." More black and whites of a congested scene: rows and rows of laundry strung over a labyrinthine collection of pools in which women were washing clothes, bed sheets, and saris. "It's called *dhobi ghat,* and it is where my mother worked from the age of fourteen to seventy-eight." He used his fingers to enlarge one of his mother. "Every time I feel lazy, I pull this picture out to remind me how fortunate I am." He put the phone away and pulled his attention back. "Did you give Lupe a call?"

"Gave her the loan docs, got approved, so yeah, thank you for that." A chess player stood and shot his arms up, fists clenched, the apparent victor. "I saw her at Dolores's funeral and got her card." He now had a small collection of business cards: Morales, Jones, and Lupe, all stuffed in his wallet, and as he pulled them out and began flipping through them, Patel stuck his hand out.

"Wait." He was pointing at one of the cards. "Show me that second one."

It was Jones'. Javier handed it to Patel. "I towed the guy's car a few weeks back, and he—" Patel flicked the card making a popping sound loud enough hard to startle a few of the chess players.

"Stay away from this man, Javier." In the Shoe, these kinds of admonitions meant one thing, though Javier sensed this wasn't the case with Jones. "I'm sorry, Javier. I can't say more, but you should forget you met this man. You want an internship somewhere? I can give you a dozen names." He handed Javier the card back. "Jones is poison."

A voice came over the PA announcing to all students they had ten minutes to exit the campus. Patel watched one game end, the players shaking hands. He turned to Javier, picking up his bag. "After the game, the king and the pawn go in the same box."

CHAPTER 20

Javier climbed into the beater, an old Hyundai with over two hundred thousand miles, blown rings and a transmission that dropped out of gear when it went over fifty-five. It had been abandoned by an owner who must have known the car wasn't worth whatever it might cost to get it out of impound. It sat alone off to one side of the yard next to a stack of tires, its passenger seat forever stuck in the fully reclined position. Apart from the few days a year Javier borrowed it, the beater was used mostly for taking naps.

Javier was sitting in it now, the idle rough enough to rock the entire frame. He was one block from the construction site where he expected Jones to soon arrive. He got out and put on a high-viz safety vest, hardhat, a pair of sunglasses, and then walked through the gate and quickly slipped between a stack of lumber and another of rebar. He looked at his shoes, a pair of red Vans, and palm-smacked his forehead. No one on a jobsite wore anything other than work boots.

The goal was to clone Jones' burner, not steal it. Javier checked his backpack. Inside were two russet potatoes, a rubber mallet, and the cloning hardware Sergio had given him. The potatoes in particular made Javier nervous, the utter idiocy of this stunt starting to worm into his brain. He sent a confirmation text to Mark Bergosian who was on standby three blocks away in his flatbed wrecker and got one back.

lets do this

Jones' Cayenne pulled into the site and parked in front of Lonnie's trailer, right on time. He got out and went inside without knocking. Javier emerged from behind the lumber, casually strolled to the Cayenne then crouched down behind it. He reached into his backpack, took out the russets, turned them sideways, and hammered one into each tailpipe with the mallet. He took a peek at the door to the trailer to see if anyone was coming out, then stood as nonchalantly as he could and walked back out the gate, eyes on the ground. There were cameras all over the place, and he knew that at some point Jones would pull the footage. He was off the site and half a block away before he realized he hadn't been breathing the whole time. He texted Mark, then peered through the construction fence at Lonnie's trailer.

Jones came out moments later, got into his car, and cranked the engine several times. Javier could see the brake lights come on and go off with each attempt. On the fifth unsuccessful crank, Jones got out of the car and was on the phone no doubt calling roadside assistance without even popping the hood. The call would get routed to Mark given his proximity, and five minutes later he drove his Bergosian flatbed through the gate. He pulled in front of the Cayenne, got out, spoke briefly with Jones who was in the middle of another phone call, then backed his rig into place, ramped the bed, and started winching the Cayenne up.

As soon as he saw Mark reefing the chains tight, Javier took off and drove the two miles to Bergosian Tow where he parked again on the street then walked through the front gate. The yard was much larger than Mission's, and it was paved, a noticeable upgrade from the dirt and gravel surface Javier was used to. Bergosian also had a proper office with windows, an awning, and a soda machine out front. He ducked behind a row of cars at the back of the yard and waited.

It wasn't long before Mark drove in with the Cayenne on the bed and Jones in the passenger seat. The two got out and went into the office where Mark got busy with some bogus paperwork while Javier emerged from his hiding place, crab-walked over to Jones' car, gently opened the door, got in, and started looking for the burner. He'd given himself four minutes for the whole thing and set a timer. He checked the glovebox, the armrest, the backseat, and finally found it in a pull-out compartment under the driver's seat. He pulled off his backpack, put the burner on the passenger seat, and took out what Sergio had given him. He'd practiced the sequence every day now for a week though in the moment of truth, he saw the steps more circular and less linear. He popped out the burner's sim card and stuck it in the duplicator with another card, then pulled out the second burner which was identical to Jones'. Once the masking app was uploaded to both and the duplicate sim card was installed, there would be two identical phones on the same number. Whatever Jones sent or received would appear on the clone. He checked his timer—two minutes—then turned on his burner.

A message appeared on the screen. And then a spinning wheel. An update. Some new software had arrived overnight which, judging by the progress bar, was going to take several minutes to install. He held himself together refusing to let slip the scream in his head, the whole enterprise now lurching off into oblivion.

He could see Mark working Jones as best he could, asking pointless questions to buy time, but the Uber arrived more quickly than Javier had expected. There was no way Javier was going to finish, leaving him with two options: he could swap out the phones though Jones would eventually realize what had happened, would then retrace his steps, and would then pull the camera footage from the construction site.

Or he could walk away and try again.

Javier slid out the door, gently closing it before slipping out past the gate as Jones' Uber honked. He snuck a peek through the fence to see Jones leaving the office and walking to the Cayenne, no doubt to retrieve his burner which was now in Javier's front pocket.

CHAPTER 21

Cerberus was running circles in the gravel lot between the motor pool and the trailer, a sign the Sikorsky was on approach. He was a full-blooded retriever, could hear a deer fart a mile deep in the woods, but only ran circles when he heard the subsonic beat of the helo-blades, as if signaling to the pilot where to land. The overhead rotor wash from a hundred feet was too much, forcing him to take cover under the trailer and wait for the sound of the door opening. Jim Madison, site manager of the Narrow Ridge Shale Gas Extraction Facility, would then appear, descend the stairs, reach under the trailer and give Cerberus an assuring ear scratch. In the Bakken fields of North Dakota, the price of shale gas was experiencing an extended lull. The current glut had pushed prices down past breakeven, leaving the man-camps mostly empty.

Bakken, which was actually the name of the farmer who had owned a piece of property on which the much larger oil field sat, held two billion barrels of oil which would have stayed there had it not been for two innovations from the early 2000s: hydraulic fracturing and horizontal drilling. It turned the US into an OPEC competitor and put thousands of people to work, giving fossil fuel companies a Gold Rush moment to compete with the arrival of electric cars. Less well known about the process of hydraulic fracturing was its seismic impact. The surface above the drill pipes, usually no less than five hundred feet down, was constantly shaking imperceptibly unless you were looking at your cup of morning coffee. Or if your grain silo eventually collapsed when its foundation failed.

Fracking, as it came to be called, coincided with a string of bad harvests that forced Mr. Bakken to offer an oil lease on his property. However, before the first horizontal well was dug into his property, he made sure it went nowhere near his farmhouse. "Boys, that farmhouse means more to me than whatever you think you'll find down there."

When the Sikorsky's door popped open and the stairs came down, a man climbed out and walked across the tarmac, stock straight, the posture Jim recognized as that of a combat veteran like himself.

"George Jones." He stuck his hand out, and they shook. "Nice to meet you, Jim."

"Likewise." Corporate had sent an email only that morning alerting him to a "new opportunity." Jim led the way, the pair of them entering the office trailer under the watchful gaze of Cerberus, peering out from beneath it.

They sat at a table with chipped Formica and some pot-sized burn marks. It had been over a year since anyone had used it for anything other than draw poker, the chip caddy still in view beneath the television console. The trailer interior was as corporate as the Badlands got, worn shag carpeting, the nap matted everywhere except along the walls, faux wood paneling starting to bow in places, and a shortage of windows, giving the space the feel of someone's basement.

"Can I get you coffee, Mr. Jones?" Jim was at least ten years older than Jones, but he was never on a first-name basis with anyone he'd known less than a month.

"Thank you." Jones pulled out a chair and ran a hand over the top of the table.

Jim brought a cup and placed a stainless-steel creamer in the middle of the table. "None of that latte shit out here, I'm afraid, Mr. Jones." Jim sat and put one ankle on a knee.

Jones smiled and held up the milk. "I don't care if it's even pasteurized." The twin turbines outside hadn't shut down, telling Jim this was going to be a short meeting. He dispensed with the typical soft-start volley of jokes and weather.

"Always a pleasure to have guests, but I have to confess total ignorance as to the occasion. Corporate was a little thin on details."

"Call me private equity." He took a sip of the coffee and studied a whiteboard listing names and times. "Very private." Then he slid a card across the table. "And lots of equity." Jim picked it up, took a quick look at the name of the company and tapped it on the Formica.

"Well then, as you know, all our equity is two thousand feet underground, and that's where it's gonna stay for the time being." Jones brought his hands to his lap and folded them. "Off the books, Jim. We're not even meeting right now." Cerberus came in, did a showy lap around the table before coming to sit by Jim. "C suite said you're the guy. Said we can rely on your discretion."

It was a thinly veiled reference, giving Jim all he needed to know about what type of meeting this was going to be. Six years ago, a waste water pit with spent fluid overflowed and leeched into the watershed that supplied the local town of Rochester. Jim had made the discovery during some routine tests, quickly capped the leak, and was then instructed to sit tight. In a few days, product safety issued a report that, given the high alkaline content of the soil, the parts-per-million numbers of the contaminant, something called dimethylammonium, was still within allowable limits. Jim knew this was horseshit, knew the only valid tests had to be done with aquifer samples, but he had child support and a mother with stage three pancreatic cancer. He knew by name at least twenty families in the local town, having hired half the residents over the years. After getting the gag order, he'd begun and ended each meal every day for six weeks with Jameson in the same, unwashed glass.

Jones ran a hand over the table to wipe away some breakfast crumbs. "You are going to break camp here, truck your equipment to Los Angeles, drill under a two-block area, and simulate an earthquake with enough force to flatten each of the twelve buildings there." Jones leaned back with his coffee, his eyes taking everything in and giving nothing back. "Sandcastles at high tide."

Jim knew the ask would be outrageous and took a moment to gather some thoughts, bite back the urge to laugh. "That's an ambitious plan, Mr. Jones. But it begs the question why not buy the land and take a wrecking ball to it. Saves you considerable time and money."

"I could have bought up the whole neighborhood, flattened it in two weeks." He sat forward now. "But I'm after tax credits, Jim. Lots of them. And nothing drives up the value of tax credits than natural disasters." As if offended, Cerberus got up and went to lie down on his cushion in the corner, the two men watching him pad across the floor. "I get the best deal when things look the most desperate. That's where you and your nifty set of drills come in. I cut deals to finance the rebuild, pays me ten dollars in credits for every one dollar of investment."

People came to Jim all the time with fever dreams to make money drilling for rare earth metals or wildcatting crude based on some new ground-penetrating satellite imagery. Jim found that the longer they spoke, the greater the chance everyone would go broke or end up in jail. This guy Jones had taken less than a minute, laid out a plan to simulate catastrophic tectonic movement in a major city, and yet Jim felt certain in every fiber of his being that not only would Jones succeed but that he would be long gone before any warrants were served. The technical term for what Jones was proposing was "subsidence," but in lay terms it was a sinkhole, the same thing that formed when a water main broke and sections of roads just opened up like gateways to the underworld. And what Jones was describing was a two-block sinkhole. It would be world news.

"A little disaster to leverage a deal." Jim was now parroting Jones, as if he was actually giving this whacko proposal serious consideration. It was nuts, would cost him his license, send him to jail, and could cost lives.

Jim didn't see much point trying to argue. There were six other camps just like his, all owned by the same company. No saying what Jones would do if Jim refused. He already knew too much, and Jones didn't seem like one to leave loose ends. "I'll need a few days to drill some soil samples, work up some numbers. Most LA substrate is sandstone." He already knew it would be like sending a hot screwdriver through butter. "And I'll have to organize a crew."

Jones put a hand up. "They're on their way already. A group from the Philippines. Plenty of experience but not much English."

"I can't work with a team that needs translation."

"And I can't work with a team that goes drinking every night and posts on social media. In fact, I need a team that spends every waking and sleeping moment on-site which is where this group of green-card-hungry young men will be. They're used to it. Most of 'em live on tanker ships ten months a year. In the bottom of the hull. Pumping bilges. Four months in the LA sun will seem like a vacation for them."

Four months. Jesus. "And you want the engineers to red-tag the buildings, not launch an investigation?" He was now telling Jones what he knew he'd want to hear; the sooner he was gone, the better.

"Bingo."

Cerberus, head on his paws, stared back, his eyebrows seesawing between the two men like he was watching a tennis match.

"One minor detail. Drilling has been illegal in Los Angeles for thirty years. Someone sees us putting up a few towers, we'll be shut down before we even break ground."

"Taken care of. You'll be working out of the largest electrical substation in Southern California. Twenty acres of walled-off land full of towers and power lines. Plenty of cover."

Over the course of his career, Jim had gone from being a roughneck working oil platforms in the North Sea to being a house cat who looked at budgets and schedules, a career path he owed to his tact and discernment. Bad news in drilling and mining, he soon came to learn, was best delivered early on and unequivocally. "And when we finally turn on the pumps, some of those buildings are going to lean to the left, some are going to lean to the right, and others are going to implode, no way to prevent that." He wondered if he needed to finish the thought. "And there might be occupants."

Jones gave one more nod as if expecting this. "Second most dangerous career, Jim, as you know: drill operators, like you once were. Forty-two hundred deaths globally, and guess what, you could double that number, triple it, and you think anyone is going to slow down oil production by even one barrel? People seem to look past workplace safety when gas approaches five dollars a gallon."

Jim tried to bring this part of the discussion to a close with a wan smile. "Roger that."

"Cost of doing business." Jones stood, signaling the meeting's end. "Net results will be for the greater good, Jim. Yours as well as mine." Jim could feel Jones measuring his reaction, checking to make sure the threat had landed.

Jones stood and then Jim did. He led them back outside, watched Jones climb back into the Sikorsky. The turbos quickly revved and the helicopter jumped back into the sky, disappearing over Narrow Ridge in less than a minute. Jim stood there, the whole life-rending interlude lasting less time than it took him to finish his morning coffee.

"And this, my friend," Jim said to Cerberus once again at his side, "is why you're lucky you're a dog."

CHAPTER 22

The Panorama City Mall was half-assed and mostly vacant, whole corridors nothing but empty storefronts, armless mannequins looking like they had places to go, things to do, if only they had their hands to open the door. The one mall cop openly dozed in his chair. A central food court, a popular after-school spot featuring greasy chow mein and overly riced burritos, was the main draw. During the day, mothers came to park their strollers and let their young children ride the rocking horses, ten minutes of freedom for fifty cents, the best use of money they'd ever known.

When Javier arrived, Sergio was sitting across from a man of mixed race in his twenties. He had short hair and enough cartilage for three people, his Adams apple dominating his throat, the two garbanzo beans on the end of his nose suggesting a life walking into walls, his ears sticking out Dumbo-style. The man's eyes were like two fish swimming behind a pair of thick-lensed glasses. He wore a plain white T-shirt revealing a sleeve tattoo down his left arm, a menagerie of geometric shapes that Javier couldn't help but study for a moment. He made out a set of stairs starting at his elbow and spiraling down to his thumb.

Two days earlier during class, Javier had told Sergio the news of his failed mission. It wasn't his intention to steal Jones' burner, but now that he had, he needed options. Sergio had given the phone the once-over, checked its ports, opened it up, squinted at the board to read something. He shook his head.

"You need some overwatch." Sergio stuck the phone in his pocket. "Gimme a few days."

That was a week ago.

"Our special new friend who—" Sergio glanced over at the man who just shook his head. "Well, we'll just leave it at that." Sergio pushed a tray of fries toward Javier. "Ordered some curly cuts if you're hungry." Some East Valley kids sat a few tables on the other side of the large food court, a three-story ceiling making the whole space a bit of an echo chamber.

"Nice to meet you," Javier said, the guy clearly not looking for a handshake.

"Bob." It came out sounding as though he'd made the name up on the spot.

"I found the phone—"

Bob held up his hand and offered a curt smile. "No backstories." His voice was high-pitched, scratchy, like he'd sucked in a lungful of smoke and was holding onto it. "I'm only here to make arrangements. The details..." He shook his head, putting an end to it. "You've been walking around with a live grenade." He paused while a woman pushing a stroller passed behind him. "Slave device. Uses the old pager network." Javier and Sergio looked at each other. "Yeah, back in the day, they had these things called pagers. Popular with doctors and drug dealers. Totally different network." He folded his arms and leaned back. "FCC still requires carriers to maintain it, so lots of paramilitary use it now to avoid wire taps because it takes an act of Congress to get subpoenas for that part of the spectrum."

Javier tried to read some of the text on the tattoo now that Bob's forearm was on full display but wasn't having much luck.

"They skip frequencies, but it's old technology, full of backdoors." A homeless-looking guy with a weather-beaten face was wandering through the tables looking for uneaten food. "And you're in luck because Chechens do everything on these phones."

Javier thought he had said chickens. "Wait, who?"

"Chechens. Russian ex-military."

The noise from a few tables over rose and fell, bursts of laughter, some overhead swats raining down on one boy covering up. Javier watched, wondering how he had ended up discussing mercenaries with Dark Web Bob when most normal kids were playing grab-ass over boba like the group hooting it up at the other table. Instead, here he was listening to a stranger about to map out Javier's future against a team of mercenaries who were, at this moment, most likely breaking down their Kalashnikovs.

This wasn't him. Javier knew when he was out of his depth, and it was time to get out of the pool. He shook his head and leaned in toward Bob. "I'm sorry. We gotta turn this over, get law enforcement involved."

Sergio leaned in further. "Not how to handle these guys, Javi."

Bob took a drink of water, his Adams apple a piston, eyes swiveling. "Think about your brother, your mother, your girlfriend." He spoke with an indifferent tone. "You may think you're clever, but your man Jones has you in his crosshairs."

Javier wondered how Bob knew about Jones but chose not to ask.

Bob continued. "The only reason you're alive right now," he paused for effect, "is because the Chechens do all their business on phones—everything—and their crypto accounts..." He shrugged. "I'd have a harder time ordering a burrito from that lady." He looked toward the Mexican food stall. "I bought you some time, ransomed their accounts. Think of it like insurance. Fixed term. They'll find a work-around eventually, and you'll lose your leverage, and when that day comes, be long gone." Apparently, this was the moral of his story. Start running. He gave both Javier and Sergio long looks. "For now, the Chechens are standing down. They'll pick up another contract in the meantime. Keep a low profile, and no law enforcement." This was aimed at Javier.

"So what? Just sit tight, hope Jones moves on, takes the Chickens with him?"

"Like I said, fixed term insurance."

Sergio jumped in, sensing Javier had met his quota of questions. "What about the phone?"

Bob held his hands out as if ready to catch a ball. "What about it? It's useless. They're not idiots. One gets compromised, they switch them all out."

"So you'll get rid of it?" Javier asked.

"I need to hang on to it for a few more days." He got up, threw out his water bottle, then came, sat back down, and sighed. "Then I give it back. To him." He gestured at Sergio, apparently the reasonable one. "Listen closely. You have no reason to ever turn that phone on. Throw it in the ocean, light it on fire, whatever, but know this: the moment you turn it on, you will have signed your own death warrant. They will know immediately where you are, and they will come for you."

The two boys looked at each other, this guy Bob getting spookier by the minute.

"One more image came in on the burner last night, just before I took the battery out."

"Jesus." Javier sat forward. "What of?"

"Not for my eyes. I'll email it to you. And that will be our last communication." He stood up. "I recommend that you leave the area. The further away the better."

■　　■　　■

Cerberus sat in the shade of a fracking tower, panting in the Santa Ana heat. Jim Madison looked at him, wishing he could have left his dog back in the cooler temps of North Dakota, but he held little faith in the few men that remained behind. Most of them were day drinkers who did poorly without the structure of employment. Under the cover of darkness for more than a week, a crew of men offloaded and then assembled ten fracking towers and an equal number of hydraulic pumps that, standing next to each other, looked like mismatched dance partners.

A semi nosed its cab into the substation like the head of a dragon. The driver climbed out of the cab and walked across the yard where Jim greeted him with an envelope of cash that came with a no-questions clause. The fracking fluid would be offloaded into one of three compression tanks, then piped down the wells, first vertically then horizontally. At night, a team would trace the path of the drill heads with lawn mower-looking devices called magnetometers and spray paint glyphs on the sidewalks and streets.

Few people could decipher these markings.

But Carlos was one of them.

And none of them made any sense.

He was now standing on Van Nuys outside Mantrap Nails having surprised his niece Jasmine with a mani-pedi for her birthday. Neurotically nice, she was easy to spoil, but he quickly lost interest after giving her his two cents on the choice of nail designs. He wandered outside, bought a taco from a street vendor, and noticed the cryptic scrawl on the ground, a system of drilling symbols, which he'd needed to memorize at one point early on in his career for a special licensing certificate. He finished his taco in two bites, more interested in deciphering the glyphs. The largest, a sun-shaped symbol with a vertical line slashing through it, represented an injection well, something used exclusively for fracking.

Across the street, a truck nudged its front end out of a service alley and heaved two clouds of ink-black exhaust. A Peterbilt towing a chrome tanker, the driver had to lean out his window several times to check his clearance. It was nuts, Carlos knew, like a pit bull trying to fit through a cat door. The driver could be written up for three points on his class A license for pulling a stunt like this, but more than just reckless, it was out of place. The alley abutted the Roscoe Substation, a collection of conductors, switches, overhead buses, transformers. Tankers hauling liquids were, in fact, forbidden by local ordinance from driving within two city blocks of the place.

Carlos crossed the street, walked down the alley to the gate of the substation and peered through. Something was way off. A dozen or so twenty-foot, ready-stand towers stood paired up with hydraulic pumps, a combination that would never belong in an electrical substation.

"Sorry, not hiring," said some guy off to his left holding a clipboard and a walkie.

It took a moment to realize the guy was talking to him. "Part of the AB 482 upgrades?" He tried to come off as unemployed rather than nosey.

The guy shrugged. "I'm just doin' the logs, boss. Call your local on Monday. Lotsa work coming up in this area."

"No kidding," Carlos said. Another truck pulled up. The guy got back on his walkie, and Carlos slipped around the trailer covered in an enormous tarp winched down tight enough to bounce a quarter. Carlos took out his phone, turned on the camera, stuck it under the tarp, and quickly brought it back out. The images confirmed his first impression—stacks of perforating guns used in shale rock. He took a short video of the towers and then headed back to Mantrap.

Something was up. Fracking towers in the middle of a substation. In a city you couldn't find enough shale gas to fill a soda bottle. He pulled out his phone and sent Tasha a text asking her to call him.

■　　■　　■

Tasha saw the text, one of two hundred currently unread since this morning alone. In the past week, Senator's Rittenhouse's office had become the lightning rod of community outrage about one thing. The infernal drones, an equal opportunity nuisance, had spawned a contagion of outrage. Even the gardeners who spent half their day running leaf blowers couldn't stand the sound. A siege mentality was beginning to grip the Shoe and with it, a growing paranoia-fueled violence. #dropthedrones featured local residents of the Shoe taking target practice. For every one that fell out of the sky, two more seemed to appear.

Though Rittenhouse would never know it, Tasha had given a masterclass on damage control and client relations while the Senator had been spending the past few weeks golfing and doing fundraisers in the Nordstrom white enclaves of Orange County. He understood life in the Shoe about as well as he understood life at the bottom of the ocean. And that was fine with Tasha, for after all, that was the crux of her work, how she got her job with him. She had learned soon after being hired that he was, on his good days, only indifferent to "those zip codes."

She'd sworn allegiance to the hot comb and straighteners for this stage of her career given the office she worked in. Had she shown up to her interview in braids, she wouldn't have made it past the first round. But she had her limits. So, when the Senator picked the tennis captain to be his chief of staff, she knew it was time. Tasha had been on a Zoom listening to serve-and-volley-Barbie talk about "team work makes the dream work" when she punched in the text she'd sworn to herself she never would.

lets talk

Jones responded a minute later.

CHAPTER 23

Javier'd fallen asleep doing homework and waiting for the email from Dark Web Bob. At midnight, he'd finally texted Sergio to say he hadn't received anything. At 2 a.m., Sergio had replied.

check ur spam

It was blinking on Javier's phone the next morning as he woke up to the sound of the trash truck in the alley. He'd dozed off without an alarm, instinctively checked his phone, and bolted straight up when he read the text. He pulled out his laptop, opened the spam folder, and there it was amidst the going-out-of-business sales and offers of romance, an email simply titled BOB SENT THIS. He opened the email and then the picture.

It was Patel.

It didn't even register as shock at first. There was a mix-up. He must have opened the wrong email. But he hadn't. He checked the URL address on the email. It seemed to go on forever—probably some scammer. But it wasn't.

from the phone we discussed at the mall

Javier looked more closely at the image as if the pixels might adjust and reveal some stranger. There were the dimples large enough to stick nickels in, a picture taken in the school parking lot as he approached his car, a smiling moment of self-amusement. Javier tried calling Sergio, got voicemail, then tried calling the school but lost patience with the prompts. He grabbed his backpack, ran out the door, his brain going red, and took the apartment stairs in two steps, a sprint down the four blocks to school, his mind suddenly circling back to his last encounter with Patel at chess club, the warning to stay away from Jones.

When he got to school, he bolted past the line at the tardy window and ran straight to Patel's classroom. A substitute was at the front holding a coffee cup and a piece of paper. She turned to look at Javier as he appeared in the doorway, and as their eyes met, he knew instantly why she was there.

"No." It tumbled out of his mouth, and the rest of the class stared at him, not only surprised he was late but, given Javier's expression of dread, now doubly alert for some type of catastrophic news.

"My name is Ms. Reyes, and I will be your teacher for the rest of the semester." She stood there for a long moment. "I am sorry to tell you that Mr. Patel died unexpectedly on Saturday night." Some gasped, others froze, a few oh-my-gods, then heads swiveling, hands to mouths, the sudden vacuum of shock. The room descended into an anguished bewilderment.

Javier started squinting at the substitute like she might be an apparition, a hologram. The substitute paused and tried to get a sense of whether to stick to the script or go another way. One girl calmly got up and disappeared into the hallway like she was protesting the news. A static buzz started to fill Javier's head. He hardly knew the guy, and yet that was the thing, he did know him. On the whiteboard were Patel's graphs and key terms in his all-cap handwriting. His coffee thermos, still uncapped. His UC Berkeley pennant tacked to the bulletin board, constant reminder to the class that any reference to Cal was a surefire entre to story-time. A stack of books he had moved from the front of the large, black lab table to give himself somewhere to lean during their last meeting.

Javier, still standing at the door, took a seat in the back, the halls of his mind a set of closed doorways. He went online to confirm it and found a short obit in the *LA Times*, saw that Patel'd been admitted to a hospital in San Jose on Saturday night suffering from chest pains. He leaned over to Sergio and asked him if he could dig up anything else.

The substitute finished her statement and stood motionless, thirty disconsolate faces staring back, rug neatly snatched from beneath them. The abundant pointlessness of it, a stranger breaking the news with a pro forma condolence. Heads lolled and mostly ended up staring at the floor, out windows, at the ceiling. The substitute did her best to offer some solace and tried coaxing out some personal remembrances, but no one was ready to share. By fourth period, Enrique finally broke the ice with a story about how he once ran into Patel at a Starbucks and heard the barista call his name with a long a, like it rhymed with fatal. The story lacked a punchline though one girl broke out in laughter. Someone admitted to loving his accent. Another thought he was from Guam.

Javier wasn't listening, his head now a carousel of snapshots and snippets from his last few meet-ups with Patel. He got an idea and sent Chuey a text.

"Pulmonary embolism." Sergio pulled out his phone and showed a preliminary report from Kaiser Hospital in San Jose. Javier pulled out Jones' card and laid it down in front of Sergio.

"I'm gonna need the name of the janitorial company that cleans this address." Sergio took a picture of it. "And I need a name of the biggest Lakers fan on the cleaning crew that does that office." Sergio gave him a look but didn't ask any questions.

When the last bell sounded, the day mercifully over, Javier went back to Patel's room. Ms. Reyes was still there, flipping through a textbook, making notes. Javier sent Chuey one more text before entering.

"Ms. Reyes, I wanted to ask you a question."

She looked up and smiled. "Of course. I'm sorry. I forgot your name."

"It's Javier. Javier Jimenez."

Just then an announcement came over the PA. "If you are the owner of a car with the license plate DT3409, your lights are on."

Ms. Reyes looked up. "Did they just say 3409?"

"Gee, not sure." Chuey, right on time.

She scowled then rummaged through her bag. "I'll be right back, Javier." She grabbed her bag and hustled out and down the hall, the sound of her heels gradually fading until there was the sound of the big double doors. Javier went round the desk and got onto Patel's computer. Like most teachers, he never closed any windows, his personal Gmail account eternally open and unlocked. Javier made a quick scroll through his inbox looking for subject lines that stood out. Most of the emails were bills and advertising, a few written in a different language. He had no idea what he was looking for but started forwarding anything that looked leading: four emails from the sent folder to someone named Lorenzo Dimas at the *LA Times* and one more sent from Patel to another Patel two weeks ago with the subject line "SJ Trip." Javier heard the click of heels coming back and quickly closed the screen then got back to where he had been standing.

"False alarm." Ms. Mendez came through the door. "Sorry about that, Javier. Please, what can I do for you?"

It was a throwaway moment, his purpose already served. He'd probably never see her again. "Do you think family can sometimes hold you back?"

He expected her to act confused, to deflect, but she didn't hesitate. "Happy families are all alike; every unhappy family is unhappy in its own way." It sounded like something Patel would say. "Doesn't really answer your question, but it was written by a famous Russian author named Tolstoy," Ms. Reyes said. "I find when asked these big questions, the best answer is just to quote famous authors." She closed the textbook sitting open on the table and stuck it in her shoulder bag. "Does it help?"

Javier looked around the room as if expecting Patel to pop up from behind a desk. "Tolstoy, huh?" He tapped the doorframe as if considering her response. "I'm betting unhappy family."

CHAPTER 24

Javier got on the escalator at the Figueroa and Third subway exit, the air feeling less and less used the further he rode up. The mouth of the tunnel framed the afternoon sky, the tops of several buildings looming as if staring down the hole from which Javier was now ascending. He'd only been downtown a few times in his life, the last occasion a trip to the Grammy Museum in sixth grade where he got to record himself singing songs by someone named Marvin Gaye. He never sang, not even to himself, but when he heard "Trouble Man," he'd grown infected with the bridge which he rapped continuously for the rest of the day.

He stepped off and looked up at Three Wilshire, the most recent addition to the LA skyline. It was impossible to avoid craning your neck to see just how high it went, but in so doing, it cost Javier his balance. He stumbled sidewise, nearly colliding with a man who quickly turned his shoulder and kept walking.

He was here to meet some guy he'd messaged on Instagram yesterday. Of the six people who cleaned Solano, Jimmy was the biggest Lakers fan. Javier looked across the street. Standing outside the Starbucks where they had agreed to meet was a young guy in blue pants and a blue shirt with some kind of patch sewn on over a breast pocket. Javier studied him for a moment, noticed his hands in his pockets, a hint of gold around his neck. He wanted to measure this guy, gauge his first reflex, so he sent him a text.

5 mins

The supposed-Jimmy guy pulled out his phone and sent a reply, nothing out of place, no head nods or hand signals to someone on standby. Javier crossed Third Street, checking his coat pocket to make sure his tickets were there.

He walked up to Jimmy, giving him an up-and-down before offering his hand to shake. "Nice to meet you, Jimmy. I'm Javier." He wasn't sure if it was a mistake to use his real name. Everything else was fake. "I appreciate this."

"Hey, I get it. If my lady was getting hassled on the job, I'd wanna find out who and do something about it." The name of the janitorial company was embroidered on the patch. "You must really love this lady though. Lakers Skybox seats." He smiled and held out a clean pressed shirt and unclipped his ID badge. "You'll need these to get in. Don't worry. They never check the pictures."

Javier pulled out the tickets and handed them to Jimmy who held them at an angle to study the light pattern in the hologram. Then Jimmy looked toward someone standing alone next to the stop light and nodded to him. The guy started walking toward them. Javier considered running, certain he was about to be arrested for scalping tickets, his scholarship out the window. Jimmy recognized the panic. "*Tranquillo.* This is Raul, *mi primo.* Never know these days, right?"

Raul walked up smiling, his eyes like buttonholes. Javier guessed he spent most of his life high. "Thanks for the tix bro. All you can eat." He pulled out a large empty Ziploc bag. "Gallon size."

Javier felt his pulse come back down, his scholarship check once again back on the kitchen table. "What do I need to know?"

"You work three floors. Twenty-five through twenty-eight. Just push your cart like you're going somewhere and look busy but not too busy, know what I mean? Don't get chatty and don't get nosy. You'll need this," he pulled out a key fob and gave it to Javier, "for the twenty-eighth floor. Fools up there don't play. We get a new fob every month. Cameras up the wazoo so don't get sticky fingers.

Security is going to take your phone, so don't get bugged out. You'll get it back when you're done."

Javier had worn only a T-shirt so he could pull on the work shirt Jimmy had just given him. He clipped the badge on the front pocket and took the fob. "*Andale pues.* Send me a text when there's a few minutes left in the fourth quarter so I can get out of there and meet you back here."

"Like Cinderella," said Raul. "My money is on Cesar giving your lady the hard time. Dude's a dick."

Javier found the cart with the cleaning supplies right where Jimmy said he would leave it. It was two rolling shelves of blue plastic, neatly filled with aerosol cans, a pile of folded red rags, brown paper towels to restock bathrooms, an open box of black trash bags, and some tools inside a flip-top compartment. Clipped to the side was a manual sweeper that had a set of brushes that spun around when you pushed it.

Outside the elevator, a security officer ran a wand over Javier and asked in Spanish for his cell phone which Javier handed over. The guard waved his passkey to open the doors, and Javier got on. He pulled out the fob and inserted it in the slot next to the number twenty-eight. The chrome doors slid shut, and Javier suddenly found himself looking at the janitor version of himself, the same one he knew the people who worked in this building would assume was the right one for him. He pulled out a baseball cap and pulled the brim down as low as it could go.

He wasn't sure what he was doing, but he knew that he had to do something, that it had been Jones who was responsible for Patel's death. The burner proved it. Javier doubted he would find any evidence in Jones' office, no bloody weapon, no revealing diary entries, but he kept coming back to Patel's reaction when he'd seen Jones' card. There was history there.

The elevator shot up like a rocket, the G-force buckling Javier's knees. At the twenty-eighth floor, the doors slid open to reveal an extravagant space whose main function seemed only to appear empty. It had white marble floors almost too bright to look at and dark wood paneling along three walls. Directly in front was a pair of enormous glass doors with modest stenciling: Solano, LLC. From the corner of his eye, he could see a pair of red camera lights winking at him from either side.

He pushed his cart forward, certain this ploy would end badly. Rash acts weren't his thing, and technically he could be arrested for trespassing. And then came an image of Patel, offering one of his wife's samosas, talking photography and the push-pull of family. He swiped his key card and walked through the barn-sized glass doors. On the other side was a desk where a receptionist most likely played bouncer-in-heels during business hours.

In his entire life, he'd been to one other office, eight years ago, a doctor's visit to get his shots before enrolling in school. The receptionist there had turned her cubicle into a family altar, every inch of wall space covered with photos, preschool artwork, and a set of Mylar balloons with Happy Birthday on them. Here, there was no hint of who sat at this desk. A thin computer screen seemed to levitate, a phone console with a number of blinking green lights, and a plant spilling out of a glass bowl with no dirt. Javier wanted to touch it but kept pushing his cart.

The twenty-eighth floor was in fact an enormous open space with comfortable furniture, workstations, and long tables spaced evenly throughout. A few corner offices and one conference room were the only occasions for actual walls and doors. The entire perimeter was floor-to-ceiling glass with expansive city-to-sea views. Outside the sun had set, and the Hollywood Hills were lit with long rows of brake lights on the north/south boulevards. He'd never been this high up before and found himself overcome with a sense of awe. He could feel himself staring and got busy doing what he imagined Jimmy did every night—push the little sweeper thing, empty the trash, polish the chrome, Windex the glass, all the while stealing glances for clues. Clues to what, though? He had no idea what he was looking for. The desks were all OCD-tidy, no loose papers, screens off, keyboards stowed. Every trash can had a shredder on its top. He discretely tugged a drawer to see if it was locked; it was.

"The break room has a coffee spill under the machine."

Javier jumped at the familiar voice. It was Jones standing to his left, comparing two sheets of paper like they were flooring samples.

"Someone doesn't know how to use a filter," he said, still not looking at Javier.

Game over, go to jail, end of dreams, break your mother's heart. *"Con permiso, senior. No hablar ingles."* He gave his shoulders a little shrug, his eyes anywhere but on Jones, then quickly reaching for some towels to go attack the spill.

Jones, still absorbed in his side-by-side comparison, didn't respond but stuck an elbow out. *"Aya."* Javier, head down, another wave of panic cresting over him, busied himself with his cart, then finally stole a glance when he sensed Jones was gone. Javier finally stood and saw Jones already in the corner office. Javier pushed the cart to the break room which wasn't even really a room, just a glass-brick wall with a sink, refrigerator, and an enormous coffee machine that could have been a Mars lander. The spill had already evaporated, leaving behind a brown stain and some grounds, the office offender too lazy to wipe it up. Javier got out one of the red rags and a squirt bottle and began spraying and wiping, scanning the office as he did. People sat at their desks, most staring at screens, one guy squeezing a blue stress ball, alternating hands and bouncing it off the floor a few times as he spoke into the air. When he turned, Javier could see he was wearing try-too-hard glasses, the same guy who had arrived at the tow yard asking for Jones' phone.

There was no way to know what exactly went on in this office, with its sense of hyper-efficiency. Javier could only imagine large sums of money moving on and off the screens. No one had any less than three of them. These people here probably made more in a week—hell, who was he kidding, more in a day—than he made all year. Once more, he felt the lurking sense of impending failure, his D-league felony certain to come apart any moment now, perhaps some dark wish fulfillment of his. It was time to abort mission, head back to the Shoe, where he belonged. He finished cleaning the coffee spill, went back to the elevators, and stood in front of the chrome doors, the lit numbers overhead slowly climbing to twenty-eight.

He turned and peered from just under the brim of his cap one more time at Jones' office, now empty, door open. He stood there staring at the interior of the office, wondering if there might be something in there that could link Jones to Patel.

The guy with the stress ball started snapping his fingers like he expected Javier to come take his drink order. Chances were good Stress Ball Guy had been raised by a Central American nanny, now hired mostly Spanish speakers to do his yard work, wash his car, and generally act as a surrogate set of back, leg, and arm muscles. The man kept snapping his finger then held up his trash can expectantly. Javier stared at the guy long enough to send an f-u, then pushed his cart into Jones' office.

Javier got out the sweeper and went straight to the glass desk. On its surface sat only a wireless keyboard and mouse. No drawers with magic files, no Post-it notes with passwords or addresses or names he could take pictures of, not one breadcrumb to follow. He went to the couch to arrange some pillows, water the plant on the coffee table. Apart from a mahogany credenza and pine book shelves, the office was mostly glass surfaces and steel frames. A modest collection of pictures filled most of the far wall—Jones shaking hands with dignitaries, sometimes at formal events, others at groundbreakings. One picture grabbed Javier's attention. It was of Jones standing in front of a large office building distinctly shaped like a fish, complete with dorsal fin and gills. In front of this building Jones stood on one side of a semicircle of men in suits. There was a handwritten note at the bottom in black pen that said *Silk from a sow's ear.*

"Thought you'd be at the Lakers game tonight." Javier turned to see Jones, standing in the doorway. "Don't tell me you're a Clippers fan."

Javier stood like a pithed frog, unable to move or speak.

Jones went to the credenza. "Unless you're here to return my phone." Jones shot his eyes at Javier's red Vans. "Stick to finance, Javier. You're not cut out for this." He opened a drawer revealing a small, refrigerated compartment stocked with unlabeled water. Javier looked past Jones' left shoulder at the one door with a red exit sign over it. Jones followed his gaze. "Don't bother. It's locked." He pulled out a water and twisted the top off, then motioned to his office door. "I actually just opened it to see if you had the neck to go through with this." He took a swallow of water. "Some kamikaze shit, Javier." He sounded mildly impressed.

"You killed Dolores and Patel."

"Nope, can't take credit for either one." Security arrived at the door, Jones giving the stop sign with his eyes. "Blood and bodies, different department." Jones's phone buzzed, something on the screen prompting him to look out his office through one of the glass walls at Stress Ball Guy looking back. Jones swung his attention back on Javier. "Lots of accidents though lately, Javier." He closed the distance between them to a couple of feet then veered off toward his desk which he leaned against. "When we find whoever's ransomed our accounts—and we will—you best be back in Jalisco. Under a rock. Deep in the rain forest or whatever the fuck."

"You're gonna pay." It came out small and pathetic, a verbal BANG! flag from a cartoon pistol. The elevator chimed, and two more security officers got out, each wide enough to require them to exit one at a time.

Jones finished the water and put the empty bottle in Javier's trash bag. He picked up a scouring pad from the janitorial cart. "What are you gonna do? Scrub me to death?"

Javier sucked up a throatful of snot and shot it at Jones' chest. It clung there and began to sag. Jones didn't flinch, and security made another move, but Jones held up a hand, his face impassive. He opened another drawer, pulled out a towel, cleaned himself, and then threw the towel out. "Oh, and one more thing. My friends in the white van? On the sidelines for now, sure, but best believe, Javier, my bench is deep. You think all this stops because someone hacked a burner?"

He angled his head toward the Solano staff staring at the two of them, wanting to see how Jones responded to the interloper with the death wish. "Lucky for you we value transparency here at Solano. Too many witnesses," and with that Jones nodded at security. Javier suddenly grabbed the cart and started pushing it out the door, the deception now pointless. They got to the elevators, and one of the security officers rode down with him to the basement where he was let out. Javier pushed his cart to a corner, reclaimed his phone, and took the stairs to the street, noticing for the first time, as he pressed the release on the door, both hands were shaking.

Jimmy and Raul were there waiting for him, drunk, their faces showing signs of barbecue wings. "Fuckin' buffet, bro!" Raul pulled out his gallon Ziploc stuffed with greasy leftovers. "Want one?"

"I'm good," Javier said. He handed Jimmy his shirt, fob, swipe card, and ID badge. "You were right. It was Cesar."

Twenty minutes later, on the 402 bus back to the Valley, he sat quietly watching the street scenes roll by, scanned the faces of riders, most on their phones, some clutching bags in their laps, eyes closed, heads bobbing, one day's toil already bleeding into the next. Not a single head of blond hair on the bus, these people, his people, who came here to work whatever job was available at whatever hours were available. They'd live ten to an apartment, send half their checks back across the border, and ask Jesus on Sunday to forgive them the sin of endless work.

He searched up "fish-shaped building" and was given links to the National Fisheries Development Board located in Hyderabad. There it was, someone's idea of clever architecture. Then he pulled up the emails he'd forwarded from Patel's computer and started opening them. The emails to the reporter from the Times were encrypted and required a sixteen-digit passkey. Nonetheless, Javier sent an email to the reporter explaining who he was, how he knew Patel, and asked that he get in touch. He did some searches on the reporter, Lorenzo Dimas, and found out he was an investigative journalist with a focus on financial crimes and government corruption. He'd written a number of articles on Jones for different publications.

The other email sent to someone else named Patel didn't have any password protection, but it was short, mostly travel confirmations with dates and locations. The only clue came at the end, a final line referencing a fire. Javier recalled the pictures Patel had shared of the twisted wreckage from his home city, the fire in which his brother was so badly burned. He sent an email to this person doing his best to preempt the likely suspicion he might arouse. After twenty minutes of careful wording and hitting send, he got a reply seconds later. DNS 404. Invalid address.

Jones had been generous with his assessment. At least kamikaze pilots were clear on their missions.

CHAPTER 25

The chartered bus pulled into the parking lot one block east of Sepulveda, released its airbrakes, and opened the door. The driver got out, pulled open the giant luggage doors where the picket signs were kept, and began handing them out to the passengers. They rested the signs against their shoulders, each trying to remember what the man had told them last night at the hotel. Something about drones with special cameras and ICE.

A man holding a clipboard went around doing a head count then brought everyone together. "Just remember, you've been betrayed." He looked at the translator, hoping she could capture the subtlety of the word but having no way to check. "You have all been shopping at this store for years and years, and now they are cooperating with ICE, and you want the rest of the city to know how evil the owner is." Last night, they had watched the video of the man in the red sweatpants and Dodgers T-shirt, convinced it was real footage until the man, again relying on the translator, explained that this was part of a new reality show called "Televised Revolution," and that in addition to their daily rate, they would be earning something called residuals which required almost fifteen minutes of translation before everyone's head was nodding.

There were about thirty of them, Mexican, Salvadoran, Guatemalan, and all playing the part of the righteously outraged. They looked around at each other, everyone unsure and looking for someone to take the lead—it was an absurd moment made only more absurd by the payday that came at the end. They finally lifted their signs off their shoulders and started in with some half-hearted chants they'd learned on the bus ride over: *No queremos que nuestros tenderos ayuden la migra* all broken into rhythmic couplets.

They were going to march on this big supermarket, Valley Mercado. Their demand? That the owners of Valley Mercado stop sharing their CCTV footage with ICE and Border Patrol. According to the premise they'd been given last night at dinner, the store's footage was getting fed through facial identification software and was now being used to check for outstanding warrants, child support, and overstayed visas. They were told law enforcement were, within the context of the completely fabricated setup, looking for the two men—one shooter and one passenger—involved with the very real homicide of a border agent, Terry Price, several weeks ago, an impenetrable mix of truth and fiction. No one had been paid a dime as of last night, though the four-star accommodations with the showers that weren't also bathtubs was a hopeful sign.

They'd been instructed to make a line and walk back and forth in a tight oval. Most just stuck their signs on their shoulders and stared at the person in front of them as they paced, their lackluster chants sounding more like prayers. A car turned in, honked at the protesters which they considered a gesture of support until the car turned around in the parking lot, came back and sped towards them, causing their line to quickly split in two as if they'd just played a high-stakes game of Red Rover.

Then a parting tribute. *Fuck you beaners.*

That got things started.

A couple of the protesters got their signs off their shoulders and started lifting them up and down. Others started making eye contact with drivers who pulled in, past the picket line. Soon there were fists in the air and the noise level came close to a respectable protest. The cause, however apocryphal, was suddenly real to them.

"Make sure you wear sunglasses when you go in there or *migra* might show up this afternoon!" A few of the ladies broke from the script to take it up a notch, righteously strutting back and forth between rows of cars stopped at lights in front of the store. "*No compre en Valley Mercado. Valley Mercado es fascista!*" Some East Valley kids on the way to school noticed them and saw a good reason to ditch. A couple of posts on social media and soon a few more kids, older brothers and sisters who had grown up walking up and down the aisles of Valley Mercado. Within less than an hour, all three local networks and an even larger group of freelance journalists had their cameras set up.

I'm Jose Ramos and I'm here at Valley Mercado in Panorama City where a contingent of local residents have begun protesting the store owner's cooperation with border patrol. We spoke with one of the group's leaders earlier to better understand why they have come out today to picket.

"Last week, when the agent was shot, Border Patrol and—um—FBI started detaining a bunch of people because they said the suspect has family in the area, you know, the Shoe. And they started using drones and special cameras, and they have special cameras in Valley Mercado which tells *migra* who is illegal and who has warrants and stuff like that. So yes, we are here today to tell the owners to stop sharing their cameras with migra and the FBI and all of them because we are peaceful, law-abiding people."

I will say that NBC has been in touch with Border Patrol and that agency flatly denies any use of facial recognition cameras or drones, though we can see several overhead right now. Nonetheless, the residents here today are very angry at what they believe is a betrayal by the owners of this store. For NBC 4, I'm Jose Ramos.

The inside of Valley Mercado itself was mostly empty by 1 p.m., the owners having tried unsuccessfully to discredit the bogus allegations. At one point, management invited three of the protesters to come inside and check on their camera feeds. They brought them into the back office, offered to let them run any test they wanted, check their admin settings, pull the wiring, anything, but none of the designees from the picket lines understood anything about closed circuit television or facial recognition software. The store managers offered the three protesters some sandwiches in the hopes it might lower the heat, at least start a conversation, but all three declined and were soon back outside with the others.

The protest had gone viral by lunch. The crowd had grown to three times its original size, and this after the original "protesters" had quietly handed their signs to others in the crowd, had slipped out the sides, and were quietly back on the bus by 2 p.m. They were back in Arizona later that night, happy to collect two thousand dollars for one day of so-called work with some of that residual stuff expected to arrive soon after, once the show got picked up by a network, whatever that meant. By 3 p.m., the group had become a crowd that stretched the length of the sidewalk, and soon another, smaller group appeared on the other side of Van Nuys with signs and horns, though something had been lost in transmission, like a game of telephone, between the main group and this breakaway cell who, in their haste, had scrawled signs demanding the store "remove the campers" rather than cameras. A hyperkinetic female, a protest ringer judging by her jukebox knowledge of catchy protest chants and her actual own bullhorn, ratcheted the energy full blast, a puddle of gasoline looking for a match.

The police arrived under orders to "lose the sunglasses," work the perimeters, smile. The Chief was in a contract year and had just experienced a public reaming from the city council for some body-worn camera footage of an officer discharging his weapon on a motorist. Officers going "cowboy" would be riding desks for a month. They'd avoided the provocative use of riot-wagons, relying instead on only a handful of cruisers, lights and sirens code four, and their arrival was virtually unnoticed. They used the loading area in the back of the store to park and then casually emerged as though they'd gotten lost on the way and were just happy to be there. By 4 p.m., the protest had grown in size such that it would now need a permit, which of course no one had since none of the protesters had realized until lunchtime there was anything to protest. Law enforcement could have disbanded the whole thing right then, formed their "unlawful assembly" phalanx with their shin guards and Plexiglass. Instead, cops spent their time handing out waters, thumbs in their belts.

By 5 p.m., it had become a buzzy event with a few celebs posting about it. It was an eclectic group, immigrants and political lefties that never knew a protest they wouldn't join, working families that had shopped at Valley Mercado all their lives, a few B-list actors and their coteries doing their best to go incognito but not too incognito. At exactly 6 p.m., peak ratings, Delatorre arrived, asked to borrow the bullhorn from the chant leader whose vocal cords were mostly shot, and stood in the bed of a pickup truck. He knew the local anchors of the three majors—Jones had assured him— would cut away to feature his speech.

He didn't introduce himself, and it was doubtful more than a handful of people knew who he was. "Today, my friends, we are witnessing the arrival of the police state. We are Mexicans, Central Americans, immigrants, brown people under surveillance because of our race and our zip code. *Soy uno de ustedes.*" I am one of you. The crowd erupted. He went on for another fifteen minutes, invoking the Bill of Rights, the Mexican Revolution, Los Tigres Del Norte, and the Lakers. He leavened his outrage with the humor that was "the birthright and duty of Mexican uncles everywhere." When he punched the air, some of them punched with him. When he spoke in a humble tone, they grew quiet. No one noticed he hadn't even mentioned Valley Mercado. The crowd was just grateful for a break from the endless chanting.

He ended on a four-minute crescendo, spit flying from his mouth, his eyes growing damp with sentiment, his collar sagging under the sweat. The words found his mouth and were then lit by some new fire, and for once, the crowd was in thrall to his message, a collective gestalt emerging between speaker and audience. He'd never before known ecstasy in his life, but here it was. And just like that he finished, jumped off the truck, high-fived several of the protesters, and disappeared into the crowd. His city-issue was idling across the street. Tasha was sitting in the backseat when he climbed in.

"Jones said you'd be here." Delatorre shook his head. "Oh, how the mighty have fallen." He and Tasha'd run in the same City Hall circles ten years prior, both of them staffers for various elected officials and had briefly dated. There was a casual warmth even now.

"Someone got their swerve back," she said, shooting him a flirtatious look.

Delatorre was too annoyed to notice and pointed to the sky. "Fucking Jones."

And as if hearing his name, the man appeared, one hand on the roof, the other on the top of the open door. He nodded at Tasha.

Delatorre palmed the sweat off his face. "Get those fucking things down."

Jones took a beat and drummed his fingers on the roof. "Nice speech, Councilman. Looked like you might have surprised even yourself." Then to Tasha. "My friend over at Ways and Means even got you a parking spot under the Rayburn Building." Then to Delatorre. "Usually a four-year waiting list for one of those."

Delatorre looked over at Tasha, neither of them quite the idealists they'd once been. She got out of the car and came around to face Jones. "The Senator is bringing your little bill to a committee vote next week, so you'll have your tax credits." She wanted to push his face. In four days at least, she would be in D.C., taking her shot.

"So we're done. Quid pro fuckin' quo." She put her sunglasses on, flashed Delatorre deuces and slipped into the crowd.

Delatorre balled his towel up and tossed it in the front seat. "You know I looked this shit up. They got a name for what you're pulling, Jones. Astroturf. And I didn't get it at first, so, yeah, I went to community college, so what, but then it made sense. Astroturf. Looks like grassroots but look again 'cause it's fake. Fake as the fucking hair plugs I just sank in my head. And fake as those fruitcakes you got holding their cute little signs. Yeah, you got your tax credits and a whole lot more, I'm sure, but I'm done, Jones. Done with your parlor tricks 'cause there'll be nothing left of this place in a month."

Jones gave the Councilman a rictus smile, pulled out an envelope from his coat, and stuck it in the seat pocket. "A little something for the campaign. Governor called and wants to run you next term for Sacramento." And just like that, the Councilman felt the little belly-fire go out. "We're having lunch in a week. Be a shame to cancel." Across the street, the noise had grown, the crowd noticeably more agitated. "Apparently your constituents don't really care what kind of protest you call it, Councilman. If only they knew what was coming."

Jones pushed off from Delatorre's Town Car just as the first projectile—a full can of soda—exploded against the front of Valley Mercado. It wasn't long before someone found something with more heft and launched it at a window which cracked though didn't break. Finally, a group of young men, sensing a moment to do some justifiable vandalism, grabbed a gas grill that was part of a display for an upcoming sale, picked it up, rocked it back and forth twice, and heaved it against the glass doors.

CNN would have a panel discussion the following night on the semantics of what to call what happened next: an uprising, civil unrest, wanton destruction. Valley Mercado was in fact looted then set on fire, exactly as Jones had intended. The plans for a Whole Foods were already in place, the grand opening scheduled for six months from now. The police riot squad eventually arrived, hanging off armored trucks, and formed their line, driving the protesters off the property, a short-sighted move that only served to push the seething mob further down Van Nuys Boulevard with more things in their path to destroy. It hadn't been part of Jones' plan. He'd only wanted Valley Mercado and its *carniceria* with its five varieties of head cheese gone, but the poor planning of law enforcement ensured another ten stores were looted and three set on fire: a Payless Shoe, a phone store, and a donut shop which burned in colorful flames from the different types of sugar and oil in the stockroom. By morning, the entire block was taped off, an LAPD mobile command center parked in the middle. The mayor declared the block a disaster zone, imposed a curfew, and pledged financial aid and, most notably, a very generous tax credit package which bore virtually the same terms as the one Jones had delivered to Delatorre's office after their first meeting.

The Councilman's speech from the truck bed had nearly one million views on YouTube within days. Some reviled him for inciting the rioters; others called him a defender of the barrio. Most comments came from end-days preppers about the weapons they had on hand and the work underway to get ready for the coming race war. In the world of LA politics, the Councilman was now a rising star, relevant and trending. In his interviews the following week, he took credit for the sudden disappearance of drones, though ICE kept insisting that they had never used drones in the first place. When he met with Jones and the governor a week later, he felt both validated and disgusted, two currents that now eddied within him.

CHAPTER 26

"Lupe's house is in Studio City, Javier, you know, the hills."

"We live in a valley, Les. We're surrounded by hills." Javier could hear kitchen sounds in the background, someone shouting, oven doors banging shut, glassware on marble counters. He was on his way to the scholarship barbecue in the beater, and by the time he took a left on Rossmore and started to climb the flower- and tree-lined roads, he could see in his rearview mirror a cloud of oil smoke billowing from his exhaust. He half-hoped the beater would die on the way, give him a credible out.

"I gotta go, Javi. And Alex is already here with a friend." Leslie hung up. According to her, Lupe's board members mostly just wrote checks but occasionally liked to mix it up with the plebes. Javier knew most of the conversations would eventually devolve to food or soccer or what cities in Mexico that board member had visited. Leslie thrived in these little cultural estuaries, slipping in and out of small groups, each one like a new planet she could land on and explore. Javier, on the other hand, couldn't stand the grinding small talk and even less, the expressions of superior amusement that would no doubt be aimed his way.

The higher he drove up the hills, the further back the homes sat off the street, finally disappearing behind wrought-iron gates and Hollywood hedges and stonework with quarried rock. There was no on-street parking, no way short of pole-vaulting to get onto someone's property without getting buzzed through. Unless you lived there, were invited, or were some kind of help around the house, you had nowhere else to go but back down the hill. Javier had an aunt who was one of the nannies, all of them bus riders, who legged it the last half-mile up the steepest grades, arriving every morning at dawn, dodging sports cars tear-assing it downhill for a 6 a.m. with the trainer.

Javier found the entrance, showed his ID to the guard at the gate who then pointed where to go. A young homie dressed in a red vest waved him forward where he pulled in behind a black SUV, a Canadian flag decal prominently displayed on its bumper. It was the wrong-way driver from Denker he and Betzaida had spotted. Javier watched as someone with the appearance and bearing of a Viking come to stake out new lands got out and tossed the keys to the kid in the red vest who had to use two hands to make the grab, almost running into the passenger getting out on the other side.

A heavyset guy, also wearing a red vest, suddenly appeared and opened Javier's door. "I'm the valet." For a moment, Javier thought the guy had said ballet but couldn't see this guy and his girth getting too far off the floor. The kid kept a straight face and flat tone, aware of how much learning was going on right now. "I park your car."

Javier looked at the collection of luxe sportscars, arrayed like peacock feathers in the lot ahead. Only the prospect of good food and Alex on neutral ground kept him from pulling the door closed and leaving. He got out and handed the guy his keys. "Hey, no scratches." There was hardly a panel on the car that wasn't dented.

Lupe's house was a Spanish colonial mansion, a world unto itself plunked down in the middle of an expansive lawn rimmed with birches and pines. At the front door, a welcoming committee dressed in black and white approached Javier with some kind of drink in a fancy glass, though he declined, too busy getting sucked into the architectural details of the house. He recognized the stucco as something called lace and skip, a high-end finish that maybe one in ten contractors knew how to do correctly. The portico surrounding the main door was nearly as large as his apartment, its teak beams and Mexican tile worthy of a *casa de patron*. And the door, with its scalloped trim and bronze inlay gave it the appearance of a Mayan altar. Not only was the door a single piece of mahogany, it had been hand-carved, some type of story in bas-relief Javier would have liked to study had the door not been pulled open revealing Leslie standing there with a wide smile. She gave Javier a hug and a kiss, then stood back and fanned an arm toward nowhere in particular.

"It's called an atrium."

Javier gazed up at three stories of nothingness. "Put a hoop in here, and it's called a gymnasium." Leslie gave him a playful push and then slipped a hand into his, sending a small thrill down his back. She led him into the house, a collection of spaces within spaces much like the lavish homes on *Rebelde* where knock-out women lounged and plotted all day. There were floor-to-ceiling shelves with a thicket of book spines and a built-in fish tank the size of a bathtub, leather sofas with colorful throw pillows, and an enormous oil that spoke to some notion of the Wild West, a grassy plain with horses feeding in the foreground. The upper third of the painting was dark sky with a thin strip of golden grass serving as horizon, and once again, Javier felt himself wanting to go in for a closer look, but Leslie pulled him down a hallway.

"Over there is her office." She pointed to a pair of French doors and then swung her arm to a hallway directly opposite. "And down there is a home theater slash game room." They could hear explosions and shouting. They passed through the kitchen where a refrigerator calendar caught Javier's eye. FRANCE was written all through the next two weeks with arrows extending from Sunday to Saturday.

They stepped down a set of tiled stairs out into the back yard, the party already underway. This year's cohort of scholarship aspirants milled around, trying hard to look relaxed, the boys with their hair shellacked and the girls doing their best to balance on their heels in the soft grass. A turquoise expanse of water appeared to spill off into nowhere, giving the backyard an end-of-the-world look.

"Infinity pool," Leslie said. "Sort of a thing around here." Far off to the northwest, Javier could make out the luggage handles of Valley Savings and the Pan City Steel smelting tower standing sentinel over the Shoe. In the background, the San Gabriels offered the Valley an expansive set of shoulders.

"Valley Savings, right Javier?" It was Lupe coming up from behind. "Only place I ever found any peace in the Shoe when I was your age." Her voice was honeyed, her attention once more as intimate as a shared umbrella. "So glad you could take time off work." Javier considered her phrasing, the acknowledgment of lost wages. "And it's very nice to finally get a chance to properly meet you." They shook hands, Javier once again marveling at her appearance, her age anywhere between eighteen and eighty.

"Thank you for inviting me, Ms. Rodriguez." He sounded like a stranger to himself.

"Please call me, Lupe."

"Okay, Ms. Lupe." He never went in on a first-name basis with adults.

Lupe smiled, familiar and touched by his insistence on formality. "I have to warn you both, weak salsa." She side-mouthed and bent her head toward one of the tables with the condiments. "C'mon, got the best aquas frescas you've ever had." She waved to one of the servers who had a platter of colorful drinks in tall glasses rimmed with blue. Lupe took two, handing a dark one to Javier, an orange one to Leslie, and then took a white one for herself. "To reunions, Javier." She held up her glass and winked at Leslie.

"Kind of told her about you and Alex," Leslie said. Javier did his best to hide his annoyance.

Lupe put a hand on Javier's. "And I'm glad she did, Javier. I understand pressures at home, really. *Mi familia*," she made a face, "let's just say I bought a bus ticket when I was thirteen. Got as far as Tulsa." Javier nodded like he'd been there. "And I had an older brother like Alex." She pulled her hair back and inclined her neck toward Javier revealing the tattoo behind her ear. "*Víctor está con Dios ahora.* So when Leslie told me what was going on with you and Alex, I said it will be a condition," she looked over Javier's shoulder at Alex, "of your scholarship. Forget about everything else here today." She made a quick semicircle with her head, a gesture meant to encompass the cattle-auction nature of the afternoon's business. "You've already got my vote." She tipped her head back, slightly. "Just a little formality in a few weeks, Javier, but you need to get right with your brother."

He could see why Leslie had grown so enamored with her. Lupe could have asked him to jump in the pool, and he would have at least taken a few steps. He'd known firsthand only two examples of unalloyed talent: Sergio's ability to hack into anything, and a sixth-grade Filipina girl who ran off twenty straight minutes on the piano, all ten fingers a blur, at one point having to lean forward to reach the keys at both ends of the keyboard. And now Lupe, a walking hope-machine, whose mere presence felt like a benediction.

"I just want to make *mi madre orgullosa*," the "proud mother" refrain always a reliable way to deflect compliments. More people were lurking behind the three of them, waiting to introduce themselves, make an impression on Lupe. Javier watched them, all smiles and clear skin, portraits of optimism, upbeat and outgoing. This was Leslie's crowd, not his, leaving him to wonder if college would just be a bigger version of the same thing.

"She already is," said Lupe, giving his hand a squeeze before turning to the other students patiently waiting behind her. He caught Leslie's eye and tipped his head toward the bar where jugs of the aquas frescas now sat. They slipped off to get refills at a table where a gray-haired man in a ponytail was mixing drinks for the board members. Javier poured their refills then spotted Alex by the pool standing with another kid, a butterball, both of them thankfully wearing dress shirts. Leslie followed his eyes then patted his chest. "Just go easy," she said before walking away to the other side of the pool where Thor and his sidekick, now both wearing sunglasses, were standing.

Whatever detente Javier and Alex had achieved was the result of avoidance. They'd pass each other in the apartment on the days Alex was home which was increasingly rare. They hadn't spoken since Javier had hit him, and now seeing Alex, Javier hadn't been prepared for what he felt. They'd grown up inseparable, the two boys and Yanira, then he and Alex here in the Shoe, having nowhere else to turn than to each other in those first few years. And now this, an eggshell brotherhood. Alex was looking thinner than normal, made to look even more so next to his corpulent friend. Javier finished his drink, set it down, and made his way over.

"I don't wanna talk to you," Alex said, coughing up something and then sending it sailing over the wall.

Javier looked at Alex's friend. By middle age, this kid would have a stomach like a shelf. "You're Sergio's cousin." It was a total guess and almost certainly wrong.

"Nah." Baby Buddha suddenly grew fixated on a jazz trio setting up.

Javier watched the pool water noiselessly disappear over the edge. Without a clear line of sight to the catch basin below, it was impossible to watch this without imagining mudslides. "Cops want to talk with you."

"Not gonna happen." Alex stared straight ahead. "Snitches are bitches."

End of. It was pointless to try and convince him, the whole exchange a waste of breath. "Ma misses you, Alex." The two of them watched a plane on approach to Burbank, its ground speed seemingly too slow to keep it in the air. "Send her a text, at least. She's lost weight behind this, Alex." He kept the tone as judgment-free as he could. "Seems like you could use some home cookin' too."

"What do you want, Javi?"

"Smack you in the head." He turned to look at Alex. "I mean, guns? Really?" Alex was staring holes into the ground while Baby Buddha shifted his weight and tugged his pants up. Javier looked at the boy, not sure if he'd do better talking to him and just letting Alex listen in.

"And the thing of it is, you don't even know what you're signing up for." He paused, almost feeling sorry now for his brother. "Not sure what upper management shares with you apart from telling you where to carry their shit, but their little operation does not go unnoticed. I mean, a lab, Alex?" He took a quick look around, he and Alex most certainly the only two at Lupe's party discussing narcotics and firearms. "That's why they're called cartels. They control everything, Alex. You think Apple is gonna let you stand on the corner and make iPhones?" He felt like a hypocrite using Morales' line now. "They already got their shooters arriving, Alex, and they will stop your clock."

Alex scratched his neck and looked indifferent. The jazz trio jumped off with a tune, the singer clutching the mic stand like her balance depended on it. Something about a rainy day in Memphis. Baby Buddha, his pants already back down where they were originally, was the only one of the two showing a spark of interest.

"You don't know shit." The noise level dipped just as Alex said this, drawing a few looks from the other guests. The singer started aiming her voice at the two of them, their standoff creating a little sinkhole amidst an otherwise upbeat crowd.

"Yeah, maybe you're right, Alex." Javier feigned a dawning realization. "Maybe you're right, maybe I need to shut up and listen." He wasn't sure if he was trying to work some reverse psychology on Alex or if in fact he actually believed what he was now saying, that he should stop with the inquisition and just hear what his brother had to say. Alex lifted his eyes off the grass, belt-height. A weightless silence passed between them. Baby Buddha snuck a look at Alex.

"Whatever you wanna do, Alex. Just know we have a lot riding on this. It ain't just your ungrateful ass."

"Fuck you." And they were off again.

Javier chuckled, though once again annoyed with himself. He'd killed the moment, taken another dig sending them off on the mobius strip of taunts and recriminations. He considered an apology, some small act of humility to restart the conversation but couldn't get there. He and Alex were done for the day, their reunion having run its brief and inevitable course.

Instead, he let his attention wander across the pool to where Leslie was talking with the two Canadian mooks. As if sensing the stalemate between brothers, she looked up and waved Javier over. He shook his head, his mood having soured though even on a good day the Thor-looking dude would only inspire contempt. Leslie, seemingly determined to introduce everyone at the barbecue to everyone else, towed her two classmates over to Javier's side of the pool.

"Javier, Alex, this is Ronnie and Gito." From the neck up, Ronnie was mostly jaw, everything else stacked on top of it. He had an incurious smile, a meaningless expression of affability. His friend, Gito, had a face like a frying pan and translucent skin that appeared filmed with oil. "Ronnie and Gito, this is Alex and Javier and—" She let it hang there, hoping Baby Buddha would fill in the blank which only came when Alex elbowed him.

"Chuco." He fiddled with the bottom edge of his polo like he was drying his fingertips. Javier tried to measure Alex's response to this Ronnie guy, clearly the bulk-buyer he and Betzaida had seen driving the wrong way at the park.

"'Sup," Ronnie said, his eyes, blue as cue chalk and vacant. His friend, Gito, oddly the inverse—a whole world buzzing in his skull. "Ronnie's on the hockey team—recruited from Ca-na-da," Leslie said, trying to make it sound exotic. "Bet you didn't know we have high school hockey here in the Valley." She looked at Ronnie like he was a prize racehorse. "Quincy built its own hockey rink."

Javier had some anger to offload. "Ice in the Valley. Makes about as much sense as my nipples."

"UCLA is starting a hockey team." Leslie went up on her toes as she said it. "Ronnie and Gito are being recruited."

"Team's gonna suck, but what the hell, LA right?" Ronnie apparently could speak in sentences. Javier stared at the guy, wondering if maybe he could serve him up to Freemon and Morales in lieu of Alex. "We're goin' inside, play some GTA." Ronnie put an arm around Gito's neck, this little tête-à-tête not worth any more of his time, and by extension, unworthy of Gito's. The two wandered off, pulling Alex's and Chuco's gaze with them.

"Go," Leslie said, shooing them off toward the house. "Lupe's kids are in there, so introduce yourselves. Say hello. Don't just grab a controller." Alex looked at Chuco for the briefest of consultations, and off they went. Javier watched, now starting to feel disgusted with himself.

Leslie glanced at him. "The French call it *l'esprit de l'escalier.*" She knew that he'd gone too far or not far enough to repair the breach with Alex. "The spirit of the stairs, as in when you leave somewhere and you realize on the stairs what you should have said earlier." He resented how well she could peer inside his head. She ran her hand up and down his arm, her sympathy landing as pity.

"Yeah, well, here's a little Mexican phrase—*I gotta work.*" His mood had soured, and the longer he stayed, the more he knew he was done with this whole thing. It wasn't his world, never would be. Leslie, on the other hand, ate it up, all the chitchat and handshaking and introductions a rush of endorphins for her, and he hated himself even more for begrudging her natural talent. It would serve her well in some rarified strata of the whip-smart and socially adroit. He wondered if she knew, as he did, that their paths were forking.

Leslie looked toward the set of double doors where Alex and Chuco had just gone inside. "Just be there for him. Don't get hung up on the words." Javier watched the singer staring at the sky trying to conjure the opening pitch of the next tune. Then to the left of the trio he saw Lupe, speaking with a small group of men, each holding little white plates which looked ridiculous in comparison to the frisbee-sized plates he was used to at Mexican cook-outs. Javier noticed the man standing in the middle and squinted at him. It was Stress Ball Guy, minus the stress ball, though now wearing a new pair of polarized look-at-me glasses.

"Yeah, I'll let you know how things go. And thanks, Les, for the, you know, reunion. We'll get there, eventually." He suspected Alex would be texting her in a week or so with some told-you-so comments. "Looks like he's made a friend."

Leslie smiled, the afternoon sun catching the curve of her throat. Javier couldn't say when he'd first noticed how beautiful she was, but he felt seized by it in these types of unguarded moments. It was effortless, and having seen it the first time long ago, he had found that he only had eyes for her.

"I've already signed you up for the scholarship interview, Javi." She kissed him then whispered in his ear, "Take me on an adventure, Javi."

The thought boggled him, romantic designs like pushing rope.

"Always more room in the front seat of Delilah." He kissed her back, felt the press of her lips, wondered if she'd get in the beater with him right now and spend the rest of the day on the Ferris wheel at Santa Monica Pier doing endless rotations. No one held as much light in their eyes as Leslie, and Javier hated watching it drain out as she considered his nonresponse.

"I'll bring the popcorn." She gave his arm a squeeze, the blandest of affections, then wandered off leaving Javier marooned with his second helping of regret.

He fled the backyard, back inside the house the way he had come. The explosions and gunfire still echoed down a hallway from the game room, though the number and volume had noticeably grown. Javier spotted Lupe's office, its mullioned French doors beckoning him to come take a look inside. The doors were unlocked, inside a shrine to her duality, one wall lined with family pictures taken from the Gardens, picnics and *quinces*, the other mostly pictures of Lupe in full boss-mode signing things, pointing at things, giving a TED talk, and shaking lots of hands looking like a force of nature. He saw the image he'd seen on Carlos' phone of her stepping on a shovel in the desert, shoulder to shoulder with a handful of guys, the start of the bullet train. Sprinkled among the pictures were various accolades—plaques, proclamations. The only concession to actual work was an angled draftsman table with some architectural drawings. Stamped in the lower right, he saw Jones' address and his company name.

So what? Lupe was working with Jones. Developers did that kind of stuff.

He jiggled a mouse on a computer screen, revealing a montage of family pictures floating across and then disappearing. Another click of the mouse and the cursor was blinking inside a password field. End of the road. On either side of the doors was a set of filing cabinets, a set of bookshelves covered half of one wall, some hardcovers, a few plants, more pictures. He tried the doors on the filing cabinet, but they were all locked.

He looked back at the monitor, the screen-saver rotation of family pictures, an endless cycle of Lupe's kids and family outings. Then something caught his eye. An extended family portrait, the big semicircle, Lupe standing in the middle, one arm around a young man with a goatee, a vein of scar tissue running through it, and an 818 tattooed on his neck in Gothic font. Something in her bearing was pure *chola*, and even there in the bosom of her very extended family, her eyes were as hard as two black stones. It was the mouth-breather from Dolores's funeral.

CHAPTER 27

On the way home, Javier swung by the 7-Eleven off Sepulveda to reload his blood sugar before his shift at Mission. Truth was, he didn't have a shift. He'd lied to Leslie to get out of there, and worse yet, he knew that she knew he was lying. It had been an article of faith they'd both shared since grade school that college was the promised land, that a four-year degree was the Holy Grail, though standing there in Lupe's backyard among the Valley's high achievers, he wasn't sure it was for him.

He stood in line at the counter and checked his email, hoping to see a reply from the *Times* reporter but still nothing. Sergio had left him a text letting him know he'd picked up the burner from Bob but wasn't sure what to do with it. It was useless at this point, but Javier suggested holding onto it in the event the cops needed it for evidence at some point. Sergio went on to mention that the Chechen's accounts were still ransomed so the "cloak of protection was still in place," words that Javier had to reread more than once before he could fathom how fragile and unfamiliar his life had become. Here he was, living his life, wholly reliant on some vague assurances from a total stranger to ward off a team of mercenaries using some dark web voodoo.

At the checkout counter, Javier watched the bingo ball bounce across the screen, an apt metaphor for his life, then land on sixteen. He tried to consider if there might be some mystical message in the number but gave up when he heard someone behind him call his name.

"Mr. Jimenez." Javier turned to see Detective Freemon. "Five minutes. Across the street, Red Lantern." He chin-tilted toward the other side of Sepulveda to the strip mall where Javier could see Morales looking back, once again the sporty half of the duo. Freemon and Morales had actually done him a solid, not making a show of things in public.

He made his purchase, crossed the street, and went inside the Red Lantern. They were sitting there with a pot of hot tea between them. Javier took a seat in the booth on the opposite side of the table. The red wallpaper featured golden men in traditional Chinese garb picking rice.

"Your timing is kinda spooky." He looked at them for some kind of reaction. "I just saw my brother for the first time in a while."

They didn't seem struck by the coincidence. "Where's he at with our offer?" It was Freemon doing his best to sound patient.

Javier took a breath. "Respectfully declined."

Morales nodded. "Kinda figured." He took a sip of tea and squinted at Javier like he was trying to concentrate. "You know, what's funny is we make these offers all the time and the youngsters always wanna stand tall—at least that's what they call it—they stand tall on deals like this 'cause they've got it tattooed on their brain that nothin' sticks 'til eighteen."

Freemon shifted his weight. "We moved on, Javier. Didn't hear from you, so, you know, like we said, we got a short window here." He busied himself by running a hand over the table as if wiping off salt. "Picked up a kid, wants out so he took the deal." Javier looked at the green tea in the white cup. "Be advised. Your name is still on the knock-list now at ICE. They might come by tonight, next week...never."

"Alex's gonna have an appearance in a couple months." Morales sounded like he was explaining what to order off the menu, but his eyes told Javier this guy might have been pulling for Alex. "First offense, judge will go easy on him, but he's gonna do time at a camp." Javier heard the word camp and couldn't help but think of water sports and tents.

"Few months of juvie probably just what he needs." It was a common refrain but rarely panned out.

Morales shook his head. "News flash, *hermano*, Alex just earned a stripe. The homies are gonna shower him with love which you, big brother, can't compete with." He leaned in, elbows on the table. "I was you, Javier, grew up on Orion fifteen years ago. Most things still the same. Can't stand the shit they call music these days but same *vida loca*. Had a little knucklehead brother with a funky attitude, put our whole family at risk—'cause we were in the shadows, just like you." He poked his finger straight at Javier. "That's a special kind of stress you gotta pull around."

He leaned back, leaving Freemon to put the cherry on their routine. "Just remember this. We're trying to squash things before the bullets start flying, Javier. If I was you, I'd do whatever I could to get Alex to sit this one out or tell him to grow eyes in the back of his head. Cartels are coming hard for the lab."

Without another word the two officers got up and walked out leaving Javier wondering if he had to pay for the tea.

▪   ▪   ▪

Even though he didn't have a shift that evening, Javier went into work anyway, feeling moody and peevish. The first call was for an abandoned vehicle at an apartment complex. It was the latest part of Betzaida's evolving business plan, to offer apartment buildings preferred rates for contract business. In addition to funding her loan, Lupe had made some introductions on Betzaida's behalf to find new opportunities, and this complex was the start of this new niche. On the way, they swung past Denker and spotted Alex leaning against a tree, already back from the barbecue.

"He's on pro-ba-tion," Javier said. "Can't get to juvie fast enough."

Betzaida slowly shook her head. "I oughta go snatch that boy right now."

In the back, few of the *capitanes* leaned against fences smoking blunts. Javier recognized the one with the area code ink and the marbled goatee from Lupe's picture and Dolores's funeral. The guy's phone rang, and he stepped off into the dark. Curbside, the jugglers were a loose confederation, some standing hands in pockets, others sprawled out on the benches, the dinner rush still another hour away. And then there was Alex, motionless and not quite on-script. The other boys would laugh at something on a phone, wave him over. He'd wander over, feign interest, and just as quickly slip away. His only real payoff appeared to have come and gone already—the steady lunchtime recruitment that was now over like the first stage of a space-rocket, a boost into position and then gone.

The muzzle flash caught the corner of Javier's eye a millisecond before he heard the shots going off like fireworks. Javier and Betzaida dove down, though kept an eye just over the dash. People screamed then ran for cover, engines gunned and tires squealed. Mothers scooped up their kids and booked it across the park, leaving strollers behind, the whole place emptied in seconds. Javier clocked the park for any sign of Alex but saw nothing, just a few jugglers sprinting for the shadows, clutching their beltless, oversized pants. Against the backboard of the handball courts, he could see two bodies slumped beneath a pair of red smears, chins on their chests as if napping.

A black Ford F-150 pickup drove slowly through the park from the opposite side. It came to a stop near the handball courts where four men got out, two wearing cowboy hats, walked up to the two bodies, pulled out pistols from their waistbands, grabbed the hair of each lifeless head, and fired single shots through the mouths. One of the men pulled the wallets from each victim, took something out and held it up to the lifeless heads while another took out his phone and took pictures. All four walked casually back to the truck like they'd come to the park on the wrong day for a birthday party. Three climbed in while the fourth took his time scanning the park, quickly spotting Delilah and sending Betzaida and Javier diving back under the dash. Javier heard the engine crank then the sound of it getting louder as it came closer to Delilah then fading as it turned and left the area in no apparent rush. Apart from a few car alarms cycling uselessly through their burps and whirs, the park was silent. Betzaida wasn't waiting around. In minutes, there'd be a police perimeter, no one in or out, and they'd be forced to give a statement.

Ten minutes later, they were back in the Box where Javier went straight for a dusty bottle of Don Carlo that sat on a top shelf. He poured a set of shots for the two of them. Neither said anything until the third round when they finally made a toast to being spared from the ugly side of chance.

"Jesus, Betz." Javier thought the tequila would take the edge off, but it only served to loosen a fresh wave of panic. "What the fuck?" He took out his phone and tried texting Alex. No response. Betzaida reached for the scanner and turned it on. Dispatch was spitting out APBs with suspect descriptions, including several references to cowboy hats, cop shorthand for cartels. Betzaida looked out the window then at Javier.

She tossed a shot back and poured both of them another. "To Yanira."

When he got home that night, the decks of his mind having been swept clean from both the tequila and adrenaline, Javier checked his email to see if he'd received a response from the Lorenzo Dimas guy that Patel had been corresponding with, but there was nothing. He tried calling the *Times* to see if he might get his voicemail and got bounced around to an assignment desk which sounded like a dead end but he left his name, number, referenced Patel, and right before he was about to hang up managed to mention a fire in

Hyderabad. He then dug Alex's Chromebook out of his backpack, turned it on and scrolled through his search history. Not surprisingly the most recent searches were still back in August, six months ago, the last time he'd made any attempt at schoolwork. He clicked on two of the saved searches; one was of a site for an organization called Center for Public Integrity which was written in English and immediately struck Javier as too dense and scholarly for Alex. The second, sin-nombre.org, was written in Spanish though featured mostly pictures with captions: articles of clothing, personal effects, shoes belonging to those who had died crossing the border. The bodies of the deceased were no longer recognizable, having been left to the elements too long. The teddy bears, jewelry, dentures, pill jars, knives, and all manner of crosses found in the Sonoran sands next to the prostrate bodies, now mostly bones and hair. And there it was, at the bottom of the page, Yanira's inhaler with its daisy blossom stickers, the only bookmark on Alex's browser.

CHAPTER 28

By Thursday, Deirdre Hemingway was so sick of meetings and fires and progress reports that she had a standing hour every week with a split of Perignon and Stefan's magic fingers. Her subscription rates were twice the industry average, had been for the past six quarters, leaving her less and less runway to sustain the rate. She'd grown hostile with her staff, sharp with her friends, juggled chainsaws in her sleep, and woke every day making lists. Stefan, six floors down, was her salvation.

She took the stairs to avoid seeing anyone, unwilling to squeeze out one more clever comment in the elevator. She let herself into Stefan's office with her own pass card, something not even Stefan had as she had leased the office for herself and was now the one and only client Stefan had in the building. She pulled the split from the mini-fridge and popped the cork, letting it carom off the ceiling and land in a corner then poured herself a flute. She pulled out her phone, listened to a Bach piano cantata, one she had struggled with as a child, one of the few things she ever found beyond her abilities. Lately she'd started ignoring phone calls to finger the first four measures on the edge of her glass desk, doing her best to capture the piano forte in her mind's ear. Her mother had always said she had artless fingers.

She finished her champagne in three gulps, took off her clothes, wrapped herself in a towel, and got on the table. She lay on her stomach, her face resting in what she always thought looked like a toilet seat, staring at the floor. The few minutes before Stefan entered were often the only moments of peace she had all week.

The door opened. She neither looked up nor said anything. Some days the massage was wordless, and she hoped today would be one of those. The first hint of trouble was the way the door shut. It normally closed on its own, gently clicking, a delicate sound, but today she could hear the pneumatic arm on the door let out a slight hiss as the door was pushed closed.

The second hint was the cologne. Stefan usually wore something with sandalwood, but the aroma today was more stringent. Perhaps, she thought, he had been given a gift from his husband. She'd had that experience too many times with all three of her exes, overly fragrant scents she'd wear once out of courtesy and then flush.

A stack of papers made a thud as it landed directly below her face, giving her a clear view of something with a legal heading. Someone versus someone. And Jones' card clipped to the right corner.

"That's a grand jury indictment with your name on it," said Jones, pulling a robe off a hook in the wall. "Panama Papers...the gift that keeps on giving."

The Panama Papers were an international data-dump of over eleven million files several years ago exposing sovereign wealth holdings of current and former government officials as well as very high net worth individuals. It revealed naked corruption—prime ministers from Iceland, Mongolia, Spain, and Pakistan were forced from office. Billionaires from six continents were brought to trial on tax and wire fraud charges that led to criminal verdicts totaling over six hundred years of sentencing. The attorney general had followed the breadcrumbs now to the feet of Deirdre and twelve others—a who's who of the most wealthy and influential names in Los Angeles.

She rolled over onto her back, careful to bring the towel with her. Jones handed her the robe and turned his back.

"Do I know you," she stole a glance at Jones' card, "Mr. Jones?"

He waited for a respectful moment before turning around. "Consider this a heads-up. You have forty-eight hours to get out in front of it before the Eleventh District makes its announcement."

She wasn't accustomed to hearing someone explain her options and poured herself another glass before picking up the indictment. "I see I'm in good company, at least." The names on the indictment were all Hollywood moguls, tech leaders, the only California chef with two Michelin stars. "And where do you come into the picture?"

"I can't do anything about that." He crossed his legs and threw his chin at the ream of paper. "But it's only an indictment." He watched her review the first page. "I have a long reach, Ms. Hemingway. In six months' time, a lot can happen. Things get lost...people disappear." He studied her reaction—she gave none—and then continued. "I'll make sure the case gets dropped—for you and the rest of your breakfast club."

She took a seat, ran her eyes up and down the man in front of her then examined her nails. "I get several offers a year from fixers. I wouldn't trust them to put together a birthday party for my niece. In fact, I loathe your type because ultimately, I rely on your type...for these little moments." She tipped the last of the champagne and inspected the glass. "You need to convince me you have this...reach. I don't drive a car off the lot until I've taken it on the freeway first."

Jones put his hands on the armrests. "I don't audition, and I don't negotiate. You want a work sample, fine, but it comes with a price."

She stared at him, her face a fortress.

"You have an item coming up with the FCC in a week. Something to do with mobile data."

"Go on."

"You want modifications to rules that would keep carriers from having certain perpetuity rights to your content." Her eyes betrayed nothing, her mouth a straight line. "We both know the commissioner finds your claims frivolous. No way he approves the changes. So when I get you those modifications—and I will—I'll expect you, in turn, to reach out to the other twelve names on that indictment"—he pointed at the stack of papers—"and make sure we have a complete football team."

"What's in it for you?"

"Don't worry about me. And don't think your brand won't benefit. These next few months will be a PR coup. You're about to be part of something very special, Ms. Hemingway. You'll be the keystone to a major redevelopment project."

She tilted her head back. "Redevelopment sounds very exotic. Are we going to Haiti?"

Jones flashed a mock smile. "Panorama City. Forty-five minutes over the hill from here."

"Good lord, not the Valley." She frowned. She rarely spent any time east of the 405 or north of the 101. "What do you want, Mr. Jones?"

"You and your group of co-conspirators are going to offer six hundred of the best and brightest young people in Southern California one-year internships with the chance to go full time at each of your firms."

Her eyebrows arched. "In the Valley." She seemed still stuck on the location.

"Anyone with life science IP, two million followers, carbon capture proof-of-concept, or a fucking app for enlightenment. Get the picture?"

"Sounds like a reality show, Mr. Jones."

"Only gunners and raw talent, Ms. Hemingway, the sharpest in the shed. You'll be wondering why you hadn't dreamed this idea up sooner." She noticed Jones watching her thumb and forefinger rubbing together and immediately stopped. "But you need to put the word out, like today. Wrangle the other names on the indictment for a meeting next week." He nodded again at the ream of paper. "Otherwise, you'll be taking that long walk from the corner office, two guys in blue nylon jackets on each of your elbows." Jones let the image sink in. "I'm starting with you given your prominence, but if you wanna take a pass, I'll just try the next name on the indictment." He sat forward, getting ready to leave.

"One condition." She tilted her head back slightly. "No more kidnapping Stefan. He's the best part of my week."

■　　　■　　　■

The small conference room at the Four Seasons was done in Berber carpets and original oils. A set of linen drapes framed a view of an azure pool which, at seven o'clock in the morning, was empty apart from the pool boy who ran his sieve along the surface with the same arching stroke of a Venetian gondolier. Everyone's phone had been collected at the door. A team of three technicians, each wearing headphones, swept the room for electronics then left.

"I love you, Deirdre, and have the tattoo to prove it, but you have me confused with someone who takes meetings before eleven." This was Olaf from Facebook, his eyes hidden behind a pair of shades, slumped forward, his chin on the glass table. "I call this poodle pose."

"Actually, Mr. Ovechkin, the start time was my idea." Jones entered the room and went to the front. "And if my math is correct, we have twelve heads here, not thirteen." A few people actually started counting, though it was obvious from the one empty chair that someone was missing.

"I don't expect Mr. Sanderson to show, so I'll get started. As you all know by now, the indictments have come down, but for now, you are each being labeled as John and Jane Does. Consider that my way of thanking you for being here today." Olaf slowly lifted his chin but kept on the sunglasses. "In three months, I can make certain these charges are dropped, and you can put this little misadventure behind you. Your name need never be made public, brand intact, all that."

A few fidgets.

"Let's hear the ransom." Jean Magee, founder of a biotech firm that held over six hundred mRNA patents. She had the cracked lips of a pack-a-day smoker and the hint of an early onset wattle.

"Door's right there, Ms. Magee." Jones gave her a fuck-with-me look. "AG's office is holding the gun, not me." He drew her into a stare-off for a matter of seconds before she reached for her water.

"Each of you, all twelve, will be opening offices in Panorama City. More specifically, Barrio Horseshoe. None of you have probably been within ten miles of the place, but by May, you will each have fifteen thousand square feet of office, lab, and studio space there. You will also each create forty-five internships to be filled by the top students in Southern California."

Several around the table shifted in their seats, the outline of the proposal not what they expected. Each of them had summer programs for undergrads, mostly sinecures for the children of execs, ten times the effort for the return.

"You're a fuckin' weirdo, this is a scam, and I'm outta here." It was Lance Bedard, CEO of Synecdoche, the largest AI software developer in California. He got halfway to the door.

"Leave at your own peril, Mr. Bedard, and as a courtesy, let me demonstrate what I mean when I say peril." Bedard slowed to a stop just before the door, folded his arms, and leaned against a wall. "The empty chair." Jones nodded at it then pressed a button on the conference phone sitting in the middle of the table. "Guy owns a lithium production company called Cureon. Remember that name. Greg Sanderson, a few of you may know him, extracts lithium from the Salton Sea which is a license to print money. Didn't feel he needed to show." The phone connected, an audible click, and a secretary came on. "Go ahead for Mr. Sanderson."

"This is Greg."

"Sorry you couldn't make it this morning, but I understand you had more urgent business to take care of."

"Who is this?"

"Turn on CNBC. Some breaking news for you."

"Who the fuck is this?"

On the screen behind him, Jones clicked on CNBC with the sound off. He then swung his gaze at Bedard. "What you waitin' for Lance, parking validation?"

On the crawl, the words Breaking News suddenly appeared. Jones turned up the volume. "...the EPA has filed an injunction against Cureon to suspend all operations. According to the court filing which the EPA has just released, and I'm reading now, 'Cureon's malfeasance has jeopardized a portion of the Colorado River watershed which irrigates over six million acres of farmland.' Representatives from Cureon have not been available for comment, but its stock price has already fallen over 80 percent in early trading and is expected to sink even further. For more now, let's go to—"

Jones turned the screen off, the room stone silent, everyone looking at the conference phone imagining this Greg guy, his world suddenly imploding. Long pause.

"What the fuck did you do, Jones? What the fuck—"

"Life's full of choices, eh, Greggy boy?" Jones clicked off then turned to the others, now thoroughly chastened. "That explains the early hour for today's meeting. EPA loves to drop their bombs before eight. Shows they're real go-getters." Jones motioned to someone standing outside the glass doors. One of the technicians came in carrying a box containing the phones which were then quickly passed back, each of the eleven immediately hitting speed dials, issuing directives, setting up meetings. Bedard was back in his seat.

"Oh, and one more thing." Jones held his hand up, instant silence once again, everyone staring at him. "We're on the clock here. Shit goes live in six months. You're either in or out."

CHAPTER 29

They slept shoulder to shoulder, at least thirty of them sardine-style. The sign outside said Officina Medical, though it had long stopped providing any sort of medical care. For the past twenty years, it had served as the last lay-up before crossing the river. Javier, only eleven, lay on his back, unwilling to turn on his side since it would create a vacuum of space the large man wearing the Cruz Azul jersey would quickly fill up. Yanira, his four-year-old sister, on his other side, poked him, his signal to get up with her to go to the bathroom.

When they had left Jalisco, Mama had taken two bubble packs of pills in addition to her inhaler to help treat Yanira's asthma, always a problem in the dry heat. But during the ride north on La Bestia, the train which was both legendarily unsafe and undeniably free, Mama had been separated from her three children during a "document" check by a local constabulary. It was a shakedown, one that Mama had anticipated. She'd drilled into Javier's head that he should keep Alex and Yanira on the train no matter what, that she would be released within a few days, and that she would rejoin them on the US side of the border at a tia's house in San Diego. Most families had to split up and reunite several times on the journey north. She'd given Javier Yanira's asthma medication for just this reason.

The medication irritated Yanira's bladder so there was a nightly ritual—Javier insisted she never go to the bathroom alone. That night, when she poked him, they both grabbed their backpacks in the dark and stepped over the snoring bodies as best they could. The bathroom was really just a closet with a bucket that had to be taken outside after each use. He offered to hold her backpack, but she had become accustomed to carrying it with her at all times, her handful of possessions she'd been allowed to bring all neatly arranged inside.

The door closed behind her, and Javier could hear the sound of the lock, most likely a rusty nail stuck through some type of latch, which she had been told from an early age to always use.

Javier leaned against the door and looked down the hallway, first left, then right, one door at each end. He imagined it as it was originally designed, a place for people to get treatment, to mend and then leave. There would be families in the waiting room, monitors with their readouts, nurses with their kind, efficient manner. Instead, there were only cabinets with their doors missing and mattress springs, a calendar from 1981, and windows covered with newspaper. Javier looked down at his feet, both of his big toes sticking out of his shoes and losing their nails from the endless walking. He figured the man in the Cruz Azul shirt was lying flat on his back, now, his girth finally able to spread.

In the distance, Javier could hear a truck, shifting gears as it climbed up the hill. The engine had the familiar tone. No one would be driving the streets in this area at this hour other than the military. Javier was familiar with the drill—men in fatigues carrying rifles would show up and collect soborno. If the count looked light, the soldiers would have to flex on the coyotes, make them feel it, and fill their truck with some unlucky souls which would eventually hurt business back in Jalisco. At the end of the quarter, if their colleagues at Border Patrol were running behind on their quota, they'd snatch a truckload and drop them off at TJ or Calexico. In return, they would expect reciprocity when it came time to take pictures of impounded contraband displayed on floors, masked officers standing guard over the seizure.

Javier knew from the animated discussion going on outside that tonight was going to be one of those nights. If things between coyotes and the army went well, the small talk would be inaudible, maybe some laughs, and the men in the fatigues would never get out of the truck. But Javier could hear the doors opening and the back gate coming down. He knew the men in the fatigues would start blowing their whistles any second.

"Yanira! Darse prisa. ¡Tenemos que irnos!" The lights of some small Texas border town blinked through the waiting room window.

"Okay, I'm almost done," she replied in her small voice.

The hallway door was already wide open, but the first soldier through made a show of slamming it with the butt end of his carbine. A flashlight was fastened to the stock and swept a path back and forth, followed by more flashlights behind him. The sound of the boots coming down the hall got everyone up, and Javier started tugging on the handle of the bathroom/closet, but it was locked.

"Afuera, Yanira!"

A beam of flashlight momentarily blinded Javier, and as he brought his hand up to shield his eyes, he felt a boot push him in the small of his back. He spilled forward face first and got up amidst a swarm of people now pushing for the exits, unwilling to be cornered by federales in one of the medical offices. Javier turned to look at the bathroom door now shaking from Yanira's desperate attempts to unlock it.

"Yanira!" Javier shouted.

It was the shouting that did it. The soldiers hated loud noises at night. Javier felt his chin turn before the pain ever caught up with him. He was out before his head hit the floor. When he woke up, he was in the back of the transport, lying on the floor. He sat up slowly, felt the pain and swelling in his jaw, moved it back and forth slowly. He quickly realized he was in the back of a transport and judging from the expressions of those around him, the coyotes were not the ones driving. Two men in blue camouflage sat at the rear gate leaning on their assault rifles, their heads bouncing in unison with the rest of the passengers. Javier scanned the faces quickly for Yanira and Alex.

"Javi!" It was Alex. "Yanira's still back there." The sudden commotion drew the attention of one of the soldiers who made sure to lock eyes with Javier. He slid one hand down the stock and let it rest on the trigger. No one was going anywhere.

The man in the Cruz Azul shirt, sitting on the bench across from Javier, passed him an unopened bottle of water and a 7-Eleven burrito. He thanked him and gave them to Alex who opened both. It was then that Javier saw the lanyard on the bottom loop of Alex's backpack—it was the lanyard Yanira had made to distinguish hers from Alex's. In the dark, she'd taken his and Alex now had hers. Javier knew Alex, a sensitive kid under normal circumstances, would blame himself for the confusion. He snatched the backpack, complete with Yanira's inhaler and medicine and stuffed it in his own. He'd figure out some excuse later for why Alex no longer had any of his belongings. Alex believed everything his older brother said.

Seven years later, there on the Sin Nombre website was a picture of Alex's backpack which Yanira had inadvertently picked up. Next to it was a caption:

"Found on four-year-old female victim, cause of death: asthmatic reaction."

CHAPTER 30

The scene outside Royce Hall had the buzz of a celebrity appearance, the lines spilling through the Gothic arches and out onto the grassy quad. It was a hot ticket with free admission, the only prerequisite being a bloodlust for achievement and an outsized image of yourself rampaging behind a modest demeanor.

"My name is Deirdre Hemingway, and I am the President of Acquisitions and Production at Dispatch Films." There was a round of applause which she ignored and spoke over. "UCLA, right? So, no chance we have any writers or dare I say actors with us this evening?" Laughter, coiled and tense. Most in the crowd saw their lives as genuinely cinematic.

Like Deirdre herself, these were the souls that thirsted for any chance to prove themselves. Deadlines and applications were the gateway through which they climbed the mountain. UCLA was the last stop on the recruitment push for Can City, a one-year program for only the "most qualified"—like blood in the water for this crowd—looking to get into entertainment, biotech, fintech, green-tech, tech-tech, software development, or just about any top-tier career with the most competitive firms. They had six hundred slots and expected over ten thousand applicants. A ratio like this produced the special strain of endorphins that came only from the lowest regions of the limbic system.

"We will offer you the chance to come try a variety of fields in a short course of time, finish your university credit, and, next year, if you have what it takes, possibly be offered a position." A QR code popped up on the screen behind her, a sea of phones shot up. The starting pistol had just been fired.

Eleven of the largest Los Angeles companies had agreed, at the behest of Ms. Hemingway whose initial appeal went unheeded until she sent the first fifty pages of the indictment with which Jones had interrupted her champagne rub. Can City would become a proving ground for the most talented and most ambitious to audition for the Big Six in Tech, Big Five in accounting, Big Four in entertainment, and Big Three in pharma. Can City would be the place where scripts got green-lit, social media got monetized, biofuels went from concept to prototype, and where tastemakers wandered around with selfie sticks, a Disneyland for Zoomers who liked to "move fast and break things."

Then the coup de grace. "While we would love to accept each and every one of you, we have only a limited number of slots. There are three hundred units in those three residential towers, total." Everyone in attendance only looked at the top three floors, the balcony units, which would one day be their home. "That being said, count the nine people around you, front, back, and sides. Only one of you will be part of history." Everyone smiled, laughed, looked around at each other playing along, wishing each other good luck while privately sending their neighbors thoughts of debilitating and possibly terminal illness.

CHAPTER 31

Javier got out to survey the crash scene: a T-boned Prius, nearly cleaved in two, at Sepulveda and Roscoe, the field of wreckage wide enough to close all but one lane in each direction. The other vehicle was across the street resting on its side. No skid marks, suggesting the other driver had gunned the light, the physics of an acceleration usually catastrophic. All three occupants were "circling," EMT shorthand for likely DOAs which meant this was going to be a felony scene which meant another three hours taking measurements and pictures before anyone was getting towed.

"We're outta here," Javier said. "The sarge just called in MAIT," the police accident investigation team. They got back into Delilah just as Bergosian rolled up in a shiny new ten-ton rotator rig, big enough to pick up the 7-Eleven across the street and drop it in the middle of the road. He slowed as he approached Betzaida, rolled down his window, and honked his horn, a bone-rattling blast, then pointed at a disabled Metro bus sitting in the middle of lanes blocking traffic.

"You wanna go back and get your…oh, that's right." Bergosian, ten feet up in the cab relishing the moment, banged his hand on the side of his door and gave a little wink. Only a rotator, which cost six figures used, would be able to haul a Metro bus. "You can borrow mine if you want."

"It's your world, Kris. I'm just visiting." Betzaida whistled and spun a finger in the air, Javier saw Mark sitting in the passenger seat. They traded subtle nods out of sight of their respective bosses before Javier jumped into Delilah and heard his phone alarm going off. He pulled it out and studied a blinking red dot set against a map.

"What the hell is Alex doing in Studio City?" He'd installed another tracking app on Alex's phone with a geofence along the south side of the 101. The blinking dot was stationary, the location oddly familiar.

"This ain't good, Betz." Javier widened the map. Betzaida pulled into traffic, shaking her head, turned off the radios, and hit the strobes on the light bar. "Jesus, he's going to Lupe's." He went back through the texts from Leslie and entered the address she had texted him and punched it into the GPS. A sudden image emerged in his mind's eye, the calendar in Lupe's kitchen with the black line spanning two weeks: FRANCE. The house was going to be empty.

Javier trawled his recollections from the meet-and-greet, tried to piece together some explanation that didn't include Alex and a second felony. Maybe Lupe hadn't gone on vacation. Maybe Alex had struck up a friendship with Lupe's two boys and was playing video games with one of them. His pulse came back down, but he knew he was kidding himself. That was last year's version of Alex.

He checked Alex's search history from his phone for the past few days. He threw his head back. "He's been watching lock-picking videos." He scrolled some more. "Here's another—how to disable alarms. He's going there to boost the place."

Betzaida gave Javier a quick look then changed lanes to exit the 101. "Nice house, nice security. ADT's already calling it in, pulling up the cameras. Text his ass."

He texted Alex.

WTF

Javier pictured Alex going upstairs, tossing the bedrooms. "Denker's putting him up to this." Just prior to getting jumped in, it was customary for the initiates to rob someone or somewhere and deliver the proceeds prior to the ritual beatdown. They were turning left on Cahuenga, starting to climb the hills. Betzaida turned on the scanner to listen to the calls going out.

"Boy's got a death wish." Betzaida tapped the steering wheel with her thumb. "Real dumbass jihad shit."

They were high enough now to have a view of the Valley, the setting sun lighting up some of the Burbank high-rises, the scale and distance of things rendering them all quaint.

"I think he found out about Yanira."

Betzaida didn't say anything, just a slight shake of the head, another conversation for another time. The GPS lady, her cooing voice barely audible over Delilah's low-gear rev, was narrating a steady stream of upcoming turns and forks.

"Boy is out on bail?" Betzaida said, leaning into a hairpin curve.

"He's probably got at least one other person with him, both gonna be jumpy as hell. Probably strapped. And high." Alex was going to be in a standoff soon. Javier sent Alex another text.

cops r coming

He knew Alex wouldn't see the text, another fruitless effort, a tree falling in the woods with no one to hear it. It wasn't so long ago, though, that if the tree fell, Javier was there with a list of questions and a set of consequences. Last spring, he'd fished a pair of black socks with white stripes out of Alex's backpack.

"*Porque*?" He'd held one of the socks out with a pen, already certain it didn't belong to Alex who then confessed to a schoolyard prank that ended up with a younger boy going home barefoot. The next day, Javier had taken the morning off from school to make sure Alex made amends and took his detentions. But in the last two months, he'd lost the bead on Alex, stopped playing sheepdog, and all those little moments like threads in a tether were now gone.

They arrived at Lupe's address, the dial pad to the driveway gate hanging out by a few wires. The house and a few trees were decoratively uplit, though the house was dark inside. Javier turned the police scanner up.

"All units, 1011 in progress near Burliner and Fox. Suspect is armed." The house was going to be soon surrounded, so whatever Javier was going to do, he had to do it now. Light suddenly flashed from a second-story window, probably Alex rummaging the master bedroom for Lupe's gold. Javier punched in another text:

c ur light

No response.

"We gotta talk him outta there, Javi. Kid's not gonna do well in this spot."

The sirens were getting louder, the outcome all but certain without some type of intervention.

Javier got out and started walking toward the house. "Tell the cops I'm in there."

Javier approached the massive front door with its hand-worked bas-relief, a blinking red light letting him know he was now on camera, possibly even Lupe's phone as she biked Les Champs-Elysées. The picks were still in the jimmied lock, and the door opened with a push. Javier went through.

"Alex!" Javier stood in the atrium, the spectral glow of Delilah's headlights casting a silver wash over the interior. "Alex, listen to me." No response, but he could hear footsteps and then voices coming from upstairs, Alex and maybe Baby Buddha.

"Alex, the place is going to be surrounded in about a minute. We have to walk out together, now."

Still no response. Outside, a helicopter spotlight was waving around on the grass, the noise of the engine rising and falling with each pass.

He tried a more conversational tone. "Alex, we have a window here. Lupe won't press charges, but you have to do the right thing." He slid a living room curtain back as he said this and peered out. Two cruisers were now parked on the grass, four officers with guns drawn. Javier started slowly walking up the stairs. "Alex, please don't shoot. I'm unarmed." He was working off a lifetime of cop shows. More footsteps, voices, something falling over, then broken glass. Javier was halfway up when he saw a shadow dart down the hallway. LAPD had poured on the ultra-brights giving the scene inside a gauzy effect. The voices were now shouting at each other, a volley of accusations, this team of DIY burglars having apparently missed the videos about police encirclement.

"Alex, don't do anything stu—"

Someone came up on Javier's right while he was looking left, and pushed him down the stairs. Javier managed to tuck his head and to reach out for a banister which stopped him before he got to the bottom. A second person ran past him, down the stairs, and through the living room. Javier couldn't see who, but he knew they would be trying the back door, which was probably the first place cops had set up. The voice on the bullhorn came out like a net.

"Put your hands up!" Even without the cops, there was nowhere to go unless you wanted to go for a swim. There was only the pool and then a fifty-foot drop.

Javier was now the only person in the house, leaving him looking more like a suspect himself and less like the concerned brother.

He went to the front door and stuck his hands out. "I'm unarmed!" he shouted, certain the cops were ready to drill anything that moved. "I'm coming out!"

He waited for a response. He just hoped when he ended up face down with a bunch of knees on his back that he would be on that supple grass and not the brick walkway.

"Javier!" It was Betzaida shouting from the front of the house.

"I'm okay! I'm coming out. Tell 'em..." He wasn't sure why he was telling her, as if she were an interpreter. "I'm the brother!"

It sounded ridiculous. He stuck his head out, wincing at the glare of the lights. Then he walked out onto the portico, a small circle of lasers dancing over his abdomen and upper chest. Turning around with his arms raised, he followed the directions repeated endlessly on the bullhorn telling him to walk backward then to lie face down, ankles crossed, arms out. A part of him hated giving these officers the satisfaction of playing hero with another brown boy from the Shoe, this mistaken moment a cliché he had vowed to never be part of; and yet here he was prone on the lawn face down. The pile-on was immediate. He was surprised at how quickly his lungs compressed, how hard it was to breathe.

He was cuffed and led to a cruiser where he figured he would at least see Alex, now a repeat offender at the ripe age of thirteen. But the back seat was empty. It smelled of urine and he was told to sit. Through the windshield, he could see Betzaida talking insistently to a couple of officers. She was on and off her phone at least half a dozen times, most likely reaching out to some of her contacts in the department who might be able to vouch for her. Detectives Morales arrived alone in a Crown Vic, spotted Javier, and gave a noncommittal look before joining a huddle of officers convening on Lupe's front lawn. The jury was still out on Morales, as far as Javier was concerned. He'd been stiffed by Alex but seemed to know it was coming, perhaps a replay from his own life. It didn't mean he was sympathetic. Cops who'd grown up in the streets would sometimes get their heads bent when they stuck on their badge, every call another chance to restage whatever psychodrama really drove them. Morales went straight to the sergeant who kept glancing at Javier the more Morales talked. Ten minutes later, the sergeant came over to the squad car where Javier was being detained and undid the cuffs.

Betzaida was standing off to the side and came over once he was out of the backseat. She took his head in both hands.

"Jesus, Javi, what the fuck were you thinkin'?"

It seemed pointless to try and answer. "I guess they got Alex, huh."

Betzaida gestured toward the gate that separated the front and back of the house. "C'mon over here." They walked across the lawn and through a redwood gate to a side yard where two boys were in a seated position, hands cuffed behind their back. Ronnie the Viking, the other dude, Gito. A handful of officers milled around, one of them with his flashlight out looking for something in the grass.

Javier scanned the area looking for Alex. "Wait, what?"

"Those fools look familiar?"

"Yeah, but where's Alex? I mean his phone—"

Then it clicked. He pictured Alex in the game room with the Ronnie guy then getting a ride home with him. He'd left the phone in Ronnie's SUV knowing Javier had a tracking app on it, thus sending him on this goose chase. He could see Alex at Denker right now, laughing it up with Baby Buddha and the rest of the jugglers. He turned his eyes to the night sky, his anger now in freefall.

"We're going to the park, Betz." Javier started walking toward Delilah.

Betzaida got in front of him and tried to get her hands on his shoulders, but he shook them off. "Javi, take a minute and breathe, okay. You're—"

He turned sharply on her and stuck a finger in her face. "In case you missed it, I was just lit up like a Christmas tree then turned into a human football back there, Betz, so yeah, he and I need to have a little talk."

"I get it, but that boy is—"

"You drive, Betz, or I'll call an Uber." He stood and glared, heat coming off his eyes.

"All right, all right, Javi, just...just take it down a notch. You did the right thing tonight, and Alex would be grateful knowing you—"

"Bullshit, he'd be grateful if Officer Fucknuts back there had dropped me." He turned back to the truck and got in, slamming the door. "Cocksucker's been..." He bit it off and stared at Lupe's house. For a brief moment, he considered her disappointment when his name came up in the police report. Alex had just cost him the scholarship, the off-ramp he'd been planning on now closed with a row of traffic cones.

On the ride over, Betzaida kept talking, reminding Javier this wasn't the time to confront Alex, that he had no idea how that hockey player kid ended up with Alex's phone, that he owed it to Alex to do some fact finding, but Javier wasn't listening. He just stared out the passenger window lost in a sulfuric rage. They pulled up across from the handball courts, but before Javier could get out, Betzaida grabbed his arm.

"Just ask simple questions. Give him some space."

He pulled his arm free. "I'll give him space—between his front teeth." Alex was off to the side as usual, one foot against a light pole. He was vaping and didn't bother putting the pen away when he saw Delilah pull up and Javier get out.

"Not even on my list, Alex," Javier started. He tried counting to three, and almost got to two. "Any guess where Betz and I just came from?"

Alex exhaled a large cloud. "Pep Boys?" A few chuckles from the boys off to the right taking notice of the face-off.

"We just followed your new gamer friend to that lady Lupe's house."

Alex looked puzzled.

"That barbecue we went to, that house in the hills, the Thor-looking dude?"

"What the fuck are you talking about?"

Javier started coming toward him. "I'm talking about having some very amped-up cops aiming their guns at me because I was stupid enough to fall for your stupid fucking trick."

Betzaida got there and moved quickly in between them. "Alex, we're glad you're okay because Javier had a tracking app on your phone, and it looks like your phone was in the backseat of the hockey player's SUV, and Goldilocks there just committed armed robbery on the house where the barbecue was." She was talking a mile a minute to steal the wind from Javier.

Alex finally got it, the case of mistaken identity, and looked at Javier. "And you went up there, thinking it was me?"

Javier wanted to stay quiet but couldn't. "I went in that house, Alex, in the middle of an armed robbery because I thought you were in there."

Alex looked first at Betzaida then Javier and burst out laughing. For an odd moment, Javier felt warmed by the sound of his brother's laughter, something he hadn't heard in a long time, but in the end, it was the pin pulled from the grenade. He tackled Alex and once down, started punching him repeatedly until Betzaida horse-collared and pulled him off, some of the other jugglers coming by like a pack of hyenas. Alex got to his feet, nose bloodied, ready to charge Javier, but Betzaida was holding her arm out to ward off Alex while she stiff-armed Javier, staggering back and forth trying to get around her like a blitzing linebacker.

"Stop it you two!" Her voice had enough command to even freeze the small group of jugglers circling up with their phones out. Older sisters had a potency in the Shoe few others could lay claim to; when they intervened as publicly as this, boys took heed. She pushed Javier backward for twenty feet, in the direction of the truck. He backpedaled, leaning into Betzaida without taking his eyes off Alex. They came to rest against the hood of Delilah. Betzaida stuck a finger in Javier's face. "Do not fucking move."

Then she came back and waved Alex off to the side away from the others and started in with her most soothing version of, "All right, all right." Alex was panting and pacing, clearly aware the homies were taking notes.

"I'm coming back on him, Betz!" He spat it out. "Tell that piece of shit he better watch his six 'cause—" His voice cracked, and Betzaida took over before Alex turned into a puddle of grief and confusion. She grabbed him by the shoulders, pushed him around the handball backboard and slapped him hard. It had the immediate effect of smelling salts, his head instantly clear, his eyes suddenly dry and alert.

"Look, Alex, Javier was wrong tonight, and he knows it, and he'll come around in his own time and his own way, and you have every right to wanna come back, but Alex, no one is thinking straight right now because Javier and I just came from a crime scene where we thought you were the stickup guy, and Javier put his ass on the line in front of some very hyped-up police 'cause he thought you were in danger, and I know your head is way too hot to hear all this, but just understand, Alex, that we are both worried about you sitting up here playing Tony Montana." Alex was trying to look over her shoulder at Javier, but Betzaida stuck her face directly in front to block his view. "Not just Javier, but me too, Alex."

He shrugged her hand off his shoulder and walked away, then over his shoulder to Javier across the street. "I'm coming back on you." She wondered if this last threat was mostly for the benefit of all the others. "Lay you the fuck out," full-throated, then disappearing into the crowd of jugglers, giving him daps.

For the first time, Alex fit in.

CHAPTER 32

Javier felt something oddly comforting about the center breakdown lane of the northbound 405. The rules were different here, a temporary suspension of the norms that governed the rest of life. Every minute, hundreds of cars and trucks sped past in both directions, leaving the eight feet of pavement for disabled vehicles like an automotive DMZ. There was a thrill to it, and he never felt more alive than the moments when he'd walk up to a driver whose car wouldn't move another inch, a driver who might spend the rest of their lives in the breakdown lane waiting for a break in the traffic to cross to the other side, and there, amidst the barely managed chaos of the 405, winch the car up on the bed, and return this person and their vehicle to the relative sanity of Mission Tow.

Today, however, was not one of those days. He and Betzaida were parked in the breakdown lane in front of a disabled vehicle watching a woman in heels get out of her car and start walking towards them. She was oblivious to her surroundings, wandering across the white line into the number 4 lane of traffic, looking drunk and drawing honks from passing drivers.

The woman was driving a Cadillac Eldorado, a car that, no matter who its owner, always seemed to have an ashtray stuffed to overflowing with cigarette butts. Betzaida reached for the mic and turned on the squawk box.

"Ma'am, move over, away from the traffic." She waved an arm to indicate which way to go. The lady waved her off, went to the front of her car, leaned against it, and dialed a number on her phone.

"You gotta find Alex and figure a way to make it right, Javi." She looked at him then took another look at the car. "Need the sixteen gauge. Left-side locker," she said, telling Javier which cable to use.

A CHP cruiser pulled into the lane to do a courtesy check. Betzaida stuck her arm out the window and held up four fingers—Code 4, everything good—and the officer, apparently looking for an excuse to eat lunch, flashed her some blues and pulled in front of her.

Betzaida got out and walked to the driver of the Eldorado, now puffing away on a menthol, toy poodle in her arms, asked her a few questions, and quickly determined the problem. Betzaida lay down and scooted halfway under the car, pulled out her mag-light and was back standing in twenty seconds. "Someone's taken your catalytic converter, ma'am." She knew the lady had no idea what that was and didn't feel like explaining. "Don't worry. I can have you back on the road in two hours." Thefts of catalytic converters had spiked to the point Betzaida had ordered a pallet of them back in her shop.

The woman balked, looked at her dog, and shook her head. "No, thank you. I think I'll wait for Triple A." She lit another cigarette.

"Ma'am, I am Triple A."

The lady seemed more interested in the passing cars. "Well, then, I'll ask for another tow company." Betzaida didn't have the patience to play games. She whistled loudly to Javier and spun her index finger saddle-up style in the air. "Suit yourself."

She walked up to the cruiser, knocked on the window, and waited for the officer to roll down the window. "Lady refused service. I'm outta here."

The officer shook his head. "I don't know what it is, but you get the dumbest people on this stretch of the 405. The stories I could tell you." He fiddled with some buttons on his console then undid his seat belt to get out. "Ignorant."

Javier was already in the truck when Betzaida got back. "Look, Javier." She gestured with her hand. "Look at that lady. Doesn't know help when it's staring her in the face. Whatever world she's livin' in, she wants to do things her way. And what are you gonna do? I'm not gonna try to convince her that her car ain't going anywhere until she gets a new converter, and you know what, the next guy is gonna try to sell her a new transmission, and she'll probably go for it 'cause the advice is coming out of the mouth of some dude." She started Delilah, got some speed in the breakdown, and began her merge.

Javier sat and listened, one of Betzaida's rants that usually went nowhere but sometimes had a point. "This has something to do with Alex?"

"The boy is lost, and for whatever reason, in his bootleg world, he seems to want to crash and burn. I mean, the boy is out on bail, and he's already back on the benches, Javier, and then you run up there and wanna tap dance on his face." She was driving faster than she normally drove. "That lady back there, I deal with 'em all the time. Turn me down 'cause I'm not what they're expecting and they need something familiar, you know what I mean, some fat fuck with chains and a few jokes, and that ain't me." She usually stayed away from profanity, but Javier could feel she was working something out.

"What are you saying?"

"I'm saying Alex is so far outside his familiar that he's in fuck-it world, as in he's just lettin' it rip, and he don't give a shit where it all ends, and that, my half-brother, is a very dangerous place to be.

And you're still the best chance to rope him back in before something permanent happens to his ass."

Javier wanted to tell her he had his own ass to think about, that the chickens or whatever they were called were coming for him any day now, and the best thing he could do for Alex would be to stay away from him. Her too for that matter. His phone buzzed. A blocked number was calling. Javier let it go to voicemail, then read the transcript.

Lorenzo Dimas from the *LA Times* had called him back.

CHAPTER 33

4 a.m. in the Shoe was as much a place as it was a time, and the nightcrawlers who inhabited it moved like deep water fish, solitary and languid, pushing their carts down empty streets. When the tremors finally came, they were the first to see the buildings along Van Nuys sway, looking slightly drunk. Six weeks of fracking had finally taken its toll.

By the time the first emergency vehicles arrived, the dust cloud had turned the morning sunlight sepia-toned. Tall buildings stood Pisa-style, as if the top floors wanted to get a good look at the sidewalks. Nothing was symmetrical, no pattern that gave the eye a sense of causality, only the impressions that everything needed to come down. One whole block of commercial buildings, flat as a failed souffle, stood next to a block of retail clearly headed for demolition. Among the condemned, Mantrap Nails, a bar which hosted knife fights once a month in the parking lot, an Elks club, and a barber shop.

Six people were injured, and one elderly Black male, a veteran, sustained life-threatening injuries and was in ICU. The "Big Sink" as it was called in the news drew national and then world headlines for a day, and by the time the news cycle had moved on, so had Jim Madison. The fracking rigs had been struck and shipped back to North Dakota a week earlier to avoid any suspicions, leaving the crowning act to a half-mile cable rigged with C4 explosive. He flipped the switch himself on his phone while playing fetch with

Cerberus. He'd never liked Los Angeles, now home to his ex-wife who wrote *Keep the fuckin' dog* in the note she'd left on the kitchen island after deciding it wasn't too late to chase her dreams.

.   .   .

At the same time, another chunk of the Shoe was fated for demo as well, though in the case of the Roscoe Gardens, it had permits. Even so, when the excavators arrived, a few holdouts remained. Most eventually slunk away, leaving everything behind, though some dug in their heels and made an event out of it. One guy went viral, blathering on about the deep state and microchips, resulting in enough crowdfunded cash to buy a double-wide in Apple Valley.

Residents stood around in somber circles and watched the steel bucket teeth tear into each of the sixteen buildings that had been home to four generations. It brought out the voyeur in most of the residents, the tearaway views suddenly dioramas of some of the neighbors' lives, furniture still in place, dishes still sitting in sinks, clothes still hanging in closets, floor plants, and one cat who leaped just in time to elude the bucket. In four days, the trucks arrived to begin the costliest and longest part of the demo—trucking it all to landfill.

Someone had made a small memorial outside Dolores's unit which was quickly flattened under the wheel of an excavator which then swung its hydraulic arm on the community center. By the time all evidence of the Gardens had been erased, an eight-foot construction fence lined the place auguring some new use for the site.

Javier suspected that if anyone might know what was in store for all the real estate now suddenly vacant in the Shoe, Lonnie and her triumph of hair would be the source.

"Shipping containers, Javier. Hundreds of them, and when they get done—and I hate to say this 'cause they're friggin' firing me—it's gonna look amazing."

"You're being fired?" He said it with a mix of obligatory outrage and genuine sadness.

She waved a dismissive hand at him and turned her screen to show him the mock-ups for a new development to replace the two blocks of Van Nuys that had just imploded. "Hip little one-off Melrose stores, you know, like, all they sell is breakfast cereal. Freakin' jazz bar with those cute tables that have the little table lamps—whadda they call them, sconces?—shit ton of eateries, sit-down stand-up clothing optional." She scratched her jaw. "Not sure how hygienic that last place will be. They're calling it Can City. Get it? Oh yeah, and pickleball." She rolled her eyes and motioned for Javier to follow her outside so she could light up. She'd started smoking, or rather she'd started smoking again, the small cracks that ringed her lips starting to reappear.

"Yeah, the fuckers are cutting me loose next week," Lonnie said. She didn't appear particularly bothered by the news, pink-slips apparently a familiar part of employment for her. "Don't worry about me, hon, I already got something lined up."

"Oh yeah?" He'd only stopped in to see her five or six times, initially to pump her for information but lately to just say hello. "Where you going?"

"Santa Clarita." She blew out a cloud of smoke and tapped her cigarette. "Six Flags is expanding." She snorted. They looked out on Lake Mistake, now a proper body of water with all the amenities.

Enough sand had been trucked in to create a pseudo-beach for a long row of Adirondack chairs and rack for a few paddle boats. A twenty-foot pier gave people a place to dangle their feet and a raft was moored in the middle.

"Just wish I could have been around to see the station go in." She looked off at the expanse that had once been the Gardens. "Guess I'll have to come back to see it when it's all finished."

"Station?"

She lit another cigarette, waved her hand holding the lighter toward where the Gardens had stood. "Bullet train from Vegas. Not supposed to tell anyone. Had to sign an NDA, but what are they gonna do, fire me?" She made a puh-leez face. "Huge terminal complex. You won't recognize this place."

Javier had to say it again. "A train station?"

"And not that Amtrack shit, honey. One of those crazy fast trains."

"Jesus." Javier stood up straight. Lonnie was handing him the jackpot. "Anything you can email me? You know, for the Daily Python." He doubted Lonnie had ever believed his cover but kept the charade. "But don't worry, totally anonymous."

She made a no-problem face. "I been an email copy since the early days and never came off, so I got it all." She stuck her cigarettes back in her purse. "Be careful, Javier, intrepid reporter." She gave him a knowing look. "Jones does this shit for a living, and your little stunt with the potatoes?"

He didn't even try to pretend. "How'd he know it was me?" She looked at Javier's red Vans and made a face.

.　　.　　.

Javier went home and crossed himself when he saw the email from Lonnie. It took several hours unpacking the financials before Javier knew what the end game was. From the projections, he could see Jones intended to drive values in the Shoe into the ground. The profit and loss statement had the simple logic of red and black ink. Jones' investment showed the red tide going out. Then came the black. Jones strikes his tax credit deal then syndicates them to investors. But here is what Javier found—the inflection from red to black relied on the bullet train and its lavish station. Without it, the tax credits would be worth less than the investment. The losses would be in the billions.

Javier found Carlos' business card in his wallet, called him, and left a voicemail, reminding him who he was and asking him to call back certain he never would. Then he realized he'd have better luck if he just sent him the folder Lonnie had sent. He went online and searched "bullet train Los Angeles station" and found some dated articles. The CalTrans site had no mention of any terminals other than Rancho Cucamonga which was officially the LA terminus. He tried combing through hearings, looking for any mention of proposed route alterations, and only found pages and pages of change order documentation. Nothing about a station coming to the Shoe.

Jones' financials told a different story.

He opened a folder labeled "cadastrals" which held a collection of maps with grids, elevations, and a pair of dotted red lines going from the I-15 corridor through the Santa Susana Pass in the northeast Valley down into Panorama City. He zoomed in on the terminus and sure enough, he could see the footprints of the sixteen buildings that had made up the Gardens.

Carlos called back thirty minutes later.

"'Course I remember you, Javier. Betz's brother."

"Half-brother, but yeah, thanks for calling, and don't worry, I'm not looking for a job. It's not about work. It's something else." Javier was inching into it, hoping he'd seen the folder. "Look, I know this is gonna sound nuts. It's about the train project you were telling me about at Dolores's funeral."

"School project or something, right? No problem, happy to help."

"Little bit more than that, actually." Long pause. "Just don't hang up when you hear what I have to say." No use trying to dance around it. This guy was either going to be in or out very quickly. "The bullet train is getting routed to Panorama City, the Shoe." No dial tone. "Where the Gardens used to stand."

Pause. "Look Javier, I'm busy. You seem like a nice kid—"

"Just look at what I sent you." He did his best to sound reasonable without sounding demanding. "Please."

A chuckle then a pause. "Listen, Javier, there's no way that's happening."

"Check your email, Carlos. I'm not making this up. I sent you some files, and I wouldn't be calling unless I thought it was worth your time."

Another pause and a sigh. "What you're describing, that's like ten years of studies, another five in committees, state-wide propositions. You got at least ten agencies involved and that's just at the state level."

Javier could hear Carlos clicking his mouse. "Let me call you back."

Javier'd been hoping for a *right* back, but as it turned out, it was less than five minutes.

When he called back, Carlos sounded almost accusatory. "How the hell did you get this?" He knew better than to think Javier would rat out his source and didn't wait for an answer. "And why are you calling me? I mean, it's major shit, and yeah, of course I understand what this means, but why are you showing me all this?"

"It's not the station, Carlos. It's the guy financing it. Dude named Jones. You know him?"

"Everyone with a budget on the project knows him."

Javier had to wade into the conspiracies slowly. He started with the Gardens since he knew Carlos had grown up there. "Take what happened to Dolores, Carlos. Slim Charles worked Woodland, right? Dolores would never have been anywhere near where they found her." He could hear some affirmative sounds coming from Carlos.

Then he went into the Dogtown flood and the buses. He didn't bring up the burner, convinced any talk of Chechen mercenaries would be too much.

"Yeah, but...this? I mean, the station where the Gardens used to stand?" It sounded as though Carlos was trying to talk himself into the idea. "Truth is I've been noticing a few things around the Shoe that are definitely not right. Someone was doing some horizontal drilling under Van Nuys, right under the two blocks that just, you know, fell down." He sounded resigned to the preponderance of outlandishness. "The drilling caused all that." Carlos took a long inhale. "Check the seismograph. Nothing there."

Javier wasn't sure what Carlos was talking about. "I've seen the financials. His whole game is to stir up panic, drive down values, then he strong arms the government on tax credit deals. And the final piece to this is—"

"—the bullet train." Carlos said.

"You said you knew someone."

"Tasha, yeah, Tasha." Carlos sounded like he'd been thinking the same thing. "Lemme see if she's around."

Ten minutes later, all three of them were on a Facetime call. Carlos made the introductions, Tasha quickly getting to the point. "I know this shit already. Seen it up close. Muthafucka already put my pops in the hospital, yo. Elks Club fuckin' gone, his barber gone, that greasy spoon—what the fuck was it called—that place on the corner of Van Nuys and Roscoe—"

"Chato's," Javier and Carlos said at the same time.

"Yeah, Chaco's, all them places gone." Chato's was still there, but neither Carlos nor Javier felt like correcting her. She was getting into the back of a car now, the background noise gone. "I know Jones, and, fellas, he is a com-plete snake, and to be honest fellas, I took his bait once." She pulled a face. "Long fuckin' story I'm not gonna get into, but I know he put my daddy in the ICU for a week, so no, no, no, cocksucker got somethin' coming his way." She was getting out of the car now. "Sick of playing defense, fellas, time to get off the muthafuckin' ropes."

They spoke twice more that week and by Friday the plan was in place.

■   ■   ■

As Jones had predicted, the Councilman was in fact cutting many ribbons. Next to Lake Mistake, he announced one office building and three residential buildings would be going up on the lot, something called modular construction which would take no more than two weeks. He then fanned his arm as if he were hosting a game show. "And in the coming months, we shall see the dormant Pan City Steel once again spring to life, this time for high-tech start-ups and content creators." There was a smattering of applause as he ceremonially started a countdown timer that represented when the enormous building would reopen after decades sitting dormant.

The three residential towers were Can City dorms. There had been thousands of applications from throughout Southern California colleges to come live and work in the Shoe, and the lucky three hundred had started arriving in droves.

The party was underway. A few food trucks had quickly smelled opportunity and parked at the foot of the towers even though it was still unpaved. Some Can City engineer-types wired a compressor and refrigerant together and soon cold beer was on tap outside. A group of guys had trucked in several sheets of plywood and two by fours, a carton of screws, and now there were tables and benches. Someone strung lights from here to there and back again to give it the permanently festive look. Then the influencers started roaming the dorms and the shoreline of Lake Mistake with their selfie sticks, live streaming in such abundance you often saw on their posts other streamers walking past them doing just the same.

"Who are these people and where's the rocket ship that dropped them off?" Gio asked. "It's like an invasion, but all they do is work."

"And drink. And eat," added Javier. They were a tribe, really, that had parachuted into the Shoe with the easy confidence that made it seem so natural for them to be now living in a part of LA they had never even heard of two months prior. They were a salad ratio—white kids the lettuce and everyone else in smaller quantities, all of them purposeful and to a person, extra. Behind the four towers, Pan City Steel was now covered in scaffolding and a rotation of crews were in 24/7 shifts renovating its cavernous interior and brick exterior, small brown sandblasting clouds floating briefly out from under the green mesh covering.

"More offices, lab and studio space," said Lonnie, on a coffee and cigarette break with Javier one day on his way to work. It would be their last meeting. She stubbed her cigarette out, pulled out a handful of key cards, and handed a few to Javier. "Going-away present. I figure some of the local kids deserve a chance to check out the views up there." She looked off in the direction of the four towers standing like sentinels next to Lake Mistake. "Keys to the kingdom, Javier. Master pass to every lock on the campus. Knock yourself out." She gave him one more wink, tossed her butt on the ground, and walked out the gate. Javier could see the crown of her hair peeking over the top of the construction fence as she walked all the way down to Roscoe.

CHAPTER 34

To Javier's surprise, Lorenzo Dimas had agreed to come by Mission Tow and meet with him. Dimas had actually grown up in a Shoe-adjacent part of Van Nuys, knew the guy Janson who had originally owned Mission. Javier had heard the story from Betzaida, how she went from driver to owner in a matter of years. The guy Janson had gotten into a fight outside a liquor store and punched a guy who then hit his head on a curb, got up, left the scene, and later died from a brain hemorrhage. Camera footage from the liquor store led police straight to Janson, who had a wife, two kids, and three priors. He took a deal, got eight years in Lompoc, and then opened the floor up to offers on Mission Tow. Janson got five bidders, all of them versions of a three-year rent-to-own model. Betzaida took a longer view, a vesting schedule over eight years based on profit goals. That meant, given he'd be out in five, Janson would still have partial ownership, though she would be majority owner by then. The choice was easy.

"That was one of my first bylines for the *Times*." Lorenzo plopped down into a ripped-out bucket seat that was now part of the Box interior decor. Javier sat across from him trying to figure out why this guy hadn't taken off his sunglasses. "Tough luck for Janson, but tougher luck for the guy he punched."

Javier reached into the fridge. "Get you a water?"

Lorenzo shook his head. "Sorry, my pupils are dilated." He took off his sunglasses then immediately squinted and put them back on. "Doc is running some tests." Javier was relieved, unsure if he could trust someone who wore sunglasses inside. "I've been following Jones for a while now. Does the same shit everywhere he goes." Lorenzo seemed to be in his early forties, dressed in black jeans and a white polo which Javier noted was tucked in. "Blows up a neighborhood and then brings in a transit node. A subway or a rail stop, a freeway exit, an airport sometimes. I was pretty sure he was going to get involved in the bullet train here once it started stalling."

"Stalling?"

"Three years ago. Funding, authorizations, all that mess. Which is why I reached out to Raj."

"Who...oh right, Mr. Patel. How'd you guys meet?"

"The Indian financial markets were part of my beat many years ago, so I knew him from his private equity days. We stayed in touch, and when he told me about what happened to his brother, Jones, the garment factory fire in Hyderabad, I let him know Jones was sort of a project of mine."

"And so you'd been working together."

Lorenzo nodded. "Raj'd been feeding me documents, footage his cousins had been sending him linking Jones to the fire, and he was building a strong case. He wanted me to start publishing, lay the groundwork for a legal case. He called me a few days before the trip to San Jose. Apparently, he had copies of communications, some CCTV footage from the factory fire that all pointed indirectly to Jones. He knew a prosecutor in India who was going to put together an extradition motion if the evidence lined up."

The two sat in silence for a moment. Outside, Lester was racing through the front gates before taking a long, decelerating lap around the yard, apparently returning from a contested repo run. He'd be coming through the door in a few minutes.

"These people are still out there, trying to build a case on Jones?"

"Not only that, but the other way too." Lorenzo made a finger-gun and shot it at the facing wall. That explained the original hit-and-run on Jones. Folks were coming for him. "Look, Javier, I considered Raj more than a source. He was a friend, and he'd kick my ass right now if I didn't tell you to stay as far away from Jones as possible."

■   ■   ■

On the walk home, Javier was forced to detour off Roscoe past a small park that featured soccer games seven nights a week. As he listened to the shouts and whistles that floated over the field in the early evening air, a small peloton of boys on bikes sailed past Javier so close he could smell the bleach on their pressed T-shirts. They then quickly circled back and wove past him on both sides, cutting him off and forcing him to stop. They all stopped at the same time, though the last two, Itchy and Scratchy, stood on their pedals and coasted through a finale of figure-eights in front of Javier. And in the back, forearms on handlebars was Alex, throwing his hardest look at Javier.

"Looks like you're lost, homes." Itchy sat on his bike and shot his legs out. "Best break out that swell phone in your back pocket, ese. You'll need the *pendejo* app." His smile flattened, and he wagged his fingers gimme-style. "Your phone."

Javier glanced at the group and then stared at Alex. "Really?" He said it as if it was just the two of them. Then he took out his phone and tossed it at Itchy's feet.

Itchy ignored the phone, got off his bike, walked over to Javier with a showy roll, and quick-jabbed him in the stomach, sending him down on one knee, sucking air. He grabbed Javier by the hair and pulled his head back. "Some fuckin' respect!"

Javier tried to stand but just staggered and went back down on his knee, his breath a string of shallow gulps. There was a jagged pain in his left side like he'd been stabbed from the inside, some little creature in his stomach with a dull knife trying to cut his way out. "I told you to stay away from my brother." He croaked the words out. "Now I gotta kick your ass." He coughed up some blood and spat it out, never taking his eyes off Itchy.

Alex got off his bike, let it drop, and came and stood directly in front of Javier who was bent double, hands on his knees, gasping more than breathing.

"No fuckin' way, Alex."

Alex bent at the waist to meet Javier's eyes. "Don't look so good, Javi." He scowled with mock concern.

"You don't—" Javier grimaced and finally stood, "have to do this."

"No, but I want to."

His first punch, an uppercut, sent Javier backward like he'd walked into the wash of a jet engine. He didn't make any attempt to counter, just teetered looking drunk. The other boys pushed their bikes in, the main event underway. Javier could hear a cheer go up from the soccer game. Someone must have scored though for an addled minute he thought the cheers were for him. He knew he shouldn't, but he reached for his cheek, felt the blossoming pin cushion, the swelling nearly instantaneous. He looked at his fingers, no blood.

"It wasn't your fault, Alex. Her breather—" The next punch, a jab to Javier's jaw, his eyes now looking up at a paisley sky, hot wires of pain looping over his skull. His body arched then toppled, feeling the kicks landing pinata-style as soon as he'd hit the ground. He covered up, felt the warm moisture of blood streaming from his nose, over his lips, and he waited to pass out. Pain stretched on a line over his ribs. A boot stomped his head—Scratchy getting his payback from the beatdown at Tommy's—flickering his consciousness like a loose bulb and sending bolts of new pain ricocheting down his spine. He could feel his mind blinking on and off, the others now only fuzzy profiles going stop-action.

And then, without prologue or protest, he heard the boys climb back on their bikes, silently disappearing off into the night. He was concussed, his vision like he was looking through the wrong end of binoculars, but he could make out a group of men, all in shorts— the soccer players—jogging off the pitch and circling his limp form. One of them emptied a bottle of water on Javier's head, shrouded in pain.

"*No puedes estar inconsciente,*" Javier heard one of them say, telling him to stay conscious. "*De lo contrario, tendremos que llamar a una ambulancia.*" If he passed out, they would have to call an ambulance, and that would be expensive, would bring the police and no one wanted that. Several of them squatted, grabbed his hands, and began patting them. It felt odd and endearing and made no sense to Javier, but the sudden Samaritan attention rallied something inside him, the perdition and glory of humanity on full display in such quick succession.

"C'mon, *amigo*. They're gone. You're gonna be okay." Javier leaned to one side, threw up, then propped himself up on an elbow. He stuck a hand out for some help and was pulled up, though it was anyone's guess how long he'd keep standing.

"*Gracias.*" Another wave of nausea, one more bottle of water on his head, down his back. He could see it pool, a slightly pink shade at his feet as the pavement swam underneath him. He looked up expecting to see Alex, but saw only a crowd of soccer players staring back. "I'm good." He waved them off then took a few steps like he was on a boat broadside to ten-foot waves and decided to take a knee. A few of the soccer players patted him on the back and gave some parting words of encouragement before heading back onto the field to resume their game. Javier could taste the alkaloid flavor of blood in his mouth. He ran his tongue over the inside of his cheek where Alex had punched him and felt loose flesh and loose teeth. Amid the pain, though, he felt adrenalized relief, the survivor's rush of having withstood the worst.

One of the soccer players was an East Valley kid who knew Chuey, knew Javier was one of his friends, and had texted Chuey to let him know what had happened. In fifteen minutes, the guys minus Gio were squatting next to Javier who was once again lying in the grass semi-conscious. Without ice, the swelling had moved in, his skin starting to feel like a spacesuit, his bell-rung brain too big for his skull.

"Who," Chuey said, more command than question. He still had on his Home Depot apron, some bright pins stuck on one strap, one declaring his commitment to always smile.

Javier looked up, boggle-eyed, having lost the plot. He scowled at Chuey, fumbling for an answer. "Itchy and Scratchy...from Tommy's." Javier's left eye was already half closed.

Chuey turned Javier's head slightly to check the corneas for any signs of hemorrhaging. Nothing. "Always about numbers with those pussies. Five of us and one of you."

"Eight, actually."

"Yeah, well, I got my peoples, Javi, you know that, and one text from me, and it's our turn at bat."

"Alex did most of this."

"Tell Alex to take a hiatus." He got some looks from the other guys for his sudden jump in vocabulary. "*Pendejos*, all of 'em, only understand one thing. Overwhelming force." Chuey looked at the other guys for some amens and got a few *Fuck yeahs*.

"Don't start shit, don't take shit." Enrique nodded.

"My uncles are so ugly they don't even need to swing. Just look at you," This from Raffa, and it wasn't hyperbole. Of all the guys, Raffa's family had the most cousins and uncles who'd been in and out of prison. Javier's phone was still where he'd tossed it. Raffa picked it up and gave it to him. "Say the word, Javi."

"Guys, thanks, but just leave it. This is between me and Alex." He looked around for Gio, then remembered Gio didn't have a phone and wouldn't have received a text. "And I think technically Alex and I are even now."

Javier stood gingerly. Sergio helped him up and then shouldered one of Javier's arms. Javier dry-heaved, the blood flow to his head from standing proving to be too much. He took his arm off of Sergio's shoulders, bent at the waist and spat blood on the sidewalk. "You find anything about what happened in San Jose?" He turned his head but didn't stand up.

The other guys were already halfway up the block. Sergio blew some air out of his mouth, then dragged a hand over his face. "Patel got *got*, Javi. Nothin' natural about it. Room service, around midnight. Some *pelon* with a lotta ink on his neck. Goes in with a cart full of food and comes back out two minutes later with the cart still full. Like one of those spot-the-difference games, but nothing changed."

Later that night, once he'd taken an ice bath with the six bags the guys had lugged from 7-Eleven, Javier sat down and watched the video Sergio had sent, and for the third time that night, he got sick.

CHAPTER 35

Top of Haidu Tower @ noon

It was Javier's version of an adventure, though he doubted Leslie would see it that way, especially when he asked her for the favor which was the real reason for asking her here.

A week had passed since Scratchy had foot-stomped his head, and though the swelling had gone down, the bruising was on full display. His left eye had comically raccooned and on his right cheek was a blue-green tread-shaped welt where the boot had landed. Sitting now atop one of the three Can City towers, his appearance was the least of his worries.

Eight years of Chato's shakes and fries had gotten old for Leslie, an unspoken complaint he knew was a placeholder for a much larger issue she had with his paint-by-numbers approach to romance. And working with Lupe had lit something in Leslie. They had both assumed from a young age that they would be up and out at the same time, perhaps in the same direction, but just as puberty had come with a three-year gender-lag, it seemed Leslie's ascendency was well ahead and much more promising than his.

The roof was an enormous outdoor patio eleven stories up with no hint of the bustling world below, only expansive sky and mountain views up here. And quiet. Ping-pong tables and fire pits, and open taps of beer catered to the Can City emphasis on shared diversions. Tables and chairs formed little pods, usually centered around some mosaic tile. What shocked Javier most were the glass-doored refrigerators scattered throughout with an assortment of ready-made meals and snacks and drinks. He had assumed at first that each item belonged to someone, that they parked their food there but soon noticed people just reaching in and pulling things out. His only experience with a shared refrigerator had been in the Box where everyone stuck their lunches and even had their own proprietary sections of each shelf.

"Entitled little pricks." Javier turned and flinched. It was Jones, appearing out of nowhere like some ancient jinn. He didn't smile or offer any greeting, just flung his gaze around the rooftop implicating all the Can City kids up there, hammering away on their laptops and phones. "None of 'em have your abilities or that good ol' immigrant drive."

"How 'bout I drive this immigrant foot up your ass."

Jones made a show of noticing the damage to Javier's face. "Well on the upside, dark skin tends to hide the bruising." Jones stepped away and sat down on one of the futon-looking couches. "Got some Chato's coming in a minute. Took the privilege of ordering you and your sweetheart a plate of chili fries—they're out of nachos today." Jones, wearing a gray suit, flung an arm across the top of the sofa revealing a leather strap and holster of his concealed-carry.

"Not gonna hurt you, Javier," he said, bringing one leg up on top of the other and hitching his pants in the same motion, "not that it hasn't crossed my mind. Been trying to figure out if you might be more valuable to me alive than dead."

Javier sat down in a chair at one end of the sofa. "Dolores, Patel. And those are just the two that showed up on your burner."

"Don't do anything rash, Javier." The food delivery person arrived holding a bag up like it was a prize. Jones lifted a finger to signal it was his. "Leslie's got a bright future ahead of her." Of course he knew about Leslie. "Three of them work for me." Jones flicked his head toward the twenty or so people on the roof, the handful of middle-aged ones in sports coats looking out of place.

Jones pulled a ramekin out of the bag and held it up for inspection like it was a lab specimen. "Dipping sauce. Whatever happened to ketchup, huh, Javier? Instead, we got this aioli shit."

Jones took out a paper plate of fries wrapped in foil. "Sign of the times, I suppose. Last time I was in Chato's I hardly recognized the place. Used to be everyone at the counter had a week's worth of dirt under their nails. Now—" he tried a fry and then pushed the plate in Javier's direction. "Now you gotta have some Rumi quote tattooed on your forehead to get a cup of coffee."

"You touch Leslie–" Javier's voice was thin and serrated.

"Slow down, Sicario." Jones grabbed two more fries and dragged them through the aioli. "Let's not get off on the wrong foot." He stood, threw out the empty bag, and came back to sit down. "Probably wondering what exactly it is that I do."

"Don't flatter yourself." He could hear in his own voice the same peevish tone that Alex so often took.

"You and ninety-nine percent of the people who live in the Shoe came here for a better life. Who wouldn't? Growing up in your part of Jalisco? Your mother saw more there than anyone should in five lifetimes."

"So your solution is, what, to turn the Shoe into a food court for the dean's list?"

"Half the money that people in the Shoe earn goes straight to Mexico or El Salvador or wherever. Three-quarters of what's left over goes to rent. And the rest to pay the bills. No savings, no equity, all cash and all gone. Every month. And the promising ones? Like you, who might actually help turn this neighborhood around? Up and out at the first chance."

Javier sat there stone faced, the judgments starting to land.

Jones continued. "I monetize non-performing assets, find shitty neighborhoods and make them nice."

"Three hundred families living in the Gardens were doing okay before you showed up."

Jones wiped his fingers and put the napkin in the tin foil used to wrap the fries. "You're a smart young man, Javier, so let me pay you the compliment of being blunt. Six months ago, the liquor store on Van Nuys and Roscoe, two inches of Plexiglass on the counter. Owner bought the place because it had an oven and he loved to bake, but every time he checked on the bread, he'd turn around and be staring down a barrel with some fuckwit telling him to empty the till. Today, the guy is selling hot biscuits. Customers queue up for them. Plexiglass gone and not even a sneeze guard between him and the customers."

"Good for him." Javier knew the place, had tried the biscuits, the best he'd ever eaten.

"The guys you saw when you barnstormed my office? All they do is crunch numbers on neighborhoods like the Shoe, forgotten little zip codes, all over the world, and they look at all the usual metrics but wanna know what's the biggest giveaway here in LA?"

Javier tried to ignore the tease but couldn't help lifting his gaze to meet Jones's eyes.

"Water stores. Your people gotta have those water stores because they don't trust tap water anywhere. And if we find more than two per square mile, we start our financial modeling, put the numbers together. And here's the bitter pill, Javier. Immigrants don't push back. They can't afford to hire lawyers, and they don't complain because they're too busy doing all the shit work none of the actual citizens are willing to do." Jones fixed Javier with a long look. "And no one goes to bat for them because none of them vote."

"Buy a carwash, and go home."

That got a chuckle out of Jones. "Normally, a place like the Shoe, it might take two or three generations to see any improvement." He waved a hand in disgust. "Fuck all that inch-by-inch shit. I've trucked in an army of the most ambitious cocksuckers," he head-nodded nowhere in particular, "and hidden a pot of gold for each one of them. So good luck pushing back on that crowd. They're already putting offers in on homes a few blocks from here. Property values are going to double in three years, Javier. I've done in a few months what usually takes a few lifetimes."

Javier stared straight ahead, feeling walled in. "Where are all the little Jones-drones? Run out of batteries?"

An off-leash dog came by and started sniffing Jones. His hand shot out and grabbed the dog's snout, pulling its head to the ground where he held it for a few seconds before releasing it. The dog gave a yelp and quickly ran off. "Surveillance is a big motivator. And you know who's the first to go? Open warrants. Deadbeat dads. The same dregs I'm guessing you'd prefer would find somewhere else to live. And me and my little eyes-in-the-sky just chased a big chunk of them out of the Shoe."

"You're gonna lose, Jones. And when you do, tell your friends in the white van to get lost too."

"Know this, Javier. I handle one end of things, and they handle another. As you can see, they've given you a hall pass for the time being." He bent forward, elbows on knees. "That is not a permanent solution, Javier. Whoever ransomed their accounts must have told you that much. And here's a newsflash. They'll come for your family first." Jones let the imagery work its way into Javier's head. "And if I see you fucking with my program—." The threat flashed in his voice like a blade. "Truth is, I could use someone like you. I've seen your work, and you got chops. You want some real advice? Fuck college. Come work for me. I'll fire that goofball in the glasses, give you his desk and make you wealthier than you could imagine." Jones followed Javier's gaze off to nowhere. "Most guys would give their left nut for a slot in Solano."

Javier sat motionless, doing his best to wall his mind off to Jones' entreaties.

"You have two options. Let a team of very pissed off Chechens run you and your family over. Or hop in the diamond lane to some real money at Solano." He checked his watch. "Buy your mother a house. Take your sweetheart on a real date."

"I hope you get cancer. The fifty-fifty kind where there's just enough hope you might beat it that you spend three afternoons a week on chemo, then the other four days getting sick wishing you were dead."

"Hey, who's your friend?" It was Leslie, coming up on Javier's side, flicking her eyes between Jones and Javier.

Jones stood and flashed Leslie a smile. "Javier is as modest as he is talented. George Jones, Harvard class of '87." He pulled a chair from a neighboring table for her to sit in. "And I'm recruiting your friend to come join us in Cambridge next year."

Leslie beamed. "Oh my God, Javier! You didn't tell me Harvard was on your list." Javier could tell this type of uber-ambitious version of himself appealed to her.

"Probably quite a bit Javier hasn't shared." Jones let it float there. "It was really nice talking, Javier. Don't forget my promise." He swung his full attention her way. "Nice to meet you, Leslie." As Jones left, three men who had been scattered among the students suddenly stood up and followed him out.

Leslie watched Jones go. "How'd he know my name?"

"You see him coming, cross the street."

She bunched her brows in confusion. "He's trying to recruit you to Harvard. What are you talking about?"

"Full-on groomer shit. Boys and girls. And dogs." He pushed the plate of fries, now cold, her way. "Probably small appliances too." Leslie made a disgusted look and grabbed a fry. "Your face looks better." He knew it was a lie, though she tried to sell it by going in for a closer look. "Any word from Alex?" Javier's mind was still sifting through the warnings and offers from Jones.

He'd been piqued by the bit about water stores.

"I need a favor, Les." Romance would have to wait.

CHAPTER 36

It was a sign of the times. Joshua Tree, once little more than a wide part in the road, had exploded to the point that it now had its own fifteen-lane bowling alley, complete with a lunch counter and four beers—all domestic—on tap. It helped that the median age of the town was now fifty-six, a group drawn to the arthritis-friendly climate and now desperate for things to do and places to meet.

Gordo rolled his second strike of the night and did a butt-floss victory dance, all three hundred and ten pounds of him, that had his teammates diving under tables in a mock earthquake drill. "Jesus, it's the big one!" Two teams of six bowlers, one from construction captained by Carlos and one from survey captained by Raymond, played loser-buys every Wednesday, and the tab was once again Team Survey's.

"Where's Jenny Craig when you need her?" Raymond said, throwing down his credit card in disgust. Gordo was bowling in the 280s, twice the next best score on Team Survey. Fifteen pitchers of Michelob and twenty-three double cheeseburgers with heart attack fries was nearly a mortgage payment. "Gonna need to go on the government cheese pretty soon unless Gordo develops some tendonitis." It was nearly 11 p.m. and surveyors had to be on-site in six hours, so the men were back in their trucks driving home before Carlos and Raymond had unlaced their rental shoes. Carlos poured them each one more cup of semi-flat beer and waved to Patty at the counter to let her know they'd be gone in fifteen.

Raymond took a long pull on the beer. "To my cousin and your *abuela*."

Carlos clinked bottles with him and took a long draw. "Still nothing?"

Raymond shook his head.

Carlos had twenty minutes to sell Raymond. "Two in the tits and one in the head." He looked at Raymond. "I mean, c'mon, Ray. Those fools were on a contract, and they made sure he wasn't floating back up." Carlos drained his beer. "Someone blew the dam, Ray. Van der Lipp was old but that shit wasn't structural. It was detonated, and your cousin was in the wrong place."

Raymond gave him a crooked look. His cousin had gone missing from his favorite fishing hole and then found at the bottom of the Van der Lipp Reservoir after the dam break.

"You ever notice there were no pictures of Van der Lipp in the news? Just the flood, right, but I got some from a buddy of mine in Public Works who was doing the investigation on the down-low, which is suspicious as hell if you ask me, and the pictures of the dam show a blast pattern. An explosion. You ever watch a real dam fail structurally? You got the primary and then the secondary, but no cratering in the actual dam." He leaned forward. "My buddy found pieces of rebar from Van der Lipp two hundred feet from the dam. That's some shrapnel shit, Ray. C4. And whoever set the charge shot your cousin 'cause he was an eyeball witness." He sat up and straightened his back to deliver the punchline. "And it was Jones behind that."

Carlos had shared the folder Javier had sent with Ray. He was asking his friend to risk committing professional suicide. Ray finished his beer, grimaced, and looked at his watch. "You say the cads are gonna be stamped, embossed, and signed—wet ink— nothing to come back on me?" Cads, or cadastral maps, were the official documents issued by the State Transportation Department specifying the authorized route—referred to as alpha—for the construction of the bullet train viaduct. Raymond and his team had authority to find the best path for the bullet train within this given "alpha corridor," usually three hundred feet wide. Carlos was proposing that Raymond and his survey team send the bullet train on a path outside the corridor.

Half a mile outside.

"I've seen 'em, Ray. No way you can tell the difference. The cads look legit. Paper trail is gonna go straight up to Sacramento." The lights over the lanes went out, Patty's cue to wrap it up. "Take a look at them tomorrow and let me know. Like I said, Jones put your cousin *y mi abuela* in the ground. And the bullet train is his payday." Carlos shook his head. "Nah, he ain't gettin' it."

They bumped fists and stood. "Homie fucked with the wrong people," Ray said. They picked up his rental shoes and brought them over to Patty along with the receipt for the night's food and alcohol. "I pull this off, then Gordo's bowling for Survey."

■　　　■　　　■

The game of squash was a cultural yardstick, a bellwether of background. To have played it before or during college suggested a boarding school or Ivy League education. No one else would have heard about it, much less cared about it. Racquetball was the cousin sport meant for the masses: faster, more exercise, old guys with sweatbands. Every gym had one, but squash courts were rare. Squash required whites and a ball which didn't even bounce when dropped from waist height. Squash courts in Washington were to politicians what back rooms in Vegas were to high-stakes gamblers. Tasha had watched a few squash videos, committed some terms of art to memory. In her line of work, opening gambits were an artform.

"Mr. Secretary, he owns the T. Git yo big butt in there and push his skinny ass outta the way!" she half shouted from the viewing gallery. She was still unpacking her clothes from her move to

Georgetown and noticed a wrinkle on her pants which she tried, with no luck, to flatten.

The Secretary of Interior, a man named Will Payne, recognized her voice and smiled before he looked up. "My wife says my butt is sexy. You must be talking about the other Senator on the court." Her new boss, Congressman Blythe, Chairman of Ways and Means, shared her contempt for Jones and made the introduction to the Secretary a week prior at a fundraiser. Tasha and the Secretary hit off immediately.

Some referred to squash as physical chess, and control of the T, which was the intersection of two lines in the middle of the court, usually enabled someone to make the other player run all over the court. "I'll buy you breakfast if you can hit even one drop shot."

"You're buying anyway," he said. No one knew the score, but the two players, both in their sixties and panting for air, quickly shook hands, grateful for an excuse to wrap things up.

After he showered, the Secretary met Tasha in the club restaurant, tony enough to have waiters with white towels draped over one forearm, where she'd already ordered his freshly squeezed grapefruit juice. "Eggs over easy on the way."

"Thank God you didn't get me the oatmeal. My wife has me eating that shit four days a week." Tasha made small talk which, in this case, was easy. She enjoyed the Secretary, found his sense of humor self-deprecating, a vanishing trait among politicians. It was a waste of time diving headfirst into the real reason for her visit before a plate of food was in front of him. And with a nod of her head, the waiter appeared and dropped the plate of eggs with a side of roasted potatoes and a stack of toasted sourdough in front of the secretary.

"Appropriations are coming down to the fine print, Mr. Secretary, and the Congressman wants you to know he has put Twenty-Nine Palms at the top of his list." Twenty-Nine Palms was a Marine Base that employed a good chunk of his electorate. "We've carved out some new line items you'll be happily surprised to see." She didn't want to go too heavy with the sugar.

"Let's just leave it there then, shall we?" He smiled, knowing full well she wouldn't drag herself to the club to bring him only good news. She smiled back, dialing in enough teeth to send a teasing warmth, just south of flirtatious.

"I'll spare you the details—"

He broke in. "Good idea."

"But I need a golden ticket." They'd bonded at the fundraiser over Charlie and the Chocolate Factory. They'd both grown up on the book and abhorred the movie.

He put down his fork and wiped his mouth. "Broad strokes only, darling."

"I need BLM to assign six hundred acres in the desert." BLM, Bureau of Land Management which controlled most of the federal land in the Mojave Desert.

The Secretary snorted into his plate. "And I need a better backhand. Doesn't mean it's gonna happen."

"I dunno, Mr. Secretary, you had some corner shots that just sat the fuck down." She was working her church voice, a one-two foot stomp under the table, and a "Hand to God!" If she'd had a church crown on, she'd have taken it off and fanned herself. He chuckled at how well she worked him.

"And when they sign this parcel over, who will be the lucky recipient of all that sand?"

"The very proud Native American Chuckwalla Nation, Mr. Secretary, who have just been granted the customary door prize for a history of displacement and annihilation."

The secretary smiled knowingly. "Fourteen casinos over twenty years." He ran his toast in a figure eight through his eggs. "Got it." Then he stuffed the toast in his mouth and chased it with some coffee. "You're coming back on Jones. Good girl, cocksucker needs to be taken down a peg or two. Not that easy, though, my friend.

BLM is tighter than a clam's ass at low tide when it comes to inventory."

"I know, Mr. Secretary, and I realize this is not something I would ordinarily do, but Jones currently has a hard-on for our district and the dude is a triflin' piece of shit."

"Truly." He wiped his mouth and studied her. She knew the look, his thoughts like bingo balls rattling around the draw cage. "I'll be sure to quote you during the floor vote next week." He shot her a wink. "I despise Jones as much as you do. Normally, I could trade horses with BLM but they got some new six sigma management dickwad in there trying to make a name for himself, so I'll have to resort to less subtle means. Gimme a day, sweetheart."

That was as intimate as they ever got, and it was always just enough for both of them.

CHAPTER 37

Alex sat in the back of Manny's dark blue Impala with Chuco, slowly coming unglued. One of the *capitanes*, a human tree stump named Tony, was in the front passenger seat, one hand out the window holding a Modelo, a pair of Loks slung backward around his fat-folded neck. Manny had doused himself in cologne, dragged a comb through his hair, and had a pressed white shirt, giving the impression he would offset his evening's sins by putting on his church clothes.

The evening air was Santa Ana warm, 210 freeway traffic, the sound of AC units humming away, the whippet-thin voices of children somewhere on the other side of the wall just behind them, and Alex sat with a Glock in his waistband at loose ends with himself. He double-checked the safety, certain he was going to shoot himself in the balls, then ran a hand over the ribbed seat redolent of his father's *carcachita* where he would stuff wrappers and search for change to use at the arcade.

Chuco, his leg jackhammering, offered Alex a bottle of tequila with a label featuring a burro wearing a sombrero, now half finished. Alex tipped it back once again, felt his throat catch fire, and passed it back, though his friend shook it off leaving Alex to stick it between his legs. The silence was a heavy blanket that made him feel clammy, like he was yoked to a team of horses, each one wishing they were somewhere else.

"What time is it?" he asked, like punctuality was an issue. No one responded.

He could see across the tracks, a pickup soccer game, kids no older than himself, their shouts like sparks in the night. He went at the tequila, his throat no longer burning, a lust for action starting to fill his head.

"I mean, we're gonna do this, right, like where's the train?" He leaned forward against the top of the front bench, poking his head between Manny and this Tony guy, once again a *carcachita* rewind, Mama and Papa and a trip to the beach. The Tony guy turned slowly, his teardrop tats the nonverbal shutdown, leaving Alex now feeling a black heat of depression. He'd never gotten the full story on the teardrops, just like the sneaker fruit that hung from the phone lines; ask ten guys what it was all about and get ten answers, all part of the myth-making that sold the newcomers.

He gave up on the front seat and turned to Chuco, leg still bouncing. "You got your whistle?" Alex thought he'd try out his street-speak. Chuco gave him a puzzled face, and Alex patted his lower stomach. Chuco nodded and hiked up his T-shirt to reveal a handle-grip poking out of his considerable girth. Alex gave an approving look and realized then and there he wasn't much cut out for this life.

He could sense a grim resolve coming off Chuco and wondered if the two boys were cut from the same cloth. Theirs had been a friendship of initiates, two boys stuck on the same Denker bench whose primary qualifications were to follow orders and keep their gobs shut. They'd played their part, covered for each other, gave each other heads-up, and yet here, at the moment of truth, Chuco seemed like a stranger. Manny and Tony had pulled them both off the benches two nights ago promising a "taste to take home and spend on the ladies." Alex knew that's what most of the guys did, but it seemed like such a waste, like most of the girls who went in for that stuff were stupid and lazy. He liked the girls with hair bands, who buttoned their shirts up, not the prancing loud mouths always leaning in, uneven girls who made him feel uneven just listening to them.

"Strap up, fellas. Train's comin'." Manny's thumb started bouncing on the steering wheel. Chuco shifted his weight but didn't look at Alex.

The locomotive came into sight pulling a single boxcar behind it. The tracks ran through an open expanse of the north Valley between a set of freeways and then disappeared into the rail yard. Alex noticed a white van idling on the other side of the tracks, lights off, though the glow of phones on the inside told him someone else was here, possibly waiting for the same train. The locomotive slowed with a metallic grind that announced the beginning of whatever was going to happen. The train stopped, and the four of them stared as though expecting circus animals to suddenly climb out. Alex was now drunk and had gone fuzzy on the overall goal of the mission.

"You sure this is it?"

"Shut the fuck up." Alex wasn't sure who had said it.

The engine and the boxcar decoupled with a metallic pop, and a moment later, the engine inched away as though glad to be done with the boxcar. Another moment later, a loud clank, and the door on the boxcar slid open maybe a foot, revealing a black interior. The locomotive blew out a cloud of diesel smoke and slowly disappeared the way it had come.

"You're up."

"Wait, what?" Alex froze, Chuco already out and moving toward the train. But before Alex could argue the choice of pronouns, another car, a late model Dodge Charger, suddenly pulled up, engulfed in its own dust cloud, and out popped two more jugglers from the benches, gold swinging freely from their necks.

"*Apurate!*" Manny finally said something, telling Alex to get moving.

Alex got out, slid the gun to his back, and broke into a jog, first in the direction of the soccer game until Manny got on the horn and pointed toward the train. The locomotive was no longer in sight, leaving the boxcar looking like a Trojan horse, suspiciously abandoned, its door ajar. Alex wondered how thorough the vetting process was for Denker, how much time went into sourcing backgrounds on leads. He'd never had much cause to rely on instinct before, but he felt himself in the early stages of a doomed finale.

The two boys from the other car hadn't waited for either Alex or Chuco but were now standing on opposite sides of the sliding door. The deck of the boxcar was a lot higher up than it appeared at a distance, and the four of them had to work out a system to boost each other up, the last one getting arm-pulled on board. The instructions had been vague—find the crate, open it, and bring the contents back. Fortunately, once on board there was only one crate, wedged under one of the steel rails at the front of the boxcar. Alex walked up to it and examined it, equal parts curious and terrified. It was a locker-sized wooden crate with something stenciled on the side, its lid screwed shut with a series of brass lags.

"Who brought the drill?" Alex asked, already knowing the answer.

"*Hijo de puta!*" one of the boys from the Charger blurted out. The four of them stood their hands on hips, each waiting for someone to make a suggestion.

"Look for something to lever it open with." Alex was somehow taking charge, which made him even more uneasy. No way he should be calling the shots. The three others started searching the boxcar, grateful to have something to do.

"Over here!" It was Chuco. He'd found a metal bar and raised it proudly over his head like a prize when the left half of his face exploded, his body pitching forward like a felled tree and hitting the floor of the boxcar with a thud.

Alex dove just as the fusillade tore through the boxcar. The metallic clang of the bullets raining through the steel siding was deafening, Alex doing his best to remain flat and as far from the open door as possible. And as suddenly as the gunfire had started, it stopped. The silence was even more unwelcome, the gunmen certain to be on the move. Alex ran his hand over his abdomen, the sudden apprehension that it was blood between his fingers flipping a panic switch, a hot pain flooding his body. He'd never imagined getting shot would hurt so much; his vision went blurry, his sense of things coming in and out. He was losing consciousness but was aware of the two other boys leaping over Chuco and out the door. Alex went to his friend, stymied an urge to throw up, and managed to feel for a pulse but got nothing. For a heroic second, he considered putting Chuco's arm over his shoulder and carrying him to safety but knew right away that was out of the question.

Another shot split the air over his head, causing him to turn and see that a second door facing the opposite direction was open revealing two men with rifles next to the white van. He half jumped and half fell out of the door he had come through, landing on the ground, rolling once before staggering back up.

"Wait!" None of the others even so much as turned to watch Alex take two hesitant steps forward before falling down in the weeds, his head gone to soup in semi-conscious shock.

He sat up just enough, saw the boys getting into the Charger, already in motion, doors open, before out of nowhere, a Ford F-150 pulled up directly in front blocking its path. Whether it was instinct or la Virgin or the tequila amplified with the loss of blood, Alex lolled to one side and fell like a reluctant tenpin, looking up at the dusk-teal sky from the protective length of weeds. He heard the unmistakable sound of shotguns getting pumped, followed closely by a volley of fire. He could hear the gravel beneath the boots of the men, now walking his way toward the train, maybe ten feet from his prone form, heard them board the boxcar. A conversation in Spanish began, some loud banging and the sound of the wooden crate being dragged to the door. Alex waited, breathless and bleeding, reciting a prayer he was surprised he'd remembered.

Even lying down, he could see the cowboy hats of two of the men pass close enough to smell the gun smoke still lingering in their wake, then the sound of a diesel engine casually making its exit, leaving only the white noise of the city thrum. He propped himself up on one arm and noticed the blue Impala was gone. He managed to stand and zigzag back toward the dirt road. The Charger sat there idling, its left turn signal blinking uselessly, four doors flung open, bodies hanging out of two of them.

A faint sound of sirens, as he spun and collapsed. The last thing he remembered was noticing how dirty his Vans were.

CHAPTER 38

Mama was baggy-eyed, her face swollen with lack of sleep. She'd been awake forty-eight hours between work and the hospital. Her prayer beads wound through her hands like a bike chain, her lips whispering incantations Javier hadn't heard since she'd first learned about Yanira. They met first not with a doctor but law enforcement to explain the officer posted outside Alex's room. Detective Morales arrived soon after and explained that Alex had been caught in some drug ring crossfire, most likely one of the cartels. If and when Alex recovered, he was going straight into custody.

The doctor arrived wearing scrubs and drying his hands with a paper towel. He'd introduced himself briefly prior to the surgery and explained what the X-rays had shown and what he and his team would try to do. "The bullet hit a rib and got lodged in his femur. We removed it, no sign of infection just yet." Mama put one hand on the doctor's folded arms and another over her mouth.

"He's lost a lot of blood which isn't surprising because the bullet nicked his spleen when it ricocheted off the rib." It made Alex sound like he had bones made of steel. The doctor spoke with a practiced, even tone that could have been interpreted as either bringing with it good or bad news. "Quarter inch either way, he wouldn't have even made it to the hospital. He'll need one more surgery, so he's not set to be discharged just yet, Ms. Jimenez."

Mama crossed herself several times while thanking the doctor, most likely wanted to kiss him but was too short to really go in for one. "Can we go see him?"

The doctor nodded and waved to the nurse station. "Of course. The nurse will take you to him." And with that the doctor ducked into another room.

They found Alex looking dopey, his eyelids like window shades, an IV hanging on a stand, and a monitor light blipping from left to right. Mama bent over him and began stroking his cheeks with the back of her fingers. She spoke in a whisper as Alex slowly opened his eyes.

Javier pointed at the monitor. "You got a Baxter—the Cadillac of heart monitors." He'd done some volunteering here two summers ago, trying to see if medicine might be right for him. Too much blood for his liking. He leaned in to study the readout. "You're gonna hope you get shot more often." He nodded at the nurse who was across the room opening the blinds. "Have you had a chance to see who's changing your bedpan?"

Alex was pale and lolled his head in Javier's direction. "Only seen your ugly face."

Mama stood up, her eyes starting to flood. She was wearing the two flannel shirts worn when she worked overnights in the meat locker. Her cuffs were red-stained from pulling sides of beef for the past six hours. "*Gracias a Dios*," she murmured and crossed herself.

Alex turned his head to see her then immediately turned away and wept for the next few minutes. It was like a fever breaking, a pathogen leaving his body having set up shop for the past few months and now choosing to move on. He and Mama didn't even try to speak, palmed their eyes dry. Javier busied himself by inflating the blood pressure cuff around his bicep a few times.

"Ma pulled some enchiladas out of the freezer." He presented a tray and wagged it under Alex's face, peeling back enough tinfoil to allow the familiar aroma to escape. Alex slowly moved his eyes from the food to Javier to Mama, and then back to the food.

"I made the sauce less spicy," Mama added, reaching for his stomach, then pulling her hand back is if touching a hot stove. "I forgot about the stitches." Javier could see the morphine drip making its hourly delivery, saw Alex's lids flutter, his mouth fall open. The nurse arrived and let them know he would be out for a while and that this might be a good time to go home and get some rest.

"I'll heat the food up when he wakes up." She smiled, taking Alex's wrist to measure his pulse. "Between you and me, patients who get home cooking are up and outta here in half the time."

■   ■   ■

What little she knew about Chief Rosales, Tasha had heard that punctuality was a sign of respect she had better abide. Her dashboard clock said 2:55 and the dirt road was technically "undeveloped," which is why her satnav was no help. At 2:59, she pulled up with a bit of skid in front of the chief's house, a one-story with weather-beaten clapboard siding and an enormous satellite dish that could have doubled as a swimming pool if it had been pointed straight up. The chief was sitting on the porch with a pitcher and two glasses already out. The wind had spared the chief a mouthful of dust from Tasha's dramatic arrival, an auspicious sign that didn't go unnoticed by the chief.

"Chief Rosales." Tasha had expected something a little more stereotypical like Dancing Bear. "So nice to meet you."

The chief stood, smiled, and offered her a chair. "You could charm the pants off a donkey with that smile, young lady. Welcome to the asshole of America!" They both laughed and fell into small talk which the chief plainly relished. Tasha imagined there weren't a lot of folks around here, fewer still who were even half as loquacious as the chief. The Chuckwalla Tribe was very new by BLM standards, though its people had beaten Father Serra to California by several hundred years. The reservation had a whopping population of six, but the casino was coming, and suddenly everyone within a thousand miles claimed to be some fractional member.

"We need some frontage, Ms. Tasha. You don't see Bellagio six blocks off the Strip." He used his hands when he spoke but kept his upper body still. "I mean, you saw how long it took to get off the street to get to us. We're forty miles from nowhere."

Tasha angled herself toward the chief. "Well, here's the thing. BLM won't just sign you the deed without a predicate, which in this case will require a little...help from you."

The chief nodded. "Predicates." He squished his lips into a duckbill. "I got six boxes of 'em in the back." He gave her a wink, and they were off. His wife joined them on the porch for some dominoes while they worked out the details.

■   ■   ■

The call between Sacramento and Carlos was scheduled for three p.m. which meant it wouldn't start until 3:30. In the past three months, Carlos and Ray had sent nine piers into the ground, a staggering number not only in terms of schedule but in terms of sabotage. These piers would now take the bullet train a grand total of two thousand feet in the wrong direction. The Department of Transportation conducted its oversight by low-level satellite that took pictures of the viaduct then mapped that onto the sanctioned cads to make sure the actual construction was being done to specification. The download request for the satellite image from the previous month had mysteriously gone missing, so by month two, a Gant chart in project oversight—some guy named Leo—sent an alert that prompted the call with Carlos.

"I don't know how to say this, Carlos," Leo said, "but the viaduct is almost a mile off alpha. You're like in, in epsilon or something. I mean, I've never seen it like...this...bad."

Carlos had been practicing his surprise but had a hard time doing it then without cracking up, and had started importing grotesque mental images to stave off a laughing fit. It never worked when he practiced. "Wait, what are you...what are you talking about?" He felt the laughter coming up like a sneeze and had to mute his phone.

"I'll send you the images but we've done three low-orbit flyovers and even sent a Cessna up to confirm, but it's no joke. You're so far off alpha...well, I can't..." Alpha was the planned route, the prescribed route, the one approved by four different committees in Sacramento and two in Washington. "You're one of the best."

Carlos was touched by the praise and almost forgot to unmute himself. He had to make covering for Ray his first move. "The cads are file stamped, embossed, wet ink, everything, Leo, Ray and I conference with DOT every week—what's his name—"

"You mean Grover."

Carlos couldn't contain his snort, had to play it off as a cough. "Right, Grover. Check his phone log—we're on it every Wednesday since the injunctions were lifted."

Leo had come to the cul-de-sac in the conversation with Carlos, nowhere else to go but turn around. Leo had called looking for some plausible explanation, some escape tunnel he could take to avoid the tsunami of shit headed his way. Carlos felt a little bad for Leo, typical middle management, powerless to effect change, easy to blame, and probably one of the first casualties.

"DOT can always re-reoute it, right? Demo the piers, put the rail back on—"

"No chance," Leo cut Carlos off at the hint of a redo. Carlos already knew no one would approve redoing this stretch of rail to put it back on the course Jones had planned. Everyone with decision-making authority would have their heads on a platter. They'd come up with excuses to cover this little snafu. "Jones has already filed six lawsuits to course-correct." Carlos heard Grover shuffling some papers. "Place called Dhamma Gap. DOT has a team redoing the cads right now. "Needless to say, this is a hard stop, straight from the governor's office, tell your guys—I don't know—tell 'em the truth, I suppose."

"Of course, Leo. Wow, I still can't...unreal." They hung up, Carlos hoping Leo hadn't heard the front end of what was a long laugh.

CHAPTER 39

During the two weeks of touch and go with Alex, Javier buried himself in the finances of Mission. Lupe's loan helped pay down most of the vendors and catch up on maintenance. He put together tax returns for the past two years which included heavy penalties he figured were worth it if it put Mission in position for traditional bank financing. When he wasn't doing that, he was doing brake jobs, and when he got done with those, he was answering calls with Betzaida, seven days a week.

The ransomware was still in place, though Sergio was giving his updates with less and less confidence. The Chechens were like dogs on a rusty chain, and Javier handled his increasing anxiety the only way he knew how—by working nonstop.

"Nothing like a little near death to put things in perspective, but you seem to be doing some kind of penance or something." Betzaida was sitting at her desk, a repurposed piston head once used as an ashtray from back in her smoking days still the only thing on her desk. "No priests within a mile of this place, so I'm all you got."

He was seated on a couch below the big screen. He shrugged. "Maybe I need to stick around for a year, you know. Put college off for a bit." He spread his arms on the back of the couch crucifixion-style. "Go full time here."

Betzaida snorted. "No wrenches for you, Javi. Scalpels an' shit only." Betzaida'd got it stuck in her head years ago when he'd started volunteering at the hospital that he was going pre-med. They took three calls that night: a deuce, an 1180, and a car fire which had to have been visible from ten miles away. They were first on the scene, and the fire was just starting to spread from the engine compartment to the rest of the vehicle. Javier stood there transfixed, hoping the fire department would get stuck in traffic so he could watch the whole thing go up in flames, a guilty pleasure he indulged himself.

She dropped him at the hospital where Alex was still a few days from being released, and as she pulled into the turnout, a call came over the scanner: pile-up at the intersection on Ventura and White Oak. "Look at that. Here we are in Bergosian's backyard and whaddaya know. Got a chance to snatch one." Betzaida smiled and nodded at Javier as he got out.

At the automatic doors to the hospital, Javier got the text from Sergio that he always knew would come.

bob gone game over

*   *   *

Javier entered the hospital amidst a commotion over some kind of a billing issue with one family threatening lawsuits and the front desk attendant doing her best to hold the fort until reinforcements arrived. Javier didn't bother signing in and wandered to the bank of elevators and up to Alex's room where an officer was seated outside, the same one every afternoon. The officer bumped his head in the direction of the door, and Javier went inside where some gushy get-wells with the i's dotted with small hearts had arrived and were standing on a table near the bed. He wanted to pick one up but knew Alex would get annoyed. Instead, he pretended to peer inside the biggest one.

"Didn't know you and J-Lo were such good friends?" A pair of crutches next to his bed already showed signs of use, and a stack of clothes sat atop a chair in the corner. There was a half-eaten piece of cake on the rolling table sitting off to the side.

"She took the wrong backpack, Javi." Alex spoke in a faraway tone. "She took mine."

Javier paused, then found a chair and sat down, not speaking until he was sure Alex was done. "I know."

Alex was still staring out the window which had a second-story view of another building directly across a driveway. "Why'd you keep it to yourself all this time?" There was no edge to his voice, no hint of any trap.

"Because the breather was empty, Alex. It hadn't been working for a couple of days." Javier followed Alex's line of sight out the window across the driveway. There was a wide picture window, drapes drawn though backlit. "I'd asked the coyotes—there was one of them who said he would help—to go pick one up for us that day, but he said he had got a call from his *tia* who needed him to fix a flat tire."

"What?" He turned to look at Javier.

"Yanira never should have been with us, Alex. I should have turned back when we had the chance, but the coyote..." The room across the way suddenly went black. "We didn't tell you because we knew you'd blame yourself. We thought we were protecting you." Alex did a couple of laps around the room with his eyes casually surveying the furniture, the equipment. A voice came over the PA announcing some kind of hospital code, and soon after, a technician wheeled a large machine down the hall.

A guy in green scrubs poked his head in and smiled. "OT, but I can come back." The guy looked at Alex who nodded and gave him a thumbs-up prompting the man to return the gesture and disappear.

Javier leaned forward. "I say 'we' like Mama had anything to do with it." He tugged the bed sheets which felt like they'd work well scrubbing pots. "Can't even remember why, but I got into it with Mama, and I dropped that little bomb on her. Told her Yanira never should have been with us." The IV pump hummed away. "She'll never forgive herself, and I knew that, and I used it." He felt his mood go from dark to black and stood to go. "I'm no golden boy, Alex."

"She used to hide one of my shoes." He chuckled. "She used to— I loved that look in her eye when I asked her if she'd seen it. *Donde mi zapato*! And I'd act all crazy, running around with one shoe."

"She got all her good hiding places from me."

The PA came to life again, doctor someone needed somewhere. "Random," Alex, mostly to himself now. "Quarter inch for me and my spleen. Coyote's *tia* doesn't get a flat tire. Just...random." He'd gone philosophical, the hand of fate having swept so close he had felt its breeze. He turned his head to look at Javier. "Homies just left me there."

It took Javier a moment to realize that Alex was referring to the shooting at the railyard.

"No visits. No texts. Just...nothing."

A nurse sauntered in, not pausing to read the room. "Good afternoon. My name is Janice. How is everyone?" Neither brother was prepared to deal with her cheerfulness. She made a few small claps as if preparing to announce a guessing game. Then she took Alex's pulse. "Any pain, Mr. Jimenez?" She laid a hand on his stomach. Javier wondered if that was something they taught you in medical school, the human touch.

"I'm good, thanks."

"Okay, great. Our occupational therapist will be in later today to go over a few things to get you walking again soon. In about an hour, the doctor will be by to check on the sutures and dressing. Any luck, you'll be out of here by the weekend." She made some notations on a clipboard, hung it at the foot of his bed then waved and left. Alex's eyes followed her.

"The fuck is an occupational therapist?" He scooted up in the bed. "I don't have an occupation." Javier stood next to Alex's bed.

The Shoe could be a voracious and forgetful place for a boys like Alex. He'd never had many friends, and now he had one less.

"Sorry about Chuco."

Alex gazed up overhead at the drop ceiling.

"Yeah, me too."

Javier knew trouble was on its way, and the hospital would be a likely place for the Chechens to start looking. A nurse behind the counter picked up a phone, then stared through the window at Javier. Or was she just looking at her screen and her line of sight seemed just aimed in his direction?

"Alex, this is gonna sound—," Javier watched the readout on one of the monitors, "—strange." A pump started, its rotating arm giving it the appearance of a Slurpee machine. "I've gotten myself mixed up in something. I'll explain it to you one day, but I'm gonna have to disappear. For a bit." In twenty minutes, they'd unwound a year's worth of turned rope, and perhaps because he was still coasting on the last drips of Nembutal, Alex looked at Javier like he'd just said it was sunny and eighty degrees outside.

"You need a *cuete*?" In fact, Javier could have used a gun but not from Alex.

Javier got up and looked out the window at the traffic, every other vehicle now seemingly a white transit van. He looked at Alex, heavy lidded and slipping away. "I was never here." He walked quickly out the door, past the cop still sitting outside the door, and disappeared down the hall. He had no idea where he was going.

CHAPTER 40

Study hall, its orange bulk quite possibly visible from space, was a poor choice to begin his life on the lam, but Javier felt drawn to the familiar. He was supposed to be finalizing his scholarships, waiting on college acceptance letters, picking out his tux with Leslie for prom, showing Alex how to shave. It was supposed to be the denouement to his four-year grind at East Valley, yearbook notes with empty promises to stay in touch, a few porch parties with the guys, and then adios. Javier took a seat and leaned back, stuck his arms out along its back, his panic slowly morphing into resignation.

A raccoon skittered by, turned its head, its eyes green-lit in the dark. Behind him, a coyote tippy-toed, downwind and angling just out of sight, its snout riding low to the ground measuring the scent. Javier wanted to warn the raccoon but even more, wanted to witness the act of predation. The coyote wove back and forth a few times, trying out angles of approach, the raccoon, its eyes like two glowing emeralds still staring at Javier, oblivious to the threat on its flank. Or was it? In an instant, the raccoon rolled over on its back proclaiming that in fact it was a possum not a raccoon, resorting to its almost comical you-can't-kill-what's-already-dead pose. The coyote closed cautiously, ears pointed, then sniffed the prone possum and quickly recoiled. Confused, the coyote picked his head up as if someone might be playing a joke, looked around. He sniffed the possum one more time, then sneezed, inched back, looked around some more, and finally wandered off into the night. There was no shortage of prey for an enterprising coyote. Lake Mistake now drew almost anything with a tail and four legs at night.

Javier watched the possum scuttle away, then recoiled in shock. "What the—"

Gio was standing there like he'd been beamed down from a spaceship.

"Neat trick, huh?" Gio motioned toward where the possum had been. "Little fuckers even secrete the hormone that comes right before death. Makes 'em stink." Gio reached into his hoodie pocket, produced a burrito then tossed it onto Javier's lap. He held up a folder with the other hand. "Applyin' for food stamps." He plunked down on the adjacent section of sofa and pulled out an envelope. "And Medi-Cal." He stuck his feet up on the cable spool and checked the folder for anything else. "And I forgot the other one."

"RE Grants." Javier opened the burrito. He was no longer in a position to say no to free food. "Recently emancipated, Gio. You get monthly stipends for the first six months." Javier felt buoyed by this little uptick in Gio's self-management.

"Put in an application at Red Lantern, too. All you can eat." He spread his arms wide, perhaps imagining the buffet, then took a breath and let his arms fall, done for now with contemplating his future. Javier had always imagined the worst for Gio, but he had misjudged him completely. Gio was, after all, a survivor, his life a series of depredations and betrayals, a typical head start on a life of violence, and now here he was doing the dull business of getting on with adulthood. Gio'd never really needed Javier for the practical stuff. The only thing Gio ever wanted was family.

"How's Alex?"

"Doctor says no infection, so maybe two more days." Javier finished the burrito in four quick bites. With a little Tapatio, he could get used to them. "I need a favor."

"I bet you do."

Javier gave Gio a look. "Sergio told you?"

Gio nodded, his attention wandering off in the direction of what had once been Dogtown. The scaffolding had come down off Pan City Steel, revealing vibrant red brick announcing its second coming. "Didn't go into details, but said you were...up against it, or somethin'."

Javier sat forward, grabbed a stick off the ground and began scratching a line in the dirt. "Yeah. Or somethin'." He felt leaden and old. "You were right, Gio."

Gio smiled and wagged a finger at Javier. "That phone." It was Friday night, and Can City was just coming to life. A band with a horn section had started playing, the brass floating over the rhythm section, the gimlet sounds of the work-hard-play-hard league of Zoomers just starting off the evening. The timbre of their voices suggested they were still on their early rounds. Jones had nailed that part of his plan—the Can City crowd had arrived like they owned the place and were driving the types of change Jones had predicted. Local merchants in the Shoe were already redoing their business plans to meet the demand for a whole new tier of products and services. The *lavenderia* across from Javier's was getting remodeled into a yoga studio. Bungalows with aging stucco and dirt yards were getting snapped up and redone in East Coast clapboard and drought tolerant landscaping.

"Two people dead and Alex in the hospital." Javier pictured a line of dominoes, Jones finger-pushing the first one. "I gotta lay low, Gio." He looked at him. "Like. Low low."

Gio didn't react. "I'll keep an eye on your mom. And Alex." He sounded like he'd known this was coming. Javier was struck by his instinct to watch out for his family but actually had hoped Gio might try to convince him that he was overreacting, that the Chechens wouldn't waste their time on an act of petty revenge, that Jones would pack up and soon move on, that there was nothing to worry about.

"I told her you're aging out, Gio, you know, Ma." It was a lie. "And like, her green card is finally on its way—although that's probably up in the air right now—but, anyway, she was thinking, if you were, like, up for it, maybe she could...adopt you, Gio. Make you part of the family." Javier had never discussed the idea with his mother, had never even really seriously considered it himself until this very moment. "Make you *hermano*, Gio."

Gio, mostly in the shadows, folded at the waist, his head between his knees which flopped open and closed a few times before he sprang up, and stood legs apart.

"No fuckin' way!" His arms shot straight up over his head as if he'd scored a goal. Then he reached two-handed for Javier, still seated going in for a hug, lost his balance, fell into Javier, then rolled off and ended up on the ground looking up, laughing.

"Oh my God, Javi." He sat up and stuck both arms behind himself like kickstands. "For real?" There was a note of skepticism in his voice.

"I'm moving out next year." Javier caught himself, now wondering if he might have just made a mistake. It wasn't a good time to be making long-range plans, his chances of going to college suddenly perhaps not the slam dunk he'd once thought they were. "At least, I thought I was." It was as if Javier's inventory of hope had slid out of his life and into Gio's.

A text buzzed Javier's phone. It was from Enrique.

here to help homie

A link from an Instagram account. Javier clicked it open, scanned it. "Jesus." His face quickly dropped. More bad news.

"What is it?"

If the walls had been closing in, the floor was now dropping out. "There's an APB out for me."

Jones was pulling the net closed. "Apparently, I'm wanted for questioning in a homicide." He turned the screen and held it for Gio to read.

Valley Youth A Person Of Interest In Border Agent Execution

Gio inflated his cheeks and expelled the air. "Jones just unleashed the hounds." A white van pulled off Van Nuys and began to run along the service road that formed the north boundary of the lot. "Find a hole and climb in it, Javi."

Javier stood to leave, noticing a pair of bike cops splitting lanes on Van Nuys. "I'm outta here." He tossed Gio his set of keys. "Take care of 'em." Then he broke into a jog across the lot, once again unsure where he was going.

CHAPTER 41

A small tent city had already emerged, little nylon blisters smack dab in the middle of Dhamma Pass. The protesters had emerged overnight, like desert frogs that sprout from the sand following a heavy rain. Most of them had their own civil disobedience go-bags sitting in the trunk of their uninsured cars. News crews were running around collecting B-reel and trying to find someone who might articulate why exactly they were there. They had read the call to action a day ago, clicked the map link, and had arrived within hours, leaving most of the field reporters privately wanting to ask what kind of lifestyle allows someone to drop everything and live in the desert for an indeterminate length of time.

Chief Rosales had pulled out his regalia, warbonnets and knee-high moccasins and was doing game-faced interviews with historical references and personal stories expertly woven in. The clutch of reporters nodded their heads with stern expressions. Tasha was off to the side with some of the BLM people who were getting some mileage with the land deal and a team of academics were on hand to provide the forensic proof that in fact Dhamma Pass was sixty acres of sacred burial ground, that any plans to run a bullet train coming within anything less than two miles would violate federal statutes, not to mention heap yet another indignity on a First Nation.

The burial site was staged, the team of validating academics having recently been awarded a large and unsolicited grant from the Department of Education, the type of windfall that never happened in academia, much less in archaeology. On a table to the right of the microphones was a collection of relics and a weighty tome detailing the significance of each item allegedly unearthed from this site. In truth, the only thing that had ever been buried on this patch of desert—two-hundred oil drums of toxic waste—were relics from a more recent and less noteworthy moment in history, namely the invention of nonstick pans. Everyone on hand was essentially a paid actor, the props eagerly furnished by several professors whose chairs were now endowed for the foreseeable future.

On the horizon, Tasha spotted an SUV driving hell-bent on the access road, dust coming off it like rocket smoke. She'd been hoping Jones would be here to witness the coup de grace, to watch him come to terms with the fact that he'd been outplayed. Jones pulled up, got out, and found a place in the back row. Then Tasha nodded to the Chief who wrapped up his interview and got in front of the bank of microphones.

He wasn't windy, instead going through a list of occasions where developers dug up and paved over what nearly every indigenous group regarded as the seat of its people's strength—its ancestors. Then he gave thanks to the dean and his team from UC Riverside for uncovering the site before the path of the bullet train upset the site and thereby upset the Sky Father, Weywot. He found Jones and gave him a this-one's-for-you look.

"The Chuckwalla people cannot sit idly by while the great earthmovers destroy our ancestors' final resting place." Jones' eyes went from Tasha to the Chief and back to Tasha, sending his head back with a sudden realization landing like a jab to the nose. Tasha made no secret of the fact that she was taking his picture. She wanted to show her father who was still in ICU the moment of Jones' realization. If she were honest, the whole thing felt a little anticlimactic, though in her experience, payback often came in little packages.

Dhamma Pass, the one possible course correction to still route the bullet train to the Shoe, had now been foreclosed. There was nowhere left to send the bullet train except back down the I-15 corridor which was no longer populated with migrating tortoises. A team of Chinese herpetologists had been granted visas to come reclaim the two hundred and sixty-two Gobi tortoises, each one fitted with radio beacons, which had been left to wander the Mojave.

Check and mate.

CHAPTER 42

If I catch you fucking with my program...

Jones' little admonition was now playing on a loop in Javier's mind as he slipped down a back alley that ran parallel to Roscoe. Tasha had sent Carlos and himself a picture of Jones, his eyes like a pair of flamethrowers, at the ceremony of what he knew was a staged archaeological site. Jones would want his measure of pain.

From the alley, he came around the corner of a mini mall and slipped into the liquor store where he paid six dollars for a hat that said Giddy Up, pulled the brim down, and then walked the four blocks to the Panorama City library. Users had to log in with a library card, and he figured there would be an alarm set for his card number, so he found a book and pretended to read while one of the local school kids, not playing a game but actually doing research, stepped away. Javier jumped into his seat for the balance of his thirty minutes. He opened a browser, unsure where to start, what to do, whether to buy a bus ticket or a gun or reach out to the police or the guys.

"Yo ass trendin'." Javier looked across the table. It was Oral-B, trademark toothbrush in his mouth, a winter coat, and nothing underneath.

"Five-oh done put the BOLO on blast." He spoke casually, almost a mumble, his eyes still on the computer. Javier looked around to see if anyone else had heard this, apparently his one-piece disguise not quite as convincing as he'd hoped it would be. Oral-B pointed at his computer. "Copper." Javier had no idea what he was talking about. "Six carts of fuckin' aluminum and the only thing they buyin' is copper."

Javier quickly ran a search on his name and saw in fact that he was trending in Los Angeles. Mama would be hearing all this at the plant from her coworkers during the break. The first link on his screen, *Manhunt On For Los Angeles Youth*, detailed how he was wanted for the homicide of a border agent named Terry Price. He skimmed the article, familiarized himself with his alleged homicide, dates and times in case he needed to come up with an alibi.

"Time to git to ground, homie." Oral-B hadn't taken his eyes off the monitor. Javier came around the table and looked at Oral-B's screen which showed a rate schedule of metal prices per pound. He thought of something he'd overheard Lonnie tell someone on his first trip to her trailer.

"Let's say I know where you could get your hands on some copper." Javier was close enough to read the label on the toothbrush handle—Colgate. "Lots of it."

Oral-B pulled the toothbrush from his mouth, the bristles worn to the nub, and looked at him. "Then you and I should parlay."

"You need copper, and I need...cover."

Oral-B closed the screen and gave Javier a nod, his first bit of hope all day. Like the little girl with the long braid who'd been led out of the Dogtown floodwaters, Javier had little doubt he'd found the right person for the job. They walked two blocks down Van Nuys, took a right at the railroad trestle, came to an abandoned warehouse and went inside. As his eyes adjusted to the dim light, Javier could make out personal berms of cast-offs—bike frames, door-less microwaves, car seats springs, filing cabinet drawers, road signs, legless card tables, milk crates with only three sides—giving the interior the look and feel of homesteaders come to claim their parcels. Oral-B, whose real name was Charles, as Javier soon learned, had claimed a far corner of the building. His living space was minimalist to the point of nonexistence, having only a blanket and pillow and a collection of tools arranged neatly on shelves out of sight behind a pony wall.

"Take this." Oral-B/Charles stood, arm out stiffly holding a bottle of cold Yoo-Hoo apparently conjured out of thin air like an uncle snatching quarters from behind your ear. And just like that, he slipped out a side door, leaving Javier stranded with his cold chocolate milk, looking around the warehouse, pin-drop quiet. He sat himself down against a wall, his first chance to stop and consider his gradually metastasizing life. He felt like a tourist in some parallel world. He had a test tomorrow in AP Calc and needed to pay gas and water, and here he was, his name and likeness plastered on every feed. He opened his phone to read more about himself and his alleged crimes, his high school picture staring back at him on each page. Anxiety leached up from his stomach giving him breath so foul he could smell it.

Charles returned holding a man's wig and a pair of non-prescription glasses. "Gonna need these." Javier looked at the wig, curious to know how many others had worn it. He took off his hat, pulled on the wig, doing his best to look thankful rather than worried. Then the glasses. Charles held out a shaving mirror for Javier. "Don't think you the first one to lam it on these streets, amigo."

Javier tugged at his new set of bangs and turned his head side to side.

"I look like a child molester."

He put on his Giddy Up hat, his disguise now complete. If he had already been starting to disassociate from himself, the disguise only made the break more complete. Charles put a sandwich wrapped in plastic on a milk crate and pointed at it with an elbow.

"Turn your phone off, *hombre.*" Ooof. Javier grimaced at his own stupidity. "Relax. Five-oh won't have no phone warrant yet. Just make sure you keep it off." If law enforcement suddenly came crashing through the front door to arrest Javier, it would mean everyone inside would be looking for a new squat. Javier could make out the various fiefdoms of junk within the warehouse, though one stood out for its rather functional appearance. Five or six scooters lined up along the opposite wall stood in front of an equal number of mattresses and a few microwaves. It was like a beehive, kids no older than himself, slipping in and out of the warehouse on their scooters.

Javier and Charles ate silently, Javier not wanting to crowd Charles with pointless conversation. He was a study in stoicism, a man incapable of indulgence, and without parting words, he grabbed some tools from his shelf, put them in a bag, and left through the door, leaving Javier sitting there alone. He finished his noodles, lay down and succumbed to the special fatigue that apparently came with being a fugitive. Sleep came to him like he'd dropped off a cliff, and he woke up an hour later, still very much a prisoner in his own life. Charles sat perched on his milk crate reading his phone. It was dark outside now.

"Three fifty a pound." Javier had to assume Charles was referring to the price of copper, reminding Javier of his half of the bargain, that he would take Charles to a cache of copper. He'd made the offer based on a secondhand snippet of conversation from months ago and would no doubt be sleeping on the street if they came up empty-handed. Charles' little price quotation was his way of saying it was go-time.

Javier tried to mirror Charles' style of communication and only motioned with his head toward the door. Charles nodded back, and the two of them pushed a pair of shopping carts three blocks down Van Nuys to the back of the Pan City Steel. The loading platform was well lit and red lights winked at them from a series of cameras mounted at various angles. It was a coin flip if anyone was actually watching the monitors. Javier produced the master passkey Lonnie had given him at their last meeting, trying to act like he'd done this before though it took him a long minute to get the reader to work and the door to click open. They pushed their carts inside and down a long hall then found a freight elevator which they rode down to the basement. When the door opened, they saw only rows and rows of shrink-wrapped office furniture and servers. The place had damp-smelling air, and its walls were composed of original red brick and a recently added exoskeleton of steel I-beams.

"Fort fuckin Knox," Charles said. Against the wall was their bounty, endless hexagonally shaped bundles of twelve-foot copper pipe. Javier crossed himself and said a short prayer of thanks.

Charles produced a box cutter and began cutting the binding that held the lengths of copper together, using his leg to prevent an avalanche. Javier did his best to do the same, though at one point, he mispositioned his leg, causing a dozen lengths of pipe to tumble out onto the concrete floor and clatter away. If there had been anything close to active security measures, that would have been the end of it, but no one came. In ten minutes, they'd loaded up their carts, a small fraction of the total. They took the elevator back up, then wheeled their prize to the back of the building, left through an unalarmed emergency exit and down an unlit ramp.

A block away, they stopped and shared a bottle of water. "Three fifty, four hundred, what we got here," Charles doing the math in his head, though Javier was unsure what the units were: feet, dollars, or pounds. "Can't be greedy. We go small enough to avoid notice or else they'll start putting a guard in the basement. And we don't roll back into the squat tonight looking like we won Lotto.

Comprendez?" Javier nodded. It was the first time Charles had strung together more than three sentences.

The earliest hint of daylight was just beginning to lighten the eastern sky as they pushed their carts down an alley. Charles made a short diversion to an access tunnel, a black maw that ran below a set of railroad tracks. He pulled out a flashlight and a set of keys, unlocked a fence gate where they stashed their carts, then relocked the gate. By the time they were back inside the warehouse, dawn was filtering through the windows, spreading a brackish hue on the walls and floors. Someone was snoring, another rising from behind a collection of boxes. A couple of Team Scooter members were waiting by one of the microwaves squatting on their haunches, one of them examining the back of his hands, the other staring at the ceiling as if counting the joists. The bell rang, the boys grabbed their breakfasts then rolled out the door and were gone, some new mission awaiting them. Several more dunes of clothes in the middle of the warehouse had arrived overnight. It was impossible to tell if there were people under them.

Javier'd been at large for twelve hours now and was exhausted, his hyper-alertness a mental motor that wouldn't stop. He pulled off his hat, wig, and glasses, and lay them on the ground next to an air mattress and blanket that Charles had produced. They'd struck the mother lode which meant Javier had bought himself time and cover and apparently some amenities. Charles once again disappeared without any notice, his life apparently a series of comings and goings. As the adrenaline of the night began to wear off, Javier fell back on the air mattress and dreamt that he was an amphibian, emerging from the ocean onto dry land, his front fins just beginning their transformation into legs and feet, though the toes were still missing.

A door slammed, causing Javier to bolt upright. Any number of people from both sides of the law were now looking for him. His mouth was chalky, and his back hurt, the air in the mattress having escaped over the night leaving his hip resting on concrete. A thin shaft of light lit up a column of dust motes casually swirling beneath a hole in the ceiling, giving the place the appearance of a snow-globe. Javier looked around, knew he was not alone, but had no idea how many people were still stashed away. Someone next to him emerged from beneath a tarp, shaggy-headed and crooked, took no notice of Javier and then went back inside.

A bowl of oatmeal with a spoon sticking out of it sat on a milk crate, a little something from Charles who was turning out to be quite the host. Admittedly, Javier felt touched at this gesture, and not without a measure of pride. The little offering seemed to confer a passing grade for last night's work. He'd been dropped into the hand-to-mouth world of the streets, and survived his first day. He'd always been confident that, whatever the circumstances, he could tunnel his way through life to reach the other side, then realized, as he studied the array of tools on the shelf, that Charles was someone who would do nothing but tunnel his whole life, that there was no other side.

Javier finished, went outside to rinse the bowl with some bottled water, squinting from the sudden brightness and immediately chastising himself for not checking the street before stepping outside. The hat, wig, and glasses needed to become second nature, and he went back inside to get them. When he picked up the hat, he froze. A gun sat underneath it, another little gift from Charles. Javier picked it up and could feel every fiber in his body telling him to just leave it there. He stuck it in the wall behind the loose brick he'd seen Charles pull out the previous night and was half a block down Van Nuys when he decided to go back for it.

Though it was two blocks to the library, he found himself walking in the direction of East Valley, unsure if it was his need for something familiar or just the voyeur in him, a niggling curiosity to see if his absence was noticeable in any way, maybe a "Run, Javier, Run" banner hanging somewhere. He got there before the first bell and watched from the strip mall across the street. Raffa, Chuey, Enrique, and Sergio were by the flagpole, Chuey barking at Raffa, Enrique wearing his backpack papoose-style in the front and catcalling a girl who flipped him off. Sergio looked around, perhaps sensing Javier nearby, his gaze sailing over the street. Two men in untucked flannel shirts at opposite ends of the turnout in front of the main gates essentially self-identified themselves as plainclothes officers. Half a block away, Javier spotted Gio shuffling backward down the sidewalk. Javier half-hoped Gio would turn around, spot him, maybe smile, maybe a nod. And perhaps that was why he was walking backward. No chance this way of tipping off the cops in their flannel shirts. Gio couldn't trust himself to not spot Javier.

The tardy bell rang, triggering a hiccup of guilt. Javier was now, for the first time in his four years at East Valley, going to be marked absent from class. The fact that he would be missing his AP Calc test only made the whole moment all the more surreal, his life now no different from the two kids leaning against a wall at the other end of the parking lot, blowing out vape smoke and looking at East Valley like it was the Dawn Wall of El Capitan.

The library was closed when he got there, leaving him to loiter in front with a handful of the dispossessed. They were a loose confederation, some chatty and upbeat, oblivious to their circumstances, others having already capitulated to the smoke in the glass straw. Two empty black-and-whites were parked across the street, once again law enforcement doing little in the way of setting traps. A librarian appeared from inside, unlocked the doors, and held them open while the small crowd, including Javier, shuffled in.

"Birdbath." That had been Charles' parting comment last night while waving a hand in front of his nose. "Find a sink, and ditch the stink." It had been forty-eight hours since he'd showered, and Javier could feel a film of oil on his skin. The bathroom was quickly occupied, and he could see under the handicap stall someone had set up shop, unpacking his wares like he'd signed a lease and was moving in. Javier waited patiently until one of the sinks was free, took off his shirt and splashed water on himself. A gauzy reflection appeared in the steel mirror, a pair of sallow eyes staring back. He put his shirt back on and headed for the bay of computers. One with twenty minutes still on it was already available. He quickly slid in, opened his Signal account, and noticed Alex had left him a message.

He'd been released from the hospital the day after he'd seen Javier, been taken straight to central booking, and released with an ankle monitor to await his first hearing. He'd be starting Zoom school next week and was actually looking forward to it. Mama had actually taken a few days off from work which never happened. Alex noted that Gio spent the last night at the apartment, watching *Rebelde* with her, sleeping on the floor literally against the front door. Detective Morales had been around twice on his own time to check on things. Alex had assumed Morales had shown up to work him for details, but Denker never came up. Javier sent a one-liner back to Alex to let him know he was okay and to maybe throw Morales a bone in case they needed help later on.

Javier's calendar blinked a reminder, not that he needed the prompt—an interview in two hours downtown, the last hoop for Lupe's scholarship. It was a moot point now, but he was keen to be there nonetheless. Leslie had set it up two months ago. Had she made the appointment using his name, it would have been pointless to go, but the scholarship used a number system to schedule all interviews, part of an effort to keep the process impartial. He already knew he was no longer a candidate, but he had one final piece of business to settle.

According to the office directory at the bottom of Three Wilshire, Lupe's office was, not surprisingly, two floors below Solano's, the whole thing sadly making perfect sense. As he stood there now once again in the lobby, the midday lunch exodus underway, Javier indulged a momentary video game fantasy: the elevator doors opening, Javier walking out, gun drawn, a frightened receptionist ducking for cover, and then Jones in his glass office with his point value blinking over his head.

As before, he looked at his reflection in the elevator door as it shot up to the twenty-fifth floor of Three Wilshire, his second glimpse at the what-if version of himself, this time destitute and desperate, though, like the first time, working off a half-baked plan. He was, as Betzaida had described Alex, in fuck-it world, a strangely exhilarating place where the only wrong move was to stop moving because he would lose his nerve. He could recall only one other moment like it—the day he first knocked on Leslie's door. The only difference between then and now was how much he stood to lose today.

"If you could be so kind as to write down your applicant ID number, your interview will begin shortly." The spritely receptionist sounded eerily like the voice he'd spoken with back when he'd first called Lupe's office to inquire about a business loan. Hands folded in front of her, she was doing her best to act natural, though Javier's appearance suggested he was going to ask for money. "Can I get you something to drink?"

"What do you have on tap?"

He kept a straight face for a few seconds, happy to see her smile slowly slide off her face. Her eyes skipped over his shoulder toward security, possibly signaling his second eviction from the building. "Just kidding." He came closer to her. "I only drink from cans." Her mouth started to open but quickly closed when she smelled his breath.

Two other candidates seated in the waiting area scrupulously avoided eye contact, each visibly relieved when their numbers were called. Two floors above, Jones was quite likely seated in his office working up the numbers on some new plan to uproot some unfortunate community to site a transit node.

"Mr. Jimenez, last door on your left." The receptionist pointed down a hallway, the enthusiasm in her voice gone. He sniffed his pits as he passed her, wondering what she would do if he pulled out the gun and asked her to hang onto it. He walked down the hallway and came through the door while taking off his hat and wig but leaving the glasses for now. It was a lavish conference room, at least two dozen chairs around the table, and a city view that stretched to the ocean. Javier went straight to the mini-fridge and pulled out two waters.

"Want one?"

Lupe, sitting on one side of the conference table with a legal pad in front of her, offered an amused smile and shook her head. "I made sure your interview was with me, Javier. All that number shit—" She waved a hand in the air. "And don't worry, I haven't contacted law enforcement."

He snorted. "Really." He took a seat and removed his glasses, placing them on the wig. "I wish you had. You belong in jail. You're a fuckin' disgrace."

"Careful, Javier." Something swam behind her eyes, a glimmer of the *chola* with the Glock and the bowl of cereal. She scrawled a note on a legal pad, tore it off, folded it in half, and then slid it across the table. "Four years, full ride and a little something extra for *su mama y hermano.*" She sat back in her chair and steepled her fingers. A long moment passed. "Were you a *Sabado Gigante* family?"

Javier was staring out the window. It was impossible not to, the whole city rolled out like a carpet to the ocean which blinked in the sun. "Don Francisco." Javier nodded. "None better."

Lupe paused to let the shared memory settle. "Cornball stuff, right? Big boobs for the guys, cheesy ballads for the ladies. And all the chance games for the car, nothing but blind luck, let everyone at home think they had a shot too, and every week, I watched that show because they had one game that wasn't just based on chance."

"Name That Tune." Javier was leaning back, arms folded, now staring back at her.

Lupe sat forward. "And I loved that game because I knew every tune in five notes. Some in four. Way before the contestants, who needed half the *pinche* song, you know, before they could name it. But I just knew the song. And that's been my life, Javier. Give me four notes, and I know the song."

"Yeah, well, I'm not that clever, and I'm sure there's a lesson coming up, but you can save your story, Ms. Lupe." Javier's voice was flayed and exhausted. He picked up the paper Lupe had pushed across the table, crumpled it up without looking at it, and sailed it over her head. "You would have been lucky to have one teacher even half as good as Patel."

He pulled out his phone and opened an image from the video Sergio had sent from the Hyatt. "I know Jones put you up to this." He widened the frame, pushed his phone to the middle of the table so Lupe could see it and pointed to the man pushing the room service cart down a hall. He swiped through a few close-ups showing a time code in the lower right, a floor number in the lower left, an 818 on the man's throat and a scar running through his goatee. Javier swiped to a video which showed him pushing the cart up to Room 3214, again going tight on the cart's contents which, once the cart came back out, hadn't changed. "Your fat-fuck cousin from the Gardens, but I'm guessing he's got an alibi and all that." He drank the water in one go and remained standing.

Lupe sat there impassively. "Think carefully, Javier. You—"

"Don't." He could feel his rage, a starved beast. When he pulled out the gun, he couldn't help but marvel at its logic, quick answers to life's pressing problems in one clip. He stood and let one finger curl around the trigger, then swung the muzzle back and forth pendulum-style before letting it come to rest on the table top pointed straight down as if he was ready to shoot a hole through it.

"Wife, two kids." He sat down, aware she had probably already sent a panic message to her assistant to get security. "But you were underwater with the bullet train, bit off more than you could chew." Leslie had found the files, sent Javier everything, an act of courage and loyalty he knew he would never be able to repay. She had quit Lupe's office the same day, gut-punched at the revelation. The hallowed Lupe, having moved to the hills once she'd made it, had resorted to the streets when pressed. Lupe had been leveraged to the hilt on the project, expecting the revenues to start working off the debt service within five years, but then came the delays. And then came the creditors. And the subpoenas. She was underwater with no prospects for any bailout.

"And, of course, Jones found out 'cause that's what he does, and he worked it. He put the screws to you, and you folded like a *puta*. Got your Denker cousin to fly up to San Jose, take out a...citizen. A *maestro*." He picked up his phone. "He had a brother who got third-degree burns over half his body in a factory fire, a cousin who died. Some place called Hyderabad." He leaned forward, his elbows on the table, gun aimed straight at her chest. "Your boy Jones." He checked the corner of her eyes for anything. "And Patel was about to blow the whistle."

"Know this much, Javier. You were first on the list, not the teacher." Lupe's eyes had narrowed. Javier noticed her avoidance of calling Patel by name. "But I convinced Jones to give you a pass, *entiendes*?" She'd arched one eyebrow, then her spine and held a hand up to the guard who stood outside the door clearly ready to give Javier the heave-ho. "You won't make it another day out there, Javier." He could hear a thread of genuine concern in her voice.

Javier looked at the gun again, stood up, and stuck it back in his waistband. "Tell Jones you need to meet him for breakfast in a week, Engine Company 37. Great waffles according to Yelp. 8 a.m. And if you try to get cute, your financials, that image," he held up his phone, "go straight to the Feds." He took out Detective Morales' card with his other hand and flashed it at her. It was LAPD, but he didn't care. He put on his wig, hat, and glasses and stood. A security officer put his hand on Javier's shoulder which he shrugged off as he came around to Lupe's side of the table. "Life is cheap, huh?"

CHAPTER 43

Javier couldn't deny how easily he'd found himself seduced by the gun, its unimpeachable authority. Bizarro-Javier had an evil streak, and he knew the longer he remained a fugitive, the less sleep he would get, the more desperate he would become, and something permanent would take root. He would grow used to the gun, learn to sleep with the lump it made under his pillow at night. It was time to go back, let the chips fall, and get on with whatever was going to come his way.

Over the next few days, Javier drew up his plan. As if sensing a change in Javier, Charles had left a burner with ninety minutes on it under Javier's Giddy Up hat.

He'd reached out to Morales to put a few things in place, and to his credit, the detective didn't make any quid pro quo demands. Alex had confirmed a few leads for Morales about Denker, giving Javier a credit balance in the family favor bank. He texted Sergio the warehouse address and asked him to come by and leave Jones' burner next to where Charles kept his tools. Sergio replied with a string of question marks to which Javier said that he didn't have time to explain.

Six nights into his sabbatical from reality, Javier led Charles on what would be their last trip to the Pan City Steel basement together and hiked out four more carts of copper. The fact that it was Jones they were stealing from was, for Javier, the cherry on top of a brief and fruitful partnership. Six pallets of pipe still remained, enough copper to put a deposit down on a new apartment and pay a full year in rent up front, though he doubted if permanent shelter was one of Charles' goals. While it would be hard to say anyone could actually thrive on the streets, Charles was at home there. His window for re-civilizing had come and gone; he was a cowboy who'd slept under the stars too long. In the two weeks Javier had flopped in the warehouse, he'd never seen Charles hit a flask or a pipe. He was a portrait of thrift and industry. They pushed the carts back down Roscoe, and at Sepulveda, Javier spotted a small fire lit by the study hall couches. He knew who it was, and he knew now it was time now to finish what he'd started that day Jones had darkened the Box's doorway. Javier pulled out the pass card and handed it to Charles.

"Nice doin' business." Javier knew better than to extend his hand for a shake, got a nod from Charles, which was all he expected, then waited for Charles to shove off which didn't take long. Javier watched him go, the rattle of the copper in the cart loud enough to wake the whole block. In his brief acquaintance with Patel, Javier had come to learn about the limits he'd placed on himself. In his even briefer acquaintance with Charles, he'd witnessed a life, however modest, lived free of any limits whatsoever.

Gio was sitting on the study hall couches, his profile flame-lit against the gathering dark. From a distance, Javier sensed something odd about Gio, and as he drew close, he noted the haircut. Gio had pushed the table to the side and was burning construction cast-offs, two by fours and plywood remnants. He was poking the fire with a length of dowel.

"Nice get-up, Javi." Gio hadn't even turned his head, now neatly cropped.

"Somewhere there's a family of birds without a nest." Javier recognized the hair length—same as his.

Gio looked at Javier. "How 'bout that. Me with the high and tight and you with the...creepy uncle look."

Javier sat down on the far end of the sofa. "Thought you'd be eatin' tamales with Alex and Mama. It's Wednesday." Dolores had sold her tamales on Wednesdays, and even after her death, it had remained a tradition.

"Sergio and Chuey are playing canasta with Alex and your mother tonight." He poked the fire with the dowel, sending sparks spiraling into the night sky. "Chuey's been bringing his brothers by." He didn't need to say much else. Chuey's mother had popped out the Chavez brothers in such rapid succession it had the appearance of a sales quota. "That white van? Well, those fools made a pass at your place yesterday, pulled up in front, you know, sorta sat there checking things out, and I texted Chuey, and he texted his brothers, and Jesus, Javi." Gio stopped poking the fire. "They fucked those guys up."

"Who fucked up who?"

"Chuey's brothers."

"They did the fucking, or they got fucked?"

"The first one."

It was necessarily good news. The Chechens would reload and return.

Gio could read Javier's expression. "They went to the mattresses on this one, Javi. Posted up all over the place. Twenty-four-hour watch. Those fools in the van won't make it past Roscoe." Gio chuckled.

Javier grabbed his own piece of dowel from the pile of wood and started poking. "Can't believe this shit, Gio."

"You talkin' about my hair or your life?"

Javier looked at Gio's head. "Think I liked you more with the mop."

The two went silent, each lost in their thoughts, neither willing to broach the obvious, that there were warrants for Javier's arrest and a dark web kill team looking for him. It was a Monday night and the party-sounds from Can City had migrated to the rooftops of the three residential towers like there was a competition to see who was having more fun.

"This life-on-the-run bullshit aint for me, Gio." Javier swung his dowel through the air, a neon ribbon in the darkness. "I'm gonna turn myself in. 8 a.m. tomorrow. Engine Company 37, downtown. Jones will be there and so will the goon squad in the white van."

Gio sat there unresponsive, Javier wondering if he'd even heard what he'd said. "How you making that happen?"

"I got word to Jones, and I still have the burner. As soon as it's on, the dudes in the van will know where I am and come find me. I need them on hand to witness it go down." He tossed the dowel into the fire. "Probably be on a bus back to the border by Saturday." He had no idea if any of this was true. "What are they saying about me at school? The shooting of the Border Patrol."

Gio smiled. "Most people say they thought you had it in you."

Gio tossed his dowel into the fire, kicking up a small shower of sparks. "You're gonna be all right, Javi." As the fire faded, they lay down and stared up at the few stars able to outdo the LA light-wash. The next morning, Javier woke up feeling cold. Gio was gone, and so was Javier's wallet. And so was the wig, the hat, and the gun.

CHAPTER 44

The boy lay by his scooter, his head banked against the wall at a slight angle and watched the stranger with leather wristbands and Metallica tee-shirt walk over to the far corner where the metal man kept his space. The stranger pulled something out from his pocket then stuck it on the middle shelf amid the tools. As soon as the stranger was gone, the boy was up, looking left then right before scampering across the floor. It was a phone. The guys were always looking for them, so he stuck it in his pocket.

Two minutes later the boy wheeled up to the lab, itself another brick warehouse, rang the bell on the steel-plated door, looked in the camera, and got buzzed in. Three men with automatic weapons slung over their shoulders sat in front playing cards, occasionally glancing over at a row of monitors. The boy handed the burner to one of the men who tossed it into a box with a dozen other phones. The boy got an approving nod followed by a beat-it gesture.

Twenty minutes later, a different boy picked up the box and brought it across the room to another group of armed men playing video games. The interior of the lab was large enough for a go-kart track and in the middle sat the production line, most notable for the collection of Home Depot buckets sitting astride lab equipment—glass globes fitted with hoses that were fed through a series of devices with meters, screens, and dials. Four technicians in hazmat bunny suits wearing respirators worked various stations that synthesized the precursors into pure fentanyl which was then cut with baby formula and delivered in a cart to a solitary figure, the lone female in the place, who ran the pill press, turning powder into retail product which she then wiped off the table like a croupier raking in lost bets.

One at a time, the boys playing video games would be finger-whistled, handed a phone from the basket, and then given an address. They then got on their scooters, went to a second door which had another two armed gunmen watching La Liga soccer, before exiting onto the alley to make their delivery. There was never more than one person exiting the building every thirty minutes.

One block away and across the street, the cartel hit team was sitting in its F-150 keeping tabs on the doors. The previous evening, they'd used metal snips to shorten two of the five fingers on one hand of the slowest of the Denker jugglers who finally gave up the location of the lab, figuring no woman would love a man with anything less than three fingers on one hand.

Jones' burner had now changed hands five times since Javier first pulled it out of the Land Rover's cup holder. This last transfer would prove its most fateful. When one of the Denker crew finally switched it on, the Chechens wasted little time descending on its location, unaware that in their thirst for revenge, they had actually stepped in front of the cartel shooters. When the white transit van skidded to a stop and disgorged a team of five men all dressed in black with balaclavas over their faces, the four men in the F-150 looked at each other, wondering why any team of assassins would approach a heavily armed location dressed as ninjas in broad daylight.

No one in the F-150 spoke, though they all shared a common thought. Someone else was about to do the heavy lifting. When the smoke settled, they would put down their Big Gulps, turn off their music, and finish off anyone still standing.

CHAPTER 45

Javier took off at a sprint for the bus stop two blocks away.

Last night, he'd fallen asleep in study hall staring up at the stars with Gio. This morning, his eyes had snapped open to a chorus of backup alarms coming from the construction site across the lake. It was now second nature to reach for his wig, hat, and eyeglasses though today they were not where he'd left them. He had no idea what Gio's plan was, but he knew where he'd be headed right now. Out of shape, Javier was barely jogging by the time he got to the bus. The wait for the 152 was unbearable, the clock in his head ticking away, his brain turning red. He'd told Gio the time and location of his surrender, and now Gio was going to play stunt-double for Javier. After ten years of Javier doing for Gio, it was about to be the other way around. Javier turned on his phone to check local news sites. Nothing. He called Morales. No answer. He sent a voice-transcribed text.

Detective, this is Javier Jimenez, Alex's brother. Look, I was going to turn myself in today, but a friend of mine, a kid named Gio, is gonna try to do it for me, as me, so like, get taken into custody as me, 8:00 at Engine Company Number 37. Today. I'm heading there now, but my friend is gonna be there first.

He read it over and hit send.

A minute later, just as the bus pulled in, Morales sent back a text.

on my way 2 scene

Some guy in front of Javier was taking five minutes loading his bike in the rack and then another minute fishing for exact change out of his jacket, the whole thing almost making Javier cry. Once inside, Javier looked around, people were on their phones, staring out the window, some napping, all unaware of the panic swelling in Javier's head like a balloon. The bus stopped in North Hollywood for the transfer to the subway which meant he had another sprint down two sets of stairs and another wait on for the inbound train. Cell coverage was spotty this far down, but he opened a site for a local news channel and knew right away it was happening.

He clicked a link labeled *Police activity downtown intersection Figueroa and Third.*

That had to be Gio.

Police have reason to believe the gunman is wanted for questioning in the murder of a border agent. Closed circuit images just released indicate a Hispanic male, between the ages of eighteen and twenty now believed to be Javier Jimenez.

The news anchor spoke with her breaking-news face. Over her shoulder was the high school photo of Javier mad-dogging the camera, not a good luck if things went to trial and he had to rely on public sentiment.

An idea came to him—find a cop, identify himself, explain the situation. But that was the problem. It would require too much explanation. He'd wind up cuffed in the backseat of a cruiser spouting claims of conspiracy and sabotage and a doppelganger in an armed standoff. A hot wind came down the tunnel, the signal that the train was approaching. The first car sailed past, a metallic wail from the brakes, the train coming to a gradual stop, and the doors opened. In a matter of minutes, he would be under the Hollywood Hills and would lose whatever signal he had.

A news blog was loading updates every few minutes.

Unconfirmed reports indicate that Jimenez has taken someone hostage with a handgun. SWAT on its way.

Hostage?

Another news site featured helicopter footage showing the downtown area, the traffic into and out of the three-block area already closed off. Somewhere down there, Gio was freelancing his way through an armed standoff.

Javier's cell signal cut out, the remaining fifteen minutes an agonizing ride which included eight stops, his heart doing rumba thumps the whole way there. He berated himself for not making the connection between Gio's haircut and what was now unfolding. How could he be so daft. Twenty brain-melting minutes later, the train pulled into Pershing Square, the doors opened, another dash up one flight of stairs to the next, much longer set where he could see sunlight, yellow police tape, and a string of officers forming a human cordon at the end of the stairs. No one in or out.

Most of the riders who had just gotten off started returning to the platform to wait for the next train. Javier looked around, saw an elevator off in a corner, out of sight of the officers at the top of the tunnel. An elderly man in a wheelchair had summoned the lift, oblivious to the commotion two floors up.

Javier got behind the wheelchair, made like an attendant, and rode the lift up with him without even so much as an introduction. The doors opened at the top.

"There's a police standoff. You probably don't want to—"

"Two tours in Nam, young man, and if Charlie ain't inside the wire, I'll take my chances." He turned to look at Javier through a pair of mirrored sunglasses and then pushed the joystick on his armrest forward and sped off down the sidewalk.

Overhead, a solitary police helicopter floated lazily over the scene, drowning out whatever the officer on the PA was saying. Across the street, a handful of Starbucks customers had barricaded themselves inside behind the counter, a few heads popping up. It was the same place Javier had met Luis the janitor months back and traded the Laker tickets for his passkey and uniform.

Further down the block, a line of officers had positioned themselves outside the doors to the Biltmore Hotel to ensure no one came out and walked unwittingly into a crossfire. A small team of men in sport coats talking to their wrists had sprung up as well, a security detail for an A-list hotel guest.

The streets and sidewalks, now empty of pedestrians, were eerily quiet apart from the sound of tac-teams scurrying for position outside Engine Company 37.

Javier could see the sign for the restaurant, two blocks away. He squatted below the front end of a sedan, his side of the street now completely empty apart from a homeless man sitting on the sidewalk, his head bobbing to some private music.

A blue SWAT truck barreled past, the officers hanging off the side like they were hitching a ride into town.

Javier lay down on the pavement and crawled on his stomach under three cars and by the fourth could see four legs positioned as if dancing about twenty yards away in the middle of the street. One last car and he could see Gio with Jones in a hammerlock and the gun pressed against his ear.

Gio actually looked like he knew what he was doing, his nostrils flared like an animal smelling smoke. Javier crawled forward until his head almost poked out from under the car.

Snipers were taking up positions along one of the rooftops, and on the far side of Grand Avenue, a row of cop cars were parked in parallel, doors open, guns drawn. Radio chatter echoed in the canyon of office towers. Javier heard something about a "clear shot."

Gio kept turning, perhaps wanting to make himself a more difficult target, perhaps a little overwhelmed by the response from law enforcement. It was anyone's guess, including Gio's most likely, what the end game was here. He'd left himself little room for any out. A negotiator was on a bullhorn with some soft-start lines. "Javier, no one's gonna get hurt. We're gonna work this out, so take it slow and breathe." Gio's ruse had worked. He swung his head from side to side, looking for something or someone, pulling Jones backward with him. A cop was standing close enough for Javier to make out the radio traffic. There was a "be advised" followed by something unintelligible and then "deadman switch." An ICE van arrived and offloaded a team of armed men who quickly dispersed. Javier figured every branch of law enforcement was probably on scene right now, and out of professional courtesy, ICE was going to get first crack.

Gio said something to Jones who then took his free hand, reached into his pocket, pulled out a phone, and typed in a text. Javier felt his phone buzz.

Gio was giving Javier Jones' number.

Javier scooted out on the right side of the car and checked the make and color of the car he was under then texted Jones.

under the brown honda corner of olive and 4th

"Javier Jimenez, this is Sergeant Napolitano from LAPD. You are surrounded. Put down your weapon and release the hostage now." Javier sensed the police were trying to hurry things along a little too much, that they should get the first guy back on the bullhorn and talk about breathing.

The whole street was now wall-to-wall blue and black. The helicopter made another brief and noisy appearance, drawing everyone's attention briefly skyward before disappearing again.

The scene had suddenly gone quiet and still, Gio once again scanning the perimeter before he finally found the brown Honda with Javier lying flat underneath it. He smiled at Javier who at that point was shaking his head, mouthing, "No, no, no!"

"*Hermano!*" Gio shouted in reply. And with that he put the gun up firmly to Jones' head, the angle of the muzzle now indicating more intent.

"Javier Jimenez. Drop your weapon and release your hostage. This is your final warning."

Javier could see Gio's lips moving, whispering something to Jones, then torqued his arm like he hoped to snap it off, sending Jones to the ground. Gio had started raising his hands in surrender, though the loud pop of Jones' arm coming out of its socket was close enough to gunfire to commence the fusillade, hair triggers, all of them.

Gio was dead before he hit the ground, his head snapping back savagely before collapsing on the pavement. The barrage lasted only seconds, the echo of gunshots in the office canyon on Figueroa ringing out twice as long.

Then the silence, a somber coda to what would be referred to in the news as a hostage situation. Javier leaped out screaming, raced toward Gio's body but was grabbed and taken to the ground by three officers before he could get there. He went apoplectic with rage and was rolled onto his stomach then cuffed, giving him a front row seat as the EMTs fruitlessly performed chest compressions on Gio.

The luck of the evil, thought Javier, as he watched Jones for the second time get loaded into the back of an ambulance.

CHAPTER 46

Javier was taken into custody, transported to central lock-up, and led to a holding cell at the end of a long row of locked rooms with no windows and only slots in the doors. He felt grateful to be alone, his tiny cell providing a furlough from a world suddenly without Gio. "Meet me in the cave of my insanity or meet me nowhere." He'd stumbled over the line somewhere, committed it to memory, and, as he sat on the cell floor looking up, found succor in its bleak attitude.

Once again, it took Detective Morales to run interference with law enforcement and straighten everyone out. This time, it took twelve hours to unwind the dual identities and point out that the dead boy was actually Giovannie Ojeda. When the cell door opened, Javier wasn't entirely sure he wanted to leave, wondered if there might be a crime he could cop to, and extend his lock-up or perhaps give him a seat on the bus to the border. Morales had seen the effects guilt had on survivors, the dark moods and withdrawal. He sat with Javier and shared a few updates on Alex and Mama, even Flaco. He eventually coaxed Javier to his feet and drove him home where Mama greeted them at the door. She insisted the detective join them for some posole, and though he initially declined, he relented once Mama pulled the cover from the pot.

Javier entombed himself for a week in his room, shades drawn, buried underneath blankets. He turned off his phone and skipped graduation. The guys came by, but the most he would do was a brief rollover to say hello before giving them his back. He skipped meals with Alex and Mama and ate cereal when no one was around. He watched game shows, talk shows, and cooking shows with his eyes offline, open but empty. Sergio had managed to forge an application on Javier's behalf to Cal State Northridge so that he'd have a slot in the fall. It was well past the deadline, but Sergio had worked his magic and even managed to get him a meal plan and parking for the year.

Mama drew up the adoption papers for Gio before his burial and was granted dispensation by the county to allow him to be buried as Giovannie Jimenez. Javier finally beat back his despair, kicked off the sheets, snuck into the church well before the public viewing and sat there, hand on casket for thirty minutes before leaving out the back.

Betzaida sold Javier the beater for $50, and he had the car on a lift for three days straight before getting past inspection. He drove it to Santa Monica to meet up with Lorenzo Dimas who was no longer wearing sunglasses, the bags under his eyes adding ten years to his appearance. He had just published a two-part investigative report in the *LA Times* which, among other things, established a pattern of tax credit deals between Jones' firm Solano and a string of municipalities across the globe in which he'd managed transit node projects. Most of the evidence was anecdotal, though Javier had managed to forward a number of documents that had mysteriously arrived in his spam folder soon after Gio's burial. He didn't need to guess who they were from, though he had no clue as to why.

"His reputation will start catching up with him, but to be honest, it may just boost his brand." Lorenzo was sipping tea. "He's a ghost when it comes to the bodies, so it's mostly racketeering and wire fraud at this point."

Javier had to carefully titrate thoughts of Jones lest they spawn hours of spiraling guilt. "Someone has to nail his ass."

Jones was long gone. Javier had texted Luis from the Solano cleaning crew to see if there were any signs of Jones on the twenty-eighth floor of Three Wilshire. The entire office had been emptied in a matter of days, boxed up, shipped out, not so much as a sign on the door.

He said goodbye to Lorenzo, wished him good luck. Then, he walked the three blocks to the Santa Monica Pier where Leslie was waiting for him at the Ferris wheel. Javier slipped the attendant a hundred-dollar bill and told him they'd be on it for at least an hour. The view from the apex was twenty miles in every direction, leaving Javier feeling a sad hopefulness, then feeling the warmth of Leslie's hand inside his.

"Better late than never, Javi."

One hour turned into two, and when the sea breeze kicked in once the sun began to sink, they climbed out of their gondola and found a Mediterranean restaurant, placed their order, and sat outside at a redwood table. When their order number was called, Javier went inside where, behind the counter, a television showed the scene of a train derailment, a tanker car leaking a vaporizing liquid, the men in hazmat suits spraying some type of foam. The news crawl claimed that a "massive toxic event" in Buenos Aires had forced the evacuation of more than five thousand residents from a favela where, as the closed captioning read, "people with very little suddenly had even less." Scenes of firetrucks on their way, hapless citizens running for cover, jackknifed trains in the background, a cloud of gas escaping from one of the cars.

Though the volume was off, Javier could tell the reporter was speaking urgently, and as the camera went wide, Javier saw him, in a suit with no tie, hands in pockets, standing off to the side, all alone, staring back.

ABOUT THE AUTHOR

Having taught in the LA public schools for thirty years, Morgan now writes about the people and places he has come to know in the course of his career. During the pandemic, he began writing *Gone To Ground.* At the same time, Los Angeles was going through a series of scandals involving public officials as well as an uptick in the perennial "crises" of homelessness, immigration, and gentrification. Add to this the on-again-off-again California bullet train, and you have the main threads of this novel.

Morgan lives in Los Angeles with his wife where he's trying to learn his mother-in- law's recipe for *dhaar dhokli.*

NOTE FROM MORGAN HATCH

Word-of-mouth is crucial for debut novels such as *Gone To Ground*, and reader reviews are the lifeblood of a book's success. All reviews, even one or two sentences long, are welcome at Goodreads, Amazon, and anywhere else you care to post. I read all reviews and welcome you to reach out to me on social media as well. All my links are available at www.morganhatch.net where you can get updates on the sequel.

Thanks!
Morgan Hatch

We hope you enjoyed reading this title from:

<u>www.blackrosewriting.com</u>

Subscribe to our mailing list – *The Rosevine* – and receive **FREE** books, daily deals, and stay current with news about upcoming releases and our hottest authors.
Scan the QR code below to sign up.

Already a subscriber? Please accept a sincere thank you for being a fan of Black Rose Writing authors.

View other Black Rose Writing titles at
<u>www.blackrosewriting.com/books</u> and use promo code
PRINT to receive a **20% discount** when purchasing.